D0196602

## WHAT A WIDOW WANTS

Leaning into him, she whispered, "We can renew our acquaintance in all ways that count."

"So you'll agree to bed me but not wed me?"

"For the moment." She tapped her fingers lightly on his chest. "Would that be such a hardship on you?"

Sighing, he pulled a face. "I suppose not." A flash of his boyish grin made her stomach drop. "May I woo you properly, at least?"

"Improperly would be more to my taste." Fanny returned his smile with one of her own, as sultry and seductive as she could make it. "But I suppose some decorous behavior wouldn't kill me either."

"Good." He took her hands and raised them to his lips. "I leave for Brighton at the end of the week. I'd hoped you'd be accompanying me as my wife, but that—"

"As your wife?" How arrogant of him to think she'd fall into his arms at the snap of his fingers.

"Well? Will you meet me in Brighton?" Matthew's eager voice brought her back to the dim room now filled with possibilities.

"I will be happy to journey to Brighton, my lord. If I find you there, I do hope you will attend me most earnestly . . ."

**Books by Jenna Jaxon**

*The Widows' Club*
TO WOO A WICKED WIDOW
WEDDING THE WIDOW
WHAT A WIDOW WANTS

*The House of Pleasure Series*
ONLY SEDUCTION WILL DO
ONLY A MISTRESS WILL DO
ONLY MARRIAGE WILL DO
ONLY SCANDAL WILL DO

**Published by Kensington Publishing Corporation**

JENNA JAXON

LYRICAL PRESS
Kensington Publishing Corp.
www.kensingtonbooks.com

LYRICAL PRESS BOOKS are published by

Kensington Publishing Corp.
119 West 40th Street
New York, NY 10018

Copyright © 2019 by Jenna Jaxon

All rights reserved. No part of this book may be reproduced in any form or by any means without the prior written consent of the Publisher, excepting brief quotes used in reviews.

To the extent that the image or images on the cover of this book depict a person or persons, such person or persons are merely models, and are not intended to portray any character or characters featured in the book.

If you purchased this book without a cover you should be aware that this book is stolen property. It was reported as "unsold and destroyed" to the Publisher and neither the Author nor the Publisher has received any payment for this "stripped book."

All Kensington titles, imprints, and distributed lines are available at special quantity discounts for bulk purchases for sales promotion, premiums, fund-raising, educational, or institutional use.

Special book excerpts or customized printings can also be created to fit specific needs. For details, write or phone the office of the Kensington Sales Manager: Attn.: Sales Department. Kensington Publishing Corp., 119 West 40th Street, New York, NY 10018. Phone: 1-800-221-2647.

Lyrical and the Lyrical logo Reg. U.S. Pat. & TM Off.

First Printing: January 2019
ISBN-13: 978-1-5161-0329-4
ISBN-10: 1-5161-0329-7

ISBN-13: 978-1-5161-0328-7 (ebook)
ISBN-10: 1-5161-0328-9 (ebook)

10 9 8 7 6 5 4 3 2 1

Printed in the United States of America

To my BFF Alexandra Christle just for being you.
Much love, my friend.

# ACKNOWLEDGMENTS

Many, many thanks go out to the people who made this book possible. Ella Quinn, Collette Cameron, and Alexandra Christle for their wonderful insights and advice on how to make this story work. Also my heartfelt thanks to Kathy Green, my agent, who helped beta read this book and gave me great feedback. And as ever, my wonderful editor, John Scognamiglio, who loved this story and made it happen.

# Chapter 1

Glittering candles, the flames wafting to and fro with the gentle June breeze, illuminated Lady Beaumont's ballroom just enough for Frances, Lady Stephen Tarkington, to see the other revelers near her without being so bright as to take the fun out of the masquerade. As far as Fanny was concerned, masquerades should be conducted in semi-darkness at all times, even the unmasking. So much better to hide one's identity when one wished to be a little naughty. And oh, but she wanted to be the epitome of a naughty widow.

Her husband, Major Lord Stephen Tarkington, had died at the battle of Waterloo. Tonight, after a long year of mourning his passing, she had emerged from her widow's weeds in the most scandalous costume money could buy. Aphrodite in a filmy white muslin gown, the fabric so sheer she could scarcely feel it against her body. Arching her neck, Fanny pushed her breasts forward until they threatened to spill over her tight bodice, so low cut it skimmed the tops of the dark circles of her nipples. After a year of almost no social interactions, she wanted to burst back onto the stage of *ton* life in the boldest way possible. She smiled behind her glittery silver mask. From the looks of the costumed gentlemen, she had hit her mark.

"Good evening, my beautiful Aphrodite." A tall gentleman in a black mask and the red and white tabard of a Knight Templar bowed low before her. His deep voice seemed forced, obviously disguised.

"Good evening, Sir Knight." She curtsied, giving him a closer look at her décolletage. "Are you just returned from the Crusades? You seem to have the dust of the road still upon you."

"Gads, I do seem to." The knight brushed at his shoulders and a burst of motes flew upward. "M'valet took it out of the attics yesterday and the man obviously didn't attend to it properly."

"You must smite him forthwith, Sir Knight. Such insolence from a lowly squire cannot be tolerated." Ah, Sir Arthur Fremont. His annoyance at his valet had made him abandon his deep voice. She'd recognized the man's high-pitched tone. A dead bore really, although a wonderful partner at whist.

Sir Arthur laughed. "Off with his head, what?"

Holding up her slender golden snake, one of Aphrodite's symbols, she shook it at the wayward knight. "Be sure you do, Sir Knight! Accept no insubordination."

The man danced backward, bumping into a rather plump woman in the guise of some medieval lady in waiting, knocking off her precariously balanced cone-shaped headdress.

"My steeple! You've ruined my steeple!" Clutching the hat, now dented in the middle, the woman stormed off, Sir Arthur following and spouting abject apologies.

Laughing and looking for someone interesting to talk to, Fanny took advantage of the change of sets to make her way across the ballroom toward a rather brightly costumed man wearing the traditional green and brown garb of Robin Hood. He carried a bow and a quiver of arrows on his back; however, what drew her attention was his legs. Encased in fine brown stockings, Robin Hood's shapely legs set her heart to thudding. Of course, she saw men all the time in ballrooms in pantaloons and stockings, but something about those finely muscled calves fed a long dormant hunger and drew her toward him.

"Well met, Prince of Thieves." Fanny smiled up into the masked face, trying to determine who he was. A flirtation with this handsome gentleman might start the evening off well indeed.

"Any meeting with your loveliness, goddess, is sheer fortune." He sketched a bow and moved closer to her. "Are you not afraid I will steal something of value from you?"

Yes, a gentleman willing to play and one she did not recognize. That added spice to the wager. "What thing of value might I possess that you would desire?"

"I believe you possess many delights I could fancy, goddess."

"Indeed?" Again she lifted the snake. "I have only this bauble." She twirled it around, making it catch the candlelight. Oh, but she was enjoying this.

His eyes twinkled and he smiled. "Quite a bauble indeed."

She laughed and tucked the snake into her magical girdle, a leather belt of sorts, and reputedly Aphrodite's sole weapon. "And these."

From her pockets Fanny produced two golden apples, another symbol of the Goddess of Love. She held them before her bodice, right in front of her breasts. "Might you like these, my lord?"

The gentleman's eyes widened behind his mask, then went deepest black. "Ah, yes. You do have treasures I desire."

A shiver raced down her spine.

"I believe I will steal those jewels, goddess." Swaying closer to her, he took the gold-painted apples, his warm fingers brushing hers. He clutched the fruit and her body flushed.

Lord, it had been such a long time since she had flirted so shamelessly with a man. Years before Stephen had died. She'd need to keep her emotions under control while she was learning to navigate this world once more. Almost like being out for her first Season, yet fully aware of all the pleasures that could be the result of such a wild flirtation.

"Take pity on me, kind sir. Those are all I have, save my little snake." Fanny sent a soulful glance toward the thief's face and pulled it forth. "Would you let me exchange something for my apples?"

Robin Hood glanced around and grasped her arm. "Perhaps we should discuss this in a more private setting. I'm certain something can be arranged." A gleam of white teeth behind the mask and he was tugging her toward a darkened corner.

Too fast, even for her. Fanny slowed her steps. Yes, she'd come here tonight hoping for an assignation to a dalliance. A dalliance that might grow into something more than she had bargained for. "I think we should remain here, in the light of this sconce, lest you steal something more than I can afford." She plucked the apples out of his hands and stuffed them back into her pockets. "Even a goddess must be wary of a thief, no matter how handsome."

"Perhaps you shall change your mind before the night is out. May I help persuade you during the next set?"

"Not the next, but the one after it. By then I will have my guard in place."

"Do you think yourself impervious to me?"

"Is not a goddess more powerful than a mere woodsman?" She tried to look down her nose at him, but had to laugh at the effort. A mask made the gesture ridiculous.

"Not if the woodsman can overpower the goddess." He grasped her hands, warm skin to warm skin, no proper gloves between them. Peering deep into her eyes, he leaned forward, breathing into her ear, "Let us continue this lovely interlude in a more private place. The library—"

"There you are, my dear."

Fanny jerked back from the bold gentleman, who also straightened as a demure-looking Diana, complete with quiver and bow, appeared as from nowhere. She pounced on Robin Hood, grabbing his arm and squeezing it. "I have been looking for you, my dear. Wherever have you been?" The petite blond woman, in Greek robes and a white full face mask, smiled at her prey. "Not hiding from me, I hope?"

"Never that, my lady." Robin Hood's smooth voice betrayed a hint of annoyance.

"I have just been informed that Lady Beaumont

has asked us to perform in a match of our archery skills for the entertainment of the guests. Two bowmen of strength, evenly matched." She cocked her head, cool eyes behind her mask glittering. "We don't want to keep our hostess waiting, do we?"

One lingering look from Robin Hood, then he took the lady's arm. "I am afraid duty calls, my goddess. Perhaps we shall continue our discussion of apples at a later time?"

"Assuredly, good sir. As we are promised for the third set, perhaps then." Fanny nodded to them both, thankful her silver mask hid her heated face. She made a shooing motion. "By all means, you must not let a lowly goddess keep you from the all-powerful hostess."

"I'm so glad you understand," Diana said, shooting her a nasty look that Fanny recognized at once. Lady Phoebe Campbell, who'd been out for two Seasons and had just managed to catch Lord Bayberry's youngest son. That must be Robin Hood here, to judge by the fierceness in Lady Phoebe's voice. An arranged marriage, or so her friend Charlotte had told their circle last week, which would explain why the lady wanted to keep Fanny as far away from her betrothed as possible.

"I wish you well in your competition. May the best bowman win."

The couple walked swiftly toward the doors that led to the main part of the house, Lady Phoebe grasping Robin Hood's arm in a death grip. Somehow she doubted Robin would be allowed to return for their set. No great loss if the gentleman was truly betrothed elsewhere.

Fanny stared after them, a smile forming on her lips. Where Lady Beaumont intended to hold such a match, she had no idea. Perhaps there was to be no such exhibition at all. A clever or determined woman wouldn't be above lying to secure her a husband. Fanny considered herself both, but didn't think she could stoop to lying to a man she loved. Stopping short in her musings, she shook off the image of her late husband, tall, wiry, always laughing. By the time she'd lied to him, she had no longer loved him. Anyway, that was in the past. Tonight was the beginning of her future life and she would damn well make the most of it.

With a shake that was partially a shiver, Fanny threw her head back and turned once more to the ballroom. The second set was making so if she waited just a little she could soon find an unoccupied gentleman to dally with. Even though she loved dancing and had not been able to do so for the past year, dancing was the last thing on her mind tonight. As though the clock had rolled back ten years to her own debut Season, she wanted to flit and flirt, to stretch her wings and soar amongst the *ton*'s most eligible gentlemen. She had a deal of time to make up for and the possibilities were deliciously spread out before her.

Several Greek gods in strategically draped robes—everyone from Zeus with his thunderbolts to Hades clutching a huge drinking horn to Poseidon armed with his trident—mingled along the edges of the ballroom floor. A Roman soldier in a shiny breastplate towered over the crowd in the far corner. He must be Lord Walston, the tallest man by far in the *ton*, standing head and shoulders above all the other gentlemen. Height was impossible to disguise, unfortunately. That must spoil the fun for him every time. A sprinkling of Renaissance courtiers, one of whom she recognized as her brother-in-law, Lord Theale. A shock to her, to find him in attendance. Was her sister-in-law here as well? Strike her dumb with a noodle. She'd always known him to be such a high stickler; now to see him cavorting with a pretty shepherdess made her skin crawl.

She turned away quickly. Theale was the last person she wished to encounter when she was in search of a dalliance. Something he would never approve of, even though she was out of mourning. Speaking spritely to a couple of what she assumed were gentlemen in richly colored dominos, she continued her hunt for a flirtation. She spied a lowly shepherd in rough clothing, and a splendidly dressed sultan in colorful robes and a bejeweled mask. Surely a feast for a lady in search of male companionship.

About to head for the dazzling sultan, Fanny glanced about one more time, just to make sure no one else interesting had entered the ballroom, when she caught sight of two identically dressed men bearing down on her. Dark-haired, tall, and broad-shouldered—with shoulders and arms almost bared beneath a thin cape trimmed in gold braid—their slim hips covered in a skirt resembling a pleated kilt of white linen, showing off shapely legs in white stockings and sandals, the duo was breathtaking. Before she could blink they stood beside her, true Greek gods in beauty and stature. Her evening had just taken a most satisfactory turn. A pity their faces were obscured with identical silver half-masks, embossed with a cantering horse across the forehead. She'd wager they were equally handsome underneath.

"Goddess Aphrodite, we greet you in the name of

our father, Zeus." The twin closest to her bowed and grasped her hand.

Suddenly unnerved by his very large, looming presence, she stepped back, trying to pull away but to no avail. The rogue held tight to her hand and raised it to his lips. "Do not be alarmed, my dear. We come to honor you with a request for the next set."

Warily, Fanny studied first the man holding her hand, then his partner. Twin Greek gods was an easy one to identify. "You are impertinent, sirs, as I cannot discern who is who. Are you Castor or Pollux?"

"I am Pollux, Aphrodite," the gentleman holding her hand said, giving it a squeeze that sent sudden tingles all along her arm. "My brother is Castor"—the other man bowed—"though friend, rather than brother, in earnest."

His rich baritone voice tugged at her memory, as did the deep blue eyes behind the mask. The warmth of his hand, however, addled her brain, turning it to mush. Grasping the obvious, she managed to ask, "How . . . how do you propose to both dance with me in a single set, unless one of you secures another partner?"

"An apt question, from an astute goddess." Castor grinned. "I have already captured such a lady for my dancing delight. We four shall make up a set."

"Who is your partner?"

"That very pretty shepherdess over there in pink." He pointed to a young girl in a modest costume, laughing with a group of other young ladies. Well, she'd not have much competition in keeping the twins' attention.

"I should be delighted to make up your set. However"—she turned her attention back to Pollux—"the second set has not yet begun." Fluttering her eyelashes up at the handsome man, she squeezed his hand. "How are we to pass the time until our dance?"

His sharp intake of breath made her hold her own. Even more amazing, his eyes changed from deep blue to black in an instant. The wave of his desire hit her like a tangible thing. Her mouth dried, her heart raced, her whole head heated as though it had caught fire. Who was this man that he could affect her so?

"Come with me." He pulled her toward the double doors behind them that led to the other part of the house.

Heart pounding, Fanny ran on tiptoes in an effort to keep up with him. This was madness. Wherever was he taking her? And what on earth did he have in mind? Oh, but she knew what that was. That deep desire in his eyes told her exactly where his intentions lay. Would she allow him to have his way with her? She didn't quite recognize him; the mask hid just enough of his face. Still he reminded her of someone. Someone who had been most dear to her what seemed a lifetime ago. But that man had left London, swearing never to return to the *ton* years before. He'd retreated to his country estate and had not been seen in Town for seven years.

They raced down the corridor, Pollux still in the lead, Castor right behind her. That gave her some comfort. Pollux wouldn't ravish her in front of his brother, or friend rather. Still, the urgency of his headlong flight, dodging wide-eyed guests left and right, persuaded her that this man would stop at nothing to get her alone.

He turned a corner into a deserted hall and slowed finally. Stopping at a door on the far end, he glanced around then put his hand on the latch. "Keep watch, Cas. No one enters."

Castor grinned. "Not a soul, Pol. My word as a gentleman."

Pollux pushed down the latch, opened the door into a shadowy room, and drew her inside.

The flickering fireplace across the room gave the only light. Fanny's eyes took a moment to adjust to the dimness. A moment in which Pollux pulled her hard against him, crushing her breasts against his unyielding chest. He wrapped his arms around her, pinning her to him, and sank his mouth onto hers.

# Chapter 2

Fanny's building panic subsided at the touch of his lips. Soft, warm, almost tender, he kissed her with a gentleness that surprised her after the fierce desire that had erupted in him. She slipped her arms round his trim waist, every muscle hard beneath her hands. Oh, but she had missed this intimacy for such a long time. So good to be this close to a man again.

He slid his tongue along the seam of her lips and without thinking she opened them, eager for more. Their tongues tangled, then she drew him in, drinking in the glorious feeling once more. Here was the passion she had shared all too little in her married life and seldom with her husband. Only with . . .

Realization hit like a blow from a fist. She pulled away, her hand going to her mouth. It couldn't be.

"Do you finally know me, Fanny?"

Speechless, she nodded, her heart beating oddly in fits and starts.

Pollux smiled and pulled his mask off over his head.

"Matthew." She whispered it, still unsure if it was truly him.

"Without a doubt. Did you truly not know me? I haven't changed that much, surely." He smiled and her stomach dropped. He'd not changed at all. Big, brooding, with a face like a dark angel, Matthew, Lord Lathbury, was just as she remembered.

"You vowed never to return to London." That had been the last time she'd seen him.

"I found never to be much too long a time." He stalked toward her and she retreated until she bumped into a bookcase, the spines of the books knobbly against her back. "I missed you, Fanny. Every day I missed you." His eyes fixed her like a bug on a pin. "Did you miss me?"

Fearing she'd reveal too much, Fanny snapped her eyes shut. Of course she'd missed Matthew. Had wished to see him back in Society more than once. Guilt and duty to Stephen, however, had forbidden her to even ask about him these past years. But she'd thought about him. Oh, yes. On the long, dark nights without Stephen, she'd thought about Matthew quite a lot. "On occasion I believe I wondered what had become of you." Opening her eyes, she allowed herself a careful smile. "How have you been, Matthew?"

"Tolerably well, although deathly bored by the country." He leaned a hand on the bookcase by her head, shutting her off from the main part of the room.

A thrill of excitement shivered down her body. Always a physical man, Matthew knew how to intimidate, to protect, to cherish. Sometimes all at once. "Have you truly remained at Lathbury for seven years? One would think you could travel to other places if London no longer amused you."

Shrugging, he leaned closer to her, bringing the exhilarating smell of bergamot to swirl about her head. "I spent some time shooting in Scotland each year with Kinellan. Then hunting with Braeton in Kent in the fall. I followed racing, as long as it didn't take me too near London."

"Not too difficult for you, then. The best racing's always been at Newmarket and many other tracks are far from Town." The proximity of his presence seemed to press upon her, heightening her senses. He'd always had that effect on her, from the night they'd met at her come-out ball. She'd be drunk on him in minutes. "But why stay away, Matthew?"

"You know why." He straightened and she could breathe easily again. "I couldn't remain in London and run the risk of meeting you at some ball or the theatre. Seeing you and knowing that you had decided you were Stephen's wife, not my lover."

"I didn't decide anything." Fanny retreated toward the fireplace, any place away from him.

"You chose to marry Lord Stephen instead of me." On her heels, Matthew could be as relentless as one of his hounds after a fox. "And you returned to him rather than run away with me."

"I married Stephen years ago." She glanced toward the door, but that was the coward's way. They needed to thrash this out, though why it must be tonight of all nights she didn't know.

"You never told me why." Brows furrowed, he pulled her around to face him again. "Why you would turn down an offer from an earl to marry the youngest son of a marquess."

God Almighty. She might have known that would be his first question. How could she explain a decision she'd wished to take back a thousand times? "Don't do this now, Matthew. I've not seen you in seven years. Can we not renew our acquaintance in a more amicable manner?"

Smoldering black eyes bore into her. "Just answer the question, Fanny. Why him? Why not me?"

What did it matter if he knew or not? She squared her shoulders. Time for a confession. "I was just out of the schoolroom, young, impressionable. Ignorant. Lord Stephen Tarkington personified excitement in a way no other man ever had for me. A rakehell with a reputation to make any girl swoon if he even looked at her. He danced the first set with me and it was over. I could hardly breathe when he touched my hand." Staring straight into his face, she frowned. "All my friends were jealous of his attentions to me and I lorded it over them. I thought he was in love with me, lost my head, and when he asked me I said yes."

"Someone should have been looking out for you. Someone who knew how unsuitable he was." His frown deepened, something she would have sworn impossible.

"You know what ladies always say. 'Reformed rakes make the best husbands.' "

Matthew grunted. "Pity Lord Stephen never reformed."

Sighing, Fanny shook her head. "I should have known better. My aunt brought me out, but she wasn't as worldly as she could have been. I was dazzled by Stephen and she was seduced by his brother's title. Another woman might have advised me better."

"Might have advised you to marry me."

Fanny lowered her eyes. "Yes, she might have

done." How many times had she wished that were true? "You would have been a brilliant match, I cannot deny it. You were handsome, tall, strong."

"Did I annoy you, perhaps?"

"No, you were quite charming." She slipped her hand over his chest and heat poured through her. "And very persistent, if I remember correctly. Two bouquets of roses after that first ball."

"Too persistent, then? Or too eager?" The bullish look returned to his face, brows lowered, cheeks puffed out.

"Neither." Grasping his hand, Fanny attempted to draw him over to the sofa. She might as well have been leading a statue. "You were everything a girl could have wanted."

"Almost every girl."

"I'm sorry, Matthew." She dropped his hand, now annoyed herself. "Yes, I chose to marry Stephen. I was young and inexperienced and didn't know what he was really like. Had someone, anyone, taken me in hand, I'd likely be your countess this moment and you wouldn't be standing there looking like you wanted to murder someone. And I wouldn't be standing here wanting to plant you a facer."

He laughed, and the tension eased. "I've been working out at Jackson's, so I think I can manage to avoid a blow or two."

"You do look marvelously in shape." A hunger kindled in her belly. Each time she'd touched him she'd felt the coiled steel of his muscles.

"I had to be if I was to wear this costume." His chuckle floated in the flickering darkness.

"Well, I for one am very glad you made the effort." Her eyes feasted on his form from top to toe as her hunger grew. It had been too long since she'd had a man in her bed. This man in her bed. But not here. Not now, but maybe soon. She smiled up into his face, letting all her joy shine through.

"You are very welcome." With a fingertip he smoothed back her hair and Fanny feared she'd melt into the floor. "I hope you know you still can be."

"Can be what?"

"My countess."

The air around her seemed to harden, as though she'd run into a wall while standing still. Had she actually heard what she thought she'd heard? "I beg your pardon?"

"Shall I go down on one knee, Fanny?" He suited the movement to his words and dropped to the floor, her hand captured in both of his. "You cannot be surprised, my dear. Why else would I have come to London?"

"But . . ." Gazing into his upturned face, shining with a joy she'd not seen in years, her powers of speech deserted her.

"Please, Fanny, do me the very great honor of becoming my wife and you will make me the happiest man in Christendom." Matthew's insistent tone, the look of longing in his eyes tugged at her heart. Why hadn't she seen his deep regard for her all those years ago? They both might be much happier had she never married Stephen. However, she was a different woman now.

"Get up, please, Matthew." She tried to slip her hand out of his grasp, but he held on fast as he rose to his feet.

"My standing won't change my question." He raised her hand to his lips and that wonderful, awful sinking feeling raced through her once more. "I love you, Fanny. I made that quite clear to you seven years ago."

"Yes, when you were trying to persuade me to run away with you." She wiggled her hand again, but it was no use. She might as well try to break free from a vise.

"You were terribly unhappy and I wanted to take you away. Make you happy once more. But you wouldn't let me."

"Someone had to be sensible. The scandal would have ruined us both." How had they come to reliving that wretchedly wonderful interlude seven years ago? They had been the best four months of her life, until she had come to her senses. And had made Matthew see sense as well.

"Now you are a widow, free as the air, you can marry me and we can enjoy one another as we did then. Even better, because we won't have to live in fear of being found out." He pulled her closer and seized her lips.

Bliss. Pure bliss to surrender to his lips once more. Firm, commanding, and with a flick of his tongue, he suddenly plundered her mouth. Hot and greedy he ravaged her, so insistent she could focus on nothing but him as he crushed her against his almost naked chest and devoured her. The world ceased to exist, save for one single thing: Matthew.

He slid his hands from her head down her back, each sensual inch stoking her flaming body more. Then he cupped her derriere and pressed her against him, wanting her to feel that eager, hard ridge against her most sensitive place. God, how she wanted him, wanted to give into him. She gloried in their closeness another moment, longing to be closer still. Yes, that would come to pass, and soon. And for now she would savor just one more moment until . . .

With a phenomenal strength of will, Fanny pulled away from his seductive heat. "But we are not married, Matthew. We can still be brought to ruin if we are found here."

"Not if you accept my proposal." He strode forward, lust in his hot gaze.

Retreating behind a tall wing-backed chair, she shook her head. "But I'm not accepting you."

He stopped as if he'd run into an invisible wall, his face blank. "You're not accepting me? Why not, for God's sake?"

Digging her fingers into the chair's soft leather upholstery, Fanny tried to clear her head before she spoke. "I am just come from a year of wearing widow's weeds. I expected to have time to enjoy my freedom. I had no idea you hadn't already married or that you'd be here on my first night out again."

"You want freedom? What on earth for? I'm offering you everything a woman could want: a title, social position, love. Do those things have no meaning for you, Fanny?" Hurt had deepened his voice.

"I got those same things when I married Stephen. And we both know how miserable they made me." Miserable enough to seek solace in this man's arms, despite her wedding vows.

"I may be many things, Fanny, but we both know I am not Stephen Tarkington." The black eyes and lowered brows had returned.

"Lower your voice before someone hears."

Waving her concerns away, he crossed his arms over his broad chest, muscles bulging. "The only one to hear might be Castor, and believe me, he's not letting anyone into this room. Better than Cerberus, my twin." He advanced toward her once more, stalking toward the chair.

Fanny dodged behind a table, putting the length between them. "Any man will be unfaithful given the right circumstances. My husband didn't need anything other than an opportunity."

"I disagree." Matthew inched toward the middle of the table, his gaze darting to and fro. "Only certain types of men will stray. I am not one of those."

"Please forgive me if I don't stake the rest of my life on that, my lord." Oh, she needed to get away from him, away from this conversation before she said something she would truly regret.

"You know I love you and only you, Fanny." His beseeching blue eyes would melt the resolve of a saint.

"Matthew." Hating the pleading tone of her voice, yet helpless to change it, Fanny grasped her head in her hands to stop the whirling sensation. God knew she wanted to believe him. As she had believed Stephen. She'd been young and naive then. She wouldn't make that same mistake now. "I need time. Time to spread my wings a little. To enjoy my freedom for a while at least and decide if I do wish to marry again."

He leaned back sharply and she sensed that had been a blow. "And in the meantime?"

Leaning into him, she whispered, "We can renew our acquaintance in all ways that count."

"So you'll agree to bed me but not wed me?" His frown deepened.

"For the moment." She tapped her fingers lightly on his chest. "Would that be such a hardship on you?"

Sighing, he pulled a face. "I suppose not." A flash of his boyish grin made her stomach drop. "May I woo you properly, at least?"

"Improperly would be more to my taste." Fanny returned his smile with one of her own, as sultry and seductive as she could make it. "But I suppose some decorous behavior wouldn't kill me either."

"Good." He took her hands and raised them to his lips. "I leave for Brighton at the end of the week. I'd hoped you'd be accompanying me as my wife, but that—"

"As your wife?" How arrogant of him to think she'd fall into his arms at the snap of his fingers. "Did you bring the special license with you tonight?"

He chuckled and shook his head. "I'd planned to get it tomorrow. Don't ruffle your feathers. If I thought myself sure of you, you've certainly clipped my wings. As I was saying, I leave for Brighton at the end of the week and I'd like for you to come. Not with me"—he shot the remark in before she could draw breath to protest—"but a visit to the seaside would not come amiss at this time of year, I think. Many are removing there, so you will have your pick of the gentlemen, and I may 'woo you with some spirit when you come.' "

"Am I to play Kate to your Petruchio? You see me as a shrew, my lord? Not the most flattering of compliments." She arched her neck, secretly pleased. Of all Shakespeare's plays, *The Taming of the Shrew* was her favorite. Its heroine was a spirited woman. She could see herself in that role, with Matthew attempting to tame her as he wooed. This excursion could be most amusing. She'd have to find a companion to accompany her, of course. One of her widowed friends would work nicely. Especially her sister-in-law Jane, who also had a wild streak in her. A companion to encourage seduction rather than a chaperone. How delicious.

"Well? Will you meet me in Brighton?" Matthew's eager voice brought her back to the dim room now filled with possibilities.

"I will be happy to journey to Brighton, my lord. If I find you there, I do hope you will attend me most earnestly." In a heart's beat she slipped her hands from his, pulled his lips down to hers, and sealed the pact with a kiss so warm and sweet her resolve slipped a notch. "And now if you'll excuse me?" Turning swiftly on her toes, Fanny raced for the door. As she grasped the handle, she glanced back at him.

The victorious grin on his face sent a shiver down her spine. She pulled the door open and fled into the corridor before she could change her mind.

# Chapter 3

Matthew stared at the door, his mind reeling at Fanny's capricious words. Seven long years he'd waited to make his proposal and she'd refused him in less than a minute. Why he didn't say to hell with the woman and marry someone else he couldn't fathom. Just that he couldn't. The woman had enchanted him body and soul ten years ago when he'd vowed no one else would be his countess. He'd waited this long; might as well bide his time a bit longer.

Running his hand through his hair, he glanced around the room. What kind of library had no libation in it for a thirsty guest? The refreshment room would have to do, although little hope of anything stronger than lemonade there. With a shake of his head, Matthew quit the library and headed back into the main rooms where the masquerade became even more risqué. He witnessed a couple not quite in the shadows, the woman in a Cleopatra costume with her back against the wall while a Roman gladiator kissed the tops of her mostly visible breasts.

As he passed them the woman's moans recalled Fanny to him. Damn. His member had stiffened as by magic and his thin costume wouldn't disguise it for long. He hurried on, hoping for the refreshment room and something, anything to cool his ardor. Turning sideways to avoid a shrieking medieval princess and the Zeus who chased her, Matthew bumped into another couple, a courtier and some kind of goddess in flowy white robes, their mouths locked together. God, he would go mad if he couldn't get away from all these rutting couples.

At last he rounded a corner into a room filled with long tables loaded with row upon row of delicacies. Sugary pastries, savory lobster patties, puddings and salads enough to make the mouth water. At the end of one he recognized his erstwhile accomplice.

"Abandoned your post a bit early, did you, Kinellan?" Matthew sidled up beside the tall man who could almost have been his twin in earnest.

Gareth, Eighth Marquess of Kinellan, shrugged and forked three patties and a cherry tart onto his already full plate. "Once Aphrodite fled the room, the guard dog ceased to be relevant. So I thought I'd pop along and have a feed." He glanced up at Matthew, a smirk on his lips. "I assumed you'd be along eventually."

"Indeed." Matthew picked up a plate, although still unsettled enough that the food appealed to him not at all.

"I take it things did not go as planned."

"Hardly. Had they done so Aphrodite would have left on my arm or at my side."

Kinellan cocked his head. "You proposed?"

"I did."

"And she refused you?"

"She did." Matthew speared a patty with enough force to break it in two.

"Is the woman daft?" His friend frowned as he added a slice of cake to his plate and turned to survey the room. "There, that small table in the corner."

Matthew threw several other savories onto his plate, not paying attention to which fork he grabbed, then followed him to a table scarcely large enough to hold their plates. After juggling the silverware a bit, he forked a lobster patty into his mouth. A heavenly rich sauce burst in his mouth. "Umm. Damned good, this."

"Wait until you try the capon in pastry." Kinellan popped one in his mouth and sighed. "Gods, I could live on these, I believe. Do you think I could steal Lady Beaumont's cook?"

"Huh. You'd have a better chance of stealing Lady Beaumont herself." Matthew crunched into one of the pastries. His friend was right. "Fanny's a strong-willed woman, one of the things I most admire about her. Even when she was first out, she spoke her mind, at least more so than most of the young ladies. I found that refreshing and"—he chuckled at the memory of Fanny rapping his hand with her fan—"more than a little stimulating. I love a challenge. She's never let me down where that's concerned."

"And you've been besotted with her ever since? When was she out?"

"Ten years ago."

"Gods. When she turned you down then, why didn't you offer for another lady? There must have been a few about."

Glaring at his friend over the table, Matthew gulped his lemonade, cursing that it wasn't something stronger. "Because I was in love with Fanny. When she married Lord Stephen I thought I'd go mad. But I lingered in London." Oh yes, he'd dawdled in Town for three long years. "I knew Lord Stephen's reputation. It was only a matter of time before he strayed." He carefully put the empty glass on the table. "I wanted to be there if Fanny needed me."

"And I assume she did."

"Less quickly than I would have imagined. But then they followed the drum for the first year, his cavalry regiment drilling at Windsor or patrolling the countryside. I saw her whenever he was on leave in London and she seemed happy enough." He'd known—or God help him, had he hoped?—it wouldn't last. "Then in '08 he got a long leave in London. I saw Fanny more at balls and parties, but less and less often with her husband. Each time I saw her she looked sadder and angrier."

"And you became her friend."

"I did." Matthew looked away. "I comforted her as best I could." She'd cried brokenheartedly in his arms after she'd found out about her husband's worst infidelity. "Then I tried to persuade her to run away with me."

Kinellan's eyebrows jumped an inch. "Gods, you're a crack shot."

Shrugging, Matthew crossed his arms over his chest. "I took a chance and lost. She refused me. Again. Much as she despised Stephen by this point, she wouldn't break her vows. She went back to him and I returned to Hunter's Cross, in self-imposed exile for the past seven years."

"You've more tenacity than I ever have, I must say."

Kinellan tugged at his mask. "Can we take these infernal things off, at least to eat? Damned nuisance."

"It's not midnight yet, but I don't particularly care if you do. I know you're the Marquess of Kinellan if no one else does." Matthew laughed and allowed his boyhood friend to change the subject as he ripped the glittery mask from his face and sent it sailing across the room. "I suppose there's something to be said for being recognized. You'll have the ladies flocking to you now."

"If they wouldn't have me when they didn't know me, I'll not have them when they do." Kinellan puckered his lips before biting into a cherry tart. He wolfed it down in two bites, then licked the crumbs from his fingers.

"Have you no one to feed you at Castle Kinellan?" Matthew forked up another lobster patty. Lady Beaumont did have a treasure in her current cook.

"Mrs. McGraw is tolerable, but it's very plain cooking." Seizing another capon pastry, Kinellan bit into it slowly, a look of ecstasy on his face. "I'm lucky if I get a decent pudding out of her." He swallowed the second bite and sipped his lemonade. "So now, after all this time, you intend to go after Lady Stephen?"

"Of course I do." The food must have rattled his friend's brain. "I'm going to dance with her before the night is through, and marry her before the year is out."

"Six months to convince her to marry you? Giving yourself a bit of a leeway, aren't you? You thought she'd agree to marry you tonight." Kinellan lined up a row of ratafia cakes across his plate. "Sounds like you have doubts she'll take you."

"Where Fanny is concerned, I wouldn't wager on anything." An unfortunate truth he hated to admit. But he had hopes. Her response to his kisses tonight had been sweeter than he'd imagined. Than he'd remembered. He'd woo her back into his life—and into his bed—before the summer was done. "But I've planned an assault in the event she didn't succumb to my roguish charm."

"Assault is it? Are we to launch a Widow's Campaign?" Mischief showed in his friend's dark blue eyes.

"Indeed, we are. First sally staunchly rebuffed. Second one to be more carefully planned." Matthew glanced at the lean-faced man across from him. "You'd planned to accompany me to Brighton, hadn't you?"

"Nothing much else to do until the shooting begins in August. Brighton could be a lark. Do you plan to take up sea bathing?" Kinellan leaned back in his chair, cake in hand.

"I do." Matthew smirked. "I understand it can be very stimulating."

"Gods, with the weather as cold as it is, I should say so. Even in June."

"You have no idea." Matthew laid his fork on his plate. "Now, I need a new disguise."

Taking hands again with a short, stout Cupid, Fanny tried in vain to keep her mind on the dance as they cast off then performed a two-hand turn. Matthew had no right to appear out of thin air and force his way back into her life. Neither was it fair of him to propose before she'd even taken it in that he'd returned.

"Oh, I beg your pardon, my dear." Cupid had trod squarely on her foot.

The pain registered, but only as a bare nuisance. "Not at all, sir. It was likely my mistake in the step. Do we circle right, now?" She should never have agreed to dance again tonight. Not while her mind was so disengaged. Grasping her partner's hands, Fanny managed to follow around the circle until they returned to place, which thankfully left them out for several measures.

"Are you enjoying yourself tonight, Aphrodite?" Her Cupid seemed to feel conversation necessary. Pity.

"As much as a goddess can when surrounded by mere mortals. Don't you find that tedious as well? Wouldn't you rather confer only with your fellow gods and goddesses?" She'd been keeping a keen eye out for Matthew. Had this not been her first ball in over a year, she'd have left as soon as she fled the library. But she'd be dashed if she'd let his lordship ruin her first night of freedom.

"I would indeed, if they were all as ravishing and regal as you." The little man's eyes gleamed behind his rough, white half-mask.

Lord, not another one. Well, this was the freedom she had sought. "You are kind, Cupid. But we are back in the set."

Thank goodness. They cast up and went down the set and Fanny took care to concentrate on the steps, as much to not miss them as to discourage more conversation. The set should almost be done. Another set-to with her partner, another circle right. When they reached their places, the music changed for a bow and Fanny allowed Cupid to lead her from the floor.

"My thanks, Cupid, for your nimble feet when mine seemed so clumsy." Surreptitiously, Fanny glanced about for an acquaintance. "Allow me to visit Athena there, to borrow wisdom before I commit further folly on the dance floor."

"Of course, my goddess." He bowed, a good sport who knew her interest lay elsewhere.

She dipped a curtsy and hurried toward a woman dressed in classic robes, a warlike helmet, and an owl perched on her shoulder. The woman had enough height she might be Lady Sophia Mallory, a friend of her come-out Season, now Lady Fauquier. Fanny hurried toward her.

"Aphrodite. A goddess I have long adored."

Stopping so swiftly her slippers slid on the polished floor, Fanny wavered precariously before a strong hand grabbed her arm. She spun around, lips pursed to show her displeasure if that grasp belonged to Pollux.

A breathy little squeak escaped instead when she beheld a tall man in a red domino, his face covered in a black oval mask that hid his features completely.

"Unhand me, sir. I will not be accosted by an enigma." The featureless robe hid any distinguishing characteristics, save his height. Taller than Matthew, to be sure. She relaxed a trifle. Perhaps this mysterious gentleman would take her mind off Lord Lathbury's proposal.

"Then allow me to partner you in the next set. By the end, I'm certain I'll be no more a mystery to you than your own true love."

Fanny started at his words, but the voice wasn't Matthew's. Deeper, more gravelly. More dangerous. The very adventure she'd been longing for. "You will need to be transparent indeed, Monsieur Domino, to accomplish that in the course of a single set."

"I am yours to command." He offered his arm, still clothed in the folds of the robe, and she lay her hand upon it, a thrill of excitement shooting through her. Sweeping her back onto the floor, he steered her toward the top of the line where a Longways set was forming.

"We are to be the top couple?" Fanny raised her brows, then realized he couldn't see her arch movement. Masks did have their drawbacks. Settling for dropping her hand from his arm, she straightened her shoulders and glared at him, with what she hoped was a piercing stare.

He chuckled. "You should be placed at the head of everything you do, my goddess. Do you not agree?"

How was one supposed to answer that? The gentleman was too clever by half. "Then I should be ranked above you as well?"

"Of course. I am a mere nothing. If I had my way, you would be on a pedestal, above all the mere mortals and even the rulers of Olympus." He shifted stiffly, an odd movement for one who had been so graceful moments ago. "Ah, we are ready."

The orchestra raised their instruments and called for *La Bagatelle.*

Fanny and the Domino bowed to one another, then began to set to the second lady. A very active dance for the first couple, who set to and circled with the second couple, then she joined hands with her partner and moved quickly down the center and back. A spritely dance that, because they were a lead couple, kept them in almost constant motion. That would not do. She would discover who this mystery gentleman was. No one of his height came to mind, but nothing else gave him away either. Well, he could not avoid talking to her. She'd puzzle it out from that.

"How does one address a cipher, pray tell?" she asked as they turned right, his bright robes billowing out behind him.

"However Aphrodite wishes. I am humbly at your service in all things," came the glib reply.

"I declare you will annoy me if you do not give me some hint of who you are, sir. I fear I do not know you at all." Perhaps she could shame him into giving her a clue.

They cast around the second couple and formed another set.

"Very well. I will tell you that I am of your acquaintance."

"Long acquaintance?"

"Not nearly long enough for my taste."

"Indeed." They turned to the right, Fanny thinking furiously. "Did you know my late husband, perhaps? He was in the Royal Horse Guards."

"I knew him, although we were never more than acquaintances. We were introduced more than ten years ago." His hand tightened on hers as they turned again. "Do you not know me still, Fanny?"

Wobbling with the shock, Fanny careened into Matthew's shoulder.

He grabbed her arm and they progressed down the set and were thankfully out for the next measure.

"What are you doing?" Fanny whispered, outraged that he had fooled her once more.

"Dancing with you. It has been too long since we stood up together."

She couldn't see it, but the wretch was undoubtedly smiling beneath that mask. "I thought I was to meet you at Brighton. You were to give me the opportunity to spread my wings before we spoke again."

"I don't believe that was the exact agreement, my dear; however, you did agree that I could woo you properly." He grasped her hands again as they now joined the set as the second couple. "What is more proper than having you as my dancing partner?"

Unable to speak due to the steps that took her away from him, Fanny couldn't help but smile beneath her mask. Matthew was correct about one thing. He was not Stephen Tarkington. She'd pursued Stephen perhaps even more than he'd chased her those long years ago. Now she had the opportunity to be the object of a man's hunt. Lord Lathbury's Corinthian nature would insist he did everything within his power to make sure his prey did not escape. There was something very appealing in that.

They met again, set to the first couple, and eventually turned together, giving Fanny the chance to ask something that had puzzled her greatly. "How on earth did you manage to increase your height, Matthew? I can swear you are two inches taller than when you were in the library."

His chuckle sounded loudly in her ears as they turned the opposite way. "Boots, my dear. Kinellan had a spare pair in his carriage. Fortunately our feet are not too much different in size, although these do pinch now and then. The heels gave me a bit more height than my dancing shoes."

"And the domino and mask?" He'd obviously

taken some trouble to be able to dance with her without her knowing him.

"Borrowed from Lord Beaumont. I remembered it from Lady Beaumont's last masquerade I attended. Luckily he had not disposed of it after all these years."

"You seem to have luck with you this evening." Fanny couldn't help a rueful smile. Matthew had always had a bit of luck about him.

"If I truly had, you'd be betrothed to me this minute." He bowed as the dance ended, his eyebrows rising as he offered her his arm.

"Not that lucky, then, perhaps." She shook her head and looked away. He wouldn't break her resolve so easily, although the man's determination was almost palpable. The warmth and vigor of him, lying right beneath her hand, sent pulses of desire through her, despite her decision to wait on his proposal. Might that be a mistake?

Fanny tossed her head and with it the momentary doubt fled. She must take care to become reacquainted with Lord Lathbury, to know him and his nature better than she had Stephen Tarkington's before she married him. She could not afford to make such a grievous mistake again.

# Chapter 4

Late next morning, after a successful gathering with her friends at Lady Cavendish's town house, Fanny climbed into the carriage, very satisfied with the meeting of what her hostess insisted on calling "The Widows' Club." Not an odd name exactly, for everyone in their little group was widowed. Charlotte's idea that their circle resembled the gentlemen's clubs, however, seemed rather fanciful. Still, it had given her the idea to host a house party in August. Nothing hinted at the desire for dalliance more than a house party. And she'd told Charlotte to invite Lathbury as her special gentleman. Of course, by August, she and Matthew should be quite an item among the *ton.*

Another of her friends, Mrs. Elizabeth Easton, climbed in and sat beside her, her oval face drawn in lines of grief. Elizabeth still deeply mourned the passing of her husband. Of course, Lieutenant Colonel Easton had been a model spouse, deserving of such devotion. Elizabeth had seemed ill at ease all throughout the morning, as they planned for the house party and which gentlemen they would invite. Most of the gathering were enthusiastically planning their conquests in August. But not Elizabeth.

"I think Charlotte's idea is brilliant, don't you, my dear? Summer house parties do incline people to be more adventuresome, at least in my experience." Fanny shot Elizabeth a knowing grin, hoping to draw her out of her somber mood.

"I'm rather afraid I have little experience of them, Fanny. And I doubt I will be much of an asset to this one to come." Her friend pried open her reticule and snatched out a handkerchief. "I'm more likely to be a watering pot than good company to Georgie's brother." She wiped her eyes, then fingered the small black lace edging. "She was a dear to suggest it, but I hope Lord Brack doesn't come expecting an amiable companion. He will be in for a disappointment."

"I sincerely doubt that, my dear. With your sweet nature you couldn't disappoint anyone if you tried." Persuading her friend to return to Society and the hunt for another husband would not be easy, it seemed. "You should give Charlotte's scheme a chance, Elizabeth. The party is not to be held for some weeks. As you go out more in society, you will begin to feel differently."

"What if I don't want to feel differently, Fanny?" Tears cascaded down Elizabeth's cheeks until she wiped them away with the handkerchief. "I loved Dickon and I still miss him so dreadfully." She looked accusingly at Fanny. "Just because the year of mourning is over doesn't mean my feelings have changed. Even if I wear bright clothes, they will still cover a broken heart."

Lord, what must it be like to have loved a man so

deeply? "Of course that is true, my dear. No one who knows you will think you have forgotten the lieutenant colonel. However, I doubt he would wish for you to mourn him forever. And Charlotte's party may be the easiest way for you to begin to seek the companionship of gentlemen once more. You may wish, as Charlotte and Jane do, not to marry again. But don't close every door that could lead to a change of heart." Fanny squeezed her friend's hands.

"Have you decided to marry again, Fanny?" Elizabeth asked, cocking her head.

"Not exactly, no. Why do you ask?"

"Well, you produced Lord Lathbury's name so quickly when Charlotte asked for the gentlemen guests, I wondered." Elizabeth managed a small, mischievous smile. "You said you renewed your acquaintance with him last night. What is he like?"

She'd never dreamed Elizabeth could turn the conversation expertly away from herself and fasten it uncomfortably on Fanny instead. She'd have sworn the woman didn't have a devious bone in her body. "As I said at the gathering, he's a Corinthian, always has been mad about sport of any kind. Hunting, shooting, racing, boxing. If it called for him to be outdoors, on a horse, or besting an opponent with his fists, Matthew enjoyed it."

"Matthew?" Elizabeth's eyebrows arched almost to her hairline.

"Yes," Fanny sighed. The woman would have to know she and Matthew were something more than friends. "We've known one another for years, and we became very close the year of my come-out."

"How close?" Elizabeth's blue eyes bore straight into Fanny's.

"Close enough for him to offer marriage."

"He proposed?" Her eyes had rounded now. "And you refused him?"

"I was wild for Stephen." Fanny turned away to stare out the window. "But after I married him, I . . . I couldn't quite give up Matthew."

"What?" Elizabeth gripped the edge of the seat, as if she feared she might fall off it.

"I don't mean it that way. But Stephen and I were stationed close to London that first year, so I often came into Town to dances and parties. Matthew would dance with me and escort me about. It was all harmless, but we became very close friends because of it."

"Did Lord Stephen think it harmless as well?"

"By then Lord Stephen was off pursuing his own less than harmless affairs." Fanny tried to keep the anger out of her voice, but it was still difficult. "I doubt he gave my flirtation with Matthew a second thought, if he even heard about it. As I said, it was nothing really."

"And do you now think it may become something?" Elizabeth leaned forward, her own sorrow clearly forgotten in her eagerness to hear Fanny's plans.

"I believe so."

"Oh Fanny, how wonderful! Do you think he may propose?"

"He did last night."

Elizabeth's audible gasp could have been given from the stage. Her eyes widened impossibly large and she clasped her chest as though her heart might attempt an escape. "He did! Fanny, how wonderful!

Why did you not say a word to me and Charlotte and the others?"

"Because I did not accept him, Elizabeth." Lord, her confession might not have been the most prudent thing to do. Yet, Elizabeth would need to know the truth if she was to be her companion, and look the other way when she met Matthew in Brighton.

"You refused Lord Lathbury *again*?" By her tone and dumbfounded look, Elizabeth clearly thought she had lost her senses.

"Given my experiences with Stephen for ten years, I believe I need time to be quite sure my next husband will treat our marriage vows as sacred ones."

"Oh, Fanny, of course." Elizabeth had shrunk back into the seat, her gaze on her lap. "I spoke without thinking. It is not a decision to be taken lightly, even if you are well acquainted with the gentleman."

"Once. We were well acquainted once. However, last night was the first time I'd seen Matthew in almost seven years." Although that time really made no difference. She knew Matthew from the top of his sleek black head to the bottoms of his brightly polished shoes. Unless given sufficient reason to do so, men didn't change. God knew Stephen hadn't in the ten years of their marriage. Matthew was the same now as then. Yet she still could not bring herself to accept him.

"So Charlotte's party will give the two of you time to become friends again? That is a marvelous idea, Fanny. Will Lord Lathbury accept the invitation, do you think?" Elizabeth grasped her hand eagerly.

"I daresay he will. He seemed *very* eager to renew our friendship last evening." Fanny couldn't suppress the chuckle that escaped her, remembering Matthew's body pressed to hers. "In fact, he has issued an invitation of his own."

"He did? What kind of invitation?" Her friend seemed to hang on every word. Good.

"It seems he is removing to Brighton at the end of the week." Fanny squeezed Elizabeth's hand and forced gaiety into her voice. "He has asked me to visit there as well."

"With him?" Drawing back, Elizabeth sent her hand to her chest once more. How could the woman be so easily flustered?

"He had expected I would accompany him as his wife. But now, he hopes we will meet and enjoy the delights of the seaside as friends."

"He does seem to wish to woo you properly, Fanny." Elizabeth had settled back into her cocoon of propriety. She, of course, had not seen the fire in Matthew's eyes last evening. Proper wooing had no place in his plans, Fanny would wager.

Still, she would seize the perfect opportunity. "And of course I will need a companion to accompany me, for propriety's sake. Will you come with me?"

"Me?" Elizabeth squeaked. "I'd have thought Charlotte or Jane would be better suited to such a journey."

"Not necessarily. Besides, they have to begin the move to Lyttlefield Park, so they will not be available in July at all." Fanny smiled and patted Elizabeth's arm. "The sea air and sea bathing will do wonders for your spirits and your health."

"Oh, no." Elizabeth pushed back in her seat until her head dug into the upholstery. "I refuse to sea bathe. I have never done it and I will not try now."

Fanny frowned, but shrugged. "Very well, only the

sea air for you, then. I'm not certain why you've taken bathing in dislike, but if you prefer to sit on the esplanade and watch, I have no objection to it."

At that assurance, Elizabeth relaxed a trifle. "Have you sea bathed before?"

"Of course. Mama and Papa used to take us to Weymouth each year and insisted we take the waters and bathe." Fond memories of her family, now gone, were always bittersweet. "I believe I was ten when I was first dipped."

Glancing about the carriage, Elizabeth leaned forward and dropped her voice to a whisper. "Do ladies really take off all their clothes to do it?"

Laughing, Fanny nodded. "Some do, but they don't have to. There are bathing dresses that cover one completely."

"Did you wear . . . ?" Elizabeth's cheeks turned fiery red.

"When I was a child I did." Fanny grinned at her blushing friend. "Once I married, Stephen didn't care if I wore one or not. So I didn't."

"Gracious." Elizabeth glanced all around the carriage, not wanting to meet Fanny's gaze.

"The water is quite invigorating and your bathing machine assures you of absolute privacy." Fanny doubted any amount of privacy could induce Elizabeth to bathe naked. Not even if she were the only woman on the beach. That had often been her own daydream. To be able to walk the beach at Weymouth or Brighton totally naked and free, running into and out of the water at will. Some nights she'd even imagined it with a tall, dark-haired male companion.

"Isn't the water rather cold?"

Her current companion's words startled Fanny back from her musings. "That's supposed to be why it's healthful to do it. I suspect the waters might be even warmer in July. My family always went in October."

"I somehow doubt it this year." Elizabeth shivered and pulled her cloak more securely around her shoulders. "The weather has been much colder than usual. I don't remember it ever being this cold in June."

"Nor do I. But that won't deter me in Brighton." Fanny cocked her head and fixed Elizabeth with a keen eye. "So you will be my companion in July? I hope to stay for at least three weeks. That will give me time to become truly reacquainted with Matthew and make up my mind about marrying him. Then we will have a little rest before Charlotte's house party." She grasped Elizabeth's clasped hands. "Please say you'll come with me."

"If you truly need me, Fanny . . ."

"I do. Most passionately. You can be my advisor and lay out all the reasons why I should marry again." It would take extremely good ones to overcome the lack of trust she felt for men after her husband's grave infidelities. But perhaps Elizabeth could find a way to persuade her to have faith in men again.

"Then yes, I will accompany you to Brighton." Elizabeth nodded, the frown lines in her face smoothed out. "When do you wish to leave? I will have to consult with my mother about the children, although she seems to enjoy raising them when I go away."

"Excellent. We will set the first of July for our departure and our return on the twenty-second, which is a full three weeks." The prospect of being wooed by Lord Lathbury for three weeks seemed better each time she thought of it. "And you will have plenty of time to make your own acquaintances while we are there. We needn't live in one another's pockets. You deserve some time to yourself as well."

"Hmm." Elizabeth's smile had a knowing look to it. "That will depend on how much chaperoning you need, Fanny. You don't want to cause talk about you and Lord Lathbury, do you?"

"There is always some talk about any couple seen in company overmuch." Elizabeth might prove harder to evade than she'd originally thought. "We shall see once we meet with Lord Lathbury and see what he's about."

"I am certain you will do that with the swiftness of Mercury, Fanny." Elizabeth laughed as the carriage stopped before Worth House.

"I will send you the particulars of our journey as soon as I have them fixed," Fanny called to her friend as she left the carriage and hurried up the steps of her parents' town house. Settling back into her seat, she removed a pencil and a scrap of paper from her reticule and began a list of things to be done to prepare for their journey. Every so often, she thought of Matthew and her body tingled pleasantly. July would be a very warm month for her, whatever the weather.

The carriage deposited her before the Marquess of Theale's town house in short order, just as she had begun to consider what house agent to engage. Their three weeks would be so much more pleasant if they could acquire a house in one of the more fashionable neighborhoods. And the right agent could make all the difference. She would consult with Lady Theale as soon as possible and Lavinia would ask Lord Theale's advice about the agent.

Lord Theale had always made Fanny uncomfortable, though she'd never understood why. Something strange in his pale blue-eyed gaze always gave her the jimjams. She saw the man only at meals, when he turned up for them. Otherwise, she avoided his company whenever possible.

The butler opened the door for her, and Fanny strode into the entry hall, shedding her spencer as she asked, "Noyes, where is Lady Theale?"

"Her ladyship is in the family drawing room, Lady Stephen." He took her wrap, but waited expectantly.

"Thank you, Noyes. That is all for the moment." Fanny started for the staircase.

"Very good, my lady. A bouquet of flowers arrived for you while you were out. I took the liberty of putting it there." Noyes gestured to a tall vase filled with masses of blue hyacinths and red roses with greenery shaped to look like a small tree. It must have measured a good two feet from side to side and towered over her from its place on a small table.

Fanny stared at it, dumbfounded. Who had sent her such a huge bouquet? She retraced her steps until she stood before the vase, the sweet smell of the hyacinth wafting over her. She loved hyacinth. Burying her nose in the deep blue petals, she breathed in the scent she always associated with home. Her mother's garden had bloomed with the colorful flowers all summer.

Plucking the card out of the thick stems, she turned it over and froze. The writing, familiar even after seven years, stopped her breath as she read the inscription:

*Hyacinth for constancy, roses for love. You shall have both from me always. Matthew.*

Matthew had sent them. She might have known. Still, she couldn't be upset with him. She had given him leave to woo her, and what more traditional way than with flowers? A very sweet and thoughtful gesture, for he'd remembered her fondness for these particular blooms. With a shaking hand, she caressed the soft petals, something inside her trying to break free of its icy lair. If Lord Lathbury continued his courtship thus—and knowing his determined nature as she did he would use every method at his command to make her say yes—her plan never to remarry would require some serious reconsideration.

# Chapter 5

Dancing on her toes, almost unable to contain her delight, Fanny gazed about Mrs. Townsend's well-appointed ballroom with growing excitement. Somehow the glittering gold and crystal room seemed more attractive, the Brighton crowd more elegant than those at other such entertainments she'd attended. Perhaps the cause was the new sense of freedom her widowhood had endowed her with. Or simply the sheer anticipation of seeing Matthew again. It had only been a little over two weeks since they'd met, still the time had seemed an eternity. Whatever the reason for her exhilaration tonight, Fanny's nerves sizzled from her head to her feet, so she simply could not stand still.

Lavinia had given her a letter of introduction to Mrs. Townsend, whom she and Elizabeth had called on yesterday as soon as they had settled themselves into their elegant apartment on the Steyne. According to her sister-in-law, Mrs. Townsend's parties were all the rage, and not to be missed. Fanny now saw why. Everyone of any importance in Society attended Mrs. Townsend. She'd already recognized the powerful Duke of Sutherland, the Marchioness of Trent who was a renowned beauty, the Earl of Graystone about whom scandalous things had recently been whispered in London, and the notorious rakehell Sir John Scarborough. If she wanted to acquire a reputation, she need only be seen to dally with any of the guests here tonight and the *ton*'s tongues would do the rest.

Not that she wished to ruin herself, but the prospect of such a sensational dalliance brought her to her toes, giddy with the possibility. She snapped her fan open and waved it seductively at Sir John.

"Fanny!" Elizabeth hissed, pulling her backward to stand behind several other ladies. "You will not make a spectacle of yourself. Do you know who that was you were flirting with?"

"Of course I know," Fanny said, snapping her fan closed again. "Why else would I flirt with him?"

"Fanny, you did not tell me you planned to behave wantonly when I agreed to accompany you here." Her companion smoothed out her modest high-necked gown. The pale blue color complimented Elizabeth's complexion well; it would never do against Fanny's rather dark skin. But her own gown of deep green with gold trim became her well.

"Because you would not have come with me had I told you so." Fanny peered about. Where had Sir John gone? Although she didn't want him to ruin her exactly, she still longed for the adventure of an "almost compromise." She'd not had even the prospect of anything scandalous for over a year, and oh, how she missed that excitement!

"I most certainly would not have." Elizabeth frowned sternly. If she could have wagged her finger in Fanny's face without fear of social censure, she surely would have done so. "I believed you wished to go to Brighton to pursue your courtship with Lord Lathbury."

"I have." Fanny glanced around, still unable to find Sir John. "Is it my fault that he has not put in an appearance yet this evening? I am sure if he does not appear soon, I shall have to fill this dance card with the names of other gentlemen." She fanned the delicate pages of the small paper book in front of Elizabeth showing its empty leaves.

"We cannot have that, Lady Stephen."

Fanny squealed and danced back as the large looming figure of Lord Lathbury appeared in front of her as though he'd been conjured.

Perhaps he had.

"Lord Lathbury! Wherever did you come from?" Fanny caught her breath and looked askance at the handsome rogue.

"The card room, my lady. I thought it time I claimed a dance from you before you gave them all away." His eyes twinkled as he tugged the booklet from her hand and perused it page by page. "What is this?"

"A dance card. Mrs. Townsend says they are all the rage in Vienna." Fanny shrugged, keeping a wary eye on Matthew. "She and her husband returned from there just after the war. I daresay it will catch on soon enough. A lady uses it to keep track of her partners for each dance."

Matthew continued to thumb through the empty pages. "I see I am just in the nick of time." He seized the pencil attached to the book with a thin, fine chain and wrote his name on the second page with a flourish.

Drat the man. He would come along before her card had any names at all on it.

"There and there." Matthew had continued writing his name on the fourth and the last pages, claiming the supper dance and the final one as well.

"My lord, you know we may only dance together twice or I will be ruined." Fanny managed to snatch her book back before he could mar any more lines. "That is not permitted."

"Is there no social dispensation for widows where dancing is concerned?" His brows rose innocently.

"You know there is not." Fanny longed to rap his knuckles with her fan. "You must go about and engage other ladies as well."

Lord Lathbury turned immediately, bowed to Elizabeth then turned back to Fanny. "Will you introduce me to your friend, Lady Stephen?"

Fanny glared at him. "You are bold tonight, Matthew."

"Not at all, my dear." He smiled engagingly at Elizabeth.

Mouth puckered to repress a smile, her friend nodded.

Resisting the urge to roll her eyes at his obvious subterfuge, Fanny summoned her manners. "Very well, then. Mrs. Richard Easton, may I make known to you Lord Lathbury. My lord, this is my friend, Mrs. Easton, who is my companion here in Brighton."

"Good evening, Mrs. Easton. How do you do?" He bowed and kissed her hand.

"Good evening, my lord. I am honored." Elizabeth dipped a curtsy, her eyes sparkling as Fanny hadn't seen them since her husband's death. She might be jealous if she didn't suspect her friend found their encounter with Matthew extremely amusing.

"Will you allow me the pleasure of dancing the third set with you?"

"I would be delighted, Lord Lathbury." Elizabeth shot Fanny a mirthful look as she wrote Lord Lathbury's name in her dance card.

"Thank you, ma'am. I will return shortly to claim you." He turned and offered his arm to Fanny. "I believe this one is mine, Lady Stephen."

With a rueful smile, she hooked her arm in his and he led her to the floor where the set for a quadrille was making up. They took their places as the first couple, and Fanny bowed to her corner, then to her partner, then they began the quick, light steps of the dance.

Surprisingly, Matthew kept up quite well for a man of his powerful build. She'd not danced with him for many years, and he'd been little more than a young man then, accustomed to these skipping steps. Yet he seemed not to have changed at all in that respect, for he kept pace easily with her and their second couple, though the dance was spritely. They circled, going into the promenade, where she became all too aware how near she was to her partner.

The room had not seemed so close five minutes before, however now the heat of the glittering candles and chandeliers pressed in on Fanny, intensifying the scents of hot wax, sweet pomade, and the bergamot cologne that always brought Matthew to mind. Her body began to twitch.

He took her hand as they changed places with the other first couple, coming back to their original place as the second couples began their part of the dance. Now was the time to rest, catch her breath before the second part of the quadrille commenced.

"Your gown becomes you, Fanny." Matthew leaned toward her, speaking so low she had to lean toward him to catch his words.

"You always liked me in green." At one point she must have had four gowns in varying shades of it.

"And you remembered."

Curse the man. "No, I didn't. I didn't wear this for you." Oh, but she had, knowingly or not.

"You protest too much. Is it a sin to admit you remember me?"

She caught a satisfied look from the corner of her eye and clenched her fist. A moment to recall where she was and she relaxed her hands. "Not a sin to be sure, but perhaps not wise."

"Leave the wisdom to Athena, Fanny. You should remain Aphrodite, goddess of passion." So close to her ear she could feel the rush of air, his lips lingered on the word and she shivered.

Before she could protest, the second figure was called. Matthew bowed to her, but the steps of this section required him to dance mostly with the other first lady. In the third section Fanny had to dance with her other partner until the second couples again took to the floor. Now she could tell Matthew she would have both passion and wisdom in her life, as she had not had them ever before.

Raising her chin, she opened her lips—

"Fanny, will you marry me?"

Her mouth remained open, though no words would come. She must look a right fool to anyone paying her any mind. With an effort she closed her mouth. Why did the man keep proposing? She'd already given him her answer. But before she could remind him of it, the third figure commenced and she was off, crossing the floor with her opposite partner. When she returned to her place she had to take Matthew's hand as the steps demanded. The heat of his palm penetrated her glove, shooting up her arm until it flushed her face.

At last the second couples took over once more and she smiled at Matthew, teeth clenched. "Do you intend to propose to me every time you see me, Lord Lathbury?"

A deep chuckle rumbled up through his chest. "Only until you accept me, my dear. As soon as you say yes, I promise I will ask no more."

"Then I fear I am destined to hear this proposal for the rest of my stay in Brighton, if not for the rest of my life."

"Nonsense, Fanny." His smile slipped a bit. "You said you needed to think about it. That was weeks ago. Have you not grown tired of freedom in all this time?"

"Not a bit." Fanny raised her chin. "I am enjoying myself immensely, as you can see." The fourth figure began and they parted. Sighing in relief, she smiled at her corner partner as she bowed.

She'd had no idea Matthew would be so persistent. Flattering though it was, she must be cautious. Before she consented to marry again, she must have no doubt whatsoever about the man's fidelity. Far too soon to tell that about Matthew. They'd only spoken at the ball in June after seven years' absence. The Matthew of old she knew well; this new one, however, had changes she wasn't sure she cared for. Like his persistence. He'd not been nearly this demanding of her attention ten years ago at her come-out. If he had been, her life might have been very different indeed.

The quadrille ended and Fanny curtsied to Matthew once more. With due solemnity, he took her hand and led her from the floor. "I fear the dance has been too spritely for us both. I am quite out of breath and your cheeks are as red as the roses I sent you. Perhaps a breath of fresh air will revive us both."

Before she could protest, he whisked her out through a pair of French doors that led to the formal garden. "You did receive them, did you not?"

"Receive what?" Her head was spinning with the heat and his close proximity. She had never felt so helpless at a man's touch. Well, except for Stephen.

"The bouquet of hyacinth and roses. Let's sit by the fountain." He led her down a short flight of steps to the fountain bubbling at the garden's center where they sat, quite alone. Bathed in the bright moonlight the ordinary scene suddenly seemed exotic and exciting.

"Yes, I did." Too breathless. Best not to give him false hope. "I sent you a thank-you note, if you recall." Fanny pursed her lips and gave herself a mental shake. What was the man about now?

"Ah, yes. This one, I believe." He withdrew the note she had sent him the morning after the masquerade.

He had kept the three scrawled lines? Her heart beat faster. "Yes."

Holding the paper to his nose he inhaled deeply. "You still use rose as your perfume, Fanny. It permeates everything around you, even your writing paper." He leaned toward her, until his lips brushed her ear. "I would know you by that scent even if I were blindfolded."

Gooseflesh rose on the nape of her neck and she shivered. "Matthew."

"Fanny, I love you." He dropped a kiss on her bare skin and she suppressed a moan of longing. "I have ever since we first met. I want no other woman for my countess. Please say you will."

It would be easy to do. Open her lips and say "yes." Matthew was a good man who would likely be a good husband to her and a wonderful father to Ella. Unlike Stephen, who'd been away most of his daughter's life. She hardly knew what a father was.

Just open her mouth . . .

"As I told you before, Matthew, I may never marry again."

The smiling lines on his face turned hard, brittle in the moonlight. As though his face were a mask that might crack at any minute. "Don't say that, Fanny."

"I must say it because it's true. I made a mistake once. I won't do it again." If only she could get her trembling hands under control, she might be able to put more conviction into her words. "I intend to be a little wild and wicked before I even begin to think about marriage again."

"You have always been so." Matthew relaxed, the hard planes of his face softening once more. "I wouldn't expect you to change now." He cocked an eyebrow at her. "If you truly wish to be wicked, you should go sea bathing tomorrow morning."

"Sea bathing? What is so wicked about sea bathing?" A healthful regimen that had never had a breath of scandal laid upon it.

"If you go to the beach tomorrow morning at six o'clock, you will find out. Send a note to order your bathing machine as soon as you return home. The beach in front of the aquarium is reserved for ladies at that time." His dark eyes twinkled mischievously. "I will arrange for a dipper for you."

"I do not need a dipper, thank you. I have plunged before and am perfectly capable of doing so now." What was this rogue up to? She should refuse to go, if only it didn't sound like a marvelous lark.

"I will not insist, then. But I will expect you to do your duty when the time comes." Matthew rose and offered his arm.

"I will do my duty, Lord Lathbury." She grasped his arm, glad his mood had turned. She didn't like for them to be at odds. "But where will you be? Gentlemen are not allowed anywhere near the beach while ladies are bathing."

"I do know that. So you will trust me to provide for your wicked experience even if it is in absentia."

Giggling, Fanny accompanied him back toward the house as excitement filled her. Whatever Matthew had in mind, she could count on it being an adventure, and a wicked one at that. Once Lord Lathbury gave his word on something he would move heaven and earth to make it happen.

So if he had set his heart on marrying her, she might well find herself caught out, compromised and made to marry him or lose her reputation. She'd not put that past him. Such a quality in him, however, made her want to go to the beach so very badly. Flirting with danger had always been an exhilarating experience for her. Certainly she would not stop now.

# CHAPTER 6

"He wants to meet you at six o'clock in the morning?" Elizabeth's outraged voice filled the hired carriage as they sped toward their apartment. Brows furrowed, nostrils flaring, lips pursed, she reminded Fanny of some mythological monster. "His lordship is up to something, I'll wager. He dances much too well for a large man."

"What does his dancing have to do with sea bathing?" Fanny cocked her head, eyebrows lowered as well.

"It has to do with his character. If a large man has taken the time to perfect his dancing, when he could have spent it hunting or riding or shooting, then he learned it for a reason."

"And the reason is?"

"To seduce women."

"By dancing with them?" Fanny burst out laughing. What had Matthew said to her friend when they had danced together? "Did he try to seduce you, Elizabeth?"

Even the scant moonlight entering the carriage

showed Elizabeth's glare. "Of course he didn't. But he'll try to seduce you if you don't have a care for where you go or when you see him."

"I'm only to go to the beach, get into a bathing machine—which I shall order as soon as we reach our apartment—and plunge myself into very cold water." Fanny shivered at the thought. "I won't even see Matthew once I leave the promenade. He won't be able to come onto the beach while the ladies are there."

"Then why is he even coming?"

"I'm not sure. But he promised me something wicked and I plan to hold him to that."

"Something wicked?" Elizabeth's eyebrows threatened to disappear into her hairline. "Then I refuse to be a part of any of this, Fanny. This is not what we came to Brighton for. We have our reputations to think about."

"I am thinking about my reputation and I want to be a 'Wicked Widow,' just like Charlotte."

"That sobriquet was an unfortunate mistake perpetrated by the *ton.*" Elizabeth sniffed. "Fortunately, it's died down quickly and did not seem to harm her much. I daresay her removal to Kent shortly will help people forget." Elizabeth stared her down. "Therefore you can go unaccompanied to the beach. I will have nothing to do with whatever scandalous behavior Lord Lathbury has in mind."

"Elizabeth," Fanny said, grasping her friend's hands and turning her voice soft and wheedling. "You promised you would chaperone me in Brighton, and since sea bathing is part of the world here, you are all but obligated to come with me." Fanny squeezed the cold hands. "Do say you'll accompany me?"

Sighing, Elizabeth nodded. "Yes, I will."

"Bless you, my dear." Fanny sat back, tension draining away.

"I do have certain conditions, however."

"What conditions?" She could smell trouble whenever her sensible friend had that arch tone in her voice.

"You must not bring Lord Lathbury nor any other gentleman to our apartment, save for an invitation to tea, and even that I will strongly discourage. I am not old enough to chaperone you properly, so you must act with utmost discretion, should you decide to flirt with him." Elizabeth stared at her frankly, and Fanny's stomach sank. No possibility for a discreet tryst with Matthew. She'd be lucky to stand up with him twice at a dance under Elizabeth's gimlet eye.

"I agree to that condition. What other rules do you wish for me to abide by?"

"You are not to act scandalously at any public assembly we attend."

"I do not court scandal, Elizabeth." Fanny squirmed on the seat. Apparently she'd have to curtail the glorious ideas she'd had about their time here in Brighton.

"Perhaps not, although it certainly finds you often enough." With a sniff, Elizabeth sat back in the carriage. "Do you agree to that condition as well?"

"I suppose I will have to." Brighton was becoming less a lark and more a jail. "Are there any other ways you propose to deter me from having fun while we are here?"

"Only this." Her companion laced her fingers together on her lap. "I know you are eager to venture out in society once more. Please be careful about the gentlemen you allow to court you. I do not include

Lord Lathbury in that warning, as his intentions are perfectly clear. Others may not be so matrimonially inclined, however."

"Well, thank God for that." Especially since she had no intention of marrying at the moment. "I believe I can talk and dance and flirt with a variety of gentlemen here without getting myself compromised."

The carriage pulled to a stop before their lodgings.

"You had better hope so, Fanny," Elizabeth said as she rose.

"So you will accompany me to the promenade in the morning?"

"Yes, but I will not sea bathe. I detest cold water, so you must do that alone. I'll remain on the beach so the proprieties will be satisfied."

The coachman handed Elizabeth down and Fanny followed her, outwardly sedate, inwardly dancing a jig. Tomorrow morning she would see what kind of wickedness Lord Lathbury had in mind.

A brisk breeze buffeted Fanny and Elizabeth as they stood on the promenade, the horizon lightening in a gorgeous array of pinks and purples as dawn approached. Fanny wished for a thicker cloak as she eyed the sole bathing machine sitting on the deserted beach. What scheme had Matthew devised that could be called wicked? And by whom if no one else was there to see?

"Whoever believes sea bathing is good for the health obviously has not attempted it in such cold weather." Elizabeth huddled next to her, her gloved hands clenched tightly, her teeth chattering as she spoke.

"It's hard to believe, but many people sea bathe during the autumn months. The chilled water is invigorating." Fanny tried to make her voice sound enthusiastic. When she'd gone bathing at the age of ten years old, she'd thought it a grand adventure and hadn't minded the chilly water. Later, with Stephen, the weather had been much warmer. Now the sight of the dark gray waves and the brisk breeze on her exposed face filled her with dismay.

With a skeptical rise of her eyebrows, Elizabeth tugged her cloak closer. "I'd think you'd rather catch your death of cold." She peered down the deserted promenade and nodded at an approaching figure. "I see Lord Lathbury has finally put in an appearance."

The dapper figure, sporting a light-colored coat, tall hat, and walking stick strode briskly toward them.

Throwing back her shoulders and assuming an air of disinterest, Fanny peered down the deserted beach in the opposite direction. Her heartbeat quickened and she gripped the railing, determined not to let her excitement show as the sound of his footfalls increased.

"Good morning, ladies."

The mellow voice sent a thrill through her. God, but he was an exciting man. Fixing a slight smile on her lips, Fanny turned to greet her suitor. "Good morning, my lord. I had almost begun to despair of you."

"Come now, Fanny. You know me better than that." His deep blue eyes sparkled in the brightening light. "When have I ever disappointed you?"

Well, he had her there. "There is a first time for everything."

"Indeed. I do not think we shall see that today," he said, with an enigmatic smile on his lips.

"Good morning, my lord." Elizabeth nodded to him, then turned to Fanny. "If you are going to sea bathe, my dear, I propose you go to it before I freeze to this spot."

"You do not intend to take the waters, Mrs. Easton?" Matthew eyed her gravely. "I understand the salt water is a marvelous cure for almost every ailment known to man."

"Huh." Her friend gave him a skeptical look. "I'd as soon put my head in a lion's mouth, my lord. A quicker and warmer death to be sure. I'm amazed Lady Stephen is actually contemplating it."

"Lady Stephen has agreed to it to humor me, Mrs. Easton." His warm gaze fell on Fanny and the chill wind suddenly seemed to lessen.

"You made a promise to me, my lord." She stared back at him boldly. "I am willing to endure the rigors of the water if that is what it takes to hold you to that promise."

"I assure you I will make good on it in due time." He turned to Elizabeth. "Although it is quite early, Mrs. Easton, I have knowledge of a certain bakery not far from here that opens at dawn just for the custom of those who accompany the early bathers. Shall I escort you there for a bit of breakfast while Lady Stephen prepares for her dip?"

Elizabeth's face lit up as though she'd had a glimpse of heaven. "I would be most grateful, my lord. The breeze is picking up if I don't miss my guess." She shot a keen glance at Fanny. "Why don't you abandon this foolish plan, Fanny, and come to the bakery with us?

I am certain you could benefit just as much if not more from Lord Lathbury's company there."

A very tempting scheme. Every gust of wind seemed as a knife cutting right through her clothing. Perhaps bathing was foolhardy this morning. Surely Matthew could devise another way for her to be wicked and warm at the same time. She raised an eyebrow just a hair's breadth and caught an almost imperceptible shake of his head. "You know I am that determined to see this through, Elizabeth. However, you can bring me a hot cross bun when you return."

Shaking her head, Elizabeth took Matthew's arm and they started down the promenade. "You'd best head to your bathing machine, my dear," Matthew called over his shoulder. *"Tempus fugit."*

The wretch had some mischief in mind, to be sure. But what on earth could it be? Best be off if she was to find it out. Drawing her cloak around her, Fanny sped down the stone staircase to the sandy beach and struck out for the wooden wagon awaiting her. The owner of the machine had apparently maneuvered it into position, let down the canvas hood into the water, then taken the horses and retired to some place inconspicuous. She'd ordered the machine for two hours, so he wouldn't return for some time to come.

Gingerly, she approached the waves that lapped at the wheels of the cart. Just how bad was this going to be? She dipped her hand into the water, expecting her fingers to freeze like icicles. The water washed over her, chilly to be sure, but surprisingly less frigid than she'd expected. Perhaps the salt content lessened the shock. Still, she doubted she would enjoy this escapade as much as she had at ten.

Mounting the wooden stairs to the wagon, she gazed about the beach once more. Hers was still the only machine in the water, although another one had entered the beach to her left. She ducked into the wagon and shut the door. One did not want the other driver seeing more than he bargained for.

Now out of the wind, Fanny let her cloak drop off her shoulders and draped it over a chair set out to hold a bather's clothes. A bathing costume hung behind it, but she'd not avail herself of it. One of the great pleasures of sea bathing was the chance to bathe nude in a semi-public place. Of course, no one could see you unless you hired a dipper to help you into the water. Still, having people scarcely more than a stone's throw away from your naked body lent the whole proceeding a scandalously wicked feeling. Was that what Matthew had meant by being wicked? She certainly hoped not. She'd set her heart on doing something much more naughty than just bathing in the nude.

Slowly she disrobed, laying each piece of clothing carefully over the chair. Down to her shift, she sat on the edge of the chair to pull her garters and stockings off. Only one piece of clothing remained. She grasped the hem of her chemise, but the nearby jingle of a bridle and a shout of "Whoa, horse," brought her to a halt. The bathing machine she'd seen entering the beach had apparently taken up residence directly beside her, despite the huge expanse of completely deserted sand stretching to either side of her.

Perhaps the lady inside was nervous and had instructed the driver to pull close to her for comfort. Not that she'd see the woman. Neither would the lady see her. The canvas cover over the rear of her wagon stretched into the water. The water came up over half of the ladder that would allow her to descend into the sea, so no prying eyes could get even a glimpse of her.

With a quick jerk, Fanny pulled her shift up and over her head, leaving her body splendidly naked to the cool air. Her nipples popped up immediately, the tips furled tight against the sudden chill. The dark circles around them puckered like gooseflesh. Her entire torso followed suit and she shivered, though the sensation thrilled her as well. Wrapping her arms around her chest, she rubbed her arms and back briskly. Get the blood pumping a bit faster before taking the plunge.

As she trailed her hands over her chilly skin, she suddenly imagined they were Matthew's hands, bigger, stronger. With the wide pads of his fingers caressing every inch of her. Shivering, though not from the cold, she stroked her hands down over her belly, eyes closed, imagining his warm body close to hers. She skimmed her fingers back up to her breasts, her nipples hard as granite points. Was it wicked to want him here with her? To want his hands on her? To want him to make love to her? Did she want him enough to marry him?

That brought her out of her dazed dream. She might lust after Lord Lathbury. Lust heartily after him. But she wasn't ready to commit her life to another man who could betray her as the last one had.

With a deep sigh, Fanny shook herself and plumped herself down at the top of the steps. She was here to bathe, not conjure a phantom lover. She lifted her foot above the murky water and clenched her teeth.

Just do it. Steeling herself against the bite of cold water, she thrust her foot down into the sea.

"Oooooh, that is cold." Instantly, her teeth chattered. The water she'd tested outside had not felt this cold. Swishing the foot around, she wriggled her toes. At least they hadn't gone numb . . . yet. Could she stand to put the other one in?

Lifting her left foot over the water, she sucked in a breath and braced herself for the plunge.

Beneath the water, something grabbed her right foot and pulled.

# Chapter 7

Fanny shrieked and fell backward onto the wooden planks of the wagon floor. Scrabbling for a purchase, she dug her elbows in and yanked her right leg back, trying to free it from whatever hellish monster had seized her.

The monster's grip was relentless, however. It clamped down on her ankle and refused to be shaken off. Dear God, what had grabbed her? She had to get away before it dragged her under the water. If she couldn't pull away maybe she could injure it so it would let her go. Fanny pistoned her leg back and forth, kicking it at the unseen menace. Grunting with the effort, she frantically peered about the bathing machine for some kind of weapon to use against this terror. Blast it, nothing of any use close to hand.

The chair that held her clothing stood directly behind her a foot or two away. She dove backward, shooting her hand out to grasp it. Fingers gripping the sturdy square wooden leg, she jerked it toward her but the chair moved not at all. Fanny pulled harder, but her fingers encountered the cold metal heads of the nails that fastened the chair to the wagon floor.

The murky water stirred between her legs. Bubbles broke the surface, followed by a sleek, round black form.

She screeched again, pulling herself back from the dark figure that was trying to claim her.

A black head emerged from the depths.

Drawing a deep breath to scream once more, Fanny stared at the monster climbing into the wagon and blinked. "Matthew?"

The name came out an absurd little squeak as she stared into the dripping, grinning face of Lord Lathbury.

"Are you all right, my lady?" A distant shout came from without the bathing machine. Apparently her screams had alarmed her driver and brought him to her rescue.

"The water's so cold," she called, scooting back as Matthew mounted the steps, his magnificent naked body towering over her. "I was quite shocked."

Drops of seawater slid gracefully down the sleek muscles of his chest and arms, over his taut abdomen to fall from his body onto her stomach.

"Are you ready to come out, then, my lady?"

Matthew raised an eyebrow and whispered the words "Or do you want to be wicked?"

Heat surged in Fanny's belly. "No, I believe I can get used to it," she called, raising her hand toward Matthew.

He grasped it and pulled her to her feet.

"It's just going to take me a little bit of time. I'll call you when I'm done."

"Very good, my lady."

Wrapping cold arms around her, Matthew pulled her against his wet chest. Her breasts protested the chilly contact only for an instant before the warmth of him began to seep into her skin. "You are a lunatic. I nearly died of fright."

"I had faith you were made of sterner stuff." He grinned, gently grasped her face, and brought her lips to his.

She thought to settle into a long, soul-searing kiss, one that would curl her toes and warm her from the inside out. She'd dreamed of such a kiss often since their encounter at Lady Beaumont's masquerade.

Matthew, however, had other ideas. He brushed her lips with a fleeting kiss, then pressed his mouth to her cheek, traveled upward to caress her eyelid, then breathed into her ear sending shivers of delight all along her body. With the tip of his tongue he traced the shell of her ear slowly from the top, sliding down the sensitive edge until he reached the bottom, then sucked the lobe into his mouth and kneaded it with his tongue.

Blissful shudders wracked her and she arched her back, pressing her breasts harder against his chest. "Mmm. Matthew."

His chuckle rumbled against her ear, sending another wave of shivers down her spine. "You wanted to be wicked, my lady. Does this qualify?"

Leaning her head back to gaze into his dark blue eyes—now mostly black with desire—she arched an eyebrow. "That depends on what you intend to do."

"To make love to you in this very public spot, unless you have a suggestion more scandalous than that." He sank his mouth onto hers, preventing an answer to his question.

Not that she had a better suggestion. The madness of doing such a thing thrilled her from top to bottom. This man knew her down to her adventurous soul and could match her turn for turn. The thought of engaging in such intimacy right on the beach added an element of danger that drove her wild with excitement. She grabbed him around the neck, and pulled him toward the floor.

"A moment, love," he said, disengaging them and grasping her hands. "We do not want anyone to suspect what we do. Even though the beach is mostly deserted, there may still be those taking the air who will notice if one of the bathing machines begins to rock in a very familiar manner."

"Then how—"

"Allow me to continue with my plan." He seized the large linen drying cloth, folded it, and lay it on the wooden planks. "If the sea was just a bit warmer we could simply slide into the water and enjoy a most blissful time that way." He seated himself on the toweling. "However, I fear that is impossible at present. I am quite used to cold baths since childhood, and still I doubt I could make a good showing with the water at this chilly temperature." He drew her down to him. "You must come to me at Hunter's Cross in the summer. There is a lake there, quite isolated, where we can swim or indulge in any manner of fun and interesting activities."

"I am ready to indulge right now, if you don't mind, my lord." She ran her hands over his broad shoulders, then across the dark mat of hair that made her hunger for him soar. Dipping her head, she licked an errant drop of seawater from his peaked nipple drawing a deep groan from him.

"As am I, vixen, if you hadn't noticed." Grasping her hand, he placed it on his shaft, hard and hot despite the chill in the air. "Rise over me, Fanny."

Oh, yes, she remembered this. Only a couple of times had she ridden astride, and had loved it. Without another thought she straddled his big body, poised to slide down over his fully erect cock.

"Wait." He stopped her by sliding his hand between her sex and his member, his fingers caressing her folds. "I want you ready for me, love."

"I am ready . . . oh . . . oh, yes." He'd found her entrance, slipping inside, coaxing her body to remember past pleasures. An internal flame ignited, heating her from the inside out until her face flushed and she panted for breath. Then his thumb brushed the little nub above her entrance and she flew apart.

"Now, Fanny." He withdrew his hand and slid her down over his eager cock as she shattered around his hot hardness.

"Oh, oh, oh, God," she cried out, unable to contain the ecstasy as he pumped into her again and again until with a groan he strained into her, filling her with his heat.

Heart beating almost out of her chest, Fanny collapsed on top of him. Never had she been so absolutely sated by a man.

At last Matthew raised his head. "You had best hope you have not killed me. You would never live down the scandal."

"I wouldn't need to." She chuckled, sliding her

thumb across his lips. "Because you have done for me as well." With a sigh she laid her head on his chest again, only to jerk it up as panic set in. "Do you think the drivers heard me?"

"They might have done so, although I believe you could still play it off as shock from the cold water. And my driver will be no trouble in any case."

"Why not?"

"Kinellan drove me down here. I took no chances with secrecy."

"Matthew!" Dear Lord. How would she ever face the man when she met him in a ballroom again? "He knows what we did!"

"Whatever he knows or heard, he'll say nothing. I swear it. Our secret is safe with him." Gently, he pulled her back down to rest against his chest. "Trust me."

Could she trust him? There lay the crux of her dilemma. Matthew wanted to marry her. Would he find a way to compromise her so she would be forced to wed him? Although her head said it was possible, her very bones protested the thought. He'd never played her false before. That was something. She relaxed, spreading her hands over his chest. "Ah, Matthew. I have missed you."

"And I you, love." He wrapped his arms around her, so sweet, so secure. "How long do you stay at Brighton?"

"Three weeks." Weeks that would pass all too quickly.

"We will meet frequently during that time, I hope." He tightened his arms about her.

"Only if you mean in more comfortable places than this." She laughed and snuggled against him.

"You didn't enjoy your wicked adventure, my lady?"

"On the contrary, I enjoyed it very much." God, but she'd missed the joy of intimacy so much. It had been such a long time since she'd been with a man. Even longer since she'd been with one who truly cared for her. With an effort she sat up, the chill of the wagon suddenly very apparent. "However, I believe I will trade some wickedness for creature comforts if it's all the same to you." Leaning down she kissed him briefly, then rolled off him. "Whatever made you even think of having us dally in such a place?"

He grinned at her before rising with a groan. "I remembered your love of danger and so thought such a tryst would appeal to you." Stretching, he flexed his sleek muscles. "Although perhaps a softer bed next time would be preferable."

Fanny eyed him hungrily. Broad chest and shoulders tapered to a trim waist and hips. His skin stretched tautly over all, giving his muscles a definition usually only seen in statues of Greek gods. Her Adonis. Beauty, strength, and passion in one dazzling figure. God, she wanted him even now. And he could be hers, forever, this moment, if only she would say the word.

He'd risked a lot to give her this dangerous pleasure today. Lord, how she'd reveled in it. He knew her so well. A tiny voice whispered that they could be happy together. She'd like to believe that voice. But it had whispered the same things about Stephen all those years ago. With her body still throbbing from the passion she'd just shared with Matthew, she wanted so much to believe he would never betray her.

She drew a shuddering breath and turned away

from the seductive body before her. Soon. She must learn to trust him enough or move on.

"Will I see you on the promenade this afternoon?" Matthew had moved to the steps at the end of the bathing machine, peering into the cold water. He raised his gaze to her, a sudden hunger in his eyes.

She met his gaze as her own hungers surged once more. "Yes. A bit more suitably dressed though."

"A pity." He grinned then pulled her toward him. "Fanny, you may be the death of me yet." Quickly sinking his mouth onto hers, he claimed her lips with a surety of possession that left her so weak she had to grab for the chair. "'Til this afternoon, then."

With a cocky wink, he dove into the chilly gray water, disappearing from sight like a sleek fish. Or merman, perhaps. Like a mythic creature, Matthew had risen from the depths of her past, seducing her with his charm and wit. Would she allow him to spirit her off to his world?

Sighing, Fanny tore her gaze from the murky water into which her lover had vanished and stood. Time enough to think of that this afternoon. As she picked up her shift, she hoped Elizabeth would not notice the completely dry state of her hair. Bathers usually submerged completely and here she wasn't damp at all. She struggled into her stays.

Of course, she could declare that she had decided not to bathe at the last minute, which was true enough. She just wouldn't tell her friend about the other invigorating activity she'd engaged in instead.

Shivering as he broke the surface of the damn cold water, Matthew gasped, shook his hair out of his eyes, and climbed the ladder into the bathing machine so fast his feet scarcely touched the rungs. He grabbed the linen drying cloth and commenced rubbing his arms, legs, and torso briskly to drive the blood back into them.

"Have a refreshing dip?" Kinellan turned around in his seat, warmly bundled up in a mean coat, hat, and gloves. His disguise as a driver meant he was well protected against the chilly morning air.

"God, it's been a long time since I swam in cold water." Toweling off his lower body, he tried to produce some feeling down there, then swiftly donned his drawers. He hoped he hadn't frozen his parts. That entire half of his body seemed quite numb. "Refreshing is not the word I would use to describe it."

"Let's hope you haven't done yourself 'a mischief,' as my old granny would say." His friend's voice held hardly a scrap of sympathy.

"Well, even if I had, it would have been worth it." He grinned at Kinellan. "The lady was startled, but very warm and willing after a moment or two."

"Ah, I thought I might have heard a scream or two. Wasn't sure if it was the reaction to her dipping into the water or you dipping into—"

"Watch yourself, Kinellan." Matthew paused in pulling his shirt over his head to fix the man with a steely eye. "You are talking about the future Countess of Lathbury. I will brook no lascivious language about her."

"My lascivious language? What about your downright obscene actions of the past half an hour?" Cocking his head, Kinellan raised an eyebrow. "Then she's accepted you? I'm to finally wish you happy?"

"Not exactly." Matthew popped his fine linen shirt

over his head and settled it over his shoulders. He was finally beginning to thaw. "She seemed very flattered by my attentions and by my choice of wicked ways and eager to extend the dalliance during our stay in Brighton."

"Then you are no further than you were when you met her at the masquerade."

"Indeed?" Matthew thought back to the tryst they'd just engaged in—her warm lips, her supple body that seemed to meld into his at their moment of completion. "I'd say I was much further along than in June, although I wish to be further still by the time we quit the city."

"Based on the morning activities that I could hear"—Kinellan cleared his throat—"um, surmise there was little else you could do save send out the wedding invitations."

Sighing, Matthew tucked his shirt into his breeches. "I do need her to say yes. Though I could be closer to that now than ever. If she ends up breeding, she will have to marry me."

"That is one strategy, although if you wish it to be more effective you'll have to arrange several more 'dips in the ocean.' "

"God, right now I'd rather suffer through any number of Mrs. Frangipani's arias, than get back in that blasted water again." Stomping to settle his feet into his boots, Matthew reached for his coat, finally beginning to feel some warmth in his fingers.

Kinellan peered over his shoulder. "I might have to call you on that one, Lathbury. Mrs. F. is in frightfully bad voice this Season. A quick plunge, you're in, you're out, it's over."

Matthew held out the damp toweling, shuddering at the very thought. "Be my guest to try for yourself."

"On second thought, perhaps I'll simply stick to being an accomplice. Much warmer work, I'll tell you." His friend grasped the ribbons and started the horses. They lurched forward and Matthew thumped into the chair.

In some ways, Kinellan was correct, however, he recalled Fanny's soft, burning body pressed against his, her insistent lips, her hot sheath heating him to the boiling point. A sudden stirring below assured him he'd not sustained permanent damage. He chuckled. The earldom would likely see an heir and as quickly as he could get the stubborn Fanny to agree to marry him.

Of course, she might even now be increasing. Sobering, he sat back in the hard chair and his shoulders slumped. If he'd just gotten her with child it would make his situation that much easier. For all that Fanny loved the danger of flirting with scandal, she'd abhor being the center of such a thing should she be pregnant and unmarried. He'd expect her to assume, and rightly so, that they would marry as soon as the ink was dry on a special license.

However, that was not the way he wanted to win his love.

He wanted Fanny to marry him because she loved him, not to escape ruin. She'd been deeply, almost tragically hurt by Stephen's perfidy. It was only natural now that she needed to be completely certain of his own loyalty to her before she agreed to give up a freedom she must be greatly enjoying. Her beautiful face seemed perpetually smiling or teasing him or excited with a carefree joy he'd not seen there in a very long time. He didn't want her to have to relinquish that, but rather choose to continue so with him forever at her side.

So if she wasn't increasing now, perhaps he needed to have a care during their subsequent encounters. There were things he could do to help prevent getting her with child. He sighed deeply. Such measures wouldn't increase his pleasure—far from it. But they would increase his peace of mind.

"Not going to sleep, are you?" Kinellan called as they turned onto the roadway behind the promenade. "I'll drop you at our lodgings, return this lot to Jeffries, reward him suitably, then join you for coffee and the largest breakfast you can order."

"Capital plan, Kinellan," Matthew said, stealing glimpses of the early morning traffic surrounding them. His exit from the bathing machine must be done without notice of anyone. "Bracing water and brisk exercise will give me an appetite every time."

"I suspect once you marry, Lathbury, you won't even need the 'bracing water' to accomplish that state."

"Beware, Kinellan." Matthew popped his head out of the wagon and, finding the street deserted, jumped to the ground. "You will go a-wooing in earnest one day and it would behoove you to remember that sauce for the goose makes an even more delicious one for the gander. I will have no compunctions whatsoever against bedeviling you at every chance I get."

"Lead on, MacDuff!" The earl grinned and started the horses again, their hooves clopping jauntily on the cobblestones.

Matthew adjusted his hat to hide his still damp hair and trotted up the steps to their rather grand digs. He'd rented two opulent suites of rooms for him and Kinellan, side by side, with an eye to impressing Fanny if he could find a way to spirit her up here. Not that he thought she'd succumb to mere decor or the luxurious appointments the landlord provided. Still, seduction was much easier to accomplish in attractive surroundings and while he didn't want Fanny's choice stripped from her, he'd not scruple on the lavishness of his attempts to make her change her mind.

# Chapter 8

"Lady Marchant has quite the best singers and musicians I've heard during our time here, don't you think, Fanny?" Elizabeth whispered as Mrs. Violetta Fremont's soaring voice rendered the popular Italian aria "Caro Mio Ben."

"I have to agree, my dear." Fanny peered around the crowded room, searching for a glimpse of Matthew. He'd promised her he would be attending Lady Marchant's musicale, though he'd yet to put in an appearance. "Mrs. Fremont's voice is divine, although I will confess to a preference for Mr. O'Shea's ditties. So humorous I want to laugh out loud."

"He does have a lovely tenor voice, although I think some of his selections a trifle risqué." Settling back in her chair, Elizabeth smiled but then tensed as Mrs. Fremont hit a note that quite shook the pendants in the crystal chandelier overhead and set them to tinkling. Pray God the woman didn't bring the house down.

Still no Matthew.

Tonight was her and Elizabeth's last night in Brighton. They would leave for London just after breakfast in the morning, which saddened Fanny, to her surprise. Had she realized she would have such a delightful time here she would have arranged a longer stay. At least until Matthew quit the resort town.

Matthew had proved the most charming companion in the three weeks since she'd arrived. After their tryst in the bathing machines, they'd managed to meet almost every day at some public or social function and thoroughly renew their acquaintance. Less frequently they'd met in private, although they'd managed three more passionate dalliances, one in a rather inventive place. Who would have guessed one could engage in sexual congress in a ruined castle without being discovered or tearing one's gown? Not the most comfortable of places, but the thrill of danger again made it worth the discomfort of hard, rough stone walls. Soon she'd be surrounded instead by the equally unyielding presence of her prim and proper brother-in-law and his equally proper wife. Theale was an old tyrant, although Lavinia had her good moments. Still, she could look forward to a much more constricted existence once she returned to London. She'd just have to endure and look forward with longing to seeing Matthew at Charlotte's house party.

Where was the wretch?

"Good evening, Fanny."

She jumped in her chair as Matthew slid into the empty seat she'd been holding for him. "Shhh. Mrs. Fremont is not finished."

"I beg your pardon." He straightened, his attention focused on the singer.

Surreptitiously cutting her gaze toward him, Fanny repressed a sigh. Matthew was in fine form tonight. His black evening dress was the epitome of elegance, from his exquisitely tied cravat to his impeccably cut pantaloons and white stockings that showed off his thickly muscled calves splendidly. A twinge of longing to have those solid calves entwined with hers once more smote her, heating her face. She glanced away, firmly turning her attention back to Mrs. Fremont, who held her final note another two full measures, then bowed to the company with arms spread wide.

Enthusiastic applause kept Mrs. Fremont bowing for another several minutes. Well, she deserved the recognition for such a display. To Fanny's left, Elizabeth clapped loudly, a wide smile gracing her lips. She'd wager her friend would miss this pleasant life when she returned home as well.

Lord Kinellan appeared on Elizabeth's left. "Good evening, Mrs. Easton. How nice to see you again."

"And you, my lord." Elizabeth's smile had narrowed, though she nodded pleasantly to the earl.

A touch on her hand jerked Fanny back to the man beside her. His eyes shone bright in the candlelight. "Would you care to go to the refreshment room or do you prefer to remain here for more music?"

"I think something to drink is a splendid notion." Fanny gathered her reticule and fan and rose. "Would you like to come with us, Elizabeth?"

Her fellow widow arose and glanced from Fanny to Lord Kinellan. "His lordship has asked me to accompany him to the Marchants' drawing room. There is a very fine Turner Lord Marchant has recently acquired."

"By all means, my dear. I know how you delight in Mr. Turner's works." Fanny bit back a grin as Elizabeth draped her cream silk shawl around her shoulders and gingerly took Lord Kinellan's arm. "Enjoy yourself."

The couple moved off, and Fanny turned to Matthew who was gazing at her with his piercing blue eyes. "I believe you suggested refreshments, my lord? Must I starve or need I take the lead?"

Grinning, he offered his arm. "I am yours to command, my lady."

"I should certainly hope so."

"I suspect Kinellan is about to make a conquest." He nodded toward the couple, just clearing the doorway.

"Hardly." Fanny chuckled. "Elizabeth Easton is still very much in love with her husband, the lieutenant colonel."

"But the man's been dead over a year now." Wrinkling his brow, Matthew steered them through the doorway and down a busy corridor thronged with chattering guests.

Fanny shrugged. "Not everyone was as unaffected as I at the death of their husband. Theirs was quite a love match, I understand, and remained that way until the day he died. She has told me she absolutely adored him from the moment she set eyes on the man. I don't believe she's ready to let that go. She may never be."

"But she has children, doesn't she?"

"Yes, a boy and a girl. About my daughter's age."

"Then the boy especially needs a man's influence. Kinellan would be a good one."

Fanny sent him a cool look through slitted eyelids. "Then I suppose it is as well that I have only a daughter."

He grinned, unperturbed. "And daughters need a father to champion them, spoil them. Love them."

They had arrived in the bright refreshment room and Fanny's mouth watered at the prospect of lobster patties. Spying a small table unoccupied by any save an older lady finishing a glass of ratafia, Fanny nodded to it. "Shall we sit here?"

"Excellent, my dear. I shall return shortly." Matthew carried himself off to the sideboard and was soon busily filling their plates.

Fanny settled herself and smiled at the lady who had finally set her glass down. "Good evening, Lady Hermione. I did not realize you were in Brighton. I have been here these three weeks and have not met you a'tall."

"Good evening, Lady Stephen Tarkington, is it not?" The older woman's head trembled, making the plume on her bejeweled headpiece flutter. "I had heard you were in Town from Lady Marchant, but sad to say I get out rarely these days. I am here now only because it is Sarah's entertainment. She's my cousin, though more like a sister to me. No more gadding for me. There's a pity. I come to Brighton in the summer for the waters."

"To drink them, my lady?"

The older woman drew herself up in her chair. "Indeed not. To be dipped in them, of course."

The image of Lady Hermione Rochester, clad in bathing dress or, even worse, au naturel, being dipped in the ocean behind a bathing machine struck an unnerving chord in Fanny. Unsure whether the image amused or horrified her, Fanny gave a lukewarm smile and prayed for Matthew to return before Lady Hermione could elaborate further.

"Have you availed yourself of the seawater, my dear? Most refreshing. It is an experience you will not forget." The woman's small dark eyes seemed to stare straight into Fanny's soul, as if searching for some confession.

Could the woman know something about her meeting with Matthew in the bathing machine? No, that must simply be her guilty conscience. Casting her gaze down, Fanny suddenly worried with the way her shawl covered her shoulders. "I . . . um, well, I did go out once."

"Pah." Lady Hermione pursed her lips. "You'd best go every day, if you value your health. Do not allow the coldness of the water to deter you. If you steel yourself . . ."

Desperate, Fanny looked toward the serving table. What was taking Matthew so long? She caught his gaze and smiled in relief as he turned toward her, a full plate in each hand.

"Ah, but I see where your attention lies. Very good, my dear." The sudden approving gleam in Lady Hermione's eyes took Fanny aback. "Lord Lathbury is a very eligible *parti*. You will do him credit and he you. Such a handsome couple you make."

"I . . . um . . ." Fanny desperately hoped she was not blushing. "Lord Lathbury and I are old friends, my lady. We have been reacquainting ourselves after many years apart." Why didn't the wretch come and sit down? A glance toward him and she could have screamed in frustration. Matthew had stopped to speak to Lord Daughtry.

"I wouldn't wait too long to bring him up to scratch, my dear." Lady Hermione shook her head and rumbled to her feet. "Men don't like to wait. If you dangle them along overlong they will lose interest and stray. Mark my words: strike while the iron is hot!" The elderly woman stabbed her finger in the air with that pronouncement. Then she leaned toward Fanny. "Be good for you to get out of Theale's house too. The man's heading into his dotage according to my granddaughter."

"Your granddaughter knows the marquess?" That was a bag of moonshine.

"She's married to his heir." Lady Hermione sniffed and peered down at Fanny, a look of sour lemons about her mouth.

Taken aback, Fanny's hand went to her throat. "You are Lady Craighaven's grandmother?"

"Why would that surprise you? She must have at least two grandmothers. I happen to be one. So mark my words, young lady." With a final sharp nod of her aigrette feather, she ambled off toward the card room. God help whoever the Fates decreed to be her partner.

"I remembered that you particularly liked the lobster patties, so I made sure to give you several," Matthew said, placing a plate and utensils before her.

"What took you so long?" she hissed, feeling her face with her hands. As she suspected, her cheeks were hot as a flame.

Matthew peered at her, a concerned look on his face as he deposited his own plate on the table. "What is wrong? Has something happened?"

"Lady Hermione just interrogated me as though she were a Bow Street Runner." Relaxing her shoulders, Fanny picked up her fork, determined to enjoy the patties, which were indeed a favorite of hers.

"Did she?" Matthew chuckled, the wretch. "What about?"

"Sea bathing and . . . and other things of no consequence. For God's sake, don't you do the same thing." She stabbed the lobster as though she were Neptune with his trident and popped it into her mouth. If she could just eat in peace and spend this last evening with Matthew in relative harmony, she'd be grateful.

"Well I hope you don't mind if we do talk some. I suppose I shall not see you again for some time." A shadow flitted over his handsome face and Fanny felt rather than heard his sigh. She would miss him as well.

"Do not forget, we will soon be in company together again. Lady Cavendish's house party in early August? You did receive her invitation, didn't you?"

"I did indeed." His visage lightened and he bit into a buttered roll. "I am in great anticipation." He waggled his brows, making her giggle. "Do we dare continue on as we have here?"

"Of course we do. The whole reason for the weekend is for us widows to flirt and dally with the dashing men of our choice." She arched her neck and smiled seductively at him.

"And I am your choice?" He laid his fork down, suddenly all seriousness.

"You doubt it? After these past weeks?" Did he truly have no faith in her feelings for him? Had she made him believe her regard shallow? Or had he simply not realized how deep that regard ran?

"Then why don't you simply marry me, Fanny?" The thick, dark blows swept down in a deep V. "We would need not part at all."

"Matthew." Lord, would he never cease proposing to her?

"Fanny, you must see the sense of it." He tossed his napkin onto the table.

Her appetite, so robust moments ago, had fled. "Nothing has changed since my last refusal."

"I think it has, my dear." He grasped her hand, his warm clasp filling her with excitement despite her resolve. "There is now every possibility you carry my child."

She tried to slip her hand from his, but he held on tightly.

"Can you deny it?" He had lowered his voice, and she glanced around, but no one else had come into the refreshment room. They were virtually alone.

"Yes, I can deny it."

"What?" His startled look sent a pang of remorse through her, for he looked hurt of all things.

Heat rose to her cheeks yet another time tonight. Still, after the intimacies she'd shared with this man, what was one more? "You have not seen me these past several days, I think? Not since Monday?"

"No. When I called I was told you were resting. And your note said you had a megrim." Concerned lines deepened on his face and his grip on her hand tightened. "Are you truly ill, Fanny?"

Oh, Lord. "No, my dear. I am as well as can be.

However," even though no one else was there to hear, she lowered her voice to a whisper and he leaned close, "I had my courses."

Matthew jerked back, a faint pink staining his cheeks. "I didn't think about . . ."

"Men usually don't." Fanny had been relieved when they had started. She'd been so carried away with their passion she hadn't thought about the possible consequences until afterward and then it had simply been a matter of wait and see. This time they had been lucky. She must acquire the seeds she'd used before. They had proven most effective. "Are you terribly sorry?"

Settling back in his chair he paused, as if wanting to choose his words carefully. "I am, and I'm not."

"You surprise me, my dear." She'd assumed he would long to use a coming child as the ultimate reason for them to marry.

"I hope I'm not always predictable, Fanny." A quick smile lit his face. "I want to keep you guessing." He sobered again. "I would be thrilled if you carried my child, my dear. Never think otherwise. And yet, I would not want that blessed event to be the only reason you chose to wed me." Taking her hand, he raised it to his lips. "I would have it be because you loved me and no other."

Of all the arguments to marry Lord Lathbury, his generous nature in this declaration must be one of the greatest. And harder still to refuse.

"Shall we return to the music room or would you like cards instead?" He rose and assisted her as well.

"Cards I think," Fanny said, grasping his arm with eager fingers. "I am feeling lucky tonight."

# Chapter 9

Travel sore and weary, Fanny entered Theale's family parlor late the next afternoon, dropped into a chair, and groaned. "I thought roads in a modern age would be better maintained. Our carriage bumped along as though we were driving along the ribs of a giant."

"Good afternoon, Frances." Lavinia, Lady Theale, set her cup down on the marble-topped tea table beside her high-backed armchair, carved at the top with strange shapes.

A masculine-looking chair, Fanny had always thought, with its dark walnut wood, animal hide seat cushion, and bare backboard. It looked deuced uncomfortable, still it suited Lavinia somehow.

"I hope your stay was more pleasant than your journey." Her sister-in-law looked down her long nose at Fanny. "It seems to have left you bereft of your manners in any case."

Inwardly, Fanny groaned again. A high-stickler, just like her husband, Lavinia insisted on the most correct behavior possible. Fanny and Elizabeth had grown so close they had relaxed into a comfortable companionship by the end of their stay in Brighton. Too relaxed, apparently.

"I do beg your pardon, Lavinia." Fanny sat up, immediately assuming the correct posture with shoulders straight and her back nowhere near the chair's. "Good afternoon. How are you, dear?"

"That is better. I am very well, thank you." A slight nod from the older woman indicated the lesson was over. For now. "Would you like tea?"

"Yes, thank you." Aching with tiredness, Fanny accepted the cup, hoping Lavinia would keep her catechism short this time. She always insisted on asking about every particular of each journey everyone who resided within the household made. Fanny and Jane had agreed that the woman then took all that information straight to her husband, who wanted to keep his thumb on every pulse. At fifty-five, the marquess showed no signs of loosening his grip on all their lives.

"Did you and Mrs. Easton enjoy your little holiday? Did you use my letters of introduction? There are so few people Theale and I know left in Brighton, but I hope you availed yourself of the company of those we do." Handing Fanny her tea, Lavinia raised an eyebrow.

"Of course, we were delighted to meet Lord and Lady Marchant, Mrs. Easterbrook, and Lady Hyde-Cawfield. Lady Hermione Rochester, with whom I shared a table in the refreshment room, I was already acquainted with. It was very kind of you to assist us in making so many new acquaintances." Duller people Fanny had never met.

Even Elizabeth, usually without a harsh word to say about anyone, had admitted the two hours spent at cards with Lady Hyde-Crawford and her sister, Miss Sofia Banks, had tried her soul. A little spirited conversation at the least would have lifted the curse from the evening's entertainment; however, the one lady spoke of nothing save how clever she and her husband were, while the other only lamented her lack of a husband. Each had monopolized her table, despite a shuffling of partners, until Fanny had pled a genuine headache and she and Elizabeth had returned home before eleven o'clock.

"I am so pleased you met dear Penelope's grandmamma. Such a sweet girl Craighaven has married." Lavinia relaxed her face and for the briefest moment smiled. "Lady Marchant had her come-out with my next youngest sister. Also a sweet girl." Lavinia sipped her tea, her gaze still hard on Fanny. "She wrote to me after you called on her the first time, to express her gratitude for the connection. She happened to mention also that you were often seen in the company of Lord Lathbury while you were in Brighton."

Resisting the urge to grind her teeth, Fanny instead smiled and nodded. "She is correct. Lord Lathbury had informed me at Lady Beaufort's masquerade in June that he would be removing to the seaside for some time during the month of July."

"Did you pursue him there?"

Fanny cocked her head, determined not to lose her temper. She so often said unfortunate things when riled. A fact Lavinia knew all too well. "I do not think I would characterize my actions as pursuit. Lord Lathbury is an old friend and as old friends do, we wished to renew our acquaintance after our encounter at the masquerade."

"Why did he not simply pay you a call here after that evening? Why take yourself off to Brighton for an assignation?" Her sister-in-law's pursed lips and keen glare showed Lavinia truly on the hunt for scandal. Fanny's behavior must have been called into question while she had been absent. By Theale, perhaps?

"Why would you think we had an 'assignation,' Lavinia?"

"Why else would you suddenly decide to go to Brighton? You'd never expressed such an interest before." The woman's sharp gaze darted all over Fanny's face.

"I had been in mourning for a year, if you remember." She tried to put a hint of reproach into her voice. "I'd had no chance to go anywhere or see anyone for a very long time. As you well know." Fanny paused for a sip, and inspiration struck. "And when Lord Lathbury spoke of his going to take the waters at Brighton, it recalled to me my family's outings when I was a child. We went to Weymouth each year, not Brighton, still the mention of it made me long to experience it once again."

"Then why not go to Weymouth, if that was where you were used to going?" Apparently, Lavinia was loath to let the subject go. Why?

Sighing, Fanny brought out the reason she suspected Lavinia was searching for. "As I already said, I wished to become reacquainted with Lord Lathbury. He has been very attentive to me ever since our meeting in June. You'll remember the flowers he sent the next morning?"

With a slow nod, her sister-in-law acknowledged the huge bouquet that had dominated the entry hall for days.

Swallowing hard, Fanny continued slowly. "He has also made me an offer of marriage."

The smile that spread across Lavinia's face shocked Fanny to no end. In ten years she'd never seen her sister-in-law give such a display of satisfaction. It was quite off-putting, really.

"How splendid for you, my dear." Though her words contained a modicum of warmth—another first where her sister-in-law was concerned—the woman's eyes were calculating. "You should have told me this immediately. We will, of course, assist with your preparations for the wedding."

"I have not accepted him yet."

Reaching for the teapot, the woman stopped, her head snapping up. "Haven't accepted him? Why ever would you not accept Lord Lathbury?"

"As I said, we had not met for some years. I need to know him better, need to see if he has changed at all since that time."

A peculiar look came over Lavinia's face, a flicker of impatience teamed with something akin to malice. "You should think carefully before discarding such a suitor, Frances. You do have your welfare and that of your daughter to think of."

Warily, Fanny turned the teacup this way and that in its saucer, the faint rasp of the porcelain like the gritting of teeth. What had that disturbing look meant? "I do think of my welfare, Lavinia. That is why I must be certain before leaping into a marriage with a man I hardly know. After Stephen's—" She stopped herself just in time. Lavinia likely had no idea of Stephen's infidelities, although unless the marquess had no idea of his brother's character, he must have known they occurred. Perhaps not the extent of them, however. "After having Stephen as a husband, well, I think I must take care to marry a man who will treat me even better."

"Beggars cannot be choosers, Frances."

"I hardly think I am a beggar, Lavinia." Fanny sipped her cooling tea, feathers ruffled. The terms of her settlement agreements were a sore spot with her.

"You have lived upon Theale's generosity almost since you married his brother and completely since Stephen's death. If you have the means to release us from this obligation, out of common decency you should take it." Lavinia sat back on her forbidding chair, the sour look on her face like a monarch about to order the beheading of someone.

Sliding the cup back into its saucer, afraid she would smash it otherwise, Fanny rose. "I had no idea Ella and I were such a burden to you. As you must know, the clause in my settlements was none of my doing. Because of Stephen's commission in the army, my father feared the possibility of his death and wished to provide as best he could for me. If Theale had not wanted the expense of my upkeep in the event of my widowhood, he should not have agreed to that stipulation in the contracts."

Looking down her long nose, Lavinia glared at her with a long-suffering eye. "As per those arrangements, Theale will, of course, provide for you for as long as you live, Frances, or until you marry again. Ella as well, until she marries. However, in fairness to the marquess, if you have a decent offer you should take it. I should think you would want a home of your own at last."

"I should like nothing better, my lady." These were new heights of insolence, even for her sister-in-law. The woman had ever been frosty toward Fanny, refusing to call her by any name other than Frances and making her feel most unwelcome at any of Theale's properties. "I daresay I would have repaired to another relative's home by now had I one who could take me. My cousin's circumstances forbid it, however."

"So sad for you that you and she are the only family you have left, save Theale." The archness in the woman's deep voice made Fanny bite back the sharp retort she longed to make.

"I am sure that if I could have prevented my family's deaths, Lavinia, I would have done so." Her father, mother, sister, and brother had all been caught up in the measles epidemic in 1809. Over the course of two months, her entire family had been lost. She had wanted to go to them, help nurse them, but Stephen and Theale both had forbidden it. That had turned out to be a lucky circumstance, for soon after she'd discovered she was with child. In the end, all she could do was mourn her family's loss. "I do have Ella as well, you remember."

"Such a delightful child. So very like Stephen." Lavinia's features softened, as they always did when speaking of Ella. "Save in her coloring, of course. That she gets from you."

"I daresay so. All the Tarkingtons are blond."

"Yes, all of my children were blond, thank goodness." Lavinia sighed proudly. "I've always thought pale hair against a pale face is a lovely combination.

So unfortunate Ella did not take after her papa in that respect." She glanced up at Fanny, her mouth pursing again. "The family could have been all blonds."

"Save for me." Fanny turned the screw as best she could. She'd always known the fact Ella took after her irked her sister-in-law to no end.

"Indeed. I see you stayed out in the sun far too much in Brighton. Your face is as brown as a pair of York tan gloves."

The hairs on the back of Fanny's neck bristled. Turning on her heel, she swept toward the door just as it opened on Ella and Nurse.

"Mama!" Ella ran to her and jumped into her mother's arms. "I missed you. I truly did."

Burying her face in Ella's hair, Fanny hugged her child as a wave of guilt washed over her. She hadn't seen her daughter for over three weeks. "I missed you too, my love. Every day." She glanced up at Nurse. "Thank you for bringing her down." She hugged Ella once more, then set her on the floor. "But how did you know I was here?"

The nurse gave her a startled look, then turned her head sharply toward Lady Theale.

"I told Clayborn to bring her." Lavinia rose from her throne and extended a hand toward the girl. "Ella and I have tea every day at this time. Come, Ella."

The child clung to Fanny's hand, then grasped her about the waist.

"Ella."

The imperious voice made Fanny shudder. She took Ella's hand and kissed it. "Let's go have tea with Aunt Theale, shall we?"

"You will come with me?" The hopeful blue eyes

turned up to her smote Fanny's heart anew. If she were six years old, she wouldn't want to be left alone with Lavinia either. "Yes, darling. Of course, I will. I haven't seen you in ever so long. I'm sure Aunt won't mind me joining you, will you, Lavinia?"

"Not at all." The icy look behind her sister-in-law's eyes belied her words as she resumed her regal seat.

"You see, Ella? I shall be part of the party today." Fanny smiled down at her as she steered them toward the sofa beside Lavinia's chair. Although the most comfortable seat in the room, that still didn't say much. The bright vermillion upholstery was stiff, the seat cushion thin, and the bizarre arms curled inward in such an odd fashion Fanny never wanted to touch them. The whole family drawing room gave off a cold and uncomfortable aura no fireplace blaze could counteract.

"How long have you been having these little teas, Lavinia?" And why hadn't she told her of them? Fanny settled them on the sofa. Ella's feet, encased in white slippers embroidered with pink flowers, now touched the floor. When had the child gotten so tall?

"You have been gone so much since you came out of mourning, I thought Ella might like the treat. Clayborn, ring for more tea and cakes, please, then you may leave."

"Yes, my lady." The nurse jerked the bellpull by the door, curtsied, and scurried out the door.

Fanny bit back a sharp retort. Perhaps Lavinia was truly fond of the child. "It was thoughtful of you to have arranged such a treat for Ella."

"I used to do the same with my children. We would have tea every afternoon, right here. They are grown now, all married save the last one, and she had her come-out this Season past. Never any time for tea with her mother."

The plaintive sound in Lavinia's voice brought a pang of guilt to Fanny's heart. Perhaps she had misjudged her sister-in-law. She sounded so lonely, although the woman seemed to have the busiest social life Fanny had ever heard of. Always countless calls to make every Tuesday and Thursday, committee meetings for the various charities to which she gave her patronage, *ton* entertainments by the dozens to attend, in addition to her other responsibilities as Marchioness of Theale. Still she had found time to give Fanny's daughter what should be an extraordinary treat.

"Have you told your aunt 'thank you,' Ella?"

The child bent her head, then shook it.

"That is the polite thing to do when someone does something nice for you." She really must find time to work on Ella's manners a little before she had to leave for Kent.

After a long pause, Ella whispered, "Thank you, Aunt."

"You are welcome my dear." Lavinia's voice had not warmed.

Fanny glanced sharply at the woman she'd always considered distant and aloof toward her and Ella.

Fresh tea arrived with a plate of fairy cakes.

Fanny's mouth watered. She'd not had this children's treat in a very long time. Newly baked, too, as the smell of the sweet glacé topping was thick in the air. She reached for one of the petite cakes she remembered with such fondness from her childhood.

"Wait, Mama." Ella grasped her hand before she

could take a cake. "Aunt must always pour the tea and take her cake first."

"Very good, Ella. That is correct."

Raising her eyebrows at Lavinia, Fanny eased back in her seat. "I am sorry, Lavinia. I had no idea."

"Ella must be taught to be respectful of her elders. She has made excellent progress over the last few weeks." Lavinia poured tea. "You take sugar but not milk, is that correct, Frances?"

"Yes, thank you." A glance down at Ella showed her daughter sitting with her back straight as a poker, hands folded neatly in her lap, eyes staring straight ahead. The tension in her small body seemed to roll off her in waves.

Lavinia handed her the cup. "Ella takes sugar and milk, just as I do." She dropped two lumps into the third cup, and poured again. A long stream of milk followed before she handed the brimming cup to Ella. "Be careful, my dear. Don't spill it on your pretty dress."

"I won't, Aunt." Ella maneuvered the cup to her lips, took a sip, grimaced, then set the cup and saucer on the table.

"Is something wrong with your tea, my dear?" Lavinia stared at the girl like a cat about to pounce on a mouse.

"Oh, no, Aunt." Shaking her head, Ella was quick to deny it.

Perhaps too quick.

"It was hotter than I expected is all." Resolutely, the child picked up the cup again, sipped, and smiled.

Fanny set her tea down, slowly. Although she'd not had tea with Ella in months, she well recalled that the child had always taken it as she did, without milk.

Fanny herself had never been fond of it and Ella had seemed to follow suit. Why this sudden affection for it now? Her daughter looked positively bilious. "Don't drink too quickly, darling. You'll make yourself ill."

"I won't, Mama."

"Take one of the fairy cakes. They look delicious."

"But Aunt hasn't—"

"I shall put one on a plate for Aunt Theale." Fanny slid a petite cake, glazed with pink sugar icing, onto the saucer and thrust it at Lavinia. "There."

Caught off guard, her sister-in-law had no choice but to accept the cake. Her eyes narrowed at Fanny.

"And I have my cake, so you may have yours as well." With a deft hand, Fanny distributed the confection to Ella in the proper order of rank. Was that the lesson Lavinia was trying to teach her daughter? At what cost to the child?

Ella, her eyes pools of blue on a field of white, shot a frightened look to her aunt.

Lavinia nodded, although her mouth looked as though she'd bit into an unripe persimmon.

"Thank you, Mama." Moments later Ella was nibbling the cake, some of the tension in her slight body eased.

Almost as though the strain of this encounter had flowed from her daughter to her, Fanny tensed, gripping her cup so hard she feared the handle could snap off in her hand. Better if it did. That would keep her from pitching the lot—tea, milk, cup, and saucer—at Lavinia. She'd been torturing her daughter in the name of good manners. Well, manners did not dictate the inclusion of milk in tea just to honor the hostess. And although the order of service might be decreed, to deny a hungry child a treat had nothing to do with manners.

She must remove Ella from this hateful household. Lavinia had taken advantage of her absence to impose these arbitrary rules on her child. That would cease from this day forward. At least she would attempt to put measures in place. Drat. She would be leaving in a week or so for Kent and could scarcely bring her child with her. With no one to intervene for Ella, the girl would be at the mercy of Lord and Lady Theale.

Relaxing her grip on the cup once more, Fanny sipped the cooling brew. At last she had hit upon a completely different reason for marrying Lord Lathbury—security for Ella. Matthew would be an excellent father, Fanny was certain of that, though she'd never heard him speak of children, nor seen how he fared in their company. He would take both of them away from Theale's repressive rules and none too quickly, apparently. She would have to arrange a meeting between Matthew and Ella to see how they got on. If she were to marry the man, he would thereafter be her child's guardian. A godsend, perhaps, or a nightmare.

Yes, she must consider Matthew, or any man, carefully. More than one life was at stake.

# CHAPTER 10

"Jane." Fanny embraced her sister-in-law on the steps of Lyttlefield Park's spacious portico. "How good to see you again. I've missed you."

"Hello, Fanny. I've missed you as well." Lady John Tarkington, widow of Stephen's second-eldest brother, returned the hug. "You have managed to keep busy these last months, I understand. Your stay in Brighton was invigorating, I hear."

With a sigh and a laugh, Fanny swept past Jane and into the foyer. "Very. Has Lavinia been filling your head with my scandalous behavior?"

"I daresay she could have done, considering what transpired there. Have she and Theale had the whole story from you, then? Elizabeth is my informant, though she said nothing of scandal." The petite blonde sidled up to Fanny as the butler took her spencer. "We must catch up this instant." She gestured to the staircase rising to the right of the foyer. "Will you take a moment to freshen up or shall we go straight to the drawing room? Charlotte is to gather her guests there."

"Oh, please," Fanny said, heading straight for the stairs, "if a meeting with Lord Lathbury is imminent, I must repair these travel-weary looks."

"Charlotte did not have time to inform you." Jane mounted the stairs behind her. "Lord Lathbury sent his regrets at the very last moment."

Fanny stopped, her heart giving a huge thump as though it had rolled over in her chest. "Regrets?" She whirled around. "He's not coming this weekend?"

Shrugging, Jane motioned for her to continue upward. "I'm sorry to be the bearer of ill tidings, but no. Some urgent matter has called him to Hunter's Cross, his primary estate in Buckinghamshire."

Stunned, Fanny grasped the handrail and began to climb once more. All the joy she'd anticipated in seeing Matthew again this weekend evaporated the moment Jane spoke the words, leaving an emptiness the size of the ocean inside her. "Did he say why?"

"No. The letter arrived yesterday, saying he was terribly sorry, but he was heading north that very day."

A bitterness flooded her mouth. She hadn't understood just how much she'd been looking forward to seeing him again. To being intimate with him again.

"Are you all right, Fanny?"

Jane's question brought her back to herself. They had reached the first floor and she stood unmoving, completely unsure what to do now. "I am fine. I simply don't know which way to go."

Her sister-in-law motioned her toward the corridor

on the right, and she followed her, barely aware of her surroundings. What was she to do this weekend, then? She knew none of the other gentlemen, and wasn't interested in getting to know them. She wanted Matthew, and now couldn't have him.

They stopped halfway down the corridor and Jane opened the door on a cheerful room of pale green, the color of a ripe pear, furnished with charming white furniture in the French country style.

"Charlotte remembered how you liked the color green. Shall I send the maid to you or can you manage?" The ever efficient Jane turned to go.

"I can manage. I'll be down shortly." Still rather dazed, Fanny pulled herself together enough to send Jane a reassuring look before she closed the door.

Finally alone, she sank down onto a chaise whose green-flowered cushion would have normally brought a smile of delight to her lips.

She had nothing to smile about now.

What business in Buckinghamshire could have made Matthew renege on his promise to attend the house party? She'd lack a partner the entire weekend, as everyone else would be paired off. Unless she could entice a gentleman away from one of her fellow widows. Not a noble thing to do, to be sure, but if she became desperate enough, she might try. The idea filled her with despair. She didn't want another gentleman. She wanted Matthew.

How infuriating that she had become dependent on the favor of one man so quickly. She'd believed she'd spend her widowhood happily flitting from one companion to another, sampling them like a bee in a vast field of flowers. As Stephen had done with the women of her acquaintance.

Fury, fueled by disappointment, brought tears to her eyes. She dashed them off and breathed hard through her mouth to stem the tide rising behind her eyes. No tears. She'd have to make an appearance downstairs in a little while and she'd not have everyone wondering at her red eyes and splotched face.

Rising, she sought the wash water and basin to cool her face, then stripped down to her chemise. Her cosmetic case lay on the bed and she took some time to repair the ravages of her distress. When the image in the mirror had a new sparkle in her eyes—and skillfully placed artificial roses in her cheeks—she rose and dressed in a simple afternoon dress of green sprigged muslin. That should do for now.

She grabbed a shawl, bit her lips to bring color to them, and sallied forth, determined to forget about Matthew and enjoy herself this weekend, if it killed her.

With a smile carefully hiding her pain, Fanny went through the steps of "Grimstock" with Lord Fernley, determined never to repeat the experience even if she had to leave the party completely. She'd danced with unskilled partners many times; never had she stood up with one so utterly inept on his feet. Her entire left foot ached where the man had stepped on it with his full weight—apparently more considerable than he looked—and her right shin smarted from a kick she'd received as he'd attempted a flourish of his foot when they cast down the first time.

Finally Charlotte played the last note of the wretched song and Fanny curtsied to her partner, feeling as though she'd come through a battle, wounded but alive. Before her friend could begin the next song, Fanny seized Fernley's arm and dragged him over to a chair pushed up against a wall. "I really must rest a moment, my lord. I am quite fatigued by that lively dance. I'm not used to dancing much after being in mourning for so long."

"Ah, I do understand, Lady Stephen." He bobbed his red head, a kindly smile on his eager face. His deep blue eyes were his best feature, to be sure, for his wide nose was absurdly long and his ears stuck straight out from the sides of his head like handles on a pitcher. "May I fetch you some wine to help you recover?"

"That would be very kind, my lord."

He rushed away, leaving Fanny a moment to breathe and plan a strategy. She'd have to sit out the next dance, just to assure Fernley of her sincerity. Afterward, however, perhaps she could encourage Lord Wrotham to ask her to dance. He'd partnered little Mrs. Wickley in the first dance, smoothly guiding her step by step in a dance she obviously had never done. Yet he made it look as though they had danced a hundred times together. Clearly the best dancer in the room, he was also the most handsome, for her taste. Not that he held a candle to Matthew.

Drat. She'd vowed not to think of him tonight. Shaking her head to dislodge the image of Lathbury dancing with her, she gazed about in search of another partner.

"Here you are, Lady Stephen." Fernley had returned with a glass of something that was definitely not wine. "I'm sorry it's lemonade, but there was no wine to be had. Will you please excuse me? I am promised to Lady Georgina for the next dance."

"Thank you so much, my lord. Enjoy your dance." God save Georgie.

He scampered over to his prey and Fanny relaxed, sipping her drink, watching the others pair off for the dance. Charlotte had been snared by Alan Garrett, and didn't look particularly pleased about it. The *ton* had been buzzing about them ever since that dance in June, the night she'd met—

Drat. She would not think of that man. Why the blazes had he not come to this party? If only she'd have gone to the ball and fete instead of the masquerade, she would not have met Matthew and stirred up old passions. Instead, she might have caught the eye of this charming rogue.

Not overly tall, but with nice broad shoulders, Alan Garrett looked the epitome of an elegant rake at first glance. Curly blond hair that gave him the air of a cherub, deep blue eyes that sparkled with mischief, and a full, sensual mouth that made a woman want to beg him for a kiss, among other things. Perhaps she could entice him or Lord Wrotham to partner her next. They were the only men here with whom she'd even entertain the possibility of a tryst. Lord Brack was too wholesome-looking, Fernley too odious, and Lord Sinclair, although very handsome indeed, had been very adamantly claimed by Jane.

The music ended and Fanny rose, determinedly trying to catch Lord Wrotham's eye. That gentleman, however, had eyes for no one but Charlotte. He pursued her to the refreshment table, whither she'd fled from her partner at the dance's end. Poor Charlotte. She'd protested an affinity for Mr. Garrett earlier; apparently the sentiment still held true. Perhaps Lord Wrotham would prove a more agreeable partner for her friend.

"Lady Stephen."

The deep, sensual voice in her ear made her jump and turn toward Mr. Garrett, who had appeared seemingly out of nowhere. She could have sworn she'd seen him heading toward Mrs. Wickley after Charlotte had left him on the floor.

"Mr. Garrett." She nodded her head, giving him a knowing smile. With very little effort, she supposed, she could have this man in her bed in two or three hours' time.

"Are you engaged for the next, my lady?"

"I am not, sir."

"Then would you give me the privilege of partnering you?"

"I would be delighted."

Garrett took her hand, smoothly twined it in his arm, and led her toward the dance floor. "In more than in a dance, perhaps?"

The rogue wasted no time, that was certain. Still his question thrilled her. It was wonderful to be desired, even more so to be pursued. "Whatever do you mean, my lord?"

"I believe you understand the question too well, my lady. Ah." The first strains of music filled the air and Garrett glanced toward Elizabeth at the pianoforte. "Mrs. Easton has decided to assist me. She is being scandalous."

"How so?"

"She is playing a waltz." He seized Fanny's hand

and put it on his shoulder then placed his hand firmly on her waist. "You are familiar with the steps?"

"Of course." A flicker of competitive spirit rose in Fanny. *Let us see who seduces whom, my lord.* In pretense of adjusting her grip on his jacket, she squeezed his trim waist. "I have waltzed more than once, and with more than just my husband."

They began the steps, gazing intently at one another.

A gleam of desire darkened his eyes. "A well-educated woman is always a delight, Fanny."

"As is a knowledgeable man, Alan." On a first-name basis before the dance was scarce begun. A pleasurable thrill chased down her arms. "Shall we compare our educations this evening?"

"I can think of nothing I would like better." He took advantage of the next steps to pull her sinfully close.

Her breasts grazed the front of his jacket, turning her nipples hard. Heat shot into her cheeks. Thank goodness they had already been rouged. Never let a man see just how much you desired him, though she didn't think it would matter a jot with Mr. Garrett. "Then we must find some time alone to . . . converse."

"Yes, we must," he whispered when his lips came close to her ear again. "Shall I come to your room this evening?"

The heat of his breath in her ear made her shiver. This surrender would be hot and sweet. "I would like nothing better. The green room, first-floor corridor on the right, the door halfway down on the left."

A jangle of keys from the pianoforte brought the dancers to a sudden halt. Cheeks reddening, Elizabeth gathered the scattered sheets of music. "My pardon, ladies and gentlemen." She hurried from the instrument and Georgie sat down, immediately beginning a mazurka at breakneck pace.

"Shall we perhaps sit this one out? I can think of much more pleasant ways to expend our energies." He motioned her toward a small chaise moved out of the way to accommodate the dancing.

"As can I." Fanny dropped demurely down upon the chaise, her gloved hands clasped in her lap. For the evening she had chosen her favorite gown of deep green, sprinkled with yellow buds and a stunning embroidery of flowers at the hem, as though she wore a fantastical garden. Its very low décolletage had turned Matthew's head when they were in Brighton—

As though she'd conjured him, his image rose before her eyes. Thick, silky black hair, unruly as always, clear blue eyes, wide nose, and full sensual lips that begged to be kissed.

"What is wrong, *chérie*? You look as though you've seen a ghost." The concern in Alan's voice brought her back to Charlotte's drawing room, to the chatter and laughter in the room that had gone stale to her.

"A goose walking over my grave, I suspect. Will you be a dear and fetch me some lemonade? And if you find a bottle of brandy along the way, a drop of that in it would not go amiss." She must stop recalling every single thing she had done with Matthew, although the same unfortunate type of memories had occurred the last time they had parted, seven years before. For months afterward certain items of clothing, a particular silk fan, blue hydrangeas, and seed cake, of all things, had brought his face to mind as vividly as though he stood before her. That must not happen again. She was bound to no man now. And she would take advantage of it as this party intended.

"Are you fatigued? Would you prefer to retire, my dear?" Leaning close, he nudged her ear and gooseflesh rose on her neck. "Make your excuses now. I will follow in half an hour's time."

Gazing into the handsome face filled with desire for her, Fanny's resolve strengthened. If she shared her bed with another man it might make it easier to understand her mind regarding her feelings for Matthew. Make it easier to remain independent. Or perhaps allow her to discover once and for all if independence was what she truly desired. "A capital idea, my lord. I will say good night, then."

"A very good night to you, my lady." His cocky grin split his face as he bowed and turned toward the refreshment table.

Fanny rose and immediately glanced about for Charlotte, who proved to be nowhere in sight. Drat it. Where was her hostess? She must make her excuses for leaving the party at such a wretchedly early hour. Ten o'clock had scarcely struck. Still, she must leave now so Alan's departure would not be remarked upon as too soon after her own.

Jane. As Charlotte's companion, she could stand in as hostess. Keeping her strides short and slow, Fanny ambled toward her sister-in-law. "Jane, dear. Please make my excuses to Charlotte. I have a sudden headache and think it best I make it an early evening."

"I am so sorry to hear that, my dear." The soulful look of concern that deepened the lines on Jane's face were immediately replaced by one of annoyance as she steered them both toward the door. "If you are thinking of a tryst with Alan Garrett, Fanny, you'd best be on your guard. The rogue has been bedeviling Charlotte for months. If he's moved on to different game, I say good riddance, for the man is a scoundrel." She grasped Fanny's hands at the threshold. "However, if there is anyone here, other than me, who can sheathe the lion's claws, I will wager it is you. Enjoy your evening, my dear." Jane rapped her furled fan smartly on Fanny's arm and turned back into the room.

Mouth open, Fanny resisted the urge to call Jane back. To be given dispensation to bed Alan Garrett and outright approval of the deed stunned her. Was independence always this thrilling? If so, she'd begin planning a long and healthy widowhood.

By the time Fanny reached her room, she'd decided to call off her assignation with Alan Garrett at least three times, though currently she'd decided to allow the tryst to take place.

Needing to be alone as quickly as possible, she dismissed the maid saying she didn't need further assistance, and all but pushed the girl out the door. After pacing the room several times, she'd at last settled down to brush out her hair, though somehow she'd managed to tangle the bristles in her hair so badly she had to yank some of her thick locks out to free it. Why was she nervous? She wanted this rendezvous with Alan. Didn't she?

Banging the brush down on the table, she rubbed lotion on her hands and arms, then climbed into the pristine bed and stretched out, stiff as a ramrod.

Relax. She must relax. Taking a deep breath, she lay back on the soft mattress, the crisp linen sheets and beautifully embroidered counterpane pulled up to her chin, her gaze firmly attached to the door. Waiting for Alan.

She'd never had such qualms about Matthew coming to her bed. In Brighton, they would have been in each other's arms constantly had she not insisted on discretion. If the wretched man had just appeared this weekend, they'd be here together now. Her heart gave a lurch at the remembrance of Matthew's strong arms cradling her, his big body covering her, entering her, loving her. That was what she wanted.

Thoughts of Alan Garrett touching her that way made her clutch the covers closer. This was wrong. She could not go through with this assignation. Head clearing for the first time since she left the drawing room, she threw off the counterpane and sheets and slid to the floor. She would write a note to Alan telling him she'd become indisposed in earnest. A weak excuse, but at the moment, with his knock about to sound at any minute, she wasn't going to try to be inventive.

Seating herself at the toilet table, she rummaged through her case in search of her writing materials. Paper, pens, ink, penknife, she spilled the implements onto the table, seized a pen and paper and began to scratch across the smooth cream surface, so frantic she didn't stop to mend the pen. How he'd ever read the splotchy words she didn't know. But she mustn't lose a second. Scrawling her name at the bottom, she grasped the sheet, ink still wet and dripping, and raced to the door.

Charlotte had told her all the gentlemen had

been housed conveniently down the opposite corridor from the ladies. Ironically, Alan now occupied the room Matthew would have had. Brushing that aside, she grasped the latch just in time to hear a soft scratching and whisper.

"Fanny?"

Gritting her teeth, she slowly turned the key below the latch, praying it made no sound. Gaze locked on the handle, she held her breath and stepped slowly backward until she bumped into the foot of the bed.

The handle rattled and her heart seized as though the hand on the other side of the door had it in its grip. The chattering of the latch sounded as loud as gunfire.

*Please go away. Just go away.*

One final jiggling of the latch that almost started a scream out of her, and the handle went slack. The faint sound of footfalls faded to nothing and Fanny slumped onto the end of the bed. She drew a deep breath after what seemed like an eternity, and lay back on the counterpane, still clutching the note to Alan.

Somehow she didn't think she'd lived up to Jane's expectations in this affair. However, her heart and conscience were clear.

Groaning, she sat up and tore the note into shreds. Striding to the fireplace, she tossed the scraps on the cheerful blaze and watched the hungry flames devour the evidence of her folly. At peace now, she returned to the toilette table, straightened her writing accoutrements, and went about the business of mending the pen. There was one more letter she needed to write tonight.

# Chapter 11

Sunlight poured through the bank of windows, flooding the breakfast room of Hunter's Cross with a pearly morning brightness that made Matthew's spirits soar after three days of unrelenting rain. Sipping his coffee, he gazed outside at the dazzling day and smiled. He'd already called for Spartan to be brought around front. Morning rides were most invigorating here on the estate and he'd missed his sorely these last few days. It would be even better with a companion, but Kinellan had continued to his estate in Scotland after accompanying him this far from London. He wouldn't see his friend again until he went north for the grouse shooting in September.

He'd have to look in on Lord Skelton, his longtime neighbor, and let him know he'd returned to Buckinghamshire. If Skelly was home, he'd at least have a companion to knock about with while he sorted out the mess his estate agent had left him. Mr. Farrow had given his notice not quite a week ago, which had precipitated Matthew's unexpected return to Hunter's Cross when by all rights he should have been heading to Kent for Lady Cavendish's house party.

And Fanny.

It had hurt abominably to write to Lady Cavendish at the last moment, bowing out of her invitation—Fanny's invitation so she'd told him in Brighton—and the chance to see his love again. The ache in his heart whenever he thought of Fanny only stiffened his resolve to see her ensconced here, mistress of his estate. He gazed at the empty place beside him, imagining her sitting there, his countess talking with him, laughing, teasing him as she sipped her tea and they spoke about their plans for the day. He must write to Fanny as well, explaining his absence this past weekend and perhaps inviting her to come to Hunter's Cross for a visit. Once here surely he could persuade her to say yes to his suit.

"Good morning, Matthew." His sister, Lady Beatrice Hunter, sailed into the breakfast room, dressed in a deep red riding habit, and sat down in the very seat he'd been thinking of as Fanny's, bursting that bubble of whimsy.

"Good morning, my dear. You are riding this morning?"

"Of course. Aren't you after three dull days of sitting around?" Bea raised her eyebrows, giving him her *don't be a fool* look from crystal blue eyes. At the impossible age of seventeen, his oldest sister had insisted on leaving the schoolroom and taking her place next to him and their mother in the household and in local society. God help her suitors next year when she made her come-out.

"Yes, I've called for Spartan and am about to ride out to the Downs, to see if Lord Skelton is at home."

Beatrice wrinkled her petite nose and waved her hand in dismissal. "Do not worry on that account. Lord Skelton hasn't gone anywhere in an age. His sister Sarah complained to me last week that he never goes anywhere after the Season, making her life a misery." She paused to signal the footman. "James, a plate full with tea and toast, please."

"How can Lady Sarah's life be a misery? Skelly dotes on her and their mother." Matthew swallowed the last of his coffee.

"Too much doting is not a good thing. He's always underfoot, she says. She can't pay a call but he's escorting them, then holding them to his schedule. The same thing if they go into Aylesbury, he tags along. Why can't he take himself off like you do and let them have some peace?"

James entered with her plate and Beatrice eagerly slipped her napkin into her lap. "Thank you, James."

"More coffee, James, please." Matthew indicated his empty cup. "Well, Bea, I was going to ask to accompany you on your ride this morning, but now I dare not for fear of making your life a 'misery.' "

"Brother, you would have to remain here longer than two weeks for Mama and me to even realize you are in the house." She forked a bite of eggs and sausage into her mouth and chewed vigorously.

"Well, I may have to do just that. Mr. Farrow's departure has made it impossible for me to leave until I can get a new manager installed here. The estate will not run itself, you know."

"You cannot blame Mr. Farrow, Matthew. I'm sure

he would have prevented his wife's father dying so suddenly if he could. As it was, they had to go and quickly, for her mother was in such a state of grief Mrs. Farrow believed she would die herself if they did not assist her."

"I don't fault the man. Family needs do come first, however, it could not have come at a worse time." Both for the estate and his personal life. Matthew accepted his coffee and savored the hot bite of the dark brew. "Ahh."

"Ugh, how can you drink that without anything in it, Matthew?" Beatrice shuddered and grabbed her teacup, sipping her well-sugared tea avidly, as if in fear someone might force coffee down her throat instead.

"It is an acquired taste, I grant you, but I enjoy its invigorating effect very much. Do you wish to ride with me to Skelton's?"

"Yes, please. Sarah will be happy for the visit and your company is always much better than riding with a groom. I will tell Perkins to tell Mama when she wakes so she will not fret about me." Her plate almost empty, Beatrice patted the napkin to her lips and rose, bringing Matthew to his feet as well. "I'll meet you in the front hall."

"In ten minutes or I leave without you. We're missing the best part of the morning." He grinned as she strode out of the room. Bea was a dear and he'd be sorry to lose her next year. He couldn't help but think some gentleman would snap her up before the first month of the Season was out.

"The post, my lord." His family's butler of twenty years presented several letters on a silver salver.

"Thank you, Gates." Picking up the lot, Matthew

glanced at each before setting them on the table. Time enough for them after his ride. The handwriting on the last one, however, caught his attention. No one of his acquaintance made their *Ls* with that swooping elegance save Fanny. He plopped back into his chair and popped the seal, his heartbeat speeding inside his chest, and began to read.

Matthew seethed during the entire, interminable ride to the Downs, anger and fear warring within him by turns. Fanny's letter, while gently admonishing him for his absence at the house party, had made one thing abundantly clear: She held no loyalty to him whatsoever. The woman he loved, who he knew loved him, had made an assignation with one of the worst rakehells in London. That she had not gone through with the tryst was immaterial. The shock of the betrayal had hit him so hard he'd sat in a daze until Beatrice had come in search of him.

The letter made it absolutely clear that Fanny was determined to live an independent life, one in which he would figure only as a lover, not a husband. He wanted nothing more than to curse loudly into the refreshing morning air that washed over him as they galloped across the fields of Hunter's Cross. Beatrice's presence precluded him from such a wild display, so he urged Spartan on to greater speed. How fortunate his sister rode as well as any man and therefore kept up with him easily, though he might have to answer a pert question or two about his hell-bent flight when at last they arrived.

That Fanny might never become his countess twisted his heart. He'd wanted nothing more ever since he'd first met her, at her come-out ball over ten years ago now. Ten years of bitter hurt beginning with her refusal of him and her marriage to Lord Stephen. God, but he'd been patient. With the war raging, he'd bided his time the first few years. Tarkington had been a reckless fellow, a known risk taker within his unit, so there was every chance Fanny would end up a widow sooner rather than later.

When she'd come to him three years into the marriage, her tender heart gravely wounded, he'd comforted her in every way possible, and rejoiced anew. Divorce was unheard of, a scandal to ruin them both, still he'd begged her to run away to the Continent with him. With any luck, Tarkington would divorce her, then they could marry and live quietly at Hunter's Cross. The *ton*'s censure meant nothing to him if Fanny would be his wife.

Instead she'd returned to the blackguard after four months of absolute bliss spent with him. Her family had contracted measles in the epidemic that had raged that year, dying one after the other. In her grief, guilt over her affair with him had overcome her and she'd broken with him and returned to Tarkington. He'd understood the reason for her actions at the time, still, her desertion had cut to the bone. Returning to his estate to recover, he'd eschewed London in fear of seeing her again. Out of sight, out of mind, they said. They'd been wrong. Not a day had gone by that he hadn't thought about her, missed her with a depth of longing that had harrowed his soul.

By rights he should have moved on with his life, taken a wife and done his duty to the earldom by putting an heir in his nursery. But the hope of winning Fanny simply wouldn't die. So he'd avoided entanglements with the daughters of his neighbors and thrown himself instead into the pastimes he loved: shooting, riding, racing, and boxing. When Kinellan had sent word of Stephen Tarkington's death at Waterloo, he'd been mad to race to London and declare himself, but his friend had counseled caution, which Matthew, once again full of hope, had heeded and bided his time throughout Fanny's year of mourning.

Now it seemed his patience had, in the end, come to naught. He'd declared himself to Fanny time and again in these past months to no avail, yet still he'd hoped. This latest betrayal, however, had finally killed hope. Fanny would continue to refuse him, more enamored of her freedom to flit from man to man than of the one man who loved her. At last, it was time to let her go.

As they approached the winding driveway to the Downs, Matthew pulled Spartan down to a smart canter, then a quick trot, and finally to a walk.

Beatrice rode up beside him, a perturbed frown on her face. "What hellhounds did you think were chasing you, brother? I've never seen you push Spartan that hard outside of a hunt."

"He's in fine fettle after three days of no exercise. I gave him his head, is all."

"Well, you could have had a care for my welfare. I was hard put to keep up with your breakneck pace." Bea's reproachful look might have touched his heart, had not her eyes been shining with the exhilaration of the ride.

"You do not seem unduly distressed, sweet sister. But if your riding skills are lacking, do not blame me. You are perfectly capable of riding when you will. If you've lately taken to mainly indoor pursuits, such as reading those dreadful romance novels, you can scarcely be surprised." Matthew grinned, and narrowly managed to avoid a blow from his sister's riding crop.

"Wretch. What else am I supposed to do when it rains?" Beatrice settled back in her saddle, walking her horse alongside him. "I can hardly play billiards by myself when you are gone. Mama won't play and the younger girls are too silly to learn."

"Give them a chance, Bea. They are scarcely ten and twelve."

"I am certain I was never so giddy when I was that age."

"You have never been giddy, I grant you that," Matthew said as they came in sight of the Broadmans' stately manor house. "Stubborn, yes, giddy, no. I shall be sure to tell your future husband that when he asks for your hand."

Bea dismounted, then glared at him. "I'll thank you to keep your observations to yourself where my 'future husband' is concerned or I'll thwart you and elope to Gretna Green."

"And then I'll take a riding crop to you, my girl. Just see if I don't." Chuckling, Matthew swung down from Spartan, good humor restored by their always spirited banter. Despite his words, he'd sorely miss Bea when she did marry.

The butler showed them to the drawing room where the family had gathered for tea.

"Lady Beatrice, what a lovely surprise." Lady Skelton beckoned to her, smiling warmly. "Good day to you, my lord. It is good to see you again."

"Good morning, Lady Skelton." He and Beatrice

spoke as one to the lovely woman, their neighbor of long acquaintance. Sarah and Beatrice had grown up together, and though Jonathan Broadman, now Lord Skelton, was much younger than he, Matthew and the tall, thin, good-natured earl had always been on excellent terms.

"Skelly, well met." Matthew turned to his friend, who stood next to the fireplace, a teacup in hand.

"Beatrice!" Sarah Broadman squealed and rushed to embrace her friend. "What a lucky stroke that you have come just this minute. May I take Bea to see my new gown, Mama?"

"Sarah, did you forget to speak to Lord Lathbury?" The viscountess gave her daughter a stern gaze.

"I'm sorry, my lord." Dipping a quick curtsy, Sarah smiled brightly at him. "Good morning. Thank you ever so much for bringing Bea with you. I really must show her my gown for the ball. Come with me, my dear." She grabbed Beatrice by the hand and tugged her toward the door. "You will be astounded at what Mrs. Comfrey has managed to devise."

After her daughter disappeared, Lady Skelton shook her head. "Skelton, I fear it will matter not at all how many balls we give for Sarah, she will not secure a husband if she does not try to attract one." She looked pointedly at Matthew and sniffed. "Her second Season is likely to be as dismal as her first."

"Take heart, Lady Skelton," Matthew said, moving quickly toward Skelly, who had put his tea down on the mantelpiece and stood with hands on hips, a belligerent set to his lips. "Beatrice will be out as well next Season. When the gentlemen compare Sarah to my sister, they will undoubtedly flee Beatrice's tart tongue and flock to your vivacious daughter instead."

As long as Lady Skelton didn't look on him with a matchmaking eye. Sarah was practically the same age as Beatrice, and flighty. Not at all to his taste. "Is she looking forward to London again so soon? She spoke of a new gown for a ball."

"Yes, and a pretty piece of folly it is too." Lord Skelton glared at his mother and straightened the candlesticks on the mantel. "There are few local gentlemen my mother would deem grand enough a match for Sarah, save you." Skelly raised his eyebrows hopefully. "You aren't by any chance interested in her, are you, Lathbury? It would make my life a deal easier, I tell you."

"Alas, I seem to have a toe caught in the parson's mousetrap. I proposed to a lady when we met in Brighton, but she has yet to give me her definitive answer. Until I am certain of that outcome I could not, in good conscience, raise your sister's hopes." Hoping his description of his current state of affairs with Fanny didn't stray too wide of the mark, he sat in the rather ornate, but extremely comfortable Sheraton armchair.

"Didn't think so." His friend sighed. "My luck's out completely. Will you at least put in an appearance, Lathbury? Pay Sarah a bit of attention if you would. Dance once or maybe twice with her even. Perhaps if the other gentlemen see you dancing attendance on her, they'll try to swoop in and steal her away from you. Worth a go, don't you think?" Skelly's dark eyes pled as though his life depended on it. "I cannot endure chaperoning the girl in London for another three or four months. Not and retain my sanity."

"What has she done, Skelly?"

"What do you think she does, old chap? The same as your sister will come next April. Gad about to every ball, picnic, theatre performance, musical evening, and firework display at Vauxhall Gardens. Not to mention having to shepherd her on sightseeing trips to museums, libraries, exhibitions. And the shopping trips." His face grew pale. "You would not believe it, Lathbury. Four and a half hours to bespeak a gown!"

"Sarah had not been to London since she was a child," her mother put in crisply, "and certainly not since coming out. What did you suppose she would do for clothes in Town, Skelton? Be satisfied to make over some of my old gowns?"

"No, Mama." Lord Skelton glanced away quickly from his parent, who had started to frown. "But it was the better part of an entire day." He turned to Matthew for sympathy. "I missed the races at Newbury because of it."

Matthew shook his head as if to commiserate, his mind furiously racing down another track entirely. What if the tables were turned? "I can see why you would take every opportunity to avail Sarah of the opportunity to find a husband. I wonder if I might be of some service after all."

Eyes suddenly bright, Lady Skelton leaned toward him. "How kind of you, my lord. But what are you proposing, may I ask, if not marriage?"

"A house party, my lady." Matthew smiled evenly at his neighbor. "The lady I spoke of earlier had just attended one at which the ladies were able to make the acquaintance of new gentlemen in a secure environment. Young girls would be chaperoned by a family member, but would still have better opportunities to converse with gentlemen. And," he continued smoothly for the *coup de grace,* "I would be able to invite a variety of gentlemen, and ladies, of course, who might be suitable, yet from a different social set than that Sarah is accustomed to."

Matthew could almost see the cogs in the neatly oiled great wheel that was Skelly's brain as it ground to the perfectly logical conclusion: Lady Sarah making the acquaintance of someone new, who didn't know the girl, but might be attracted to a large dowry.

"We thank you so much for that generous offer, Lord Lathbury." Lady Skelton spoke first, with a regal nod of her head. "I hope you will find the house party as advantageous to you."

If Matthew could manage to invite the precise group of people necessary, this house party could prove not only educational and entertaining, but also devious enough to win him a wife.

# Chapter 12

As the carriage sped along the well-maintained roads of central Buckinghamshire, Fanny gazed eagerly from one window to the other, drinking in the sights of woodlands, parklands, and grassy meadows. She'd not been out of London since her journey to Kent, and although she'd always thought herself a creature more of Town than country, the bucolic vistas flying by spoke to her of a peacefulness not found in the city.

"Do sit still, Fanny." Jane, her companion for this weekend at Hunter's Cross, had withdrawn to the corner of the Marquess of Theale's huge carriage, eyes closed. "I am worn out with your bouncing about."

"You mean you are worn out fuming about your quarrel with Lord Sinclair." Fanny smirked, then sobered. Her sister-in-law had unexpectedly returned to Theale House two days before, withdrawn and upset by something that had happened while she'd been staying with the earl. Fanny had suggested she accompany her to Matthew's party mainly to cheer her friend. If Jane was going to wear a Friday face the entire time, however, Fanny would quickly rue her kind offer. "Come, you must not show your grumps to company. I'm family. I don't mind."

Jane cocked one delicate eyebrow, and glared at her. "I'll remind you of that generous offer at two o'clock in the morning when I need a friendly bosom to cry upon."

"I will be happy to oblige you from sinking further into the doldrums as long as I am not otherwise entertained at that moment." Taking Jane's hand, Fanny squeezed it and shook it ever so slightly. "Any Widows' Club member would come to a fellow member's rescue at the drop of a hat."

"As long as it wasn't a particularly fetching hat, I suspect," Jane murmured, her good humor a little better restored.

They passed through the entry to the driveway, a pair of ancient stone crosses, gray and pitted but somehow still majestic, standing on either side of the crushed gravel drive. The crosses for which the estate had been named, Matthew had said, when inviting her to this party. She'd been surprised, nay shocked, when his invitation had arrived, without a word of reproach for her actions regarding Alan Garrett. In her letter to him, she'd felt she must tell Matthew what she'd almost done and had expected a severe dressing down from him via the return post. Instead, his charming letter had arrived and enclosed an invitation to a house party of his own. His lack of concern had hurt her more than upbraiding her would have. The more she'd thought of that cheerful invitation, the more wary she'd become. Did her almost betrayal mean nothing to him? Had he tired of her refusals and given up his pursuit of her? But then why request her presence here? Did he intend to break with her and wished to do it to her face? She'd not brooded over meeting him again. Until now.

"Now who's the fount of despair?" Jane poked her shoulder and rose. "Are you going to sit there and moon over God knows what—or whom—or get out of the carriage?"

With a start, Fanny came back to herself. "After you, dear sister-in-law. Precedence must be observed or Lord Lathbury will think us quite barbaric."

Her friend looked wary of the sentiment, but accepted the handsome groom's hand without a qualm. Fanny clambered out after her, also availing herself of the strong arm of a footman. With all these attractive men running about, how were women ever supposed to seriously consider the gentlemen attending the party?

Catching Jane's gaze and dragging it away from the groom, Fanny laughed and tried to indicate with a sharp inclination of her head that the lord and the countess had appeared to welcome them.

"Good afternoon, Lady John, Lady Stephen." Matthew's deep voice rumbled and Fanny's heart leaped in her chest as though it were a stag being chased by a pack of hungry hounds.

"Good afternoon, my lord," they replied in concert, dipping a curtsy in unison as well.

"You seem well rehearsed, ladies." Matthew's gaze took them both in, but it seemed to Fanny he lingered on her a bit longer than her companion. "Perhaps you will entertain us during the weekend with a scene from Drury Lane."

"I've often thought, had my circumstances been

different, Lord Lathbury," Jane favored him with a pert smile, "I might well have made a career on the stage. So exciting to go before people and tell them stories. Quite like being out in Society, if you think of it that way."

"Lady John, I daresay you would charm any audience, whether from the Lyceum stage or at Lady Jersey's latest at home. Mama"—he turned to the gracious silver-haired lady beside him—"may I present Lady John Tarkington? Lady John, my mother, the Countess of Lathbury."

"My lady." Jane dipped her curtsy.

"I am delighted to meet you, Lady John. I believe I knew your mother, Lady Munro. You favor her about the eyes." The countess smiled and nodded, then looked expectantly at Fanny.

Unaccountably, her mouth dried as though she'd swallowed a handful of dust.

"And this is Lady Stephen Tarkington." Matthew grasped her hand and drew her toward his mother. "I have spoken to you of her several times."

At those ominous words, Fanny stumbled forward, grabbing Matthew's hand in earnest. "My . . . my lady." She coughed slightly to clear her throat. "I am so pleased . . ." The words came out in a croak. What must the woman think of her? She swallowed, desperately trying to moisten her parched throat. "I am so pleased to meet you."

"And I you, Lady Stephen." The countess's brilliant blue eyes, an exact copy of the ones that looked out of Matthew's face, took her in from top to toe. "My son has spoken of you often, in most glowing terms. I am happy to meet you at last."

Afraid to try to utter another word, Fanny dipped

a curtsy. Thankfully, Matthew took her arm and steered them all toward the house. "Mrs. Donnelly will see you to your rooms to freshen up, ladies. Then we are gathering in the drawing room for tea."

"Are we the first or last to arrive, Lady Lathbury?" Jane had fallen into step with the countess. "I fear we started rather late from London this morning."

"Somewhere in the middle, I believe." The older woman smiled and raised her China blue skirts as they mounted the steps of the portico. "Although we have several guests staying at Hunter's Cross this weekend, many are local families who will attend the festivities, such as dinner and dancing this evening, or the shooting tomorrow, but who will return home at the end of the night."

"I'll see you once you are settled," Matthew said, giving her hand a squeeze. That was encouraging. In ways she couldn't quite put her finger on, he'd seemed somewhat distant since greeting them. Had his affections turned away from her because of her dealings with Alan Garrett? If so, her moment of folly in Kent might cost her dearly.

They were shown to their chambers and Fanny resisted the urge to sink down on the bed and not arise, but that was the coward's way. If she'd lost Matthew's regard, then by God she'd make sure to get him back this weekend. She quickly washed the grime of the road from her face and hands and summoned the maid to assist her into a new day gown, a green and gold stripe trimmed in gold lace that she'd bespoke specifically for this weekend. The cut of it subtly accentuated her breasts, as low-cut as possible for a gown worn during the day, with shirring at the sides to draw the eye to their fullness. She'd designed it with Matthew's hungry eyes in mind so she'd put it to the test as soon as possible.

The drawing room teemed with people, enough to make the large, long room seem small. The walls of Pompeian red, framed with polished walnut wood, created the perfect setting for this gathering. Fanny paused on the threshold, taking in the sight, especially noting the number of young ladies attending in all manner of brightly colored pastel gowns, as though an army of bright butterflies had flown inside and now flitted about the room. Were these schoolgirls her competition?

It certainly seemed that way. Matthew glided around the room, the genial host, laughing with this one, chatting avidly with that one, smiling into the face of a chit who must surely be no more than twelve years old? Fanny gritted her teeth, forced a smile, and headed for the tea table, wishing she could drown her sorrows properly. Unfortunately, tea was the strongest beverage available. In order to drown anything, she'd have to pour all the cups into a tub and stick her head in, as though she were bobbing for apples.

"Lady Stephen?"

She turned. Dear Lord, one of the butterflies had fluttered down beside her. A pretty one, with dark hair and eyes as blue as . . . the countess. And Matthew. "Yes?"

"I know we've not been properly introduced, but I wanted to speak with you." The girl dropped a quick curtsy, impatience with the formalities in every graceful line, and smiled. "I'm Lady Beatrice, Lord Lathbury's sister, the eldest one of them still home. How do you do?"

"Quite well, thank you." Fanny's spirits, so glum a few moments ago, now took a turn for the better. Lady Beatrice's straightforward manner acted as a tonic to her. It could be simply she was a connection to Matthew, but she didn't truly think so.

"Would you care to take a turn in the garden? It's so crowded and noisy here. I told Matthew he was inviting too many people, but would he listen to anything I said? No. This way, my lady." Lady Beatrice led Fanny out the French doors, along the veranda, and down a short flight of stairs that opened onto a vast garden of blooms.

Overgrown, with riotous color everywhere, these blooms put the young ladies inside to shame. Neither was it a staid garden, with paths of exact measurements that crossed with military precision nor with shrubs clipped into precise geometric shapes, as they were in the backyard at Theale House in London. All over the Theale network of estates across England, if truth be told. None of her brother-in-law's estates included a garden such as this. This garden felt alive in a way no other ever had to her eyes. The unrestricted colors, plants unrestrained by borders or shapes made the whole area seem a living thing in a way the formal gardens did not.

"How absolutely charming, Lady Beatrice." Fanny wandered off the rustic path that wound through the wilderness and stooped to smell an exquisite tall purple flower. "What a delicious smell! Vanilla and cherries together."

"Heliotrope, my lady. One of my favorites." Remaining on the pathway, Beatrice looked on as Fanny sniffed her way across a bank of purple, yellow, and pink blooms, each more fragrant than the last.

"Lord, I could camp right here and be happy, I believe." Fanny raised her head from a showy pink damask rose and waded over to an unfamiliar, strangely stringy yellow plant. "I know the rose, but what is this one?"

"Witch hazel. Not only a pretty flower, but Cook makes a face wash from it."

"Indeed." Fanny sniffed again, a fresh, clean scent wafting upward. "Lovely." She waved her hand across the expanse of colorful blooms. "Is this your handiwork or the countess's?"

"I wish I could take credit for it; however, I do not have the patience for such meticulous design." Beatrice shook her head.

"Meticulous design? It all looks as though it came up quite naturally."

Lady Beatrice chuckled and beckoned Fanny to her. "Matthew says that for anything to both look natural and be pleasing to the senses, it must be designed to do so. For example, to insure the display you see here, the different plants are put into the ground at particular times, during different months even, so they will bloom together to make this perfection."

"Matthew says? He planted this garden?" Gazing again at the glorious blooms around her, Fanny was suddenly reminded of the bouquet of flowers he'd sent her after the masquerade. That too had been perfectly arranged with all the flowers she loved best.

"He has a passion for it." Lady Beatrice nodded and grasped Fanny's arm, propelling her farther down the path.

Stunned by this revelation, Fanny would have blindly followed Lady Beatrice into the River Thames.

Matthew had an enthusiasm for gardening and flowers? How had she never known this about him? When had she ever given him a chance to reveal it?

"Speaking of which . . ." Lady Beatrice stopped them in a little clearing, drawing Fanny to a rustic wooden bench to one side, next to a cluster of hydrangeas. "Are you in love with my brother?"

Caught in the act of seating herself on the bench, Fanny thumped down on the hard plank, once more astounded by Lady Beatrice's words. "I . . . I beg your p-pardon?"

With a merry laugh, the girl sat beside Fanny, seemingly pleased at the mayhem she'd caused in her guest's heart. "I do apologize, but Matthew instructed me to ask you that question."

"He did?" She didn't know whether to be flattered or outraged.

"I'm not to press you for an answer; however, he does wish to know."

"Then why does he not ask me himself?" If Matthew would play games, he would find her a willing participant, but likely without the result he desired.

"Perhaps he will." The girl shrugged. "Although he is much taken up with his other guests at the moment. My friend, Miss Broadman, had a ball given in her honor several nights ago in hopes she would discover a suitor to her liking. It could be my brother is introducing her to the eligible gentlemen with whom she is not already acquainted." Lady Beatrice raised her eyebrows and glanced to the side. "Of course when last I saw him, he was conversing with Miss Gadhill."

"Which young lady was she?" Fanny tried to recall all the little butterflies in the drawing room.

"The one in deep rose, with blond hair and—"

"And a predatory gleam in her eyes when she looked at your brother." The young lady had clung to Matthew's arm as though she were a permanent attachment.

"The very one." Lady Beatrice sniffed. "I must confess I have never liked her. Her laugh is false."

Lady Beatrice was no fool. Fanny would have to beware of Miss Gadhill and hope to stay on Matthew's sister's good side. "Should we return to the house now? I do wish to have ample time to dress for dinner."

"By all means, my lady."

As they returned to the house, Fanny's every step was plagued with doubt about Matthew's intentions toward her, and even worse, hers toward him.

A quick tap on the door of Fanny's room sent her into a flurry of activity. "Come in, Jane. I am almost ready."

"Why can you never manage to be ready on time, Fanny?" Jane strode into the room, straight to the fireplace. "Lord, these rooms are cold. I shall have to request another cover tonight." She cut her gaze toward her sister-in-law. "Or find some other means to warm myself."

"Jane! You waste no time a'tall, do you?" Fanny fastened her gold and amethyst earrings, then slipped her matching necklace around her neck. "Come help me with the clasp and we can go down."

"The maid could have assisted you." Her sister-in-law fussed even as she reached for the clasp.

"Not when she's already assisting ten other ladies as well. Does no one have their own lady's maid anymore?" Fanny shook her hands, hoping the fluttering in the pit of her stomach would magically disappear when she stepped into the corridor.

"Apparently not. Stand still or we will miss dinner all together." Jane fussed with the clasp, pulling a stray strand of Fanny's hair.

"Ouch!"

"If you'd stopped fidgeting that wouldn't have happened. There." Jane patted the back of her neck. "Ready to be ravished."

"What?" Fanny jumped back, perhaps because that had been her own thought.

"Isn't that why you're here? I'm certain it is not for the grouse shooting tomorrow."

"Jane . . ." Touching the necklace's teardrop-shaped pendant, Fanny gathered her courage. If anyone could give her good advice about Matthew, it was her friend. "What should I do? I believe he still wants to marry me, although to see him flirting with all those young ladies this afternoon, I have to say I'd not be as sure as I once was, except . . ."

"Except?" Jane faced her, giving her full attention, albeit with a cynically arched brow.

"He wants to know if I love him."

"And what did you tell him?"

Sighing heavily, Fanny grabbed a silk shawl and draped it over her shoulders, careful not to look at her friend. "He didn't ask me. His sister did."

"Lady Beatrice?" Jane's brows swooped up alarmingly. "How terribly odd. Why would she be interested in that question? She did not strike me as the kind of young lady who meddled in love affairs not her own."

"Her brother asked her to ask me." Unwilling to meet Jane's gaze any longer, Fanny hung her head.

"And your answer?"

"I told her I would inform Matthew of my answer myself."

"Well, I am pleased to see your wits are not completely addled," Jane said, laughter bubbling up out of her. "Fanny, you really need to just marry the man and be done with it."

"But how can I be certain I won't end up in another marriage I'll live to regret making?" The misery of all her years as the poor, neglected wife of Stephen Tarkington returned with a force that overwhelmed her and she clutched the back of the vanity chair. Pain at the memory of the sympathetic eyes of the *ton* as they sought her out at parties and whispered whenever she went by washed over her. No matter how she tried, she could not banish the fear of walking by a crowd of people to hear the low, insistent whispers of "Poor Lady Lathbury. I hear he's been seen with that opera singer . . . with Lady Margaret Seacole . . . with—"

"You can never be completely sure of any man, short of the grave, my dear," Jane broke in on her spiraling thoughts of impending tragedy. "However, for as much as I have observed, Lord Lathbury is as different from Stephen as two men could be with regard to their faithfulness. Lathbury has never enjoyed the reputation your late husband did, before or after his marriage." She embraced Fanny, hugging her tightly. "I, who know full well Stephen's perfidy toward you, say that if you believe you love Lord Lathbury, you must summon the courage to be brave and embrace it and him." She retreated a step and peered deep into Fanny's eyes. "Do not allow Stephen to rob you of happiness twice."

# Chapter 13

Under brilliant sunshine the next day, the shooting brake that conveyed Fanny, Jane, and the other women of the house party bumped cheerfully along the rough road before striking off across the fallow fields toward the shooting range, from which direction faint gunfire could be heard. The day had dawned clear and the ladies had been informed at breakfast about the picnic lunch arranged for them with the gentlemen in the afternoon. An outing Fanny approached with some trepidation.

Last evening had proved frustrating in the extreme. While Matthew had spoken to her several times, he'd not singled her out in any special way to indicate he wished an answer to the question his sister had posed. Instead, he'd talked and laughed and flirted with every woman in the room. If she wished to be generous, this behavior could indicate he favored none of these women or girls, her included. However, generosity was furthest from her mind this morning, and she nursed a growing resentment toward her host. Had he brought her here to show her she'd missed her chance, his sister's question notwithstanding? Either that or he was punishing her for telling him about her regrettable dalliance with Mr. Garrett by showing her two could play at that game. She'd not have thought that of Matthew, still what other explanation could there be for his behavior?

The brake slowed in a grassy field near a small stand of tall oaks under which several tables had been arranged, complete with snowy white tablecloths, china service, and footmen running to and fro setting out various dishes. In the distance, a line of male figures, dark against the bright sun, made their way toward them. On the far end the tallest and broadest of the gentleman strode quicker than the rest, forcing his nearest companion to lengthen his strides to keep up. Matthew seemed in a hurry to greet the women of the party. Fanny grasped a footman's hand and descended the brake, unsure for perhaps the first time in her life, what to expect from this man. Seizing Jane's arm as soon as her feet touched the ground, she steered her toward a table on the far edge of the grouping.

"Are you trying to hide, my dear? I seriously doubt it will work." Jane seated herself on the cushioned chair and looked about expectantly. "I suspect Lord Lathbury will have designated a special place for you to sit with him. I am actually already claimed by Lord Kinellan. He sent me a charming note this morning, asking for my company at lunch."

"Kinellan? From Scotland?" Matthew's particular friend was drawing Jane from her side. Another example of loyalty, as when he guarded the door at the masquerade or his part in their tryst on the beach?

Perhaps Matthew would spirit her away for another tête-à-tête. One in which she would give him a good piece of her mind. "Did you enjoy his company so much last evening?"

"He is quite amusing, my dear." Jane gave her an arch look. Her sister-in-law's idea of amusing differed from most people's. "And we have discovered a connection. His great-grandmother was a Munro who married a Graham, which is his clan. Quite a handsome man, all in all, don't you think." Jane gazed across the field as the man in question broke away from his companion, scanned the tables then strode purposefully toward her.

If one looked with an objective eye, Lord Kinellan could, indeed, be called handsome. Wavy auburn hair, piercing blue eyes, and a chiseled profile Fanny would know immediately by his long straight nose. Tall, though not so tall as Matthew, broad shoulders, though not so deep through the chest. His legs bulged with muscles, likely from so much riding. Just like Matthew's.

Hoping no one had noticed her staring at Lord Kinellan, Fanny gazed around the picnic area, trying to locate Matthew. She could have sworn he'd been beside Kinellan before that gentleman had headed toward Jane. Then she spied him on the opposite side of the field, speaking with his butler. Likely making sure everything was proceeding smoothly. Somewhat mollified, she took her seat just as Lord Kinellan arrived.

"Good afternoon, Lady John, Lady Stephen." He nodded briefly to Fanny then turned a genuine smile on Jane. "Did you receive my note, my lady?"

"I did, my lord. How thoughtful of you to ask to

partner me at luncheon. We would be delighted to have you join us." Jane's smile managed to convey her willingness to be coaxed to a more secluded spot. Fanny had always marveled at the woman's ability to convey more meaning without words than most people did with them.

"I would like nothing more; however, I believe Lord Lathbury has arranged for us to sit with another of our kinsmen, Lord Selkirk."

"Cousin James is here?" Jane looked around avidly. "I did not see him last night."

"He arrived late this morning and joined us directly in the field."

"And how is he your kindred, Lord Kinellan?" Jane rose, suddenly intent as she took the earl's arm. "You will excuse us, Fanny?"

"Of course, Jane. My lord, so nice to see you once more." She nodded pleasantly to the Scotsman, still unsure how much he knew about her escapades with Matthew.

"And I you, my lady." He nodded again before leading Jane toward a table some little way from her and seating her beside a gentleman with dark hair whose smile split his face when he saw her.

"Good afternoon, Lady Stephen."

Fanny looked up into the pleasant face of Lady Skelton, a neighbor of Matthew's to whom he'd introduced her last evening. "Good afternoon, my lady. We are having a wonderful day for a picnic, are we not?" Whenever in doubt, the weather was a comforting if dull topic of conversation.

"Might I join you here?" The lady scarcely waited for Fanny's nod before seating herself facing the rest of the company. "There is much more shade this far beneath the trees. One must always think of the ravages of sunlight, no matter how comforting the heat may feel."

Glad that her spencer covered her arms, Fanny gave thanks the tan she'd gotten in Brighton was finally fading, though her face remained the color of cream into which a dollop of coffee had been poured. She must try harder to avoid the sun.

"Indeed, a lady's complexion is the truest reflection of her refinement, don't you think, Lady Stephen?" The countess's attention seemed focused on her daughter, Lady Sarah, sitting two tables away.

"It is certainly a mark of favor with many gentlemen." Fanny searched the tables hoping to discover where Matthew had again hid himself. "Some I know do not hold it as an irreparable barrier to marriage if a lady is a little tanned."

"The less discerning gentlemen, perhaps. I have been extremely careful to keep my daughter's complexion as milky white as the day she was born." Lady Skelton nodded toward Lady Sarah, who had just smiled a greeting into the face of Lord Lathbury.

Fanny's heart skipped a beat as he seated himself next to the girl, chatting with her as though he'd known her all his life. She gripped her napkin in her hand, then forced herself to calm. Lady Beatrice had said Lady Sarah was her best friend. Presumably, Matthew *had* known the lady most of his life as well. Slowly exhaling, Fanny loosened her grip on the square of linen she'd been wringing.

"They will make an excellent couple, do you not think, Lady Stephen?" The countess nodded toward her daughter, who chose that moment to lean toward Matthew, laughing at some private jest.

"Is Lady Sarah not a trifle young for Lord Lathbury?" Fanny prayed her panic didn't show in her voice.

"Why would you say that?" Lady Skelton turned wide eyes on Fanny. "He's but one and thirty. A perfect difference in age I would say, for he is old enough to have gotten over the wildness of youth. And while she may be a little behind him in years, I have always believed a woman ripens best when married to a man who will steady her, guide her into a maturity of his own fashioning. I suspect Lord Lathbury has finally arrived at that same conclusion."

Swallowing hard, Fanny breathed slowly, trying her best to release the rancor building within her in some way other than becoming a spectacle at a picnic. This woman wrongly assumed Matthew would offer for Lady Sarah in order to mold the girl into the wife he wanted. Well, there might be such men in the world, but the Matthew she knew was not one of them. Opening her mouth to suggest that very thing, a voice of caution whispered in her ear and she paused. Was this the Matthew she knew, or thought she knew? Or had he grown too frustrated with her and turned to a more malleable woman?

"Lord Lathbury would be fortunate to have her." The proud mother smiled and nodded at the couple, just as Matthew rose and raised Lady Sarah's hand to his lips.

"Yes, I do see your point, Lady Skelton," Fanny said, sending the woman a cool, appraising look. "However, a woman already mature, especially one who had been widowed, say, could be an immediate asset to a man of Lord Lathbury's stature. She could step into the role of wife, chatelaine, and mother in an instant. Do you not agree?" Fanny arched her neck and fought not to smile at Lady Skelton's livid face. "There is the matter of the earl needing an heir. An untried virgin is a chancy thing where getting children are concerned. But a woman who already has a child would be much more apt to produce more of them, wouldn't you say?"

"My dear countess, Lady Stephen." Matthew stepped toward them, making his bow, his gaze darting between the two of them as if assessing the situation. "I had hoped to speak to you both before the shooting resumed. I was just saying to your daughter, Lady Skelton, that I hoped she would honor me with the first dance this evening."

Eyes gleaming in triumph, Lady Skelton leaned toward the earl. "And did she agree to that dance, my lord?"

"She did indeed, my lady."

Fanny bit her lips until she tasted blood, but she refused to make a sound. That would only give the wretched woman and her daughter the greater victory over her.

Matthew continued to smile at them, but peered closer at Fanny's face. "Are you quite all right, Lady Stephen?"

Breathe. She must remain in control of herself even as she fled this disastrous scene. "I am well, my lord, save for a sudden headache. I believe I shall ask to return to the house ahead of the others. I would not wish to spoil anyone else's outing."

"I am sorry to hear this, my lady. May I escort you to the brake? I'll instruct the driver to return you as quickly as possible." His gaze held a modicum of concern and perhaps a flicker of triumph.

"There is no need, my lord." Fanny rose, straightening her deep emerald spencer and smoothing her green muslin gown. Anything to avoid meeting his eyes.

"But I insist." The hard edge to his voice brought her head up. "If you will excuse us, my lady?" He dipped his head curtly in the direction of Lady Skelton, then grasped Fanny's elbow. She scarcely had a moment to make a partial curtsy before he propelled her not toward the field where the conveyance stood, but into the stand of trees behind them.

He continued to march her away from the picnic spot, away from eavesdroppers who might hear his devastating words as he told her he was now preparing to marry Lady Sarah. Well, if he wanted a simpering young fool for a wife, it was just as well she had not accepted him earlier this summer. It would have been the disaster she'd been trying to avoid. What did it matter that her heart was breaking?

Suddenly, they burst through the stand of trees into a meadow filled with sunshine and birdsong. He'd dragged her all the way out here just to throw it in her face that he didn't want her any longer. Well, she'd not give him the pleasure of seeing his words affect her. No, by God. She'd rather die than cry in front of him. Blinking rapidly to keep the tears at bay, she pulled her elbow from his grasp. "Let me go."

"If you wish it, my lady, I will do so."

She gasped, whirling around to face him. "What?"

"I have come to tell you, Fanny, if you truly do not wish to marry me, I will cease my pursuit of you."

In the deadly calm that followed his words, Fanny heard her heart break. "I see. You no longer want me." Pain exploded in her chest, forcing out the tears she'd been trying so desperately to control. "You wish to marry Lady Sarah instead."

He jerked her toward him. "You're a damned fool if you think that."

Throat choked with tears, she could scarcely understand him, scarcely speak. "What?"

"I have waited over ten years to marry you, Fanny. Do you honestly think I would throw that over in a day for a scatterbrained child?" His harsh tone cut through the fog that had enveloped her brain. "Do you truly think me so faithless?"

Unable to stop them, tears gushed down Fanny's face. Then he pressed her against his chest and she watered his hunting jacket amid the acrid smell of gunpowder and the comforting scent that was purely him. At last the watering pot ceased to water and she stepped back from him, wiping at her eyes with her gloved hand. "No."

"No?" He stopped in the midst of passing her his handkerchief, his tone deeply shocked.

"No, I don't think you faithless. Not anymore." The watering pot upended again, and she clutched the handkerchief to her streaming face.

With a deep sigh, Matthew gathered her to him again, rocking her gently. "Does this mean that you are prepared to say yes to my proposal?"

Relief stealing through her, Fanny nodded, suddenly overcome with a peace and joy she'd never experienced before.

"I think I will not take a nod nor a handshake on this agreement, my dear." He pulled her head up to look at him, and she discovered the joy in her heart reflected back to her in his eyes. "I wish to hear the words, please."

"Yes, Matthew, I will marry you." Sweet words that had taken too long to come.

He pulled her against him once more and his lips met hers, hungry and possessive in a way they had never been before. Of her own accord, she opened her mouth, moaning loudly to urge him to enter. No further encouragement needed. Grasping her head, he plundered her at will, tasting her mouth as though they'd never kissed before. When he tried to step back she slid her arms around his neck and held on, lifting herself off the ground in an effort to maintain the kiss.

He laughed and she took the moment of distraction to thrust her tongue into his mouth, holding on as she stroked his mouth with fierce, light caresses. His arms came around her, pressing her to his body, the stiffness of his cock a hard presence between them. He managed to disengage their mouths long enough to say in a husky voice, "Either we stop now or I take you here on the ground, Fanny."

Much as she would love to have him lay her down here and now, it would not do to appear before the rest of the company with grass stains on her gown and her bonnet broken. She backed away. "Little as I wish to, we had best refrain for the moment."

The hunger in his eyes lingered, but he breathed deeply and walked a little bit away, his hand massaging the back of his neck. He'd have to retie his cravat; everyone would notice how it had been pulled askew. When he turned back to her, he'd gained control of himself and came toward her, hands outstretched. "Name the day, Fanny, although by God if you make it longer than three weeks I won't be held responsible for anything I do."

Fanny took his hands, holding them lightly. "I would have us married as soon as possible; however, I feel you must come to London to meet my daughter, Ella."

"Does she have the final say in the matter?" His tone was light, but contained an edge of concern. "What can I do to win her regard?"

"For heaven's sake, she's six years old, Matthew. And no, I have the final say in whether we marry or not." He smiled at that, though she was serious. "But from the moment we marry, you will be her guardian, her new papa. I want her to love and respect you as I do."

"Then I will come as soon as I can possibly manage it." He wound her arm through his and began to walk them slowly back into the woods. "This party leaves on Tuesday; however, I am to go to Scotland for a month for some shooting with Kinellan."

"And you would indulge in that form of sport rather than another that we both could take pleasure in?" Fanny gazed up at him innocently, then licked her lips.

Matthew groaned. "I've been promised to Kinellan since Brighton. If I renege, he will call me every foul name from a turncoat to a slubberdegullion."

"Just think of what I'll call you—in bed. That should take away the sting of his epithets." Squeezing close to him, Fanny rubbed her shoulder against his. "We could celebrate our betrothal tonight, in fact."

"Tonight?" His voice deepened and a tingle shot down Fanny's spine.

"You disapprove?"

"Not in the least." He squeezed her hand. "I am delighted at the prospect. Shall I come to your room or you to mine?"

"You come to me—after you tell Kinellan your plans have changed."

"Although you may have the winning cards now, my love, the play goes around the table." He stopped them and folded her in his arms. "And eventually the dealer will take all."

Grinning at how wonderfully well his hard body fit against hers, Fanny relaxed in his arms. "Any words of wisdom before tonight's play?"

"Yes. Pray my mother does not catch us."

# Chapter 14

The gentlemen's after-dinner conversation that evening centered chiefly around the day's shooting. Comparisons were inevitably made between the before-luncheon and after-luncheon counts and every man had his own theory about how much a full stomach helped or hindered his aim. Matthew attempted to keep the conversation on an even keel, although Lord Selkirk would always advance the same opinion.

"Cheese and bread and a pint of ale out at the stands," he thundered from the far end of the table. "That's what we had when I was a lad, loading for my father. The counts don't lie, Lathbury. All this heavy food at mid-day does nothing but put a man to sleep. Can't shoot birds in your sleep."

"You've advanced that theory time and again, Selkirk," Matthew spoke up before anyone else could take the bait. "But I will tell you my numbers after lunch were almost double those of the early morning. Perhaps the quality or quantity of food has little to do with the skill of the hunter. However, gentlemen, I fear we have waxed too long on this subject." He raised his hands as if to shoo them from the room. "I know my mother will send Gates to fetch us if we do not turn up shortly."

Fleeing the wrath of the countess, the gentlemen headed out the door and to the right toward the central drawing room where the ladies had repaired over an hour before. Matthew hung back, allowing the rest of his guests to precede him. He sipped the last of his brandy, watching the parade of noblemen file out of the dining room, biding his time. When Kinellan spoke a final word to Selkirk, set his glass on the table, and looked to him expectantly, Matthew beckoned him away from the door. "A moment, Kinellan, before we join the ladies."

"Knew it. You've had that hangdog look about you all night." With a heartfelt sigh, his friend shook his head and cast his gaze on the decanter once more. "She's turned you down again, hasn't she? Your much touted plan didn't work. Be done with her, Lathbury. You've taken up too much of your life with this woman."

"On the contrary, she's agreed to become my wife." Matthew couldn't help a smug smile.

Hand outstretched for the brandy, Kinellan stopped halfway to the sideboard, his face quite comical in its surprise. His mouth dropped open, and he turned his head from side to side like a dog not sure of its master's command. "She's accepted you? Just like that?"

"Afraid so. Will you wish me happy?" Matthew's ear-to-ear grin almost hurt his face.

"Will I wish—" In two strides his friend reached him, grasped his hand, and shook it with a force that could have cracked bones. "I'll dance a jig at your wedding. Well done, old chap." He clapped Matthew on the back. "When's the happy day?"

"Soon, I earnestly hope. I came perilously close to taking her in the meadow when she accepted me." Matthew snared the decanter and poured them each a good amount.

"A gentleman goat, indeed." Kinellan laughed and accepted his libation. "But if she's accepted you, why the glum countenance?"

"There's a condition to her acceptance."

"What?" The earl frowned so deeply his brows almost touched his nose.

"Don't look like that. It's a reasonable request." Matthew tossed back the contents of his glass, then poured another one. "She wants me to go to London to meet her daughter. Once we marry I will become her legal guardian and Fanny naturally wishes for us to meet before that. It won't change the outcome of our marriage, but I couldn't refuse such a request without sounding churlish."

"I see. Well, put that way, I can't see the hurt in it either. That still doesn't explain your gloomy mood this evening." Kinellan took a long pull at his glass.

"As we wish to marry with all speed, I'm heading to London with Mother and Beatrice next week, so I'll have to cry off shooting with you in Scotland."

Attempting a cry of protest, Kinellan choked, coughed, and spewed Matthew's best French brandy all over the table. "No," he wheezed at last. "You don't mean to say you're going to give up some of the best grouse shooting in all of Scotland to go to London to see a baby?"

"Not a baby. The child's about five or six years old."

"A boy?"

"Girl."

"Pah." Kinellan poured more spirits and gulped it down. "Make sure she gives you a boy right off."

"I assure you, we will try our absolute best to oblige you as quickly as possible. And therein lies the reason for our haste. We wish to be married the soonest possible, so once I meet the child and we are seen to get along fairly well, you will receive a summons to St. Georges." Matthew winced, but continued. "If all fares well, you may need to cut your shooting trip short as well."

"What?" The spray was confined just to the earl himself this time.

"Need you to stand up with me, Kinellan. No other man for the job."

A sigh came from deep in his friend's soul. "It is a sin, Lathbury, a downright sin for a man to let a woman come between him and his shooting party. Mark my words"—Kinellan struck a pose, one finger raised—"forever after this, no woman will ever come between me and my shooting pleasure."

"I will bear witness to it, old chap. But I will make your excuses if you wish to change before joining us. I'd like for you to be there for the announcement of our betrothal."

"Certainly, certainly." The earl waved him toward the door. "I have aided you twice in your wooing and now in wedding as well. Will you also require my assistance on the wedding night?"

Matthew burst out laughing. "In that, Kinellan, I can assure you, your services will not be required."

* * *

The drawing room at Hunter's Cross teemed with the after-dinner chatter of women. Sipping tea, they broke into small groups of twos and threes for the most part, discussing the picnic, clothes, the coming Little Season in London. Fanny sidled up to Jane, who had gotten into a lengthy conversation with Lady Pamela Guire about the latest fashions in bonnets. Raising an eyebrow at her sister-in-law, Fanny tasted her tea, only to exclaim, "Gracious, there's no sugar in this tea. Do pardon me, ladies."

Hurrying away to the tea table, she hoped Jane would follow her soon. "No sugar" was their signal for need of a private conversation. By the time she'd pretended to chip off some small lumps of sugar, Jane was at her side, gathering a fresh cup for herself.

"Where have you been all afternoon?" Fanny began as her friend poured. "I tried to find you after the luncheon but you were nowhere in sight. I didn't even see you in the brake on the way home."

"Lord Kinellan invited me to come to his stand during the afternoon shooting." Jane sipped her tea, made a face, and added more milk. "Scandalous, I know. Shooting is such a man's sport, and they are usually so secretive about it, I really felt as though I should go, if only to experience it once." She sent a subtle sideways glance to Fanny. "Although now, I suspect I shall have more opportunities."

"Indeed?" Fanny led them to a chaise in a relatively secluded corner of the drawing room. "Have you made yet another conquest, my dear?"

Jane's soft laugh brought a twinkle to her eyes. "I

suppose one could call it that. He's invited me to his shooting party next week in Scotland. There's to be two weeks of it, which may prove frightfully boring. This afternoon watching him shoot was fascinating, but it is a very loud business and I suspect the fascination will pall quickly."

"If you fear you'll be bored, why attend? You could have pled an obligation in Town."

"Yes, but I believe there will be sufficient compensations. At least during the nights." A self-satisfied smile appeared on Jane's lips. "Perhaps beginning tonight."

"Of all the members of our club, you are certainly taking advantage of your widowhood, my dear." Fanny could scarcely believe how many men her sister-in-law had reputedly dallied with since June.

"As have you, I believe, if Elizabeth is to be believed about your exploits in Brighton." Jane's arch tone said Fanny might tread on delicate ground.

"I doubt she knows all that occurred there, but yes, I have had a bit of fun." More than a bit, and more to come. "But only with one man. You, on the other hand, are beginning to seem like a lady rake."

"A lady rake!"

"Shhh." Lord knew who might hear them.

"I like the sound of that." Jane settled back with her cup, seemingly delighted with the term. "Why should men have all the fun?"

"Because men do not increase. A reason you need to heed well lest you wish to become a wife again. Although"—Fanny set her cup on a nearby table, finally ready to tell Jane her news—"that constraint no longer concerns me."

Jane jumped and her cup rattled in its saucer. She set it aside and clutched Fanny's arm. "Fanny! Tell me you are not with child."

"Heavens, no." Fanny frowned, appalled that her friend would think such a thing. "I have had my courses since the last time I was with Matthew and I did not dally at Charlotte's." *Thank goodness,* she added silently.

"Then why are you not concerned about getting with child? I will simply not believe you have sworn off men or are about to take the veil."

"Nothing so unlikely," she said, taking Jane's hand. "I have agreed to marry Matthew."

"My dear, how wonderful!" Jane threw her arms around her. "I am very happy for you both. You deserve true happiness after the hell Stephen put you through." Sitting back, Jane took her hands once again. "What changed your mind about him? The last time we spoke of it you were still unsure of Lord Lathbury's ability to remain faithful to you."

"I know. I have had grave doubts about all men in that respect."

"And no one who knew your circumstances could blame you for those doubts." Jane waited, then prompted her. "So what has changed?"

"Not my reservations on men's fidelity. I still have those and likely will until I am old past caring." She hesitated, wringing her hands, the horrible sensation of irreparable loss she'd experienced earlier stealing her breath once more. She hadn't lost him. He was hers, soon forever. "However, I realized at the picnic today, that I love Matthew. I watched him talk and flirt with many of the young ladies last night and today and was overwhelmed with the sense that I'd lost him through my own folly." Tears threatened again. Perhaps they would do so every time she thought about what she'd almost thrown away. "And suddenly it didn't matter so much if he'd be faithful to me if we married, only that I would be truly miserable for the rest of my life if we did not. And when he asked me for the fourth or fifth time, I said yes."

"Bravo, my dear." Jane patted her hand and offered her handkerchief. "I believe you will find Lord Lathbury nothing at all like your first husband. Do you announce your betrothal tonight?"

"We had agreed to do it tonight, but now I am not certain we should." The company would be appreciative, she was certain, save Lady Skelton perhaps. She'd be hard-pressed not to gloat when accepting the countess's best wishes. However, until she and Matthew had settled things officially, with the settlements drawn up, perhaps it would be prudent to wait. "I have accepted him on the condition that he meets Ella in London next week. I don't feel I should marry him without seeing how she takes to him. And Theale will have to arrange for the settlements, I assume. I have no other male family members."

"Yes, in those circumstances, perhaps you should speak to Lord Lathbury before he makes the announcement." Glancing toward the doorway, Jane nodded and smiled. "Right on cue, here they come. Go speak to your betrothed. I declare I feel quite among the elite in having knowledge of a wedding that no one else does."

Throwing a smile at her sister-in-law, Fanny rose and sauntered over to the doorway where a stream of men had slowed to a trickle. Where was Matthew? She checked the room again. Easy to do when looking for a man who literally stood head and shoulders above the rest of the company. What was he playing at? A glance back at Jane saw her shrug her shoulders and mouth the word *Kinellan.*

Jane was correct. Neither Matthew nor his friend had returned from the dining room. Were they perhaps hatching a scheme regarding the announcement of the engagement? That must not happen. A quick look at the room showed no one marked her and she slipped out of the doorway. Tracing her way back toward the dining room, she turned a corner and ran slap into a tall, inflexible body.

"May I help you, my lady?" Matthew peered down at her, eyes hungry like the wolf in the Little Red Riding Hood tale.

"Yes, you may." Fanny pulled him to her, resting her head on his wonderfully firm chest. "I think it best if we do not announce our betrothal tonight."

"Why not?" The wary tone jolted her and his body tensed. He pulled her away from him, his eyes now glittering and hard. "Have you reconsidered?"

"Good Lord, no." Shaking her head, she pushed his arms away again and burrowed against his chest. "But until the settlements are done and the question with Ella settled, I'd just prefer to keep the news between us two. Well, and Jane. I told her."

"I told Kinellan, but he'll keep the secret."

"Where is he?" She looked around the dim corridor, but they were alone. "Have you two been plotting something?"

"Nothing so sinister. I told him you'd agreed to marry me and he almost drowned in his drink." Matthew laughed, and the vibrations coursed throughout her like a plucked harp chord. "When I also informed him

I wouldn't be shooting with him next week, he baptized himself anew with my best brandy. He's gone to change before the announcement. I'll have a word with him when he returns."

"And will you have a word with me later?" Fanny rubbed her breasts against his chest, making his cock stir.

"Trust me, I'll have more than a word," he replied, and sank his mouth onto her to seal the bargain.

# Chapter 15

Smoothing the Milk of Roses lotion over her face, Fanny gazed determinedly into the mirror sitting atop the toilette table. A snowy linen handkerchief in hand, she compared her skin to the fabric's intense white and frowned. Her trip to Brighton had ravaged her appearance. She'd relaxed her guard while at the seaside, lulled by the coolness of the weather into thinking that the sun's rays had weaker power somehow. As a result, her face had become more than a few shades darker than the other ladies of her acquaintance. Compared to the handkerchief she looked like a pair of York tan gloves. Such a trifle had never bothered her before, but Lady Skelton's comments today about a tan complexion had brought the point home. Ladies were supposed to be pale.

Did Matthew consider such things important, as Lady Skelton had implied? She hardly knew what he thought of her appearance, for he'd always simply wanted to be with her. Should she begin to take more care of such things? Had she done so during her marriage, would Stephen not have strayed? For the first time ever, she contemplated that her husband's actions might have been partially her own fault. In any case, that pain was done. She'd look forward now, to a life of love with Matthew.

Wiping her hands on the handkerchief, she rose and tossed the scrap of linen onto the table. The maid had unlaced her stays, helped her on with her pale green dressing gown, and laid out her nightgown before departing to help the other guests. Fanny removed the two simple combs that had held her hair out of the way while she had primped and her thick dark hair cascaded over her shoulders and halfway down her back. Matthew had always loved her hair flowing around them as they joined together.

The memory of them in bed in his old bachelor rooms in London made her breathe deeply. At any moment she could recall the first time she'd seen the tall mahogany bed with the deep maroon coverlet. Her cheeks must have been as deep a shade of red, so embarrassed had she been to be there. But enraged enough at her husband to go through with her seduction of Lord Lathbury. She'd known him only from the dances and conversations at balls they'd attended when she'd had her come-out, and the proposal she'd refused. Still, she'd instinctively known of his deep desire for her.

The seduction had been quite easy, in fact. She'd seen him across the ballroom at Lady Beaumont's, summoned her courage and all her charm, and strode up to him. His eyes had widened when she proposed a stroll in the garden. The weather had cooperated, that night in late May being pleasantly warm. Moonlight streamed over the precisely clipped lawn, almost as light as day. Light enough that she could see first shock, then desire in his face when she suggested she accompany him home from the ball. Most likely he'd heard the gossip, for he never asked why she'd come to him.

Perhaps Matthew had dreamed of them doing this, for he immediately took charge of the plan, explaining how she should take a hired carriage to his rooms, how to disguise herself to avoid recognition. It had all gone as though the gods approved their joining, for no one had discovered their deception for the entire four months of the affair. But that first night had been the most special.

Once she arrived at his apartment, covered in a cloak she'd borrowed from Lady Beaumont with a plea of a fever, she'd turned shy. She didn't recall that they had talked very much. He'd taken the cloak, asked if she wanted some lemon water, but she'd shook her head, too nervous to speak by then. So he'd gathered her into his arms and kissed her. At his touch she'd melted inside, his profound desire for her so apparent she could feel it in her bones. A feeling she'd never experienced before, not even with Stephen.

Gently and slowly, Matthew had undressed her and placed her on the tall bed, where she lay trembling until he joined her. She'd been more nervous than on her wedding night, wanting so much to please him. If she pleased him it wouldn't matter that she was using him to exact revenge on her husband. She still remembered the slow, almost reverent way he'd covered her, then entered her, as if worshipping her with his body. He'd filled her so entirely she'd cried out in completion on the very first thrust, sobbing as she shattered around him. When he'd finished, he'd gathered her into his arms and held her while she'd cried. Tears of hurt, anger, and despair had flowed onto his comforting chest, washing away everything save the regret that she'd married the wrong man.

They'd had four months of love in that comfortable bed—and other places. Then as now they had gloried in finding unexpected and even dangerous locales in which to enjoy one another. And even though tonight they would meet in a conventional bed, at the conventional time for love play, still she could not wait to enfold him in her arms again. The place didn't matter; the man did.

The image of Matthew naked before her, his lean body with smooth skin stretched over taut muscles, his cock jutting straight out to her, made her sex weep, and her breasts swell in joyous anticipation. Her nipples furled tight, poking the delicate green silk outward like two flower buds about to burst.

The clock on the mantel struck one o'clock. He should be here soon. God, let him be here soon.

She moved the fine batiste nightgown to a nearby chair. She'd not need that before morning. Checking the decanter on the bedside table, she unstoppered it to discover an excellent cognac. They'd always wanted a libation afterward if possible. Matthew truly thought of everything.

Nothing else to do now but wait.

Restless, she wandered the room, peeping out the window into the inky blackness. No romantic moon tonight. Not that they needed one. Why didn't he come?

A scratch at the door sent Fanny scrambling to

open it. Hand on the handle, an inner voice cautioned her to be sure and she called, "Who is it?"

"Me." The deep baritone sent a chill down her spine.

Thumbing the latch, she opened the door a slit and Matthew sped in, still fully dressed from dinner.

"What is wrong?" She pushed the door closed, turned the latch, and hurried to him.

"Why would something be wrong?" He took in her appearance from top to toe, his gaze lingering on her bare feet. Dipping his head he tasted her lips, his own holding a lingering sweetness from his after-dinner brandy. "Everything I see is very, very right."

"Why are you still dressed? I expected you to arrive ready for bed." Not wearing so many clothes it would take an hour for him to divest himself.

"I think I will be less conspicuous in these clothes if I am caught going from your room to mine. Wearing this"—he motioned to his formal attire—"I can plead a cranky guest needing some small notion from the kitchen. Attired in a banyan, no matter how innocent the circumstance, I will be thought on my way to or from a tryst." He ran his thumb down her cheek, along her jaw. "And as we have not yet announced our betrothal, I would rather my future wife not have a scandal attached to her when we wed."

Glorying in his touch, she rubbed her cheek against his hand. "Well, then, I am satisfied."

Matthew chuckled and clasped her face in both hands. "You, my dear, have no idea of the meaning of that word. Yet." Drawing her to him, he seized her lips once more, drinking her in until she gasped for air.

"Did you not eat enough at dinner, my lord? You seem ravenous now."

"A different dish for a different palate." He lifted her, set her on the bed, and slid the silk fabric of her robe up her thighs.

Groaning, Fanny fell back on the bed as his hands continued upward until she lay bare and exposed to him. Cool air wafted over her as he blew gently, ruffling her dark curls. His thumbs brushed through the thicket, stroking the flesh of her entrance and drawing a guttural moan from her. Matthew had always had an instinct for what a woman wanted.

"Relax, love. Allow the pleasure to draw the tension from you and allow me to give you the pleasure." He spread her folds and kissed her deeply, his clever tongue touching her pleasure spot just enough to prompt another whimper. "Does that feel good?"

"You know it does." Fanny wriggled her hips, wanting to push against him, but knowing if she tried to go too fast he'd simply withdraw. Still, the frantic pulse in her core spoke of a need deep inside her. Begged for its fulfilment. "Can't we—"

"Shhh." The shushing became a subtle vibration on her pleasure nub, sending her head spinning, her need soaring.

"Ohhh, damn you, Matthew."

The vibration increased until her legs clenched around his back, her toes curling.

Slowly, he eased his thumb into her channel, circling it around her entrance while his tongue danced on that special spot above.

The tension began to spiral upward, bringing Fanny close to the edge. "Yes, yes, Matthew. Don't stop, please don't stop."

"I wouldn't dream of it, my love." The words were muffled, but his mouth maintained the promised contact. Then he withdrew his thumb, replacing it with two fingers sliding slowly and deeply into her, shattering her self-control.

Her body uncontrollably gripping him, Fanny abandoned herself to soft squeals of bliss until she sagged onto the mattress. Her lover continued to lick and stroke, until she ceased shuddering and lay boneless on the bed.

Vaguely she noted he now stood before her, but she was too busy gasping for breath, which gave way to drowsing once her heartbeat returned to normal. The bed dipped and she was sliding over to one side of the bed.

"It's a chilly night, my love. Let's get beneath the covers."

Sated and unwilling to move, Fanny found her bottom lifted and the coverlet and sheets dragged back. Then she was underneath them, pressed to a warm, naked body. "Ummm. I like that," she said, stealing her hand across his broad, sleek chest.

"Anything in particular?" The playful lechery in his voice helped rouse her from her passion-drunk state.

"Humm. All your parts are impressive, my lord." She rolled up onto her side, staring into dark blue fathomless eyes. "However, I can think of two or three that are especially nice."

"Pray continue. I am all ears."

"I think not, my lord." She rubbed the dark hairs on his chest, brushing over his small, erect nipples. "You have many more parts than that."

"Continue." He traced a finger down her breast,

lingering on her nipple until it perked up, as rigid as his. "My particularly impressive parts."

"Your wit of course." Fanny kissed his forehead. "A remarkable part indeed."

"If it delights you, I will not deny it, although I thought surely there were other parts that impressed you more." Sliding down until his head dipped beneath the cover, Matthew traced a circle around Fanny's nipple with his tongue, then latched onto it and sucked.

"Oh, yes." Fanny purred, her breasts swelling with the tender manipulation. "You do delight me in many ways, my love. Let us see if I can reciprocate." Slipping her hand across his chest, over his hard stomach, to the proud staff, standing at full mast. She grasped him eagerly and Matthew gasped, then nodded for her to continue.

"Is this another of my impressive parts?" His eyes closed and his arms came around her.

"Very impressive." Fanny slid her fingers up and down his cockstand, attending not only to her strokes but to his face to alert her to the signs of his approaching pleasure. "I would rank it as most impressive, my lord, save there is one part yet that I would deem so extraordinary it must overshadow this magnificent beast." She squeezed him, stroking faster, making it his turn to groan aloud.

"Oh, Fanny, you will kill me." Matthew rolled on top of her, rucked up her gown, drove his shaft between her thighs, and impaled her on his rampant cock.

Nothing like their first time together; however, the magnificent feel of his claiming her fully was the same. And now they could go forward—he pulled back and thrust into her again and again—as husband and wife, perhaps as it should have been from the very beginning.

He strained above her, his face beautiful in its concentration. Eyes closed, Matthew thrust and thrust in a powerful rhythm that once again wound her up to the point at which she must shatter or die.

"Fanny, oh, Fanny." His face contorted with effort, Matthew drove into her one final time, spilling his seed into her.

The heat of him set her on fire.

"Matthew." She convulsed around him, anchored to him through more than the mere physical aspect of love.

Slumping on top of her, Matthew sighed and grunted, then rolled over and lay panting, an earsplitting grin on his face. "I cannot wait to discover what you think my most impressive part."

When she could speak again, Fanny propped herself up on her elbow and looked him in the eyes. "Your heart, my love. Nothing is greater or more generous, or nobler than your heart, which is the sum of your parts, I believe." Leaning over, she kissed him sweetly on the lips. "I thank God, and you, for giving it to me."

"It has been and always shall be yours, love." He gathered her to him, nestling her warm against his side, head pillowed on his shoulder, her long hair fanned out across his chest.

Contentment as she had never known before stole through Fanny, relaxing her into a lovely, drowsy state. Her view of him from this vantage point was magnificent. Gazing across the expanse of his body, she noted the fine sheen of sweat glistening on his chest and down his ridged stomach. That she had caused that patina to appear filled her with happiness. The carelessly flung sheet hid more interesting matters, but as much as she wanted to renew their passion, for the moment she was spent. She yawned, kissed his shoulder, and closed her eyes. "Wake me before you leave, my love."

"You may depend upon it." His deep voice rumbled in her ear. "Shall I blow out the lamps?"

Yawning, she shook her head. "Don't get up. I'm so very comfortable just like this."

"Your wish is my command, as always."

She smiled at that. Not quite the case always, but she'd not fuss about it now. Perhaps in the future they would make together it would be.

*Tap, tap, tap.*

With a gasp, Fanny shot up, tangled in the covers and her bedclothes. She turned wide eyes to Matthew who sighed, and flung an arm over his face.

"Who the devil is that at almost two o'clock in the morning?" Matthew whispered vehemently, his eyes piercingly cold.

"How should I know?" she whispered back, rapping him smartly on the arm. Did he dare insinuate she'd invited someone else to her bedroom? "You are the only one I expected tonight. Maybe if I don't answer they will go away."

They maintained silence for what seemed an aeon, but was likely only several seconds, and the tapping was repeated, along with a muffled voice calling to her.

"Did that voice sound feminine to you?" she asked, untangling the covers then sliding to the floor.

"It was indistinct, but I would say so."

"Then it's most likely Jane."

Dark eyes on her, he tracked her carefully as she moved toward the door, but he'd relaxed nonetheless.

Lord, was Matthew to prove a jealous lover now that they were about to be wed? If he thought her infidelity to Stephen was anything but revenge for his odious transgressions, then her betrothed was a fool. She tiptoed to the door and called, "Who is it?"

"It's Lady Lathbury, Lady Stephen. May I come in?"

# Chapter 16

Fanny sent a stricken look to Matthew, who had bolted up at the name. *Oh, dear Lord,* she mouthed at him. *What do we do?*

He scrambled from the bed and bent to snatch his clothes from the pile where he'd disrobed.

"Just a moment, my lady. I'm not dressed." A quick glance around the room showed nowhere for Matthew to hide. Neither the wardrobe nor the screen were large enough, and the latter was raised on legs so his feet would be seen in any case. She rushed to him and whispered, "What can we do? What will she say if she finds you here?"

"Nothing you would want to hear in polite company, I imagine." He'd managed to draw his shirt over his head, but his entire bottom half was bare. "Mother isn't a high stickler; however, finding her son in a woman's room in absolute disarray will bring down a firestorm upon my head, and a chastisement upon yours, that we do not wish to experience. Trust me on this if on nothing else."

"What if we tell her we are betrothed?"

"No difference. Except additional consternation that we hadn't told her already that we were engaged." He strode to the window and peered out. "I doubt the fall would kill me, although I might need to say my wedding vows from a sick bed with broken bones."

"I forbid you to go out that window, Matthew."

"I see no other choice, my dear."

"Lady Stephen?" The door handle rattled. "Are you quite well?"

"Dear God." Fanny grabbed the clothing Matthew was clutching to his chest and threw it under the bed. "Get under there."

"I won't fit." Still he dropped to his knees, then flat to the floor.

Unfortunately, the bed was not as high as some others she'd been in, but there was no time to lose. She put her hands on his derriere and pushed. The uncarpeted floor assisted their efforts and Matthew disappeared beneath the low-hanging blue coverlet. Tossing his shoes after him, she called, "I'm coming," and hastily spread the covers up, desperately trying to make it seem that only one person had been in that bed.

Thank God she'd never taken off her dressing gown. She pulled at it to make it hang right, then tying the belt, ran swiftly to the door, turned the lock, and opened it.

"Good evening, my lady," she said, in what she prayed was a calm voice. "Is there something amiss?"

Attired in a pink and gray silk dressing gown, Lady Lathbury stepped over the threshold, calmly peering around Fanny's room, a frown on her face. "No, nothing of any serious import. I had gone to see to a guest who had complained of a headache and was returning to my suite. Passing by your room I noticed the lights on and thought you might be restless."

"Oh, no." Fanny feigned lethargy by pretending to stifle a yawn. "I read for a while and had fallen asleep without blowing out the lamps."

"I see." The countess smiled and turned toward the door.

Fanny had just sent up a silent word of thanksgiving for the near escape when Lady Lathbury turned back to her.

"As I am here now, perhaps you will indulge me in a brief chat, Lady Stephen. I have been so taken up with my other guests I fear I have not had the opportunity for us to become better acquainted."

"Of course, my lady." Drat. Putting on the best cheerful face possible, Fanny motioned the countess toward the toilette table. "Please have a seat."

"Thank you, my dear."

As Lady Lathbury settled herself, Fanny drew a straight-backed chair from the writing desk and placed it opposite the bed. If the countess would be here, at least she'd face away from Matthew's hiding place. "Was there something in particular you wished to speak to me about, Lady Lathbury?"

The countess smiled. "I suppose I wish to know everything about the woman my son wishes to marry. Rowley has told me of your circumstances. My condolences on your late husband."

"Thank you." Good lord, but Stephen was the last person she wanted to talk about tonight. Fanny cocked her head. "Did you say 'Rowley,' my lady?"

"My husband's family has held the Viscountcy of

Rowley since the seventeenth century. Therefore, my son's title at birth was Lord Rowley. I have always called him that." She pursed her lips. "He has also informed me that he has proposed to you and you have refused him—three times." Hard blue eyes met hers with the warmth of an icicle.

Swallowing convulsively, Fanny scarcely managed to answer, "Yes." Every time she came within the woman's presence her mouth dried up as though she'd bitten into the tartest lemon possible.

"Four times if you count his proposal before your marriage to Lord Stephen."

If only she could hide under the bed as well. "Yes, my lady."

"Do you have some aversion to my son, Lady Stephen?"

"Oh, no." Fanny leaned over and grasped the woman's hand as it lay rigid on her lap. "I love your son very much. Truly, I do."

"I must inform you, my dear, refusing his suit so often does not incline me to believe you."

Shaking her head, Fanny summoned all her strength to try to make her understand. "I will admit, when I first turned Lord Lathbury down, I was very young and inexperienced in the ways of Society. I had no one to guide or advise me and so made a horrible mistake. Had I not, I would have been your son's wife these ten years."

"Inexperience can be forgiven. Most women have made at least one grave mistake as a result of ill advice." Lady Lathbury's tone had softened. "That does not, however, excuse your continual refusal of him during the past two months. I will warn you, Lady Stephen, when Rowley told me of your refusal when he returned from Brighton, I strongly urged him to abandon his efforts to secure you and turn his eye elsewhere for a wife."

Fanny hung her head, consumed with guilt. She'd been in the wrong to keep Matthew on her hook for so long. Admitting that now would do little good as far as his mother was concerned. If she could tell the countess of their betrothal it would perhaps put her in a better light, but she'd promised Matthew not to breathe a word of it to his mother. So what defense could she summon? "I do not blame you for that, Lady Lathbury. A mother must continue to look out for her child even after they reach adulthood. I have already told Matthew the reasons for my hesitation, now mainly having to do with my daughter."

"You have a child, Lady Stephen?" The countess leaned forward, an appraising light in her eyes. "Rowley did not mention that."

"I do not think he knew about her until quite recently. We had fallen out of touch before her birth."

"A daughter, then?"

"Yes. Ella."

"Pretty name." She nodded in approval. "She is how old?"

"Six this past May." The pleasantries were nice, and the countess's interest in Ella was a credit to her, but Matthew must be freezing on the cold floor under the bed.

"But you have reservations about Rowley's care of the child should you marry?" The harsh tone had returned.

At least Fanny could refute this area of consternation. "Not reservations, my lady. I am certain Matthew will be a wonderful father to Ella, but I have asked him to meet her before I can agree to marry him. I know you are aware that if a woman marries she relinquishes guardianship of her children to a man who is no blood relative to them."

"That is the law of England, my dear. No one would challenge it."

"Nor will I. However, I will feel much easier in my mind if Ella can meet the man who will be her new papa before it is irrevocable. I believe you might insist on the same condition were you to consider remarriage."

"Rowley retains guardianship of his sisters until they reach their majority or until they marry, of course. So my circumstances are somewhat different than yours, although I do take your point." The lady's brows that had furrowed, now smoothed themselves out. "And has he agreed to meet your daughter?"

"Yes, he has. Next week or as soon as possible after this house party."

Lady Lathbury shook her head and rose, a rueful smile on her lips. "My son goes to Scotland for a shooting party with Lord Kinellan next week. I am afraid he will not put that off."

"But he already has."

"I beg your pardon?" The countess stopped in the midst of reaching for the door handle.

"He informed Lord Kinellan this evening that he would not be attending the shooting party." Although Fanny had known Matthew enjoyed his sport, she'd had no idea asking him to cancel his plans to attend Lord Kinellan's shooting party would be considered such a privation. Did he truly wish to attend? His meeting with Ella could be put off another week or two. There was no hurry, save now she wished to marry him with all haste.

Turning back to face Fanny, Lady Lathbury grasped her arm. "I believe I had not correctly gauged the depth of his regard for you, then, Lady Stephen. Rowley has almost never postponed or cancelled a sporting trip, particularly not when it was shooting in Scotland." She gave Fanny's arm a friendly shake. "I would ask if my daughter and I could accompany Rowley to London and meet your daughter? If their approval of one another is all that stands between you and a betrothal, then by all means, let us make haste to Town."

"You will certainly be welcomed at the Marquess of Theale's town house, my lady. That is where I currently make my home with Ella." Fanny laid her hand over the countess's. "I would be delighted to see you and Lady Beatrice in London when Matthew comes to call."

"Just so. But I have trespassed on your time long enough. You must get some rest. Tomorrow is another full day." Lady Lathbury nodded and headed to the door. "You may come out from underneath the bed now, Rowley. You must get your rest as well."

Fanny's jaw dropped and she clutched her dressing gown to her as though it were a shield. "Wha . . . what do you mean, my lady?"

A fiendish grin flickered on and off the countess's face so fast Fanny could scarcely be sure she saw it. "So difficult for a large man to hide completely under that bed."

Pivoting, Fanny stared at the floor, confounded at how their subterfuge had failed. At last she spied

Matthew's pale foot, wedged against the dark leg of the bed in plain sight. She'd thought it a discarded fichu the maid had missed. The countess had known the whole time. His mother had known about . . . Her cheeks burned with a fire she wished would consume her on the spot.

"Good evening, my dear."

Fanny stood staring at the telltale foot until the door closed behind the lady. Dear Lord, what must she think of her? Not that she even had to ask in truth.

"Get me out of this bloody place before I freeze my bollocks off and no one will have to worry about marrying me," came the bellow from under the bed.

Fanny scrambled to help Matthew inch his way out. His hands were cold, his flesh where he'd lain on the floor was cold and clammy. As he got to his feet, he began to shiver.

"D-d-don't just stand there, woman. I'm f-fr-freezing."

Throwing her arms around his body, she rubbed up and down his front, pressing her warmth to him. After a minute of vigorous rubbing, at least one part of Matthew was no longer chilly. She peered up into his grinning face.

"Please don't stop, love. I'm not quite warm enough yet." He leered at her, then grabbed her behind and squeezed.

"Matthew!" She squealed, then shushed. "Your mother was here."

"I know. I heard every word." Pressing her to his swiftly hardening erection, he walked them backward toward the bed.

"She might return." Fanny wiggled in his grip, but that only made him harder.

"I sincerely doubt it. And in any case, she's as much as given us her dispensation." He bumped into the bed and stopped. "Otherwise you'd be packing to leave and I'd be standing before her explaining myself instead of—" He seized her lips and fell back onto the bed, Fanny sprawled on top of him.

"Ummm. How will I ever face your mother again?" Heat enough for two between them now, Fanny pulled her dressing gown over her head.

"With my heir in your arms, she won't say a word, for there's only one way to get one." Matthew lifted her and slowly impaled her on his shaft and groaned. "Many positions, but one way only."

# Chapter 17

***London, late September***

"Beatrice, if you are not here in two minutes, I shall leave without you," Matthew muttered to himself. He pulled out his pocket watch, wound the stem impatiently, and fumed. He'd already assisted his mother into the carriage five minutes ago, and they should have left for Theale House five minutes before that. Just one more in the host of interminable delays he'd suffered since his house party almost a month ago. Had he known he'd not be meeting Fanny again until today, he would not have cut his shooting trip short after all.

In the aftermath of his mother's early morning conversation with Fanny, she had insisted he attend Kinellan's party, despite the fact Matthew had expressly told her his absence there did not matter a jot to him. What mattered was marrying her, by God, and he had meant every word. The woman had, however, got the bit between her teeth and absolutely demanded that he attend the shooting in Scotland.

Never let it be said that a Hunter turned down an opportunity to hunt when so commanded. The first week had been excellent, save his yearning to have Fanny at his side anytime but when he was out in the field. Even there he'd been reminded of her for Kinellan had invited Lady John at the very last minute. Had he known that, he'd have begged an invitation for Fanny as well. Lady John had accompanied them out to the shoot each day, unheard of in Matthew's book. He'd come to suspect, over the course of that week, that his friend was a touch enamored of the pretty widow. None of his affair, if so, but Kinellan had best see to his nursery with a woman of a better childbearing age.

Matthew shook his head and peered up the staircase. "Upton." The butler had been hovering this morning. "Send to Lady Beatrice that I will be leaving in one minute by the clock whether she is here or not."

"I am here, Matthew. Have I set up your bristles?" Bea tripped merrily down the steps, pulling on her gloves, as carefree as a lark.

"You have made us unconscionably late for tea with Lady Stephen." He grabbed her arm, none too gently, and escorted her to the waiting carriage.

"Would you really have left me if I'd tarried just one more minute?" Eyes tip-tilted up at him, dancing with mischief, made Matthew pity the poor soul his sister finally brought up to scratch.

"I would have left you in the dust without a qualm." He handed her in and climbed in after, taking the backward-facing seat and rapping on the trap in one hurried movement. "Theale House in Mayfair, Harris."

"Very good, my lord." The horses moved off at once and Matthew leaned back in the soft leather seat. Almost there.

"I don't see why you're fretting so, brother. In a little while you will be seeing your love every day of the year. I doubt you'll be so impatient then." Grinning at him, Beatrice fairly shook with glee at his annoyance.

"That obviously shows you have never been in love, Beatrice." Their mother spoke up with an indulgent look at her daughter. "If you had been, you would understand how painful it is not to be with that person. Your brother has shown remarkable restraint over the past several weeks."

"Especially since, had it not been for you, we should have made this journey the moment I returned from Scotland." He stared determinedly at Bea. She should be made to feel uncomfortable.

"I could not help that Sarah insisted on getting married so quickly. And you know I would never miss being her bridesmaid, no matter what you said, Matthew." The stubborn set to Beatrice's jaw had not changed since she announced her friend's coming marriage and her own role in the ceremony. "It's your own fault for holding the house party in August. If you hadn't, Sarah would never have met Lord Malin and fallen in love."

Lady Skelton had been in alt ever since Malin, a marquess Matthew'd known at university, had asked Skelly for permission to marry his sister. Always an impetuous chap, Malin hadn't wasted a moment after that first evening. The couple had married immediately and were currently touring France in wedded bliss. In less than three weeks. At the rate Matthew was courting Fanny he might hope to be married within the next three years.

The carriage slowed and Matthew's heart beat painfully in his chest. If the meeting with Fanny's daughter went well, could he possibly convince her to marry him by special license tomorrow? He'd be in alt if he could just have everything settled and Fanny as his bride before the month was out.

For what seemed like the hundredth time, Fanny peeped out of the window of the small, front receiving room in Theale House. Matthew, Lady Lathbury, and Lady Beatrice were supposed to have already arrived, although she'd been expecting Matthew for so long, and been constantly disappointed, she almost despaired of ever seeing him again. Letting the curtain fall back into place, she sighed and resumed pacing about the room.

When she'd left Hunter's Cross in late August she'd imagined they would be married in a matter of weeks. Those weeks had turned into a month, and although the explanations for the delays had been understandable, she wanted the waiting to be over. Each successive day without the hope of seeing him had brought growing pain to her heart. Today, after he met Ella, she would insist they make their final plans for a quick ceremony and a long wedding trip. She didn't care where they went, as long as they were together and alone.

The sharp *clip-clop* of horses' hooves rang out on the pavement below and she darted back to the window in time to see the door to a large black landau open. Matthew emerged and her mouth dried instantly. Her stomach fluttered and her heart pounded. Lord, this was no time to swoon. But looking at his handsome face, after all this time, sent an aching need through her that wiped away all other discomforts. She drew back before he could notice her and moved to stand near the doorway, trying hard not to fidget.

He was here!

Noyes entered and bowed. "Lady Lathbury, Lady Beatrice Hunter, Lord Lathbury, my lady."

The room seemed to explode with chatter as Beatrice darted forward to embrace her. "Fanny, I am so happy to see you again at last. I have told my brother repeatedly for the past few weeks that we needed to make this visit, but he has constantly dragged his heels about it."

"Beatrice," Lady Lathbury stopped her daughter with a word, "you may sit in silence until I give you leave to join the conversation."

With a mischievous glance at Fanny, Beatrice retired to the chaise, her mouth puckering but effectively mute.

"Lady Stephen, so nice to meet you again." The countess curtsied and sat on the sofa. "Please, come sit beside me. We have so much to catch up."

"I believe I will say good afternoon to Fanny before she does so, Mother." Matthew drew her to his side, his eyes blazing with a desire that made her weak. He raised her hand for a kiss. "Good afternoon, my love."

At the touch of his lips on her skin the walls around them wavered. She needed him to take her away and fill her body with his powerful essence, to make her whole and them one again.

"Soon, love, I promise," he whispered in her ear.

She nodded and stepped back from him, cheeks heating. If her need had been that apparent to him, had it also been to the others? What must his mother think? Well, after their early morning encounter at Hunter's Cross, she knew very well what his mother thought of her. Resisting the urge to fan her face, she smiled serenely and went to sit beside Lady Lathbury.

"I am sorry our visit was so delayed, my dear," the countess began. "First, of course, Rowley attended Lord Kinellan's party in Scotland."

"And returned earlier than originally planned in order to leave for London." Matthew broke in, taking a seat opposite them.

His mother glared at him. "I am speaking, Rowley."

"My pardon, Mother." He threw up his hands and sat back in the chair.

Beatrice giggled, but a glower from her brother silenced her again.

"Yes, he did return to Hunter's Cross around the eighth of September only to find—"

"To find my best friend, Sarah—" Beatrice interrupted her mother this time. "You made her acquaintance, Fanny, I believe at Matthew's party—"

"Beatrice!" Lady Lathbury actually snapped the word, hard enough that her daughter drew back in her chair. "Lady Stephen will believe that I raised children with no sense of how to behave in polite company. I beg your pardon, Lady Stephen, for this disgraceful behavior." She looked askance at both her offspring, pausing as if expecting yet another disruption.

Both remained mute, and the lady continued. "Sarah Broadman, who you may indeed remember, had an offer of marriage from Lord Malin on the Sunday of the house party. She insisted on having the banns read, rather than securing a special license, so the wedding did not occur until September fifteenth."

"I am so happy for her." Fanny attempted enthusiasm, however it was hollow. She had hoped her own wedding would have taken place by now.

"And Beatrice must attend the wedding as the bridesmaid, of course. They have been friends from the cradle." Lady Lathbury waited, apparently for her daughter to make some new rapture, but Beatrice sat still, thank goodness. "Then we found the carriage in need of repair, which took almost a week. And so we have come, at last, to meet your daughter."

"And I am so glad to have you here." Fanny smiled broadly, ringing the bell for tea before Lady Lathbury could begin again. "I have told Ella of your visit today. She will be brought in presently. She is a little shy with strangers, but I have talked with her about you and especially about Matthew"—she sent a special smile to him—"and the role he is to play in our lives shortly."

"Then you have settled it between you?" Beatrice bounded up in her chair, unable to sit still any longer. "You will marry?"

"After today's visit with Ella, we will know better," Fanny replied cautiously. Smiling at Matthew, who nodded, she grasped his hand. "But yes, we are to be married."

"Oh, splendid!" Beatrice jumped up to hug Fanny about the shoulders. "Allow me to be the first to wish you happy! Well done, Matthew. Now I will have a sister with whom I can talk as a friend. You cannot know, Fanny, how dreary it is to have sisters who are so very much younger. They cannot understand anything I tell them about, well, anything." She shrugged. "But now I can confide in you and you can give me advice next spring when I have my come-out."

"Fanny can help with your come-out in fact, Bea." Matthew had on a very self-satisfied expression.

"We shall see about that, Rowley. I would not like to impose on Lady Stephen so soon after her marriage. Being the wife of an earl will be much different from being the wife of the third son of a marquess."

Fanny managed to maintain a pleasant demeanor, but the words ate at her. Her life had better be much different than her previous marriage.

The footman entered and placed the tea on the table next to Fanny. "Thank you, Thomas."

"My lady." He bowed and left, shutting the doors.

"Do you take milk and sugar, Lady Lathbury?"

"Yes, thank you. Two good-sized lumps, please, and a trickle of milk." The countess gazed about the small but well-appointed room.

Fanny had chosen it over the larger receiving room because it was a soothing pale blue color and the furniture looked brighter as it was seldom used. She hoped its small size would foster a sense of intimacy between herself and the countess. And not overwhelm Ella as the family drawing room was wont to do. The child should be here at any moment.

Remembering how Lady Beatrice and Matthew took their tea, she hurriedly poured and fixed them, handing the cups round with an efficiency that she seldom achieved. She had just poured her own cup and dropped in the sugar when the door opened, and Fanny sent up a heartfelt prayer that nothing would go amiss with this meeting.

# Chapter 18

Hand clasped firmly in Nurse's, Ella walked through the door in her white new gown, trimmed with pretty crocheted lace and a delicate pink sash. With her fair complexion and dark hair she looked like one of the pretty porcelain dolls in her room. Eyes wide, staring at the strange people before her, Ella started to tremble.

Fanny caught her eye and put her fingers to the corners of her mouth, to remind the child to smile, as they'd rehearsed just that morning. Then held her hand out to her daughter. "Ella, my love, I would like for you to meet some friends."

"What a lovely child." Lady Beatrice smiled encouragingly.

Letting go of Nurse's hand, Ella ran toward her mother, until remembering her manners, she slowed to a walk. Once she stood before Fanny, she curtsied prettily. "Good afternoon, Mama."

"Good afternoon, my dear." Fanny smiled and nodded. So far, so good. "I would like to introduce you to some of my friends. Would you like that, Ella?"

"Yes, Mama." The child sighed gravely.

"Then first, Lady Lathbury, may I present my daughter, Miss Ella Tarkington? Ella, make your curtsy to Lady Lathbury." Fanny held her breath.

"How do you do, my lady?" Ella carefully bent her knees, her face tense with concentration.

"I am very well, Ella." Lady Lathbury peered at the girl. "How old are you, my dear?"

With a quick look at Fanny, Ella straightened as tall as she could and said, "Six years old."

"You are quite tall for your age, I see. I would have thought you at least a girl of eight years." The countess continued to peer at the child. "You have your mother's coloring, I see. Unless your late husband was also dark?"

"No, my lady. He was very fair." Fanny hastened to add, "But she takes after him in other ways. Lady Theale often remarks that Ella is very like Lord Stephen, save in the color of her hair."

"I see." Lady Lathbury sipped her tea, her gaze still on Ella.

"Lady Beatrice, my daughter. This is Lady Beatrice, Lady Lathbury's daughter. And this"—she steered Ella toward Matthew after she'd bobbed another brief curtsy—"is Lord Lathbury, Lady Lathbury's son. We talked about him, do you remember?"

Ella nodded then craned her head back to look up at Matthew. "You're tall."

"I am indeed, Ella." He grinned down at her. "As my mother pointed out, you are tall as well. So is my sister. And your mother is taller than most women." Suddenly he stooped and scooped her up in his arms, making her shriek with laughter. "Now you are as tall as I am."

"I am, I am!" Ella gazed about from her new vantage point, a grin reaching from ear to ear. "Can I be taller than you?"

"Well, let's see."

"Matthew—" Fanny tried to intervene before the visit spun out of control, but Matthew ignored her.

"Let me lift you, there." He raised Ella until her head inched just above his. "Now you are the tallest in the room."

"I am, I am." Ella giggled and threw her arms around Matthew's neck. "We are the tallest people in the world."

"And the smartest and the prettiest." Matthew laughed along with her, his face pressed close to Ella's.

Struck dumb, Fanny froze, her hand gripping the back of the nearest chair.

"Lady Stephen, did you wish me to take Miss Ella up for her tea now?" Nurse's question finally penetrated Fanny's fog-filled mind. Still unable to summon words, she nodded and turned away lest Matthew or Beatrice see her face.

"No, Mama!" Ella cried. "Let me stay here. You said I could have tea with you and Lord . . . Lord . . ."

"Lathbury," Matthew supplied. "Perhaps I could have my tea in the nursery with you instead, Ella. Would that be all right?"

Not knowing what to say, Fanny looked at Lady Lathbury, whose cool eyes had missed nothing. "I think that a splendid idea, Rowley. Beatrice will go along as well for company."

"But Mama—"

"Beatrice." The commanding tone in the countess's voice brooked no dissent. "Go with Matthew and the child. I believe Lady Stephen is overwrought and needs a moment."

"Fanny?" Matthew's concerned voice sent a shiver of dread down her spine.

Gathering her wits, she put on an unconcerned smile and turned to him, Ella still in his arms. "I have done too much preparation for this meeting, I fear, Matthew. That is all. I am fatigued and overcome with an attack of vapors. It will pass." She tried to smile to reassure him. "Go have tea with Ella. I think you have made yet another conquest."

The concerned look did not leave his face. Gently, he slid Ella to the ground. "Wait with Nurse, poppet. I must speak a word with your mother."

As Ella ran to her nurse, Matthew took Fanny's arm. Out of the corner of her eye Lady Lathbury drew Beatrice to her.

"Fanny, is something wrong? You look as though you've seen a ghost." He kissed her hand passionately then squeezed it. "Have you discovered that you are increasing?"

She blew out the breath she'd been holding. "No, my dear. Unfortunately that is not the case." She lowered her voice to a whisper, glad to be able to tell him some truth. "My courses finished yesterday and always leave me somewhat weak. That is likely the cause of my dizziness just now. So please go, have tea with Ella. That was the plan, was it not? To see how you get along together. I think she's very taken with you."

"And I with her." His gaze strayed back to the doorway where Nurse waited with Ella hopping impatiently from one foot to the other. "Such a lovely child, Fanny. The spitting image of her mother."

"She has some of her father about her as well."

"I see nothing of Stephen in her." Matthew grimaced. "Let us hope she does not take after him in other ways."

"No, I pray God she does not."

"I shall return to you shortly, although I fear I must accompany Mother and Beatrice back to Hunter's Terrace. We are dining tonight with friends of my parents. Perhaps tomorrow you will ride in the park with me. You and Ella."

"No!" Fanny caught herself and laid her hand on his arm. "I am sorry. I am still overwrought, I fear. Likely I will need a few days in bed to recover completely."

"I do not understand why you worked yourself into a state about this meeting, my love. Ella is a delightful child. I trust I have put all your fears to rest on that account."

Gazing at him, her heart aching with love and despair, Fanny simply smiled and took his arm. "You should go before she becomes impatient."

"As I said, very like her mother." With a quick kiss on her lips, Matthew joined Ella and took her hand. "Lead the way, Nurse. Our tea awaits."

"I can show you the way, Lord Laffbury." Ella tugged at his hand and they, with Beatrice bringing up the rear, moved down the corridor where Ella's sweet, high voice drifted back. "Why did your mama call you Rowley?"

As soon as they disappeared, Fanny dropped down onto the chaise and buried her face in her hands.

Oh, dear God, how had this happened? What was she to do?

"I take it, then, that you did not know that Ella was my son's child, Lady Stephen?" The countess's voice brought Fanny's head up with a jerk. She'd quite forgotten the woman was still in the room.

Could she perhaps deny it? One look at Lady Lathbury told her this was out of the question. "No, I had no idea until a few minutes ago. When did you discover it?"

"Almost from the moment the child walked into the room. She is very like Rowley when he was her age." The countess sat, hands in her lap. "I spoke to Beatrice. She will not say a word to him."

"She realized it as well?"

"Of course she did. Anyone with an eye who has met Rowley, would see it. Except, apparently, you." Suspicion gleamed in the woman's crystal blue eyes. Matthew's eyes. Ella's eyes.

"I swear to you, my lady, I did not know she was Matthew's daughter." Fanny grabbed a napkin from the abandoned tea tray and wiped her eyes. "Three years into my marriage my husband was unfaithful to me, in ways that hurt me very much. I sought to get revenge on him by having an affair with Matthew, who had, as you know, offered for me before I accepted Stephen. I believe we were discreet in the extreme. No one has ever even hinted about the affair, which lasted about four months."

"You must have indeed been more discreet than most. I heard not a word bandied about you and him." She sat unmoving, unblinking, her gaze trained solely on Fanny.

"After three months, I began to feel guilty about

the lie we were living." No need to tell her about her family's deaths. That pain, at least, would remain private. "I wished to break it off, but Matthew wanted me to elope with him to Italy."

"A very foolish notion. Neither of you would have ever been received in Polite Society again."

"I told him that, but he did not wish to hear it. I feared he would become even more belligerent and challenge my husband to a duel. So I broke with him, refused to see him, and returned to my husband's bed, trying to atone for my sins." She wiped her streaming eyes, the pain she'd suffered in leaving Matthew almost more than she could bear to recall. "A month or so later I found I was with child. I'd no reason to think it Matthew's. We'd been together for months and I hadn't conceived, but as soon as I returned to my husband, I did. It seemed obvious it was Stephen's. When she was born she had dark hair and blue eyes, but so do I. Others said they could see Stephen in her, so that is what I believed. I never saw Matthew again to compare them until this June."

"When you did see him, I find it difficult to believe you weren't struck by their resemblance." If words could drip ice, these would.

"Seeing them together, it seems ludicrous that I did not see it. But again, after six years of believing one thing, why would I suddenly believe something different? Until I was faced with the undeniable proof." Proof of her infidelity that anyone in Society would see whenever they were in public together. God, what could she do?

"You will have to tell him. He has a right to know she is his child."

Inflexible words that were only the truth. "I know. I will."

"Today? It might be best. If anyone sees them together, they will be bound to say something to him. And then it may go worse for you." The unexpected flicker of pity from the countess took her by surprise.

"I have told him I am indisposed for the next few days, then we are to go to a house party in Kent next weekend. Perhaps it will be best to tell him there, in a different setting." She'd never believed herself a coward, but she could not tell Matthew today. She must have a few more days of happiness before it all came crashing down. "I can keep him away from Ella until then." What Matthew would say when she told him, she had no idea, save it would not be pleasant for her. Nor would the aftermath, for somehow she must find the strength to tell him and then to walk away from him yet again.

# Chapter 19

The lengthy carriage ride to Kent through the crisp October air had been chilly, but Fanny had scarcely noticed, until she discovered her toes were numb when they stopped to change horses some hours into the journey. Instead, she'd been all consumed in devising when and how during Charlotte's house party to tell Matthew that he was Ella's real father.

If she were an optimistic ninny, she'd expect he would clap his hands and jump for joy to find the girl he'd thought the daughter of his rival was actually his own. And take pleasure in the fact that he had thoroughly cuckolded the man he'd been jealous of for so many years. Matthew might indeed feel smug and vindicated, but those would not be his initial reactions to the news, she feared. Fury, betrayal, and condemnation were more likely the first responses she would have to counter with assurances that she had not known the true circumstances of Ella's birth.

In truth, had she known at the time she might

very well not have told him. What good would it have done, save to incite him to challenge Stephen in the hopes of killing him so he could take his place as her husband. The scandal of that would have ruined them as surely as their eloping to the Continent. She'd been hard-pressed to make Matthew see reason on that front. Had there been a child to consider he would never have stopped trying to press for their marriage.

Now, however, even with the circumstances changed by Stephen's death, the situation was fraught with peril. If Matthew could believe that she'd not been hiding Ella's parentage from him on purpose, he'd likely still wish to marry her. And although she would love to do so, she must think of Ella's future in all this. Anytime she was seen in public with Matthew, people would notice their resemblance. How could they miss it? Now that she'd seen it she could never un-see it. Talk would inevitably ensue. The *ton* would erupt with gossip about her and Matthew. Their affair all those years ago would come to light and the *on-dits* would fill the newssheets. It could become bad enough that they would not be received in some homes.

Theale and Lavinia had spoken of one such incident years ago, an acquaintance of Lavinia's who had come to grief in a similar manner. The lady had taken a lover while still married and had borne a child who looked remarkably like its father. Lavinia had given Fanny to know that after it came out, as it must for the resemblance was so great, she had given the woman the cut direct and refused her entry to Theale House.

Dear God. What would happen to her if Lavinia or

Theale found out? She couldn't even begin to imagine their horror. Of course, Theale would likely insist she be removed from the house, although her settlements stipulated it remain her home until she married. Would she then need to marry Matthew in order to escape Theale's retribution—and that retribution would be harsh she had no doubt—for bringing such scandal and shame onto his house? What a diabolical tangle she'd gotten herself into.

Worse than what might happen to Fanny, however, was what might happen to Ella. Legally, she would always be considered Stephen's child as they had been married at the time of her birth. In the eyes of Polite Society, however, what if she were looked upon as no more than Matthew's by-blow. What that might do to her social life, her ability to make friends, or her prospects for a good marriage Fanny had no idea. She'd often heard whispers about this child and that one being a "cuckoo" in the nest, but had paid relatively little attention to such things that obviously didn't concern her. Pity she hadn't been more attentive.

So not only did she need to tell Matthew he was Ella's father, but she must make it clear that they could never marry and expose the girl to ridicule and a life of shame. The prospect of a life without Matthew could scarcely be borne, still she must be strong. She had tried to persuade herself that she could keep Ella and Matthew apart in public, easy enough to accomplish once Matthew had been apprised of the risks of their being seen together. However, upon further reflection, she'd come to the unfortunate conclusion that it was probable that people who saw Ella would, as Lady Lathbury had, see the resemblance between the two even if they weren't together. And if she and Matthew married, the association between Ella and Matthew would already be in place.

Fanny had hit upon the suggestion of sending Ella away to boarding school abroad to return in ten years' time. A quick Season and marriage and the scandal might not touch the girl very harshly. A possible plan, but one Fanny was loath to enact. Ella was the innocent one in all this turmoil. To have her sent away, as though it were her fault entirely, was wrong. The guilt was Fanny's, almost entirely as she had initiated the affair with Matthew in the first place. It would be up to Fanny to bear the brunt of the pain caused by the remedy, although Matthew would suffer as well.

Oddly enough, once assured Fanny did not intend to keep Ella's parentage from her son, Lady Lathbury had seemed unconcerned about the situation. She'd remarked that such things were not unknown in *ton* circles and though there might be some talk, there would likely be no lasting repercussions for Fanny or Ella. Fanny had gazed at her would-be mother-in-law, astounded by the declaration. The only reason for the countess to make such a patently false statement must be her motherly desire for Matthew to be happy by marrying the woman he loved. Such a sentiment seemed more and more unlikely every time she thought of it.

As the carriage pulled up before Lyttlefield Park, Fanny still had not decided when she would inform Matthew of these life-changing matters. In an effort not to spoil Charlotte's party, perhaps she should wait a little. Savor her last moments together with

Matthew. Experience his love one last time before learning how to live the rest of her life without him.

"Fanny, how lovely to see you. You look marvelous this afternoon." Charlotte greeted her warmly with a hug as she entered the cozy drawing room. She'd gone straight to her room upon arrival and dressed in a new green silk gown with stripes of gold and maroon running through it. It truly became her well and she wanted to look especially good for Matthew.

"You are kind, Charlotte. Thank you so much again for inviting Lord Lathbury and me. He was still distraught that he could not attend last time." Peering around the room she frowned. "Am I the first to arrive?"

"You are, although I believe you will have company in a few moments. I see Fisk approaching." Her friend nodded toward the open door where the butler stood.

"Lord Lathbury, my lady."

Fanny's heart gave a funny beat, making her catch her breath. Matthew.

Elegantly attired in a plum-colored coat, striped waistcoat, and fawn-colored breeches, he filled the doorframe briefly, then doffed his gray silk hat and handed it to Fisk. "Lady Cavendish." He smiled broadly and bowed. "My heartfelt thanks for inviting me this weekend. Allow me to in some way make up for my absence from your August party."

"There is no need, my lord. I am so very pleased you could attend now. I think you know Lady Stephen?" Charlotte's eyes laughed as she bowed and turned to greet other arrivals.

"Fanny, why the devil have you been hiding all week?" He frowned at her, his lips pursed in displeasure. "I called twice and was told you were indisposed."

"You know I was overwrought from the visit with your mother. Have she and Beatrice returned to Hunter's Cross?" Changing the subject would work for a short period only. She'd have to answer his questions sooner or later. She greatly preferred later.

"Yes. They left two days ago, and while I would not wish them away, I must say they have been acting peculiarly ever since our visit last week." Knitting his eyebrows, he gestured for her to sit on the sofa, then joined her. "Beatrice has done nothing but laugh and giggle every time I come into a room. Extremely strange behavior, even for her. And Mother has talked of nothing but the wedding and your moving to Hunter's Cross, although she's gotten the oddest notion in her head that you will be sending Ella off to school in Germany or Switzerland."

"We had spoken of that while you were at tea with Ella. I am not, however, highly in favor of such a scheme." At least she could be honest about that.

"Well, I am happy to hear it." His frown relaxed, and he slid next to her. "I would like to keep her with us, have my younger sisters' governess take over her care as soon as we marry, rather than send her to a boarding school here in England." He shook his head. "My mother has some odd ideas. I am surprised she didn't try to send Beatrice off to a school in Germany."

"We needn't talk of such things this weekend, do we?" With her life spinning wildly out of her control,

Fanny needed some other type of distraction. "I'd hoped we could take this time to enjoy ourselves."

He slid closer, his mouth so close to her ear his breath heated her neck, causing all the hairs on her nape to rise. "I'd hoped we'd make plans for our wedding now that the question of Ella is settled."

"Oh, there is Georgina." Springing up off the sofa as if launched by a catapult, Fanny waved to Georgie as though she were a long-lost relation. "I have not seen her in an age. I must go speak to her." She sped across the room, praying Matthew would not follow. Grasping her friend's elbow, she continued toward the doorway.

"Fanny, how nice to see . . . where are we going?" Georgie's comical look of surprise would have made Fanny laugh, had not the circumstances been so dire. She could not allow Matthew to discuss plans for a wedding that was not going to take place.

"Far enough that Lord Lathbury will not pursue me." She cast a glance back toward him, but Matthew had reseated himself, his eyes narrowed and the ends of his mouth drifting downward.

"A lovers' quarrel? Shall I go cheer him up?" Georgie asked, helpfully.

"You'll do no such thing." With a firm hand, Fanny caught the bow at the back of her friend's blue sprigged gown as she teasingly turned to go.

"What's the matter, my dear?" Turning back, and drawing Fanny a little farther away, Georgie leaned close to her. "Has he done something to upset you?"

"No." The plaintive sound of her voice made Fanny even more distraught. She wasn't some weak-willed miss who couldn't handle a man. Especially one she loved. "There are things that must be said between us that I would rather be left unsaid. Once they are spoken, I do not think anything will ever be the same again."

"Can there be no remedy for the situation, Fanny? You're always so clever with men there must be something you can do. I quite envy your abilities that way."

"Do not envy me, Georgie." Fanny shook her head, resisting the urge to look at Matthew. "I have thought myself clever in the past, but I now find revenge is a two-edged sword, just as apt to bite you as the one you wield it at."

Georgie frowned, her ginger brows furrowed over her petite nose. "I cannot know what you speak of, of course, but I believe that true love will always triumph, no matter what's at stake. Choose love, Fanny. It's the only thing that truly matters." A toss of her head and her eyes lit up. "Jemmy is here! Please excuse me, Fanny."

Two very handsome young men had just entered the drawing room. Lord Brack, Georgie's brother, she'd met at the party in August. The other devastatingly attractive gentleman was a stranger. Another time she'd have followed her friend and begged an introduction. Now she wanted nothing more than to return to sit with Matthew, smooth the brooding lines from his brow, and plan a future together with him. Was there a way through this tangle she'd not considered? Could they marry and be happy without a scandal or the ruin of her child's life?

Every instinct told her that a life without Matthew would be widowhood all over again, with no hope of putting off her mourning in six months or a year. Grief she hadn't felt at Stephen's passing would now consume her for the rest of her days if Matthew was not at her side. By God, she would find a way to make the impossible possible.

Straightening her spine, head held high, Fanny strode back to the sofa where Matthew sat, his face still morose, his countenance sad.

He gazed up at her, a wariness not usually in his eyes now apparent.

Smiling, she seated herself on the sofa so close to him their hips touched. "Now that that is done, I think we can proceed. Did you wish a country wedding at Hunter's Cross, or a more fashionable one at St. George's in London? We must think carefully and come to an accord, for I swear before God, this is the last time I intend to go through with such a ceremony."

Lord Kersey's chin hit seven steps as he tumbled down the staircase shortly after dinner that evening. Matthew and the other gentlemen had been drawn out into the entry hall by a thunderous crash upstairs, followed shortly by the sound of someone bumping down the stairs.

"Is Lord Kersey drunk?" Fanny led the women who poured out of the drawing room as the unfortunate earl landed with a loud thud on the floor.

"I've no idea," he replied, alert for some other explanation of the carnage. He'd been in Jackson's enough to recognize when a man had had a good drubbing. The question now was with whom had he gone several rounds?

Immediately behind Kersey, Lord Wrotham trotted down the staircase, murder in his eyes. That look would certainly account for the downed lord's appearance.

"What's going on, Wrotham?" Lord Brack bent over, peering into the fallen man's bloodied face.

The other ladies hovered around the body, exclaiming loudly at the unfortunate sight or offering advice.

"Is he conscious?" Fanny called over the din of voices.

Grasping her arm, Matthew pulled her aside. "He's breathing at least. Do you know what caused Wrotham to draw his cork in the first place?"

"I have no idea. We were in the drawing room, sitting down to whist when the commotion started. I wish we'd come out sooner. It seems pretty much over now." Fanny sounded put out that she hadn't seen more.

Raising his hands, as if to quiet the crowd, Wrotham spoke again. "Let us say Lord Kersey insulted me in a manner I will take from no man."

"Devil the man. Sounds like he had it coming." Matthew shook his head and gulped from the glass he'd brought out with him when summoned by the noise. "Are Lady Cavendish's parties always so lively?"

"This is a new height, I must admit." Excitement had brought a pretty blush to Fanny's cheeks. "Last time all that happened was Lord Fernley kissed Charlotte and Wrotham threw him over a balustrade into a rosebush."

"Indeed." Considering Kersey's condition, the man had likely done much worse than steal a kiss from his hostess.

"Alan!" A shrill female voice brought their attention

back to the staircase where a small woman, dressed only in a blue dressing gown, raced toward the fallen lord. "Alan, who did this to you?"

"I believe we may be in for act two of this Drury Lane drama. Who is this woman? One of your circle of friends?"

"Yes, well, no, not really. Maria Wickley. She is a widow and a distant relation of Jane's who she invited to the last party. What is the woman doing?" Fanny stepped forward, looking ready to join in the fray, as Mrs. Wickley drew back her hand to take a swing at Lord Wrotham.

"I think we've had enough uproar for one evening, my love." Executing a neat strike, Matthew snared Fanny's arm and propelled her, protesting, toward the now empty drawing room. Once inside, he closed the door and leaned against it. "I would, however, be ready for excitement of a completely different sort."

"That sort being?" Her tone was biting, but she came willingly into his arms.

"One for your eyes—and body—alone, my love." Enfolding her against his chest, Matthew pulled her lovely face up to his, still in awe that she had finally consented to their marriage. "Although we did not discuss the wedding trip, my dear, I do have some thoughts on the matter. I suggest we remain at Hunter's Cross for a week after the wedding, then travel on to whatever our final destination may be."

"Why stay at home for a week?" Her puzzled frown delighted him.

"Because I vow to you I will not let you out of my bed for a solid week after we are wed."

"Matthew!" She squealed and hit his chest.

"So if we will see nothing but the inside of the

earl's chamber, I see no reason to spend good money on—"

"Wretch." Settling her head onto his chest once more, she stroked his arm in sudden silence. "Matthew."

"Yes, love?"

"If I told you an awful secret, something truly dreadful"—the stroking stopped—"would you be able to forgive me?" Fanny tensed in his arms and waited.

"I suppose that would depend on what the secret concerned." A deep foreboding raised its head. What had Fanny done? His mind leapt to the obvious, most devastating conclusion imaginable: She had in fact lain with Alan Garrett at the first house party, had lied about it to him, and now carried that man's child. That might account for her odd behavior of late. A phantom hand squeezed his heart until it hurt to breathe. "Does it involve Lord Kersey?"

Fanny jerked back, her face screwed up in disgust. "Lord Kersey? No, of course not. What secret could I have concerning Lord Kersey of all people?"

"Well, you did say dreadful, so I thought you might have—"

"Good Lord." She dissolved into giggles, all her tension draining away. "Are you still bothering over a rendezvous that never took place?" Shaking her head she slipped her arms around him, pulling him closer. "Your jealousy is very sweet, Matthew, but I have truly desired no man save you in seven years."

"Is that so?" Relief washed through him, bringing a surge of passion to his cock that swelled it in moments. "Would you care to demonstrate your desire?" He claimed a kiss, and his hunger for her soared. "Now?"

"Mmm. Now, but not here. The others will certainly be upon us shortly. Come to my room as soon as you can." She kissed him again, stabbing her tongue inside him, hardening him fully, then she was gone.

Exhaling shakily, he prayed he made it to her room before he burst. He'd go now, find his hostess, and excuse himself from the rest of the evening. That should cool him down a bit. It dawned on him, as he left the drawing room, that Fanny still had not told him her dire secret, but no matter. If it did not involve another man, it was likely not as calamitous as she believed. As with her, he could forgive anything save infidelity.

# Chapter 20

"If you had told me Lady Cavendish's house party was going to be a debauch to rival the Hell Fire Club, I'd have said you were daft." Matthew pulled Fanny toward the circle of torches that ringed the Harvest Lord and his four prospects for the title of Corn Maiden.

Wrotham Village's Harvest Festival today had been a merry time for all the house party members, enchanting them all with stalls of local goods, games of skill, and the awarding of prizes for best produce. Now, however, the festival would close with a pagan fertility rite called the Crowning of the Corn Maiden and the mood of the spectators had sobered strangely into something darker, more sensual than Matthew would have thought possible given the cheerful atmosphere of the day.

The Harvest Lord, a strapping lad named Michael Thorne, ogled the four young girls—not one of whom looked over sixteen—who were all swishing their skirts and holding bouquets of flowers in front of their breasts. Oh, yes, Mr. Thorne was getting an eyeful, as was every other man with enough age on him to know how to use his member. Matthew, who'd thought himself impervious to anyone's charms save Fanny's, found he needed to adjust himself now and then to disguise his erection.

"I don't see anything so scandalous happening. The Harvest Lord will pick a Corn Maiden, he'll give her a kiss and it will be done." Fanny tried to act nonchalant, but her pulse raced beneath the skin of her wrist where he'd clasped it. Was she feeling some of the power of this ceremony? God knew he was

"He used to give her more than a kiss, so Wrotham was telling the gentlemen after dinner." Waggling his eyebrows, Matthew drew laughter from Fanny.

"Tell, tell." She wrapped her arms around his, her giggling doing nothing to allay his predicament down below.

"The Harvest Lord claimed his Maiden, gave her a kiss to seal the temporary marriage, then the couple retired to a bridal tent made of sheaves of wheat draped with sheets washed in a local well. The couple spent the night there, in the field, the Harvest Lord sowing his seed with the Corn Maiden to bless the ground and increase the harvest for the next year." Perhaps there was something to the ancient rite. The stirring in his groin had grown most urgent just describing the event.

"So they had sexual congress and then?" Fanny's arms around him heated him to an inferno pitch.

"If the Corn Maiden caught with child, then the lord married her. If not, they did not. A man wants to sow in a fertile field." That was certainly what Matthew wanted to do—this very minute. He checked the crowd, but every eye was on Michael Thorne, who looked ready to make his pronouncement. Now would be the best time to slip away with Fanny and complete their own fertility rite.

"As the seed goes to the fertile ground, so goes the Harvest Lord to his maiden . . . Nora Burns."

The Wrotham tenants cheered as Thorne claimed his prize, drawing her to him, his attention so keenly focused on the brown-haired girl he'd just chosen Matthew doubted the man even noticed the noisy crowd around them. He'd not be surprised if Thorne lowered the girl to the stubbled ground and mounted her this moment.

Mother of God, his own need had become so great he'd burst if he didn't have his own Corn Maiden and quickly. The rite had not finished, but if he stayed he'd surely make an embarrassing spectacle of himself. He grabbed Fanny's hand. "Let's go."

A quiet moan from Fanny, staring at the Harvest couple, engorged him further. She turned to him, eyes wide and deep black with desire. They needed to leave now. He pulled her to him and she followed willingly, even eagerly, as he headed them for the only secluded spot around, a tree line above the cleared field. Matthew only hoped they would get there before the lust that filled his entire being overcame his better judgment and he took Fanny in plain sight of the entire village of Wrotham.

Once out of the immediate vicinity of the harvest rite, his primal urges eased, but only minimally. He wanted to sink himself into Fanny's warm sheath so badly he ground his teeth in the effort not to give into it. Not far now. Moaning to their left brought him up short. He stopped, peering into the darkness.

The moon had sailed behind a cloud, so Matthew could only see the outlines of a man and a woman, in the throes of passion, lying on a blanket on the ground. A powerful rite indeed, for these were not the country people of Wrotham. In fact, if he didn't miss his guess, the couple was the newly betrothed Wrotham and Lady Cavendish. *As the seed goes to the fertile ground.*

His own seed now urging him onward, Matthew continued to run toward the trees. The sound of panting in his ear as Fanny strove to keep up with his breakneck pace only served to enrage his blood more. A sound reminiscent of those she made when in the throes.

As they reached the trees, he dropped his hand to his fall, frantically working the buttons. With his other hand, he groped at Fanny's long skirt. "Help me."

"Wait." She shook her head and pointed to the edge of the tree line some ten yards to their right.

A streak of errant moonlight suddenly illuminated another couple, arms entwined about one another, kissing passionately. The damned rite must be powerful beyond belief to affect all these people.

"This way." Fanny grabbed his hand and dragged him out of the moonlight and into the woods.

The sudden darkness blinded him, but he strode onward, his need for Fanny too great to deter him. The lack of light never hindered this act. He bumped his shoulder against a tree and froze, pulling Fanny to a halt beside him. "Now. I have to have you now, Fanny."

She launched herself into his arms, her mouth claiming him in a bruising kiss that drove him over the edge of sanity. With a deep growl he spun her around and pushed her against the tree. "Hold on."

Nodding, she thrust her bottom at him, legs apart, and raked her skirts up.

Groaning from his soul, Matthew freed his member, guided it to her waiting channel, and thrust home. The intense relief of claiming her almost made him spill his seed on the first stroke, but he calmed a measure and paused, glorying in their joined state.

"More, Matthew. I need more." Fanny's voice broke his state of bliss.

He leaned over her back, straining into her until he could whisper in her ear, "You feel the power too, don't you?"

"Yes."

He nudged further inside her.

"Yes." More insistent now.

Withdrawing almost completely, he then surged forward to the hilt, every inch of him on fire for her.

"Yes, oh, yes, Matthew," she cried out, arching her back like a wild creature.

All semblance of civility fell away and he abandoned himself to the raw sensuality of the moment, thrusting faster and faster, deeper and deeper until they both cried out as he spilled himself—forever it seemed—inside her. Knees buckling, he wrapped his arms around Fanny and eased them to the ground.

They lay together panting, slowly coming back from the brink of madness that had consumed them.

"Lord Wrotham should have warned us this might happen," Fanny said at last. "It seems to have affected at least two couples. I couldn't believe Elizabeth Easton had her lips glued to Lord Brack's. I thought she was still mourning her husband."

"Three couples, my dear. Did you not see Lord Wrotham on the ground as we ran by?"

"With whom?" Fanny sat up as though alarmed.

"Lady Cavendish, I am almost certain. Who else, since they just announced their betrothal. Which reminds me." He pulled her back against his chest, secure in his arms. "You have yet to name the date for our wedding. We agreed it would be at Hunter's Cross, but not when."

She went still in his arms, for such a long time he'd have thought she'd fallen asleep, except her body remained tense. At last she sighed and sat up. "I must consult with Theale about drawing up the settlements, and with Lady Theale about arranging for my personal possessions to be packed and sent to the estate. Allow me to complete those tasks before we proclaim a date."

"Do not take too much time over it, my love." He drew her back down to him and nuzzled her neck. "Not only do I want you with me as soon as possible, but after this evening, I would not at all be surprised if you are not with child." He shook his head. "In truth, I'm surprised Wrotham Village isn't threefold as large as it is if this rite is performed every year. I wonder if most births in the vicinity occur in June or July."

"I do not think we need worry on that account. I have been drinking the herbal tea suggested by a midwife my cousin in Copsale uses since just after we met in June, with no ill effects. I'm certain we are safe."

"I didn't know you'd been doing that." Not sure if he was appalled or grateful for Fanny's forethought, Matthew laid his head on the ground, the dead leaves crackling in his ear. "Is that why you didn't conceive when we were together in London those four months?"

A long pause before she whispered, "Yes."

He'd wondered at the time if perhaps she was barren, for he certainly took no precautions to avoid getting her with child. After the first month, in fact, he'd hoped against hope she'd conceive with his child, a strong argument for her to go away with him. But it hadn't occurred until . . . "You stopped taking it after you returned to Stephen?"

After a while, when he believed she wouldn't speak, she said, "Yes," very low. "I felt so guilty, I thought if I gave him a child it would assuage the remorse I felt."

Sighing, Matthew sat them up. No need to wish back deeds long past. They must move forward, put their past to rest, and create a family of their own. "We should return to the field. The others will have gathered at the carriages."

He stood, then helped her to stand before adjusting his clothing.

"Can you brush the back of my pelisse? I hope it's not ruined." Fanny had turned away from him, industriously patting the front of the garment.

"I believe it is fine. It will be dark in any case. No one will see a stain or two." He grabbed her hands, stilling them from their insistent brushing. "We will meet in London next week, after our return. I leave Kent on the morrow. When will you follow?"

"I am promised to Charlotte until Tuesday." She seemed to shake off her melancholy spirit and smiled. "With all the hullabaloo that took place last night and tonight, I believe she will be in need of assistance from all members of the Widows' Club."

Matthew had to agree. If ever there had been a chaotic evening, tonight had been it. The robber gang that had apparently been plaguing Kent, and more particularly the estates of Lyttlefield Park and Wrotham Hall, had finally been apprehended when they tried to break into Wrotham's manor house. To add an even more bizarre twist to the story, Lady Cavendish's stepson, Sir Edgar Cavendish, had turned out to be the gang's ringleader. His capture, just before dinner, had put a thrilling cap on the evening. Or so they had thought. Shortly after he'd been taken away, Lady Cavendish and Lord Wrotham had announced their betrothal. That, along with the wildly sensual pagan rite of the Harvest Festival and Fanny's earlier acceptance of him, had made this evening one of the wildest Matthew had ever experienced in his life.

"I will give you time to return and settle in, then I will call upon you for tea on Friday next. By then I hope all your tasks will be complete and we can name the day and announce the betrothal." Offering her his arm, Matthew drew her arm through the crook of his, and moved off toward the bright moonlight showing at the edge of the trees. It could not be too soon before Fanny stood beside him as his wife. Then life could begin for them in earnest.

# Chapter 21

Fanny sat once more in the small front receiving room of Lord Theale's London townhome awaiting Matthew's arrival and dreading it. She'd not accomplished any of the tasks she'd told him she would be taking care of because she still feared Matthew's reaction to her news about Ella. That he would be angry she knew; how angry he would be was the question.

In any case, she would not have had much chance to speak with Lady Theale this past week. Lavinia had already begun the process of the removal of the family to their primary estate for the coming Christmas season, and so Fanny had scarcely seen her since her return from Kent.

Pouring more tea, and dropping in her customary two lumps of sugar, Fanny kept rehearsing what she would say. No matter how many times she said it, it never sounded very good. Pray God he could get past the initial shock so he could help counsel her on what then to do with Ella. She'd come to believe that a governess for the girl at home at Hunter's Cross would help keep the scandal at bay for a while at least. Perhaps in the quiet society of Buckinghamshire Ella could find friends and perhaps a husband who would overlook her mother's sins.

"Frances?"

Fanny jumped at the sound of her sister-in-law's voice in the doorway. Dressed in her most fashionable brown pelisse and hat, Lavinia had stopped apparently on her way out, and now stood, head cocked. "Are you taking tea alone, Frances? Why ever are you not in the drawing room?"

"I'm waiting on a caller, Lavinia. He should be here at any moment now." Fanny set her cold cup back on the saucer.

"He?" Her eyebrows rose over dark, disapproving eyes.

"The old friend I told you I had become reacquainted with this past summer. Lord Lathbury."

"Ah, yes. The earl you met in June. Have you quite made up your mind about him, I hope?" The marchioness would never let that go, apparently. Well, she'd be happy when she found out the truth.

"I believe Lord Lathbury and I are about to come to an accord. That is the reason for his visit today. He met Ella several weeks ago and she seemed very taken with him, so we are proceeding with a conversation regarding the possibility of a marriage."

"Why was Ella's acceptance of him a possible impediment?" Lavinia gazed at her as though she belonged in a lunatic asylum.

"Because I would not have my daughter made miserable living with someone she could not love and respect." Fanny fisted her hands so tightly she feared blood would begin to flow from her nails digging into her flesh. "But as I said, she is quite taken with Lord Lathbury and he with her. That will not be an obstruction to our marriage when or if the time comes."

"Please do not hesitate to ask my assistance in gathering and packing your belongings once things are settled between you and the earl."

"Thank you, Lavinia. Perhaps after our meeting today I will be able to seek you out for that very purpose." A devil flew up on Fanny's shoulder. "And Ella's belongings as well. She would be removing with me, of course, if I marry Lord Lathbury."

"Naturally." The woman's expression changed not at all; however, her normally pinched lips quivered slightly as though trying to smile. "Well, please inform me of your plans when I return."

"Lord Lathbury, my lady." Noyes showed Matthew into the room where an awkward silence ensued.

"Lady Theale, may I present Lord Lathbury, my longtime friend? My lord, Lady Theale is my sister-in-law." Why couldn't the woman have been gone before Matthew got here? Now they'd likely never be rid of her.

"My lady." He bowed politely, although his eyes and smile were for Fanny.

"My lord. Lady Stephen has informed me of your impending marriage." Shooting Fanny a look of triumph, Lavinia tugged on her gloves. "My heartfelt congratulations. But if you will excuse me, I must go. I am on my way to a meeting to raise funds for the Magdalen Hospital. There is always so much need." She curtsied. "I will see you at dinner, Frances. Good day, my lord."

Slumping in her chair, Fanny prayed she and

Matthew could come to an accord so she could remove herself and her daughter from this hateful household.

"She's a bit of a harridan, isn't she?" He sat beside Fanny and kissed her cheek. "Thank goodness she's no blood relation of yours, or I'd fear to wake up one morning some twenty years hence and find her likes in bed with me."

"God forbid." Shuddering, Fanny rang the bell for more tea. "And I vow I did not tell her that we were getting married, Matthew, only that we were considering it."

Waving his hand, he stripped off his gloves and laid them in his lap. "I would not find it amiss if you had, love. We have done all save set the date. Some women pride themselves on having such news first."

"No, Lavinia does not care for that sort of thing, at least I don't think so. She just wants to know when I will be moving out of her house so she and Theale won't have the care of me and Ella." She couldn't bear this, couldn't bear him not knowing any longer. He had a right to know Ella was his, even if it resulted in his leaving her. She must tell him. No more delays.

"Well, and that is fine. They will not have the care of you and Ella very shortly. Where is she?"

The footman entered with the fresh tea and Fanny seized on it as a drowning man does a lifeline. "Thank you, Thomas." She busied herself pouring tea and adding sugar. Anything to keep from answering his question. "You take two lumps, is that correct, Matthew?"

"You know it is, Fanny. You've been making me tea for months now." A shake of his head, and he took the cup and sipped. "Delicious as always." He set the cup in its saucer and took Fanny's hands. "Why are you so nervous? It's not as though I'm your first beau at a dance or your first man on your wedding night."

"I know." She couldn't wait. She must do it now. "It's about Ella, Matthew."

"Why isn't she here?" He glanced at the door. "I wanted us both to tell her that I am to be her new papa. She isn't ill, is she?"

"No, she is quite well. But I need to tell you something about Ella." Squeezing his hands, she said, "You are her father, Matthew."

He shook his head, gazing at her in confusion. "Yes, I know that, but she does not. I wanted us both to tell her of our marriage and that I will be her papa from now on."

"No, you don't understand." How could she make him comprehend? "I didn't realize it myself until you came for tea with your mother. And then I saw you and Ella together, and couldn't help but see it."

"See what? You're not making sense, Fanny." He shook off her grip.

"See that you are Ella's father, not Stephen."

His brows wrinkled into a deep V and he shook his head in little bursts, as though shaking water from his ears. "No. You can't mean that. It's not possible."

"It is possible. She looks just like you. No one who sees you together can think anything else. Your mother saw it immediately. And Beatrice." Miserable, Fanny rose and paced to the blazing fireplace, feeling not an iota of warmth from it.

"No." He rose and followed her, his steps thudding loudly on the polished wooden floor. "They would have told me." Staring at her with the coldest eyes she'd ever seen, he said, "You lie."

Tears trickled down her cheeks, her worst fears about this moment coming true. "No, I do not lie. If you like, I will have Ella brought here, a mirror fetched, and show you both faces together and see if you wish to deny it."

"Why didn't you tell me?"

"Because I didn't know! I never saw the two of you together until that day." All the things she'd thought to say over the past weeks came pouring out. "I told you, when we were together back in '09, I found out about the herbs to prevent children and I took them. I drank the tea every day until the day I left you because I didn't want this kind of complication. When I returned to Stephen's bed, I stopped the herbs. As I told you in Kent, it was part of my atonement to him. Two months later I realized I was increasing, so I believed it was Stephen's. When Ella was born I thought nothing of the fact that she didn't look like Stephen. She has my dark coloring so again, why would I suspect?"

"How do you explain why your herbs didn't work? If you took them every day when we were together, why would they not work this one time?" Pacing back and forth, not giving her any room to move, Matthew at last halted in front of her, his glare accusing.

"God knows, I have thought back to those days many times since I discovered the truth, trying to understand what happened." Her own folly, in the end, had tripped her up. "As I recollect, my supply of the herbs, they are seeds really, had come to an end as I was grappling with the decision of whether or not to leave with you. I didn't think missing a day or two would make much of a difference, and I wouldn't need them once I returned to Stephen." She waited, wanting to ask a question but not quite daring to until she could stand it no longer. "Are you angry because you didn't know, or are you angry because you are Ella's father?"

Jerking his arms behind his back, Matthew strode to the doorway and back again. A fierce glare at her and he paused. "I am angered to find more than six years of my daughter's life have passed without my knowing that she was my daughter. I still find you at blame here, Fanny. Did you have no notion at all that the child might be mine?"

"None. I swear to you on any holy thing you will name," Fanny said, tears in her eyes.

"And if you had known? Would you have told me?"

Should she tell the truth when a lie would be so much more convenient? What did it matter at this point what she would have done in her wretched state seven years ago? Now a better life hung in the balance for her and her child. Their child. Opening her mouth to speak, she stared into his accusatory eyes then hung her head. A slight shake, a world of betrayal. She raised her head to find herself gazing into the eyes of a stranger.

"Well, then." He turned sharply on his heel and strode to the doorway.

"What good would it have done, Matthew?" She had to stop him. They could find a way to make everything all right, if only he wouldn't leave her. "I was married to Stephen. No matter what I told or who I told it to, that fact could not be altered. In the eyes of the law she will always be Stephen's daughter."

"Oh, no." He wheeled about again, pacing toward her so quickly she backed into the chaise and sat down hard, jarring the tea things on the nearby table. "If you had come to me as soon as you knew you were increasing, we could have gone to Belgium, or Germany. Anywhere. We had proof of our affair, right there in your belly. Stephen would have divorced you before the ink was dry on the confession. Then we could have been married and began a life together." He leaned down until his face was within inches of hers. "But you didn't want that. You wanted Stephen, though God knows why. Perhaps because he treated you like the mud beneath his boots." Matthew rose. "Perhaps if I treat you that way, you'll come running after me."

Heart hammering, Fanny sat stunned, unable to speak, to call him back as he spun around and strode out of the room, without a backward glance.

# Chapter 22

November had ushered in weather even colder and wetter than they had suffered at the end of October, if that was possible. A more miserable month Fanny had never experienced, but not only because of the dismal weather. She hadn't seen or heard from Matthew since that terrible day six weeks before when he'd walked out of this very room. After the first week of waiting for him to call or send word, she'd taken to having tea in the small receiving room. It made her horribly sad, but also helped her feel closer to Matthew as well. She'd just sent for Ella to have tea with her, in the hopes that having their daughter here would give her some comfort.

In less than two weeks' time she would return to Kent for Charlotte and Nash's wedding. By now she'd thought she and Matthew would be traveling there together as husband and wife. Instead she'd be going alone, and returning to London. Only a week ago, Lavinia had informed her and all the members of the household that Theale had decided not to journey to Northumberland and his primary estate there for Christmas.

No explanation had been given, but Fanny had written to Jane, still at Lyttlefield Park assisting Charlotte with preparations for the wedding. She'd given her the latest decree from their brother-in-law and asked what she thought might be the cause of this drastic break with family tradition. Jane's response had been a tale, almost a scandal in fact, regarding Theale's acting drunk at several parties and balls and accosting young women. An occurrence completely out of character for the marquess, who had always enjoyed a sterling reputation as a teetotaler and a man who never looked at a woman other than his wife. This odd behavior on top of remaining in London for the holiday did not bode well for any of them. As Shakespeare was often famously quoted, something was rotten in Denmark.

Little as she wanted to admit it, Fanny's life, so recently like a straight path lined with gold, had now spun out of control and threatened to crash like a runaway carriage. Powerless to make any changes, she would live at the whim of the Marquess of Theale for the rest of her days unless she managed to find someone to marry her. She sighed and distractedly poured milk into her cup of tea, stirring as the white swirls made pretty patterns before muddling into a bland tannish color. Much like her life now. She raised the cup to her lips, tasted the milky brew and grimaced, but swallowed. Where was her mind to have put milk in her tea? Woefully fixed on her predicament.

It might be possible to catch another husband. She still had her looks, and if she took a little more pains, she would do well enough she supposed. However, her heart was simply not engaged. Flirting had not even held any charms for her recently. She'd have sworn she'd enjoy that pastime until the grave, but nothing about talking to or teasing men appealed to her now.

Not since Matthew.

Why had she not accepted him and married him in June when he'd asked? Or in Brighton. Or even in Kent in October? Had she not hesitated, had she not wanted her daughter to matter in her decision regarding her life . . . Had she not told the truth, she'd likely be married this moment to Matthew and happily ensconced at Hunter's Cross. And even if not happy, then at least tolerably situated and with the ability to win him back.

So what was she to do now?

"Frances. Why are you in this small room again?" Lavinia's voice grated on Fanny's ears worse and worse these days. "Why are you not in the family drawing room with everyone else?" Her sister-in-law came quickly into the room, frowning at the tea service. "Laying tea service in two different rooms is a wasteful extravagance. I am surprised you haven't heeded my warning about that already. Theale says this room should be closed up during the cold months unless we are entertaining, which we so seldom do these days. It will save on the household expenses tremendously, he says."

"I didn't realize the Marquess of Theale had financial worries, Lavinia. I will, of course, do my best to save him a penny or two by remaining in my rooms at all times." Fanny could have bitten her tongue. Such outbursts did no good whatsoever and only tended to make Lavinia even more unpleasant toward her.

"Temper will never do, Frances. I will tell Mrs. Gaines to have another pot of tea sent up to the drawing room for you. We are all gathering there shortly." Lavinia stepped to the door. "Unless you would like to go directly to your room to dress for dinner."

What she would like was to be left alone by this harpy, but that was impossible. "May I please have the tea and cakes brought here? Nurse is bringing Ella down for us to have a tea party and I think this room is much more suitable for a girl Ella's age."

"Ella is coming down?"

"Yes. We have tea quite often now." Now that Fanny was home almost constantly.

"Would you mind if I joined you? I have not been able to see Ella as much as I used to. The household seems more difficult to run to Theale's taste recently. I'd planned the move to Northumberland, had even had the packing begun, and he decided to stay here." She clasped her hands together, wringing them to and fro.

In all the time since her marriage, Fanny had never seen Lavinia so distraught. That alone unnerved her more than anything Theale himself had done. Perhaps her sister-in-law needed some time away from her myriad duties as marchioness. "Certainly, Lavinia. Please have a seat. Nurse should be bringing her any moment."

Taking the Queen Anne chair—not nearly as imposing as her one in the drawing room, but much more comfortable looking—Lavinia looked around the small room as though seeing it for the first time.

"I hadn't noticed how intimate this room seems. I have seldom had the need to use it."

"It's quite my favorite of the public rooms here just for that reason."

Silence fell between them, broken only by the scrape of porcelain as Lavinia set her cup in its saucer and the clink of Fanny's spoon against her cup. Not a companionable silence either. Conversation, no matter how banal, would have helped, but Fanny hesitated to offer any for fear a quarrel would break out just as Ella appeared. Her times with her daughter were very precious, more so because she had had no contact with her father in weeks. Ella was her only link to him now.

The soft pattering of feet on the hardwood floors down the corridor made Fanny sit up suddenly and force a pleasant smile onto her lips. Lavinia's effort actually looked more genuine.

"Mama!" Ella's voice held the joy that always stopped Fanny's heart. To be so loved by her daughter, when she certainly didn't deserve it, made her most humble indeed. The child raced into the room, face wreathed in smiles, only to skid to a stop at the sight of Lavinia.

"Good afternoon, darling." Fanny motioned the girl to her and hugged her tight. "Don't be afraid," she whispered. "It will be all right."

Ella nodded, then put on a smile of her own and curtsied to Lavinia. "Good afternoon, Aunt. I didn't know you would be here today."

"I didn't know myself, my dear, but isn't this a pleasant surprise?" The older woman smiled warmly at the child. "I haven't seen you in quite some weeks. I shall be glad for us to take tea together again. I hope your manners have not suffered because of my absence."

"I have seen no problem with her manners since we began our parties, Lavinia. You taught her well." The words galled Fanny to no end; however, they might go some way to smoothing the way for a tolerable teatime today. "Have a seat by me, my love, and I'll pour your tea."

"Children do need strict instruction if they are to get on well in Society. So often they do not receive it." Lavinia raised her cup again, her gaze still on Ella.

As discreetly as possible, Fanny put two lumps of sugar into the cup, poured the tea slowly, and gave the cup to her daughter.

"Thank you, Mama." The child's eyes widened, but Fanny gave a slight shake of her head, and Ella avidly sipped the tea without milk. "This is very good."

"I'm glad you like it." Perhaps the milkless tea would slip past Lavinia's notice if she distracted her. "Have you been able to assist with your charity at the Magdalene Hospital recently, Lavinia? I know you have been extremely busy here at home."

"I have not, Frances, and that has been a sadness to me." Lavinia turned to Fanny, lines of fatigue deeper than usual in her face. "I know the Magdalene Hospital is one of the most important charities in London. These poor women, sunk into such depravity, most through no fault of their own, have proven they can be rehabilitated, if only we will take the time to help them relearn the Christian values of good, honest work and teach them the skills to accomplish it."

"It is a noble cause. Perhaps I can assist you with it." Not that she particularly wished to work with her sister-in-law, but the charity itself seemed well worthy.

"I would be happy to have you along the next time I go to the board meeting. Sadly, I've not been able to go for several weeks."

"The last time I heard you mention you were going was the day . . ." Her heart stuttered. It had been the last day Matthew had come to call.

"The day I met Lord Lathbury, before his defection." Lavinia's face pinched. "You still have no idea why he ceased his attentions to you? You had given me to understand you were about to announce an engagement."

"I liked Lord Laffbury, Mama." Ella had drained her cup and now piped up. "Why has he not returned?"

"I suppose you could say he and I quarreled. As ladies and gentlemen sometimes do from time to time, Ella. I hope we can make it up at some later time." Wishful thinking at best. Unless his conscience got the better of him and he wished to see his daughter again.

"Can't you tell him you are sorry, Mama? He was ever so much fun at tea." Ella smiled excitedly. "Did you know he looks like me?"

Fanny froze, afraid to breathe. "Why would you say that, my dear?"

"When we were having tea that day I saw us together in the mirror. We look just alike."

Think, think, she must play this off as best she could. "I suppose you both have dark hair and blue eyes, but so do I, poppet. And I do not look anything like his lordship, do I?"

A frown twisted Ella's small face. "No, you don't look like him at all."

"But you do look like me, don't you?" Fanny cut her gaze over to Lavinia, who was also looking at her with lowered brows. A storm obviously brewed from that direction.

"Yes, Mama. Everyone has always said I looked like you." Ella nodded, then her gaze followed Fanny's to her aunt and her small face suddenly pinched with worry. "Is that a bad thing, Mama?"

"No, of course not, darling. Children are supposed to look like their . . . mothers." The word "parents" had almost slipped out, which would have been disastrous. "Or sometimes fathers, although your father had blond hair like his father and brothers. But that happens in families. Sometimes." The more she talked the more she seemed to be digging herself in deeper.

"Clayborn." In a strained voice, Lavinia called and the nurse, who'd been waiting in the corridor, entered. "Please take Miss Ella back to the nursery." The look of outrage she turned on Fanny made her stomach sink. "I think our teatime is ended."

Instantly, Ella jumped up and rushed to throw her arms around Fanny. "Mama, I'm sorry. I don't want to go back to the nursery. I want to stay with you." Hiding her face in Fanny's bosom, the child began to sob.

"Hush, sweetheart. Don't cry." She pulled Ella's head up and smiled into her face. "Go with Nurse now and I'll come up in a little while to play. We'll read a story or maybe we can take a short walk in the garden before it gets too dark." She wiped the tears from the girl's cheeks with her napkin. "I promise."

"Truly? You're not angry at me?"

"No, darling. Of course I'm not angry with you."

Ella shot a look at Lavinia, but nodded. Head hanging, she marched over to Clayborn and took her hand.

"Close the door, Clayborn." Lavinia sat back in her chair, watching until the door shut, then turned a malevolent gaze on Fanny. "Why does Stephen's daughter look like Lord Lathbury?"

Head suddenly cool and mind focused, Fanny shrugged. "I don't know what you mean, Lavinia. The child saw a similar coloring between her and the earl, nothing more. She's too young to understand anything other than that."

"But I do understand, all too well now." The marchioness rose, her lips pulled back in a grimace. "When I met Lord Lathbury something nagged at me. I'd not met him before, yet he seemed very familiar. And as soon as Ella pointed it out, it became obvious. He looked familiar because he looks like her. And he looks like her because he is her father. They favor one another much too well beyond just their coloring." Trembling, she drew herself up. "How could you betray Stephen so? Betray the Tarkington family so?"

Clenching her fists, Fanny rose. She could continue to deny the accusation, but Lavinia would never believe her. She'd always disliked Fanny, so nothing she said now would change that in the least. Time at last to set the record straight. "How could I betray him? Better ask your precious Stephen how he could betray and dishonor me."

"Stephen would never—"

"Oh, wouldn't he? You may have no idea what

Stephen Tarkington did and did not do during the course of our marriage, but everyone else in the *ton* certainly knew it. After the first year of our marriage I could not set foot in a ballroom without the constant whispers. *'Do you think she knows?' 'Will she make a scene?' 'Did you hear he was almost caught by the woman's husband?'* I tried to ignore the whispers, ignore the nights Stephen did not come home, ignore the smell of women's perfume and powder on his uniform whenever he did come home."

"Men cannot be held accountable for their baser transgressions. And you must have known his reputation when you married him, my dear. He was never a saint by anyone's estimation." The cool defense of her philandering husband by a woman who'd never experienced such shame enraged Fanny even more.

"I knew he was a rake, but I believed he would change after our marriage." More fool her. "And even . . . even after I realized he would never change, I would not have betrayed him had he not dishonored me in the vilest manner." The memory of it even now made her ill.

Suddenly wary, Lavinia drew back. "I doubt Stephen would have done anything as wicked as you claim. Men simply have greater needs than women do."

"Then he should have eased them with a light woman in a brothel, or procured a mistress. Someone I would not have to meet socially." Chest heaving with pain and anger years old, Fanny fought back tears in a fight she would not win. "But he chose to dally with women of the *ton.* Married women bored with their own husbands, who allowed themselves to be seduced by a handsome face in regimentals."

"You are mistaken, my dear." Her sister-in-law's

smile had slipped, but she insisted on denying the truth. "Stephen would not have risked bringing scandal to this house by consorting so with decent women."

"Why do you insist on defending him?" The woman would drive her mad. Had she really never known of Stephen's unfaithfulness? "If you don't believe me, you can ask your husband. I'm certain he remembers. I believe he may have paid off a husband or two so they wouldn't call Stephen out. So the affairs never became full-blown scandals, although rumors of them circulated a great deal. The worst infidelity drove me to seek my revenge."

"Lies, all lies." Lavinia's voice rose shrilly. "Can you name these ladies you claim he . . . he dallied with?"

"Lady Godwin was the first I knew of, almost a year after we married. A fleeting transgression that I forgave him for. Then a somewhat longer affair with the Countess of Alnwick, after which he was so contrite I forgave him again." How many more might she have forgiven him for but for Selena? "The one I could not forgive, will never forgive him for, was his affair with Selena Prothroe."

"Selena Prothroe?" Lavinia's jaw dropped. "Wasn't she . . ."

"The maid of honor at our wedding? Yes, and my friend since childhood." Had she any opportunity to do bodily or other harm to the deceitful Selena, she would have sold her soul to do so. Unfortunately, no such chance had presented itself. Yet. "She married soon after I did, to a man with much less exalted connections than Stephen. Perhaps she was jealous of me. I know she was smitten with Stephen. We both were. In the end I suspect no one could say who seduced whom."

"Why have I never heard of any of this?" The demanding tone in her sister-in-law's voice made Fanny want to laugh.

"God knows, Lavinia. Everyone else did. Except for his affair with Selena. In that instance Stephen exercised some discretion at least. Perhaps he believed if I found out I would not accept it quietly as I had the others. I might not have ever known of that dalliance except—"

Try as she might the memory of that night would always haunt her. Lying in their bed, her husband on top of her, riding her to a fiercely passionate conclusion, only to call out the wrong woman's name . . . Shaking her head to clear the image from her mind, Fanny drew a deep breath.

"Except what?"

"Except for a chance mention of her name. When the truth came out, I was hurt and angry enough to exact my own revenge on Stephen. Lord Lathbury had shown great interest in me before my marriage. I managed to kindle those feelings once more." Would that she could do so again. "We saw one another for almost four months; however, my conscience wouldn't let me continue the affair when he wished us to run away together and I broke it off. After I returned to Stephen, I discovered I was increasing and simply assumed the child was his. Until last month when I saw Ella and Lathbury together."

"Does Lord Lathbury know?" Her sister-in-law's words dripped ice.

"Yes."

"But he does not wish to marry the mother of his child?" The marchioness's frown transformed her face into a gargoyle's.

"He was incensed that I hadn't told him about her, even though I swore I didn't know. We quarreled and I have not heard a word from him since that day, so I assume he has done with me, despite his connection to Ella." Drained by the whole dismal recitation, Fanny sank onto the chaise. If she never had to rise again she'd be delighted.

"That at least is a blessing." Lavinia's pronouncement brought Fanny's head back up. "You can never marry Lord Lathbury, Frances. Do you not see that? If you and Ella lived with the man it would be inevitable that people would see them together and realize what you had done. The entire Tarkington family's reputation would be irreparably soiled. It is only by the grace of God no one has made the connection yet." The marchioness's eyes bore into Fanny. "We will not allow your misbehavior to ruin Theale, to make him and Stephen a laughingstock before the whole *ton.*"

Fanny winced. Lady Lathbury had told her the matter was of little consequence. She'd doubted it at the time, but had grown to hope it was true, as that would have made her marriage to Matthew much easier.

Lavinia's outrage at the situation, however, was completely genuine. Matthew's mother must have lied, as she had suspected, in order to get her to agree to marry him. By moving Ella into the country, she must have hoped the prying eyes of Society's gossips would not see the resemblance. At least now it seemed a moot point. Matthew had broken with her, likely for good.

Shaking off the dread that had taken hold of her, Fanny stared calmly back at her sister-in-law. Life for her in the Theale household from now on would be an unmitigated hell.

"Mark my words, Frances, Theale will hear of this outrage. Such a scandal has never touched our family and for you to do such a thing is unconscionable." Lavinia nodded so violently her cap came askew. She turned, heading for the doorway with a determined walk. "I tremble to think what Theale will do."

"Indeed, so do I when he hears." Spoiling to give the woman her comeuppance, Fanny tried to make her voice as sympathetic as possible. "He has been so . . . disturbed recently."

Her sister-in-law stopped and turned slowly around, her jaw clenched.

"Even the servants have spoken about his outbursts of anger and"—she hushed her voice—"other things." She shook her head. "I daresay something like this might unhinge him completely."

The color drained from Lavinia's face. She stared at Fanny, wringing her hands, then drew a deep, shuddering breath. "I had best get back to making arrangements for the family to gather here during the holidays." Lavinia backed toward the door. "It is rather inconvenient to spend it here where we have fewer rooms than at the estate in Northumberland; however, I will make accommodations." The marchioness sped out of the doorway, her heels clacking down the corridor until the sound was finally lost.

Fanny sat back in her seat, all her bravado fled. Tears trickled down her face and she let them fall. She would never marry Matthew now, that much was certain. Despite his mother's claims to the contrary, infidelity, and especially infidelity that resulted in a child not of her husband's body, must be an abomination. His own absence these past weeks proved he no longer wished to have anything to do with her. He would not risk the scandal their alliance would surely create.

Lavinia certainly believed disgrace was imminent. Fanny herself didn't recall hearing such things spoken of in *ton* circles, but then she'd paid less attention to gossip unless it concerned her own reputation. She'd been much more intent on the next *on-dit* that linked Stephen's name to another woman rather than one about what another woman was doing to her husband. Nevertheless, what she'd done had been a sin in the eyes of God and in the eyes of the *ton*. Her only doubt, in the end, was who would sit in stricter judgment of her.

# Chapter 23

As his valet put his cases down in the small dressing room adjoining the bedroom, Matthew stripped off his gloves, uneasy to be back in Wrotham. He'd been in two minds about attending Lady Cavendish and Wrotham's wedding in the first place. They were Fanny's friends more so than his, although his invitation had been addressed to him alone. He couldn't assume Fanny had told her friends about their estrangement, although if they had been informed it had not been reflected in his lodgings. Lyttlefield Park apparently housed friends of the bride and groom, while Wrotham Hall accommodated their family members. Despite that assignment, he'd arrived determined to be pleasant no matter what.

He should not have come at all, but he'd not been able to resist the chance to see Fanny again. His head had cooled long since the day he'd strode out of the receiving room at Theale House, incensed at her confession. Still, her absence from his life had made it a merry hell. He missed her every day, just as before, but would not allow himself to entertain the idea of seeing her again. Her betrayal bit deep into his soul, in a place reason couldn't reach. Once or twice he thought he'd caught a glimpse of her about London—shopping or the like, but had forced himself to ignore her. As a result, he'd been moody and ill-tempered to the staff at his town house, to members at his club, even to his family when they arrived in London for the Little Season. His refusal to accompany them to *ton* events had infuriated Beatrice and grieved his mother. But he'd feared a chance encounter with Fanny would shake his resolve.

Therefore, he didn't understand at all what he was doing in Kent, where he certainly would see her. Had that been the plan in his heart ever since he'd received the invitation? The urge to come to the wedding had been undeniable. Did that mean he was ready to talk with her? To take her back? Would she have him at this point? Never certain about anything regarding Fanny, Matthew sent up a prayer for a clear head and a steady hand.

Dinner that night was a lively event. Wedding guests and family had converged on Wrotham with a vengeance, causing some room mishaps in both houses. From Lord Brack he understood that his sister Lady Georgina had actually been moved from her room at Lyttlefield Park, where she'd resided for some time, to share a room with her brother. Upon hearing that, Lady Cavendish had instead proposed she give up her chamber to Lady Georgina and move into her soon-to-be-husband's suite. It had all been sorted out eventually, making for an amusing story and Wrotham's excellent wine and spirits had flowed well into the night. Matthew hadn't been able to speak to Fanny, although he'd admired her from the far end of the table.

Dressed in her favorite green, this time an emerald velvet that shone richly in the candlelight, she had laughed and talked with a handsome young man Matthew didn't know. Tinges of the green monster rose in him, jealous of the man's close proximity to Fanny. He'd better simply admit he was still besotted with the woman and be done with it. His heart beat madly whenever he gazed at her and any resolve he'd maintained in London had long crumbled. Best make his peace with her either tonight or before the service in the morning.

Having come to this conclusion, he allowed the evening's jocularity to raise his spirits and give him hope of a civil meeting between them on the morrow. What he wanted to say to her, however, still eluded him.

Next morning, turned out in a dark blue square-cut jacket, striped waistcoat, and pale gray trousers, Matthew stood in front of the tiny St. George's church in Wrotham village, gazing about for someone to talk to before heading into the church. Everyone hurried about, seeming bent on duties to which he was not privy, leaving him literally the odd man out in the proceedings. Almost of a mind to take his seat inside, Matthew paused as a carriage swept up before the door. Moments later Lady Georgina, Lady John, and Fanny alighted all chattering and laughing together.

The pang of remorse that shot through his heart made him wince. Beautiful as always, in a leaf green pelisse, she made every reason he should still be angry with her fly out of his head, as he'd known she would. He'd wanted to hold on to his anger, for not being told of her pregnancy, or about the existence of his daughter for the past six years had hurt abominably. Whether or not he believed she had not known seemed irrelevant. She should have realized it was a possibility from the beginning and informed him. Seeing her now, well, the need for her to admit she'd been wrong seemed childish. He started toward her, but she had turned together with her friends and headed into the church. No matter, he'd speak with her after the ceremony. A happy time when they might set their differences straight and look toward the future once more.

Wedding guests poured out of St. George's as though fleeing a dragon, though the cause for the exodus was thankfully much less dire. Mrs. Easton, apparently overcome by emotion at the wedding, had swooned. While she was being seen to by her group of friends, Matthew had taken charge and shepherded out as many wedding guests as he could, giving the tiny group huddled around Mrs. Easton the chance to revive her. The woman likely needed a bit of rest and some fresh air to set her to rights. Ladies, in his experience, swooned often and usually at the most inappropriate times.

Most of Lady Wrotham's family in attendance had left in their carriages while the local parishioners had set out on foot toward Wrotham Hall for the extravagant wedding breakfast prepared there. Matthew, however, elected to remain until Fanny emerged. Perhaps she would agree to ride back to Wrotham with him.

"I must say I did not expect to see you here today, Matthew."

He spun around to encounter hard blue eyes gazing at him from Fanny's unsmiling face. "Fanny. I . . . I'd hoped to see you here."

"You did? I might ask why." The harsh planes of her face retained their beauty, though it was a terrible beauty all the same. "A trip to Kent seems rather a lot of trouble to go to to see me when you could have made a ten-minute carriage ride to call on me in London." Her mouth hardened. "Why are you here, Matthew?"

"I wanted to know how you were doing. You and Ella."

Her delicate eyebrows swooping up, Fanny laughed. The shrill sound sent a shudder down his back. "After you abandoned us, you mean? Fine, we are just fine. Are you satisfied? I wish you a pleasant journey all the way back to London." She turned on her heel.

"Fanny." He grasped her elbow, spinning her back to him a bit more forcefully than he'd intended. The woman could infuriate him more than anyone of his acquaintance and still he wanted her. Proof of his love for her if ever there was one.

"I will ask you to release me before I cause a scene. One more sensational scene today will likely go unremarked, but one never knows. You might get the reputation you deserve after all."

"I had no idea my company was now so abhorrent to you." Releasing her arm, Matthew stepped back, hands raised. "Please forgive the mistake. It will not be repeated." Clenching his teeth to prevent railing at her even more, Matthew bowed and strode off in the direction of his carriage.

A quick trip back to Lyttlefield Park and a hasty retreat before the situation became even uglier. What had turned Fanny so completely against him? True, he'd not attempted to visit her in the past month, but after that confession at Theale House, how could she think he'd immediately wish to see her again? Neither had she attempted any contact with him during the ensuing six weeks. Was there something other than his lack of attendance on her mind? Had she perhaps had another offer of marriage and intended to accept it and so was breaking with him for once and all? Although it was early afternoon, by the time he could be packed, it would be too dark to leave. He would remain overnight and discover the truth behind her scorn if he could before leaving tomorrow. Forever.

Heart thumping all the way back to Charlotte's carriage, Fanny flung herself into the conveyance and burst into tears.

"Fanny! My dear, what has happened?" Elizabeth, who had revived, leaned forward and grabbed her hands.

"Are you all right? Are you hurt?" Putting her arms around Fanny's shoulders, Georgina hugged her tightly.

"My dear, was that Lord Lathbury?" Jane peered out the window. "What has he done?"

"Nothing." Wiping at her cheeks, Fanny tried to stem the flow, but the frustration of weeks of waiting for Matthew to contact her had built to a boiling point. His cavalier attitude just now had pushed her to goad him into that ill-considered action and now he would likely never speak to her again.

"This hardly seems nothing, Fanny. Here." Jane passed her a handkerchief. "He must have done something."

"We were to be married."

"What? How splendid, Fanny." Georgie squeezed her tighter.

"Why didn't you tell me?" Elizabeth gave her a chastened look. "I suspected this would happen after Brighton."

"You said 'were to be married.'" Jane sat back on the black leather seat. "Does that mean he's jilted you?"

"I wouldn't say jilt, for it was never properly announced; however, he apparently has no plans to marry me, because I picked a quarrel with him a few minutes ago. Now he'd rather die than marry me." Sobs tore from her throat, making it difficult to breathe.

"Why pick a quarrel with him in the first place, Fanny?" Jane frowned, still looking directly at her. "If you wanted to marry him, you should have avoided a quarrel, at least until you were married."

"I don't know. It seems so stupid now. But he hadn't called or written for almost six weeks and then he showed up here . . ." What had come over her? All she'd wanted to do when she'd seen him standing outside before the wedding was rail at him for not calling on her or even inquiring about Ella. She was his daughter and he couldn't trouble himself at all about her welfare. She'd told him the truth about Ella. If he couldn't accept that she didn't know her parentage until recently, then he needed to stay away from them. But that's not what she wanted either. Their predicament concerning Ella's parentage had also slipped her mind. Of course she couldn't marry Matthew, though she might die right here to think so.

Something was wrong with her. Her head had swirled in a muddle so she'd had to search and search to find Elizabeth's coat. It had slid under the pew when they were trying to revive her and by the time she'd retrieved it she'd come upon Elizabeth confessing to Jane that she was increasing. That explained Elizabeth's peculiar behavior in London and the reason for asking her help with Lord Brack, assuming he was the father.

She couldn't imagine who else it could be. Elizabeth hadn't looked at another man since she'd made Lord Brack's acquaintance in August. The way they'd kissed the night of the festival should have made it obvious, but she and Matthew had been quite occupied at the time to be gazing and remarking about the other people they'd stumbled over that night.

That night had been strange beyond belief. Charlotte and Nash, Elizabeth and Lord Brack, she and Matthew had all been wildly passionate after the crowning. The only time Elizabeth and Brack had indulged according to what she'd told Jane. Would Charlotte also catch with child that quickly? Thank goodness she'd been drinking her tea at the time. Else she might have . . .

"No." It wasn't possible. Not like last time when she'd not taken the tea toward the end. She hadn't stopped drinking it this time until two weeks after the last time she'd seen Matthew.

"What do you mean by 'no,' dear?" Jane's eyes were bright as a hawk's.

The woman was worse than a bird dog after a scent.

"Lord Lathbury has certainly showed up here. What is it you would deny?"

Fanny stared at her, trying hard to remember the last time she'd had her courses. She'd been so upset the past weeks that she'd not really paid attention to such things. There were other things she had noticed, however. A tiredness every morning when she awoke, as though she hadn't slept well. Sudden bouts of heat, like the one Elizabeth had had in church, where her head felt like a flame. Soreness in her breasts she'd thought caused by her courses, though her courses, she now realized, hadn't come on her since before her last journey to Kent. "My folly," she answered at last. "I may have driven Matthew away for good when I need him more than ever."

"Shall I speak to him this evening, Fanny?" Georgie laid her head on Fanny's shoulder once more. "I have managed in the past few months to help bring Charlotte and Nash together when they certainly seemed at odds with one another."

"Georgie, I do not think this is the time for such . . . measures." Elizabeth spoke up, shooting Fanny a worried look. "You look very pale, my dear. Are you sure you are all right?"

Scrubbing her hand over her face as the telltale heat flushed her cheeks, Fanny shook her head. All she wanted was the quiet of her room and some time to decide what to do . . . and when to do it. She must tell Matthew of her suspicions, although after this afternoon's encounter she had no idea if he would listen to her. "I simply need some time to rest, ladies. The wedding and Elizabeth's collapse would have been quite enough to stir one's emotions without the encounter with Matthew. I'll skip the breakfast, have the coachman take me back to Lyttlefield Park with Elizabeth, and rest in my room until dinner. I daresay all will be fine by then."

"If you are sure, my dear?" Staring at Fanny as though trying to see into her soul, Jane finally sighed. "I will come see to you first thing when I return to dress for dinner."

"And I, Fanny." Georgie nodded determinedly. "I will talk to Lord Lathbury during the breakfast if I can. Men always seem to want to confide in me."

Lord help her if Georgie managed to wheedle anything out of Matthew, although a confession of his love would not come amiss presently.

The graying light around the edges of the curtain was enough to wake Fanny, who blinked and stretched. She had needed that nap more than she'd known. Sinking back into the warm mattress, she dreaded rising to get ready for dinner and another confrontation with Matthew, but it must be faced. She sat up and lit the lamp beside her bed. Time to make herself as ravishing as possible and try to win back her love.

Slipping her feet to the floor, she padded over to the window and pulled the curtains back to stare out at the gray landscape, a few tendrils of fog twining around a carriage stopped in the driveway. A late return from the wedding breakfast? It must have been a merry time, one she was sorry to have missed, but her head was much clearer after her rest, ready to take on the world—or at least Matthew.

She pulled the bell rope beside her bed, and pondered which gown to choose. She'd yet to wear the green with gold overlay she'd bespoke after her shopping trip with Elizabeth early last month, before her troubles with Matthew had begun. She'd made it with him in mind, of course. A very fetching garment that accentuated her breasts, always the way to claim his attention. Wandering back to the window, she noted the carriage now heading down the driveway. Returning to Wrotham Hall, perhaps, though dinner was supposed to be here tonight. A ray of sun shot through the clouds, brightening the landscape and bouncing off the shiny black lacquered body of the disappearing carriage.

Brightening? Fanny peered out the window again. The light was getting brighter, not dimmer with the failing of the light as she'd supposed.

"Good morning, my lady." Sarah, the upstairs maid tending to her during this visit, suppressed a yawn. "You're up early this morning." She lifted a large pitcher. "I've brought your washing water."

"Morning?" Dazedly she turned around, the room getting lighter by the second. "It can't be morning. I was supposed to be awakened for dinner. Who let me sleep?"

"Lady Cavendish . . . that is Lady Wrotham. She gave orders you and Mrs. Easton were not to be disturbed last night. I came with a tray about ten o'clock, but you were still asleep, my lady, so I came away."

"Dear Lord." Fanny sat on the bed, her head spinning. She must dress and seek out Matthew without delay. Perhaps she could meet him in the breakfast room and beg a private interview. If he would give her the chance, she would gladly apologize for her behavior and words yesterday. Why must she ever act foolish when dealing with him? "Please fetch my green lutestring with the gold trim. Is anyone else stirring this early?"

"No, my lady. No one save the one gentleman who left just now." Sarah headed into the dressing room.

"Which gentleman?" Dread seized Fanny's heart. It couldn't be . . .

"Lord Lathbury, my lady," she called from within the chamber. "He didn't wait for breakfast. His gentleman said he wanted an early start for London."

All the strength draining out of her, Fanny sank onto the bed. There was an end to it. He obviously did not wish to see her. That much was dreadfully clear. And yet, she must see him, tell him her suspicions, and pray that he would take pity on her and marry her. If he would not, she had no hope of avoiding the scandal of bearing a bastard child.

"On second thought, Sarah, bring my blue traveling dress. I believe I too must set out for London posthaste." If she did not overtake him on the road, she would seek an interview with him tomorrow in Town. She could not allow this impending disaster to hang over her head for very long. Her life, along with Ella's and this child's, were now irreparably linked to Matthew's. Pray God he did not fail them now.

# Chapter 24

Weary enough to drop down where she stood, Fanny knocked on the door at Theale House after an all-day journey in the carriage. Try though she might, she'd never met Matthew at any of the coaching inns where they'd changed horses. Perhaps he changed his less frequently or simply chose different inns. At any rate, she'd have to write to him tomorrow and ask for an interview. If he refused the audience or didn't answer her at all, she didn't know what she would do.

The butler opened the door and Fanny trudged in. "Thank you, Noyes. Can you please have Cook send me up something on a tray? I'm not very hungry, but I'm so fagged I cannot see straight."

"Lord and Lady Theale are in the drawing room, my lady. His lordship requested that if you happened to arrive this evening, I was to direct you to him." Noyes took her pelisse and bonnet and bowed.

"Very well." Straightening out her travel-stained gown as best she could, Fanny headed toward the odious room. Why couldn't the summons have come tomorrow, once she'd gotten the rest she so desperately needed? She'd dozed most of the day in the carriage, but it felt as though she hadn't slept in days. Mounting the stairs by dint of will alone, she dragged herself down the corridor to the family's gathering place. Best get this over with. She hadn't a clue what the summons was for. Likely something to do with the coming Christmas holiday.

The door had been left ajar so she walked in. Theale and Lavinia were seated side by side, Lavinia on her "throne," her husband on an old tufted, black leather chair that had seen much service. The two shared a glance when Fanny marched toward them.

"Lady Stephen," Theale intoned in his gravelly voice. "Will you be seated, please?" He indicated a smaller chair, drawn up before the two of them.

Like an inquisition. Somehow she doubted now this tête-a-tête had anything to do with the holidays. Warily, she lowered herself onto the chair, gaze flickering from one unfriendly face to the other. "Good evening, Theale, Lavinia. I am just this instant returned from Charlotte's wedding in Kent." She made sure to let them know she'd been travelling all day long. "Thank you so much for the loan of the second carriage. It made the long journey that much more pleasant."

"Well I hope something pleased you, my lady, for nothing about you pleases me." Theale's voice cracked from the vehemence in it.

"I beg your pardon, my lord?" Fanny remembered the servants' conversations about Theale doing and saying strange things. Perhaps this was more of the same. "How have I displeased you?"

"Harlot!"

The exclamation, thrown directly at her from Theale's distorted mouth, stabbed her like a knife. Shocked, she drew back in the chair, as though she'd been slapped. "What?"

"Do you deny it? Lady Theale has told me about your confession to her. That you had an affair with another man while you were married to Stephen. You had a child by him and foisted his by-blow off on my brother."

Grasping her throat, her pulse beating wildly beneath her fingers, Fanny stared at her sister-in-law, absurdly hurt and angry at herself. The betrayal astonished her, for she'd believed her threat about Theale's sanity should have sealed Lavinia's lips. It could even be true. Her brother-in-law's eyes seemed ready to pop out of his head. He reminded Fanny of nothing so much as a big bullfrog sitting in the chair. His gaze wandered, darting to and fro, as if suspicious of something or constantly searching for some danger. Worst of all, a thin stream of drool crept out of the side of his mouth.

Fanny narrowed her eyes and stared Lavinia down. "What I told the marchioness, I told her in confidence. I am very disappointed to find myself betrayed."

"I decided the family must come first, Frances. The betrayal was yours alone." Lavinia shot a glance at Theale, then slid into the farthest corner of her chair. "I asked him if what you'd said was true, about Stephen. And the other women. You said he would know. Then he asked me why I asked about such an unfit thing for a lady's ears, and I told him what you'd said." The marchioness's voice died away and she turned to stare wide-eyed at her husband. "I'd never have said such a thing, my dear, if Fanny hadn't told me first."

"So you will allow your wickedness corrupt my wife?" Doddering, he rose out of the chair, fist raised in the air. "You'll see what I can do. You'll be sorry you ever cuckolded my poor brother."

"Poor brother?" Outraged at that characterization of her philandering husband, Fanny unclenched her hands, and gripped the chair, holding herself back from the devil. "Your brother was poor in nothing, save Christian charity and the ability to keep his wedding vows. Otherwise he had all the wealth he could want, a career he loved for its excitement, and a wife who wanted nothing more than for him to come home to her at the end of the day. Your brother lacked for nothing, Lord Theale, save human decency."

Waving a hand, Theale scoffed at her. "Merely a high-spirited boy sowing his wild oats."

"You call blatant affairs with women of Society, under the very nose of his wife, 'wild oats'?" Unaware of how she'd gotten there, Fanny stood in front of Theale's chair, her fists clamped in balls that hurt where her nails dug into her flesh, restraining herself from planting the old scoundrel a facer. "If you call having sexual congress in my bed, with a woman who was supposed to be my friend, 'sowing wild oats' then I say, 'As you sow so shall you reap.' " Her voice bounced off the ceiling and echoed down the corridor.

At a gasp from Lavinia, Fanny whirled on her. "No, I didn't tell you that little piece of the story, my lady." She stabbed an accusatory finger at Theale. "His brother violated this house, your home, by bringing that woman here."

"You lie." Theale squinted at her, but his tone had no bite. She'd wondered, over the years, if her brother-in-law had been privy to the details of the affair. Too much had hinged on the family's absence for him not to know.

"I do not. The family had removed to Northumberland early for the Christmas season that year. Stephen was on maneuvers so we weren't coming to you until later. I had gone to stay with my parents rather than remain alone in the house. So Stephen brought her here."

Tears of rage and grief trickled down her face. After all these years, the anguish of that betrayal had not diminished.

"You cannot know that."

"I do know it. My husband very happily confessed to it, after I'd found him out. He seemed to delight in torturing me with the details. So do not tell me that Stephen Tarkington didn't deserve his cuckold's horns. I only wish he'd learned the extent of them, that Ella wasn't his. My affair with Lord Lathbury was at least discreet—neither you, nor Lavinia, nor Stephen nor apparently anyone else in the *ton* knew of it until now. It would have been so easy for us to let them know. Lathbury urged me to run away with him." She dug the dagger even deeper into Theale's heart. "How badly would that scandal have tarnished the family reputation if I had agreed and all the dirty details had come out? You should be thanking me for my mercy. I know I would have been a happier woman had I left."

"Then I will make you supremely happy now, my lady." Theale fixed her with a baleful eye. "You, and your fraudulent offspring, will leave this house immediately, never to return."

"What? You cannot do that." Startled, Fanny took a step back. "My settlement specifically states—"

"Settlement be damned." He pounded the arms of the chair like a child in a rage, his face turning an alarming shade of red. "When you dishonored your husband you forfeited all rights to his bed and board. If you wish to contest it, I suggest you seek justice in the courts. In the meanwhile, pack your things. I'll send them after you."

"You will turn me and my daughter out in the streets in the middle of the night? And just what will the *ton* make of that, my lord? Especially when I tell them why I am being summarily turned out?" The threat was empty. She wanted the circumstances of Ella's birth exposed about as much as Theale did. Fortunately, he didn't know that.

Lavinia laid a hand on her husband's arm and leaned toward him. She whispered something in his ear, and the color in his face ebbed a bit.

"The marchioness has graciously suggested that you be allowed to spend a single additional night here, to put your affairs in order. Pack your trunks and your daughter's. Make arrangements for where you will go and I will see your things sent along behind you. In the morning, Davies will take you in the small carriage and be done with you."

"Thank you so much, my lord. You are too kind." Turning on her heel, Fanny stalked from the room, fuming at the man who would rather act dishonorably than admit the wrongdoing of his brother. Fine, she would shake the dust of this house from her shoes and be glad of it.

Picking up her skirts, she raced up the stairs, her head spinning with all the preparations she must make. First, she must write to her cousin in Copsale, alerting her to her impending arrival. She wished she were confident enough to have the coachman take her directly to Hunt House, but caution stayed her from that line of action. She didn't like to imagine that Matthew would turn her and Ella away; however, they were currently at such great odds, it might be best to simply write to him.

Once in her room, the idea of having to pack up every possession, both hers and Ella's, was more than daunting in her exhausted condition. If she did it quietly, perhaps she could enlist the help of one of the housemaids to help her get the trunks ready. With trembling fingers, she rang the bell. By the time the maid arrived, Fanny had just finished mending her pen.

"You rang, my lady?" The girl, one of the many maids assigned to attend to Fanny's needs, curtsied and looked away. So the staff had already heard of her departure.

"Yes, Meg. Would you please have Thomas fetch my traveling trunks here? Miss Ella's should be taken to her room as well. And then can you help pack Miss Ella's clothing and toys?" Fanny drew the sheets of paper out of her letter box. "I must attend to some letters, but will find you shortly."

With a fearful glance out the door, Meg nodded, then turned and scampered off, bent on delivering her message. All the better to be able to write her letters in peace. The first one took little time to compose. Her cousin was a sweet woman whose large family kept her ever busy. She would welcome Fanny and Ella, but they dare not stay long with the family in such straitened circumstances. Setting the first letter aside to dry, Fanny drew another piece of foolscap to her. How on earth did she begin such a letter?

She must write from her heart. Was she sorry for her behavior in Kent? Yes. Was she sorry he'd not known about Ella from the beginning? Of course. He must know these things already. Did she love him? With all her heart. Had she ever told him so? Perhaps once. Was it time for her to do so again? Absolutely. The pen flew over the paper, her hand pouring out the words her mouth could not say easily.

Still, her most urgent message she hesitated to write. A nagging suspicion that her brother-in-law might open the letter forced her to be prudent. No telling what he might do should he find out how matters now stood with her. She'd never seen him as incensed as this evening. Not only angry at her past betrayal of Stephen, but enraged at her suggestion of the possible disgrace she could heap on the Tarkington family itself. Thank goodness she would soon be away from his sphere of influence. Besides, she wanted to inform Matthew she was increasing while she could look into his eyes. Then she would know if he rejoiced in the news or whether he accepted it as mere duty.

Carefully, she sanded then folded the sheet, fastening it with her red wax and the embellished "T" seal. As proud as she had been to first use that seal, now she longed to change it for the "L" designating Lathbury. If only Matthew would propose again, he'd not be disappointed with her answer. Pray God he followed her to Copsale to allow that last chance.

# Chapter 25

The sun had just peeked over the horizon when Fanny, holding Ella firmly by the hand in the heavy, damp air, climbed into Theale's coach the next morning. Days were now so short, the morning's activities had been well begun before it became light enough to begin their travel. Though she'd insisted Ella eat a hearty breakfast, Fanny had only had a cup of chocolate with a piece of bread and butter. She might feel more like eating once they had boarded the stage coach and stopped at the first leg of their journey. They had packed all their necessary things into one small trunk, much more manageable on a public coach. The larger trunks would be sent to Copsale, presumably by other conveyance.

Settling Ella on the plush seat beside her, Fanny wished for the heated bricks at her feet she'd always had on her other journeys. This morning, of course, they would not go far enough to warrant them and would certainly not have such a luxury on the stage coach. She pulled a warm blue carriage blanket around Ella, who yawned and snuggled beside her. "It will have to be a short nap, my love."

The child nodded and burrowed deeper into Fanny's side.

Slumping into the seat, Fanny attempted to relax as well. Her letters had been given to Meg for early morning posting. If she was lucky, her cousin would get a few hours' notice of her arrival before she actually appeared on her doorstep. And Matthew would know her whereabouts even sooner, as she believed him still in Town. If he heeded her summons might he actually overtake them on the road? A happy daydream of Matthew sweeping them both into his carriage and taking them off to Hunter's Cross ensued until she glanced out the window at the unfamiliar buildings. Surely the inn where she would get the coach would be closer to the bustling center of the city. She moved the sleeping child over to lie on the seat and stood slightly to rap on the trap. "Davies."

She sat back down and the trap opened. The middle-aged coachman bundled up in coat, hat, and gloves against the cold peered down at her. "Yes, my lady?"

"Have we missed the stage coach station? I wouldn't think it so far from the city's center."

"No, my lady. You're not wrong about that; however, his lordship instructed me to take you to Copsale myself rather than put you and the child on the coach. Chancy things are stage coaches. Our first change is at the Duke of Welling Inn in Mickleham, about two hours now." With a nod of his head, he lowered the trap door and Fanny sat back, pleased and surprised by Theale's unexpected largesse.

Perhaps he'd had a softening of his heart, although she'd rather lay odds that Lavinia had talked him into this kindness. Surprising, considered their stormy skirmishes throughout the years. Of course, it likely stemmed from the marchioness's fondness for Ella rather than any sympathetic feelings for her. Whatever the circumstance, Fanny thanked her sister-in-law with all her heart. She drew Ella back to her and pulled the blanket over them both, relaxing enough to allow her utter fatigue to claim her at last.

Spreading marmalade on a piece of toast, Matthew contemplated the half-eaten plate of food before him with loathing. The smoked herring had been too salty, the sausages burned, the cold veal pie a congealed mess, and now he feared the toast would be stale. Nothing tasted right this morning. Nothing had been right ever since he had broken with Fanny.

He'd fled Lyttlefield Park at first light, still incensed by Fanny's high-handed manner. The carriage had made excellent time, due to a lucky decision to give the Three Pigeons his custom. They had been able to change the horses immediately, thus continuing without any significant loss of time. Once they'd arrived at Hunt House mid-afternoon, he'd called around to his club, but it was deadly dull. Most chaps had already left Town for their country estates for Christmas, which it was high time he did as well.

Although he had planned to leave for Hunter's Cross this morning after breakfast, he found himself dragging his feet. Thinking about Fanny and their latest quarrel. Perhaps he'd been wrong to have waited to see her. It must look to her as though he'd abandoned her and Ella, but that wasn't true. He'd simply needed time to wrap his head around the notion that Ella was his actual daughter, an amazing notion when he stopped to think about it. Even if he had missed much of her babyhood, he could still be a part of her life forever, if he only could make peace with her mother.

Even after his ire over the situation had cooled, his desire for Fanny certainly hadn't. Seeing her in Kent had answered that question once and for all, for he'd been uncomfortably aroused during the wedding ceremony, thinking that if it had been their ceremony he'd have forsworn the wedding breakfast and spirited her away to ravish his bride without a thought for propriety. Their argument had cooled his ardor, but only for as long as it had taken him to arrive back at his empty town house. He wanted to be married to Fanny, and no other.

Tossing his napkin over his ill-fated breakfast, Matthew rose, determined to make an end to his misery. Had Fanny left yesterday as most of the guests had planned to do? If his luck was in, she might be breakfasting at Theale House this very moment. He'd send a note, asking to call. Striding out of the room, in search of his writing materials, Matthew halted in the corridor. Plague take it, he wanted more action than writing a damned note. He stepped back into the breakfast room and rang the bell.

Upton appeared precisely a minute later. "Yes, my lord?"

"Have my horse brought round the front. I need to go out this morning after all."

"Very good, my lord."

Matthew raced up the stairs to his suite to change into riding boots. A short ride would tell him if

Fanny were home or not. If so, he would insist on seeing her and would not leave until they had reached an accord. If she had not arrived yet, he'd continue to Hyde Park and work off his excess energy there on Spartan. Whistling a bawdy drinking tune, he blew into his empty chamber. It might be empty now, but by God it wasn't going to be for much longer.

The slowing carriage woke Fanny, who stretched and sat up. They were pulling into a coaching inn to change the horses. She'd ask to go in for a few minutes, to get some tea and bread and butter for her and Ella. She rubbed the child's back. "Wake up, sleepy head."

With an amazing yawn, Ella sat up. "Where are we, Mama?"

"At a place called the Duke of Wellington Inn, my love. Do you see the sign?" She pointed at the placard hanging over the door with the duke's coat of arms painted on it. "We are here to change the horses and stretch our legs. Want to come with me to find something to eat?"

The child nodded happily, and Fanny pulled her coat around her, then helped her from the carriage. "We will be back shortly, Davies," she called as they trudged across the cold courtyard.

Presently she and Ella were sipping tea and chatting over a plum tart, although Fanny could only nibble hers. The swaying motion of the carriage had made her stomach queasy, likely because of the child. Another child for her and Matthew. It scarcely seemed possible. She must pray very hard that he forgive her folly and come to her in Copsale. The alternative, to bear this child without benefit of a husband, she refused to think of.

They finished quickly, then stood for a moment, stretching their legs before returning to the carriage. The sun was not quite directly overhead as they swept out of the inn yard. Still many hours of travel ahead of them. Perhaps she could take her mind off of Matthew and her queasy stomach. "Shall we sing songs for a while, Ella?"

"Oh, yes, Mama." The girl sat up straight, blue eyes sparkling. "What shall we sing? Do you know 'London Bridge'?"

"Yes, lovey. Why don't you start it?"

They whiled away the hours singing and playing clapping games until Ella fell asleep again, leaving Fanny to drowse against the carriage door until she roused when they stopped at another inn, the Chequers in Southwater. Again she and Ella went in although this time Fanny requested a room for an hour so she and Ella could use the necessary, wash up, and have a real meal.

All too soon they were back in the carriage, now a bit more uncomfortable than before from the weariness of travel, and on their way on the last leg of the journey. By Fanny's estimation, they should arrive at her cousin's home in Copsale in time for tea. Nothing would be more welcome than to cease moving and truly rest. She did hope Cousin Harriet had received her note. Otherwise she and Ella would be quite the surprise.

Fanny must have dozed off again, for the slowing of the carriage made her eyes flutter open. She sat up, moving Ella who slept with her head in her mother's lap.

"Are we here?" She spoke aloud, easing her daughter onto the seat beside her. Expecting a row of houses, she peered out of the window. To her surprise, all she saw were trees in the afternoon sunlight. Peering and squinting to see in front of the carriage, she could discover no reason why they should have stopped. Had the horse thrown a shoe? The carriage seemed level, so they likely hadn't broken a wheel. She knocked on the trap. "Davies! What seems to be the matter?"

The carriage door nearest her opened and the coachman peered in.

"Why have we stopped?"

"You need to get out, my lady." He shot his hand forward and grabbed her wrist.

"What? No! Let me go!" Fanny pulled against him, outraged. Had the man gone stark staring mad? "What are you doing?"

Releasing her arm, he threw her back against the seat and grabbed Ella instead, who shrieked and tried to scoot backward.

"No!" Fanny lunged at him, striking him on his shoulder.

He flung her off, slid his arms around Ella, and hoisted her into the air. She kicked out wildly, her heels striking him in his chest. Still nothing deterred him and he dragged the child out of the carriage and dumped her onto the grass.

"Lord Theale will have your guts for garters when I tell him what you have done." Fanny scrambled out the door and swooped down, putting her arms around her weeping child. "He has never brooked such disrespect from his servants."

"Little you know about it, my lady." The man sneered and dragged her small trunk from the back of the carriage. "His lordship was the one told me to do this."

"What? He never would have ordered such a thing." A trickle of fear slid down her spine, however. Theale had been incensed by her infidelity to Stephen. Would he have gotten his revenge in such a horrible fashion?

"Seems he did." Davies dropped the trunk in front of her. The lock popped open and some of her clothing fell onto the grass. "He said when I left you to tell you this was with his compliments and a fitting end for a disloyal wife." With those words, the coachman leaped back up onto the box, gathered the ribbons, and started the horses. They turned neatly in the field—Fanny shielded Ella as the carriage careened on the uneven grass behind them—then steered back onto the road and disappeared in a cloud of dust.

"Mama, where's he going? Why is he going without us?" Ella's tearstained face stared up into her own.

"Someone has played a very nasty trick on us, lovey. Here, let's get up from the cold ground." Fanny helped Ella to her feet, then stuffed her clothing back into the trunk. Once it shut, she sat down on the lid, all the strength running out of her legs. She stared down the road at the vanishing carriage, hatred for her brother-in-law raging forth as she called every evil curse she could think of down on his head. How could Theale do something like this to her? To her child? The old scoundrel must be deranged.

"What are we going to do, Mama?"

Their prospects were bleak at best. The road was empty and though the sun still shone, night would come all too soon. Still, she must put on a good face for Ella. She didn't want her daughter to be afraid. "Let Mama catch her breath, my love. I'll think of something."

# Chapter 26

Having handed his horse to a groom, Matthew ran lightly up the steps of the portico, raised the shiny brass lion's head knocker, and let it fall with a series of loud *booms* on the plate beneath. Theale House sat on the far end of Hanover Square in Mayfair, an imposing three-story structure of whitewashed brick that had stood since the square had been created almost a hundred years before. A more prestigious address would be hard to find.

The door opened on an impeccably attired butler. The marquess had the reputation of being a stickler, insisting everything be perfectly correct, from his servants' livery, to his house's door knocker, to his pedigreed wife, to his own flawless dress.

"Good morning, my lord." The man bowed, a precise movement that he must practice in his spare time.

"Good morning. I am Lord Lathbury. Might I inquire if Lady Stephen is at home?" Matthew stood poised to continue into the house.

The little man's mouth tightened. "I am sorry, my lord, but I have been instructed to give no information about the lady."

What the devil? Frowning, Matthew stepped back. "You cannot tell me if she is here? I believed she would have arrived yesterday."

"I am sorry, but I cannot say." The butler refused to meet Matthew's eyes.

This was all deucedly odd. What had happened to Fanny? Cocking his head, Matthew stepped toward the somewhat flustered butler. "Who has given you this instruction? Your master?"

"That is correct, my lord." Fear shown in the man's wide eyes, almost completely white with only a dot of brown in the centers. So Theale was behind whatever had happened to Fanny.

"You refuse to tell me where she is." Matthew pushed inside the doorway, the butler giving ground immediately.

"I am sure I don't know where she is, my lord." The small man put up a hand as though to ward off a blow.

"Then who would know?" Taking shameless advantage of his height and size, Matthew loomed menacingly over the man now cowering before him.

"His lordship." The whimper was almost too low to hear.

Something was terribly wrong. A pit opened up in Matthew's stomach. "Take me to him."

The butler closed the door and scurried away, all his former aplomb dashed to bits. He led Matthew down the corridor, finally stopping in front of what looked like a library or study from the glimpse he got of shelves of books. Trying to shake off his unease, the man straightened his coat, raised his chin, and marched into the chamber. "Lord Lathbury."

Striding in, Matthew assumed an air of disregard, as though he had no care in the world. He'd made the acquaintance of the marquess many years ago, though they had not met for some time now. A much older-looking Theale, cheeks jowly with deep lines about the mouth, sat behind a long desk at one end of the cramped room, in an overly large chair that seemed to diminish him further. A fire crackled in the grate behind him, framing him in flames. He bowed. "Lord Theale."

Narrowed eyes met him over a mouth that snarled. "You are bold as brass to come here, Lathbury. Did you think that strumpet who married my brother didn't tell me of her perfidy with you?"

Hair bristling on his neck, Matthew clenched his hands, lest his temper get the better of him. For sixpence he'd drive his fist through the marquess's sneering face. "I will thank you to keep a civil tongue in your head, my lord."

"You dare preach to me? Defiler of wives. Seducer of happily married women." Theale seemed about to warm to his subject.

Matthew cut him short. "I don't give a tinker's damn what you say about me. You're more than likely right, although I'd not say that Fanny was ever a happily married woman." He held up a hand to stay Theale's protest. "But she is a sweet, loving, and kind lady and you will not abuse her either behind her back or to her face. Not while I am within earshot of you." He grinned. "My lord."

Theale beat upon the arm of the chair. "Do you deny you cuckolded my brother?"

"Why bother to deny what you already know?" Matthew shrugged. "I comforted Fanny when her husband had hurt her most grievously. He had a treasure that he threw away with both hands. Do not blame me if I saw its worth and picked it up for my own." Pray God he had not thrown the treasure away as well. "And why blame Fanny? Your brother was certainly no saint. His infidelities were legendary, both in scope and number. All the *ton* knew what he was. It's only a pity Fanny did not until it was too late."

"You will not disparage Stephen in this house! I will not hear it." Rising from his chair, the marquess shook with anger.

"Then I suggest you stop your ears, because I intend to enlighten you about your precious brother, although I suspect you already know about his escapades." If the marquess didn't know the extent of the merry hell his brother had fashioned for Fanny, by Jove he shortly would.

Theale held up a hand. "Spare me your sputterings. Of course I knew about Stephen's indiscretions. Some from him directly, some from rumors in the *ton*. He was a man. A man has needs beyond the marriage bed."

"Not all men." Matthew cocked an eyebrow. "Or do you speak from experience, my lord? I've never heard your name bandied about in the *on-dits* of *tonnish* circles, but perhaps you've been very discreet as well."

"By God, you are impertinent, sir!" Red splotches appeared on Theale's face as his eyes seemed ready to pop from his head.

Much as he despised the man for ignoring Fanny's pain, he didn't want the marquess to have an apoplexy—at least not until he'd told him of Fanny's whereabouts. "I have done with you, my lord, if you will kindly tell me where Fanny is, I will remove myself before my impertinence grows."

The marquess's lips cracked open in a mirthless laugh. "You can go to the devil, and that harlot with you, if you can find her. I have no idea where she is at the moment. Running from you, perhaps?"

A qualm of doubt flickered across Matthew's mind, then he brushed it away. Fanny would not have done such a thing and left Ella behind in this house. If Ella was here. There was one way to find out. "Doubtless running from you, I suspect. Did she take *our* daughter with her?"

Theale leaped up as though the chair had catapulted him. "Do not mention that bastard spawn to me. I rejoice in one thing alone—that Stephen did not live to hear that his daughter was your by-blow."

Though cringing at the word, Matthew made himself affect a more casual attitude. "As I intend to acknowledge her as my child, I would like to see her now, if I may."

"No." The clipped word spoke volumes.

"She *is* my daughter."

"Not under the law."

"I would think you'd like to rid yourself of her," now to deal the most punishing blow, "since she's no part of Stephen at all. In almost ten years of marriage he couldn't quite pass muster in the getting of children, could he?"

"You filthy cur. How dare you—"

"Tell me where Fanny and Ella are and I will be happy to leave." Matthew placed his hands on the desk and leaned forward.

"You'll do as I tell you, happy or not," the marquess snapped. He opened a desk drawer and withdrew two letters.

Recognizing Fanny's handwriting, Matthew's heart skipped a beat.

"The strumpet gave these letters to a maid to be delivered this morning. Good thing the girl knows who holds the purse strings in this house and gave them directly to me. One"—Theale waved the folded letter as though it were a flag—"is of little importance to anyone." He tossed it over his shoulder and it landed in the fire.

Matthew raised up, trying to make out the direction, but it had fallen facedown and all he glimpsed was the blob of red sealing wax, already beginning to bubble in the intense heat.

"The other one, however, may have some value to you." The marquess held it up.

Heart hammering, Matthew read his own name and direction. "I'll have that, my lord, as it's addressed to me."

"Yes, I'm sure you would like to get your hands on it." Smiling, the older man caressed the paper, running his fingers around the precise edges. "I've no doubt she wrote telling you where to meet her. Once a harlot, always a harlot."

Matthew lunged for the letter.

The marquess whipped a diamond-tipped cane up from his side, striking Matthew squarely in the stomach. The blow was weak, but unexpected and he went staggering backward. "Pity you won't be able to find her." With a cackle, Theale turned and tossed the letter into the flames. "My justice is swift. I wager she's sorry she dishonored my family now."

"What have you done with her?" Straining over the desk, Matthew seized the marquess's shoulders and shook him like a terrier with a rat. "Where is she and my daughter?" It took all of Matthew's strength of will to refrain from seizing the man by the throat and snapping his neck like a stick of kindling. He threw the evil lord back into the chair.

Theale straightened his coat, eyed him, and continued his raucous laughter.

A measure of dread filled Matthew's heart. What had this fiend done with Fanny? "If any harm has come to her or her child, old man, I vow by all that is holy I will see you crackling in the flames of hell."

Spinning on his heel, Matthew strode out, the sinister laughter unnerving him further. What had this lunatic done? If neither Fanny nor Ella were in the town house, then Fanny must have arrived yesterday and been sent away this morning. How could he find out for certain they were not still here? He could barge upstairs, but he had no idea where their rooms might be. Constables could be called to restrain him and he couldn't afford to lose either time or his freedom. If Theale's menacing demeanor was an indication of his abhorrence of her, Fanny might have need of him even now. The butler was obviously of no use to him, nor the servants in general. They lived with the marquess and likely understood his rages all too well.

The grooms, however, might be a different story. He'd fetch Spartan and discover what he could in the stables.

Matthew walked around to the mews at the back of the house and entered the stable where he'd left his horse scarcely a quarter of an hour ago. A lifetime ago it seemed. Smiling and again affecting a nonchalant demeanor, he entered the stable.

A stable lad of about fifteen bounded up to him. "Can I help you, milord?"

"Yes, I believe you can. I left my horse a short time ago but my business is conducted so I need him now." Matthew cast his gaze around as the rich familiar smells of leather, straw, and manure proclaimed a well-run establishment. "Where is Spartan?"

"The tall bay, milord? Harry's walking him up and down the mews, cooling him down a bit." The lad sounded eager to please.

Matthew hoped that was the case. He drew out a bright gold sovereign and began to flip it in the air. "You seem like a lad clever with horses. What's your name?"

"William Carter, milord. They call me Will." The boy tried to look him in the eyes when he spoke, but his gaze kept straying to the flashing gold coin.

"Will. A good, honest name. And you could tell me, Will, about the horses and carriages Lord Theale has, is that right?" A soft, interested tone worked wonders for gathering information. Of course, so did the sight of money.

"Oh, yes, milord. I've been with his lordship almost three years. You can ask me anything about his equipage."

"I see these two large carriages here, so he must have at least six horses, I'd say?"

"Ten horses all told, milord." Pride in his master's wealth made Will's eyes bright.

"Ten horses, indeed." Matthew started down the row of stalls. "There's a pair of grays, a pair of bays . . . these three blacks and a dappled mare." Rubbing the mare's nose, Matthew turned back to the lad. "But that's only eight."

"There's two lighter grays out with the small carriage."

"Ah. That explains it. I daresay Lady Theale is tooling about the park. It's a brilliant day for it, if a bit chilly."

"Oh, no, milord. Davies took Lady Stephen and her daughter out early this morning."

"Did he?" The sovereign landed in Matthew's hand and it was all he could do not to squeeze it in his fist. Damn Theale. Had he sent them away or had Fanny gone of her own accord? He held the coin out to Will. "Did Davies say where they were going?"

"Here we go, Will. I'd say he's cooled down enough." Harry had returned, leading Spartan. An older lad of perhaps twenty, he looked Matthew up and down, his gaze coming to rest on the coin in his hand. "What's this, Will?"

Slowly, Matthew closed his hand over the gold and stared idly at the lad.

"Nothing, Harry." Will grabbed the reins from the other groom and ran a sure hand over the horse's flanks. "His lordship was waiting for his horse. Right as rain, milord. He's fit for anything you set him at."

"Very good, Will." Damn, he'd been so close. Without the direction, however, he might just as well sit at home and wait for Fanny to call on him. She'd wanted to tell him something; the letter Theale had burned proved it. Why write if only to say "I'm going away, don't follow me"? Now he might never know what had happened to her. Burning with frustration, he took the reins from Will and put his foot up in the stirrup.

"Beg pardon, milord, but you should see this place on your saddle girth." Will's eyes looked innocently up at him. Too innocent.

"Of course." Hope dawning, Mathew hopped back down, following Will around to the far side of Spartan.

"I saw this worn place when you left him with us. Right here." Will pointed to a perfectly smooth section of the leather girth. "I'm not sure what could have happened to it." The boy lowered his voice. "They were heading for Copsale, Davies said. By the post road."

Relief swept through Matthew and he drew a deep breath in thanksgiving. "Thank you so much, Will. I'll postpone my trip and have that replaced today. Good lad." Matthew flipped him the coin, and swung into the saddle. "Good day to you, lads."

"I didn't see no worn place." Harry poked Will with his elbow.

"Then you need sharper eyes, Harry."

Smiling, Matthew trotted Spartan out into the cobbled lane of the mews. Copsale was almost a day's ride to the south and a bit east from London. The sun stood directly overhead now. If she'd left at first light she had perhaps a four-hour head start on him; if he was lucky only three, accounting for the stops to change horses. He could push the big bay a bit so at a canter he might overtake her before nightfall. If he did not, he had no idea with whom she planned to stay in Copsale. Little matter. Turning the horse toward the south, he set out at a brisk trot. If he had to knock on every single door in Copsale, he would find his lady and their child.

# Chapter 27

Forcing herself to rise, Fanny peered down the road at the vanishing carriage. So help her if she ever saw Theale again she would haul off and slap him for doing this. A nice, meaty slap that would leave her handprint on his withered cheek for a good long while. The fanciful thought buoyed her for a moment, but grim reality lay all around her. She was stranded in the middle of a field, miles from either Southwater or Copsale, late in the afternoon of a cold day with a young child. Time for her hero to appear, like they did in those bad Drury Lane plays, just in the nick of time.

Where might her hero be? If Matthew had received her letter, might he not be pelting down the post road even now toward her? Despite the foolishness of the whim, she walked to the road and stared down it, looking for him. If wishes could come true she'd hear his hoof beats and he'd appear to sweep her and Ella up onto his white charger, just like in the children's stories. Unfortunately, she had no idea that even if he'd received the letter he'd come to Copsale.

And then, of course, villains also might ride into sight. That practical thought sobered Fanny quickly and she headed back to her daughter. She must find some place for them to hide until Matthew, or some other kind soul, could come to their rescue. Kneeling down before the trunk, she opened it and began rummaging around.

Ah, there it was. Her jewelry box. Not that she owned many costly pieces. None of the family jewels came to the wife of a third son, but Stephen had bought her a few good pieces. She gathered them in her reticule, a jeweled hair comb, a pearl and emerald broach with matching earrings, and a sapphire ring. All the rest was paste and she closed the box on it. This should be enough that if they found an inn she could barter for food and a night's lodgings as they waited for Matthew to come.

"What are we doing, Mama?" Ella had been quiet so long, Fanny jumped at the sound of her voice.

"You startled me, lovey. We are going to have to take a very long walk in just a little bit." What else in the trunk might she use? Poking through the jumbled things she'd thrown together last night, she wished first for something warm. The cold had begun to seep through her heavy traveling gown and she was certain Ella must be chilly. The wind had not risen, but the cold was damp and would feel even more so after the sun set.

Fanny glanced toward the sun, riding low on the horizon. Not much time at all. She dug frantically through the clothing, pulling out a fan, a petticoat, a pair of lace gloves. Finally in the very bottom she found a thick woolen shawl and pulled it out with a crow of pleasure. "Come here, Ella."

Dutifully the girl stepped forward, her cheeks red with the cold.

"Here, let's put this around you, lovey." She draped and tied the brown shawl around Ella's shoulders. It hung all the way down the back of her coat, which would help keep her warm. "Now, grasp the corners of the shawl and hold them tight over your chest."

"Like this?" Ella pulled them together, the ends almost touching the ground.

"Let me fix them." A tight knot secured the garment, covering her daughter front and back. "There. Now, let's hide this trunk, so no one comes along and takes it." Kneeling down again, Fanny secured the lock, then looked around for a place to conceal it. The stand of trees behind them seemed the closest place. One old oak had a broken branch, making it look like a woman kicking her legs. She'd remember that tree. "Can you help me with the trunk, lovey?"

Ella nodded and grasped the handle, but could scarcely lift it off the ground. "I'm sorry, Mama. It's so heavy."

"It is, isn't it?" She'd loaded it down with things she thought she'd need but now obviously didn't. "Let's see if we can drag it."

Together they managed to pull the trunk, bit by bit, behind the tree where it fit perfectly into a depression in the ground. Winded by the exertion, Fanny rested on the lid again, although as soon as she ceased moving, the cold began its insidious penetration of her spencer. They had best start walking, both to find an inn and to keep warm. "Come along, lovey. I think we must walk." Fanny took her daughter's hand and headed toward the road on her left.

"But the carriage went that way, Mama," she replied, pointing the way they had come.

"I know, dear. But the place we are trying to go to, where I hope Lord Lathbury will find us, is that way."

"Lord Laffbury is coming to meet us?" Ella jumped up and down until the shawl slipped askew.

"I truly hope so, my dear." Why she had not married the man when he first asked her in June she now could not fathom. Would she ever fall into folly where Matthew was concerned? What she wouldn't give right now to be safe and warm in his arms. She gazed around the chilly clearing as the sun dipped lower in the sky. *Those who dance must pay the piper.* Her father's words echoed in her ears as she took Ella's hand and started down the cold, empty road.

Racing hell-bent down the London post road, his horse lathered and himself freezing in the damp cold, Matthew reined Spartan down to a trot so they could enter the courtyard of the Duke of Gloucester Inn in Mickleham, the third such inn he'd turned into since he set out. The other two had not garnered any results. Neither the Red Lyon just past Ashtead, nor the Dog and Duck in Leatherhead had seen any woman fitting Fanny's description with a child. They must have stopped somewhere along this stretch to change horses. Maybe the Duke would bring him good luck. It had better bring him a new horse, because Spartan, though valiant, could not keep up the pace they'd kept since the late morning. "We'll get you a rubdown and a good feed, old chap, then I'll pick you back up on the way home. Do not worry, I will not even entertain the notion of hitching you to a carriage to get them home. I'll rent one and you can lord over all the other horses as being your master's favorite."

Walking the horse to an ostler, he handed over the reins, gave the instructions for Spartan's care, and queried about another horse on whom he might continue to Copsale. The groom nodded and informed him the change would take about five minutes. Matthew nodded and turned toward the Inn's doorway.

The aroma of chicken in a country gravy assailed him as he strode through the doorway, making his feet falter and his stomach growl.

"Will you have some of my wife's chicken à la king, my lord? It's fit for the king, I'll swear upon it." The jovial innkeeper, Mr. Larch, kept up a chatter as Matthew took a seat and nodded for them to bring the dinner. "And if you please," he finally broke in on the man's tale of how a friendly game of cards ended in a man hanged, "can you tell me if a carriage passed through this morning carrying a lady with a child?"

"There've been several such, my lord. Can you describe the lady?"

"She's tall for a woman, dark hair, like mine and the child as well. Both with blue eyes."

Looking frankly at Matthew, the man finally nodded. "Aye, my lord. I believe I did see them earlier, around eleven o'clock. They came in briefly and shared one of my wife's plum tarts."

Thank God, a trace of them at last. "Thank you so

much. I'm trying to catch them up before they reach Copsale."

A silent cock of the head and Larch stepped back. "Indeed, my lord."

"A lover's quarrel only and my wife was off to visit her mother before I could make amends. Eleven o'clock you say?" It was now two. Had they stopped also farther on to make easy stages for Fanny? No way to know. He'd best not tarry here. "I believe I shall have to take bread and cheese and a bottle of ale instead of your good wife's chicken, Mr. Larch. I dare not linger here long if I am to catch them up."

The man's countenance fell until Matthew flipped him a coin worth double the price of the meal. "Very good, my lord."

Bread, cheese, and ale met him as he mounted his new horse, a black stallion that seemed eager for the road. Stowing the bag holding his meal behind the saddle, he called his thanks to the groom and swung up onto the horse. "What's his name?" he called, touching the animal's flank with his heel.

"Lucifer, my lord," the lad called as the horse shot away from the courtyard.

They turned onto the road, headed south toward Copsale, the horse straining to increase its speed. "All right, Lucifer." He eased up on the reins and the horse broke into a gallop. "Let's ride like the devil."

Less than two hours later, Matthew was trotting into the courtyard of the Chequers in Southwater, cold and windblown, but extremely impressed with the stamina of this horse. Lucifer had taken him at his word and galloped for the better part of an hour before Matthew had pulled him down to a trot. That hadn't lasted for long. The horse had eased back into a brisk canter and it had been all Matthew could do to keep him from running full tilt again. He'd make the beast rest a quarter hour at least, while he stretched and grabbed a mouthful of ale by the fire. He could also inquire about Fanny, although he assumed they wouldn't turn off this road until they saw the sign for Copsale to the east.

"Walk him, then give him water and a feed. He's earned it." Matthew patted the horse's withers fondly. He might have to buy Lucifer off the innkeeper at Mickleham. This one was a gem. He was just turning away when he thought to ask, "Has the Marquess of Theale's carriage come in today?"

"Yes, milord." The young ostler had begun walking Lucifer in circles. "Twice in fact."

Matthew spun back around. "Twice? When was the first time?"

"Some time after two o'clock, I think." Widening his circle, the groom soothed the horse when he tossed his head. "Easy, now, my fine fellow. You'll get your feed in a bit here. Beg pardon, milord."

Waving the apology away, Matthew fell into step beside him. "Continue."

"We'd just got two or three carriages and a mail coach in, so we were busy, but I took note of the crest."

"Did you see if a woman and child were in the carriage?" Matthew held his breath.

"Yes, milord. Tall dark-haired lady and a little girl just like her. They went inside."

"And you said the carriage has returned?"

"Yes, about half an hour ago. One of the horses had cast a shoe." The lad stopped Lucifer, as if his own words reminded him he'd best check that too.

Gazing up at the inn, Matthew's hands grew clammy. Fanny might be inside this very minute. He summoned moisture to his parched mouth. "Is the lady here now?"

Looking up from the hoof he'd grasped between his legs, the ostler gave a quick shake of his head. "No, my lord. Only the coachman. He's staying the night. No one else on the return trip."

A horrible sense of foreboding crept into Matthew's soul. "And you said they came through here the first time about two?" Mind racing, Matthew tried to tally the miles between the Chequers and Copsale, but gave up in frustration. "How far from here to Copsale?"

"A good twenty miles, my lord. Almost twenty-two with the way the roads curve about so. You won't get there before dark tonight." The lad went back to his job.

Something was terribly wrong. If Fanny's carriage had left the Chequers sometime well after two o'clock, and it was now almost half past four, it was absolutely impossible for the carriage to have taken her and Ella to Copsale and returned in two hours.

Dread squeezed his heart. Where were Fanny and Ella?

"I'll just go look in on John Coachman. Lord Theale is a particular friend of the family. He's the little man, Irish I'd say by the red hair and bran face." Matthew waited, praying the man would accommodate him.

"No, milord, you've mistaken him." The groom

straightened and returned to walking his charge. "The coachman that come in today was a tall, thin, older-looking man with a weathered face, like most coachmen get after some time on the job."

"So I must have. His lordship has several drivers and outriders. It's hard to keep up with such a big establishment. I was just speaking with one of their grooms this morning in London, William Carter. I thought certain he said John had taken this trip." Matthew took out a coin and pressed it on the groom. "Thank you for your good service."

"Thank you, milord." Staring at the gold, the lad shook himself, stuck his newfound wealth into his pocket, and commenced his attentions to the horse again with renewed zeal.

Rage seeping into his every pore, Matthew strode into the inn's taproom. The cozy room, filled with men drinking, eating, laughing, playing cards by the fire, exuded a homey charm and warmth. Disregarding the atmosphere that would have beckoned any other cold and tired traveler to join the company, he stalked to the center of the room, drew himself up to his full, imposing height, and bellowed, "I seek the servant of the Marquess of Theale."

The joyful hubbub of the pleasant room ceased, as though cut off by a stroke of Death's scythe. Wide-eyed men glanced at their companions, then about the rest of the room, searching. At last one man with thin shoulders clad in a black coat of quality, raised his head from his tankard and turned slowly revealing beetled brows and a weathered face. "I serve Lord Theale. Who the devil are you?"

"I am Lord Lathbury. You are Davies?"

The man nodded.

Matthew flowed forward, grasped the man's arm, and jerked him onto his feet. "Let me speak a word in your ear."

"Wha—"

"Bleat so much as one syllable that is not an answer to my questions and you'll find yourself charged with kidnapping forthwith." Matthew wrenched the rascal's arm behind his back. "You'll swing from the end of a rope before Theale can raise a hand to save you." Growling this warning in Davies' ear, Matthew hustled him out of the taproom, through the crowd of slack-jawed faces.

They reached the courtyard, and Matthew shoved his captive out into the fading afternoon light.

Windmilling his arms in an attempt to keep standing upright, the coachman staggered forward onto the cobblestone, narrowly missing falling to his knees. He righted himself and whirled on Matthew, a snarl on his lips. "You have no authority over me, my lord."

"I wouldn't count on that, Davies." Matthew drew himself up until his entire six-foot-three frame towered over the shorter man. "The law severely frowns upon men who abscond with women and children. By the authority vested in me by virtue of my title, I charge you tell me where you have taken Lady Stephen Tarkington and her daughter." His voice thundered in the cold air. "I suspect it was against their wills. Do you dare deny it?"

"I do." The man raised his head, defiance in his eyes. "I took them to Copsale, like Lord Theale ordered me to."

"You lie." Advancing on the coachman, who immediately gave way, Matthew backed him all the way across the courtyard until he ran into the stone wall of the stable. "One of the grooms informed me you came through here after two o'clock this afternoon. He also confirmed that Copsale is twenty-two miles farther on. It is now half-four and you've been here some time. Even if your carriage had been drawn by winged Pegasus himself, I doubt you could have gotten there and back again in that amount of time." He grabbed the man by his poorly tied neck cloth and twisted. "Where are they?"

"Gawp." Davies's mouth opened and closed, but no other sound came out.

Matthew hefted the scrawny servant until his feet dangled, kicking in the breeze. "Get used to this feeling, my fine lad. It's the last one you'll ever have if I have anything to do with it. If one smidgeon of harm has come to Lady Stephen, you'll be hanged man's grease before the new year." He tossed the rogue onto the cobblestones at his feet. "Speak!"

Coughing and sputtering, Theale's coachman clutched his throat, fear bright in his eyes. "I . . ." It came out a croak so he cleared his throat and began again, not taking his eyes off Matthew. "I put them out of the carriage 'bout an hour south of here."

"You blackguard." A white hot rage distorted his vision. All about him turned black, save the center in which shone the white, pasty face with two staring eyes filled to the brim with fear. Grabbing the man again, Matthew drew back his arm and planted him a facer that whipped his head back with a snap. "If anything has happened to them, by God, you'll never live to see a hangman's noose. I'll track you down and tear you limb from limb until all that's left is a bloody stump where your head used to be." He reared back his fist, itching to let fly again and again, but a trickle of reason found its way into his brain. "Describe the place to me. Exactly where did you leave them?"

"There's a clearing like, on the left side of the road." The man worked his mouth, paused, then spat blood. "You'll know the one because of the big oak. Folks about here call it the 'dancing oak' 'cause the limbs look like a lady kicking her legs up."

"And Theale ordered you to do this? Why?" He and the marquess would have some words when Fanny and Ella were safe. Words over pistols if he could arrange it so.

"I don't know meself, but he told me to tell her 'it was with his compliments and a fitting end for a disloyal wife.' He's been a queer nob the past weeks. Rantin' and ragin' at all hours of the day and night, so the footmen say." Davies gingerly got to his feet.

Ever since he'd found out about his and Fanny's affair, and Ella. So when Fanny returned, he'd thrown her out, but agreed to take her to Copsale? That made little sense. Why not just throw her out on her ear in London. He'd rather get this petty revenge? Of course, it wouldn't be deemed petty if Fanny and Ella came to grief. Theale might simply hope they caught the ague being out in the cold, though he couldn't know if they'd be out in the weather very long. A passing coach might very well take them in and give them shelter.

The marquess seemed to have aimed only for a bit of spite at Fanny, although the petty action didn't seem to fit with his dire message. Well, it would have even less sting when he arrived shortly to rescue them. Poor Ella must be frightened out of her wits. Thank God for Fanny's strength. No matter what their quarrel had been, he would see her safe and marry her tomorrow if he could only get her to agree. "I will call for your carriage to be brought here."

"What you want my carriage for? You stealin' it?" Davies had a bit of life in him yet, it seemed.

"No. I am going to rescue Lady Stephen and her daughter. For that I need the carriage." He grinned at Davies. "Poetic justice, isn't it, that the instrument of their punishment will also be that of their salvation. I'll return with it shortly and you can tell Theale how his plans were thwarted, if you dare."

"I'll do that, milord." The self-satisfied smirk on the coachman's cunning face, sent a ripple of warning to Matthew.

He grabbed the man by his throat and squeezed. "What are you not telling me?"

# Chapter 28

The clop-clop of their shoes on the hard dirt road had grown monotonous in the past hour—or hours, Fanny had no idea how long she and Ella had trudged along. A pale sun skimmed the horizon over the fields to her right. The chill damp had penetrated her spencer long ago and Ella shivered as they walked, hand in hand, silent.

Fanny had at first tried to make a game of their situation, to distract her daughter. She'd set her to counting the sheep in the fields they passed, which seemed to occupy the girl quite well. They would joke about the few black sheep dotted here and there and Fanny had questioned Ella's count a time or two, making her daughter scold her for not trusting her to count properly. It had passed the time until the fields had changed to vacant pasturelands. No fun to count bushes or trees. None of it was any fun now.

"Mama, I'm cold. When are we going to get there?"

Ella's pinched face with the red cheeks and nose smote Fanny's heart.

Her folly and hers alone had brought them to this pass. She should have married Matthew long ago, this past summer, and all of this would have been avoided. "I'm sure we will come to a house or an inn soon, lovey."

"That's what you said hours ago, Mama. I'm tired and cold and my feet hurt." Tears began to drip down her child's face.

"I'm so sorry, Ella." Fanny stopped in the middle of the road and knelt down in the dirt. She dug in her reticule and withdrew a handkerchief. Brushing away the child's tears, she peered into the miserable blue eyes. "We shall find somewhere to spend the night soon." Hugging the child, she rubbed her arms briskly, trying to warm her up. "I promise."

A promise easier said than kept. They'd seen no living creature so far along this road, save the sheep. Only the interminable fields ringed by trees. Unfortunately, there weren't even sheep now or they might have hoped to find a sheepfold. No time to go back either, even if they could. Weariness had settled into Fanny's bones until it was a struggle to put one foot before the other. Coupled with the gnawing fear that they would not find shelter before it was too late, she'd begun to shake like a leaf in a high wind. She glanced up at the darkening sky and shuddered. Soon they would be unable to see the road. Even worse, with the darkness the cold would intensify. They could freeze to death if they didn't find shelter before the light went completely.

Panic settling in around the edges of her mind, Fanny rose and looked about again, as if an inn might have magically appeared. Only blasted fields and trees, however, as far as she could see. "Let's see what's over that little hill ahead of us. Perhaps we will finally come to a farmhouse," she said with a cheerfulness she did not feel.

"Hooray! A farmhouse!" Ella jumped up and down, then took off, racing up the slight hill ahead of Fanny.

"Ella," Fanny called, starting to walk again. Dear Lord, let there be some place nearby.

"Mama, Mama. Look! Look!" The child had crested the hill and stood jumping and pointing down at the other side.

Dear Lord, could it be true? Had her prayers been answered? Fanny picked up her pace to a fast walk, then a run. Ella was still jumping up and down and laughing. Could it really be a farmhouse?

Breathing hard, Fanny reached the top of the hill. No wonder Ella had been jumping up and down. Inside, she was dancing a jig. "Thank you, dear Lord."

Not a farmhouse, but a structure at the far end of the field almost as welcome: an ancient barn with one end almost totally fallen away. New energy surged through her.

"Hurry, Mama!" Ella had climbed up on the stone wall and jumped over into the field.

Exhaustion and relief came in waves by turn. Fanny had to sit on the stone fence, a sharp edge of rock digging into her backside, and lift her legs over. With a sigh she stood and, keeping an eye on the building, started off across the field in pursuit of her daughter. "Wait for me, please."

Pausing in her headlong flight, Ella turned back then resumed jumping up and down, as if she could not stand still for the excitement.

Fanny was jumping up and down inside too. Even though the barn was disused, perhaps it was close to a house and warmth and people. And if not, at least it was shelter for the night. Reaching her child at last, she took Ella's hand, and they continued quickly, over more dead grass and hillocks, toward the looming structure.

By the time they neared the barn, daylight had waned to a deep twilight gray.

Several yards from the building, caution raised doubts in Fanny's mind. What dangers might the barn conceal? They might not be the only souls wishing to use it for a refuge tonight.

"Shhh." Putting her finger to her lips, she pushed Ella behind her. Slowly, they approached the byre. A combination of wood and brick, one end of it had been reduced to a rubble of broken sticks and sharp stones. The opposite end, however, still stood, the wooden door hanging ajar. She crept up and poked her head into the dim doorway.

After a moment her eyes adjusted to the gloom that was even darker than the failing light outside. Possibly a barn for cattle, one end held a huge pile of moldering hay, the sweetish smell still lingering in the damp air. They slipped inside, the complete silence convincing Fanny that the place had truly been abandoned.

"Can we stay here tonight, Mama? There's no one here." With complete trust, Ella peered up at her.

Fanny smiled at her daughter. She must keep Ella safe this night. "Let us see what we can find, lovey.

There may be houses and people on the other side of this barn."

Taking Ella in hand, she crossed to the other side, encountering nothing untoward, and opened a small door giving onto the outside. Gazing avidly into the darkness, she searched for the merest pinprick of light across the vast expanse of grass.

The falling darkness revealed no cheerful spark, no flame of candle or lantern, merely a vast sea of grass and trees fading into blackness. Disappointment ate sharply at Fanny. She had hoped so hard that they would find someone to succor them. Still, she would give thanks for this drafty old structure. It might be the difference between their waking in the morning cold and hungry but alive, and freezing to death in the night alongside the road.

Pulling the small door shut, Fanny retraced her steps to the large pile of hay strewn haphazardly about. Their best chance to stay warm in the chilling temperatures would be to cover themselves with the discarded fodder. It should provide protection against the damp and cold, though as she drew closer the faint sweet scent gave way to a less pleasant, moldy smell. Still, beggars could not be choosers.

"Come sit down by me in the hay, Ella." Fanny lowered herself onto the musty straw and patted the place beside her. "It will keep us warm until the morning."

Wrinkling her nose, Ella stepped back. "It smells bad, Mama."

"I know, lovey. But it's ever so much warmer than the cold air. Come, sit beside me."

"I'm hungry." The child's bottom lip poked out as she took a begrudging step toward Fanny.

"I know. I am as well." Fanny held her hand out

and Ella finally took it. She drew the child down to her, putting her arm around the thin shoulders and pulling her close. "We will go to sleep and in the morning we will walk across the fields. If there is a barn here, there must be a house somewhere near." Cuddling her daughter close, Fanny rocked her gently. "They will be country people, who are always friendly." God forgive her that lie, but she hoped whoever they eventually found would come to their rescue. "They will have a good country breakfast to share with us, homemade bread thick with butter and honey, and eggs and sausages, and lots of hot tea. Won't that be lovely?"

"Can I have some now, please?" Yawning, Ella settled back on Fanny's chest. "I would like bread and honey ever so much."

"I will make certain you have as much as you like in the morning, my love."

True darkness had descended while Fanny described the delightful breakfast. Ella sagged against her, her breathing soft and even. Poor babe. Fanny shifted her onto the hay and pulled handfuls of it over the child. The straw was stiff and scratched sometimes, but it did keep the warmth of their bodies close. She heaped it over Ella until all that showed was her head. That should keep her comfortable until morning.

The place on her chest where Ella had lain, deprived of the child's warmth, now made Fanny shudder with a newfound chill. She must cover herself before she fell asleep on top of the hay and froze. Ignoring the musty smell that intensified each time she grasped a handful of the ancient fodder, Fanny scattered several layers of straw over her legs and lower body. Pulling it over her chest and arms was more difficult, but slowly the chill receded. She glanced toward Ella, who had not moved an inch. Good, let her sleep. They would both need their strength tomorrow.

As warmth stole into her at last, Fanny relaxed for the first time since Davies had pulled them from the carriage. When she told Matthew of Theale's perfidy, he would be absolutely livid. Matthew in a rage was a rare sight to see. She would particularly enjoy seeing this one. Yawning, she burrowed deeper into the straw. Once Matthew rescued them, she would tell him she was sorry for all her dithering and accept all his past proposals to become his wife. Then she'd sit back and watch with great satisfaction as he took revenge on Theale on her behalf.

Drifting off, Fanny smiled at the image of Matthew planting her brother-in-law a facer. Ah yes, revenge against the old monster would be sweet indeed.

Fanny jerked awake, completely confused about where she was or what was going on. Prickles on her hands and neck and the musty smell of the hay brought her back to where she was with startling clarity. Stealthily, she moved her hand beneath the hay until it brushed against Ella's body, alive and warm under her blanket of straw. She eased her head back down, straining to hear any sound. Something must have awoken her, but what? No rustling of mice in the straw, no snorting of some nocturnal animal looking for shelter or a meal. It seemed the dead of night. Who else would be about? The owner of the property, perhaps, but would he come out this late to check on something? There was nothing here of value.

She settled back into the straw. This whole miserable experience had been enough to make her jumpy. Taking a deep breath she tried to relax. She'd need her strength for the ordeal yet to come tomorrow. Best get back to sleep.

The creak of the barn door sent tension flooding through Fanny's entire body. Motionless, she listened for additional rasping of the ancient hinges. The wind might have picked up enough to swing the door back and forth. Such a sound would likely have awoken her. As she was about to release the breath she held, the whisper of voices froze her heart and sent fear licking through her veins.

Men's voices, louder as they came through the door, on the far side of the room where she and Ella lay.

"I can't see anything." A man with a gruff voice whispered loudly in the darkness.

"Quiet, ye daft nigit." The insistent voice was quieter, but held more menace. "Yer wanna give 'um notice so they can squawk?"

"Let's get on with it. I told you I didn't want to get wrapped up in crashin' no woman."

The third man's words sounded ominous, especially the part about "crashin' " a woman. Fanny didn't know what that meant, but it didn't sound like it boded well for her. Breathing shallowly so as to make no noise, she prayed the three would simply miss them in the dark and move on.

"We wouldn't be in this pickle, Tom, if you'd been on time," the menacing voice growled. "I tole ye t' meet us at the Chequers at noon. Then we'd be to the dancin' tree well before the carriage arrived."

Fanny's heart beat quicker. These ruffians had planned to meet at the same inn she'd been at. Worse, their mention of the "dancing tree" shot dread through her. That was how she had described that one tree to Ella. Dear God, were these men after them?

"I couldn't help it that my wife's family arrived at dawn." The gravelly voiced man sounded put upon. "I was lucky to escape when I did. Her mother is a rare harpy. Coulda had me choppin' wood and fetchin' water most of the day."

"But if you hadn't been late, my fine fellow, we woulda been at the dancin' tree afore the bitch got there. But you were late so we had to follow her. We coulda done our work and been home afore now."

"Go explain that to my wife, then. Tell her I had to leave her and her god-awful mother to go throttle a woman."

"You'd better hope you can explain it to Mr. Davies if we don't find them."

Clenching her teeth to keep from crying out, Fanny forced herself to lie still even though fear had seized her in a death grip. Davies had arranged for these men to accost her and Ella. The ever-present question was why.

"That's one thing I don't like, Mick. Doin' for a woman, well, that ain't too bad, but killing a child just don't set right with me."

*Please let them leave. Please let them leave.* Fanny swallowed convulsively and prayed harder.

"Mr. Davies said the marquess particularly wanted the brat crashed, but don't you worry none, Jack."

Fanny could hear the evil smile in his voice.

"I'll do for the kid. Then we'll all do for the high-flyer."

Theale. Theale wanted them dead. Had he taken her words as truth, that she would advertise the circumstances of Ella's birth? Or did he simply want to erase the blot on Stephen's name permanently? Her brother-in-law must have run mad to think he could get away with this.

"You look over in that room to yer right, Tom. Jack, you check up in the loft. Mebbe they climbed up there t' get off the floor. I'll look about down here. Wish there was a moon tonight."

"How d'you know they's even in here, Mick?"

"We follow'd um from the dancin' tree, noddy. Where else they gonna go, up a tree? This is the only place they coulda gone to sleep for the night. Now get to it."

Quick fumbling sounds ensued as one of the ruffians shambled off to the right. Another set of footsteps moved restlessly, eventually retreating until that man shuffled out of the room. That left the menacing man, who moved off to the left of the pile of hay. He hadn't discovered it yet.

The man lumbered around and Fanny lost track of where he stood. Finally, the creaking of a ladder told her one of the ruffians had gone to the loft.

Forced to lie still in the dark, unable to even attempt to flee or find a better hiding place, Fanny prayed harder for the men to leave. Rustling in the hay on the far side of the pile made her hold her breath. One of the men had found her hiding place. Would he find her? She couldn't tell for sure, but she prayed none of them carried a lantern. If she were lucky they might miss her and Ella in the dark.

Suddenly the rustling stopped and someone's footsteps scraped the floor as they moved away from her. Fanny released her breath slowly. Complete silence descended upon the barn and she sent up a prayer of thanksgiving.

A hand clamped down on her leg and jerked her out of the hay.

# Chapter 29

Fanny screamed as one of the ruffians pulled her from her hiding place.

"There you are, milady." The smug voice of the menacing ruffian sent a shiver of fear running through her. "Right naughty of you to hide from us. Tom, Jack, I got 'er. Bring the lantern."

"Mama, Mama!" Ella's high-pitched shriek shook the darkness.

"Ella! Run, Ella, run outside. Hide!" Fanny jerked away from her captor, scrabbling to rise. The man hit her side, knocking her back to the ground. "Run, Ella!"

"Mama!"

Twisting toward her child, Fanny could just make out a man holding Ella in his arms.

She still shrieked and kicked, but was no match for the brute's strength.

"Let her go, you blackguard." She scooted onto her knees, trying to rise but impeded by her skirts. "If you hurt her—" Another blow laid her flat on her back.

"Where you think ye're goin', dearie?" The menacing man towered over her. "Tom. Bring your nob and the lantern over here. I wanna good look at this ladybird afore we gets started."

The man's meaning was abundantly clear. He planned to kill them under the orders of the Marquess of Theale. Could she reason with them? Bribe them, perhaps? "How much is Theale paying you to do this?"

"What d' you care? You won't live to see it hurt your purse." The one they called Mick, a burly fellow with arms the size of hams, sneered down at her. His greasy hair fell over his face, but Fanny could see the jowly cheeks, the small eyes, and the short stature of the man. A rude-looking fellow any way you looked at him.

"What if I offer you more money?" Fanny threw out the only card she suspected would interest this vulgar lot. "More money to take me and my daughter to safety?"

Mick looked first at Jack, holding the now quiet Ella, then at Tom who nodded his head ferociously. "For that much, I'd help you, milady, if you don't have none could take you to an inn or town."

"Jack!" Mick barked a warning. "We've already eaten the marquess's salt, so to speak. No goin' back now." The man with the menacing voice hoisted the lantern over her. The thin beam fell on Fanny's face and she shielded her eyes as best she could with her hand. "Not that I'd want to at any rate."

"What if I offered double what the marquess is paying you?"

That got even Mick's attention. He peered down at her and shrugged. "You got no money to be paying a brass farthing, much less what his lordship wanted to pay."

"You'll get every farthing you are owed but from Lord Lathbury, not the marquess." She must be convincing.

Eyes narrowing, Mick held the light down toward her. "How do I know this bloke will post the cole?"

"He will, I swear to you before God. He will be overjoyed to see his wife and child home and safe with him again."

"That be lot o' blunt, Mick." Tom eased closer to the surly man. "Set me up proper, it would."

The man they called Jack, who still held the quietly sobbing Ella, sounded eager. "It would, Mick. And we don't got to swing for murder if we *rescue* the lady."

"Ain't nobody swingin' no matter what." Mick stared down at her, his face settled into harsh planes in the yellowish light. "We hush the pair of 'em, ain't nobody alive to tell the tale. She's seen us now, gents. Can't let 'er tell or we all meet Jack Ketch and the end of a rope." The gleam in Mick's eyes turned her blood cold. "Hold her down, Tom. We got all night." He licked his lips and set the lantern down, then dropped his hand to the fall of his rough breeches. "No need to be hasty."

"Noooo!" Fanny jerked up off the floor, pushing a startled Tom to the side as she tried to crawl toward Ella.

"No, you don't." A big hand grabbed her leg through her skirt and yanked her backward. Her face hit the hay-strewn floor, the straw pricking her cheeks as Mick hauled her toward him. "Gonna have my fun with you afore we finish the job." With a deft hand, he flipped her onto her back and she could see his fall dangling before his gaping breeches. "Now hold her, Tom. You'll get yer turn after I'm done."

Kicking her legs wildly, Fanny connected with Mick's shin and the blackguard grunted and fell to his knees.

"You're gonna pay for that, my fine lady." Grabbing her legs, he slid her skirts up to her thighs, cold air rushing between her legs.

"You're going to roast in hell." Terror seized her and Fanny bucked, almost dislodging the cur whose hands fumbled on her cold flesh.

"Hold her down, you caw-handed fool. If you let her get away—"

"Help me! Help me! Somebody!" Screaming and twisting, Fanny dug down for every ounce of strength. She wrenched her arms up and pushed at Mick with all her might. "Get off me, you cur."

The thunderous boom of the door being blown open stopped them all.

Fanny screamed, still struggling to push Mick off her.

Swift feet pounded across the floor. A meaty *twack* and Mick sailed off her, flying into the darkness of the barn.

Before she could draw breath to scream again, Tom's body was plucked up off her. She was free. Scrabbling for a purchase in the loose hay, she slipped and trod on her gown. The rip of parting fabric didn't impede her at all as, sidling like a crab, she found her footing and staggered to her feet.

The man called Jack stood, eyes white and wide, clutching Ella to him.

Fury burning in her heart, she descended on him like an avenging angel. “Give me my daughter.”

Glancing away from her into the darkness from which arose the sounds of fists pounding flesh, groans and moans, and the crunch of bones, Jack tossed Ella into the hay, turned tail, and melted into the darkness.

Ella screamed and Fanny darted forward. “I’m here, lovey. Shhh. Shhh.” Scooping Ella out of the hay, Fanny ran for the door. Finding it hanging broken, attached only by a piece of leather hinge, she sped out into the cold night air, her child’s sobs harsh in her ear. “We’re safe now, lovey. Shhh.”

She peered into the darkness. Where to go? It needn’t be far. Doubtless the ruffians would flee as soon as their compatriot finished the drubbing they so richly deserved. Had that been Davies? The coachman had never impressed her as having much physical strength, but working with horses may have toughened him in ways she didn’t understand.

Her eyes adjusted quickly, assisted by the faint starlight, and she spied a group of bushes off to the left of the barn. She scurried over to them, ducking behind them and crouching close to the ground. Ella clung to her and she clutched her tight. “It will be all right, lovey,” she crooned over and over in a whisper. Dear God, let these men depart and not seek them out again.

A man emerged from the barn holding the lantern high.

Sucking in a breath, she whispered in Ella’s ear, “Be quiet, Ella. Not a word, not a sound.”

He swung the light to and fro, peering into the

darkness. Searching for them. Lowering her head, Fanny prayed.

"Fanny? Fanny, are you there?"

"Matthew!" The sound of the beloved, familiar voice brought her head up with a snap. She bounded up from behind the bushes, staring at her savior in the light. "Matthew, oh, God." Clutching Ella, she ran back toward the barn.

He met them halfway, enfolding them in his strong arms. "Fanny, thank God you're all right."

Stunned and completely drained, she burst into tears.

His arms tightened around them. "Hush, love. I'm here. Nothing will ever harm you again, I promise. If I have to kill Theale with my own hands, he will trouble you no longer."

The assurances only made her cry harder. This man had wanted nothing but to marry and protect her for so long. Had she not been so stubborn and blind none of this escapade would have happened. She didn't deserve such devotion and the realization made her wail even louder.

Ella chimed in with her own sobs.

"Fanny, are you hurt? Is Ella all right? For God's sake, tell me." The deep concern, something near panic in his voice forced her rational mind back to the fore.

"Yes." She sobbed and gulped, trying to stem the tears. "I believe Ella is well. Are you, lovey? Did the bad men hurt you?"

The child nodded, then burrowed her head into Fanny's shoulder. "Mama, who is it? Is it the bad man?"

"No, lovey. It's Lord Lathbury come to rescue us."

"Lord Laffbury?" Ella poked her head up. "Lord Laffbury, is it really you?" She clasped her arms around his neck and he drew her out of Fanny's arms and into his.

"I believe she's fine, as am I. A bit bruised, perhaps, but truly not harmed."

"Truly?" Lifting the lantern, he peered into her face, silently asking the question.

"No, you arrived before . . . before . . ." She shuddered and laid her head on his chest. It had been a near thing. One more minute and—

"Hush, my love. You are safe."

When had she started weeping again? "I'm so sorry." She tried to pull away and should have saved the effort. Might as well try to move the standing stones on Salisbury Plain as break his grip. "Let me go, Matthew. I can't be a watering pot, not now when Ella needs me to be strong for her."

"Why don't you let me be strong for both of you?" Dark smudges underneath his eyes, the deeply grooved furrows of his brow, and the drawn look about his mouth attested to his profound concern for her and Ella. His daughter.

Surely after this night the tale must come to light, for she would deny him no longer. If he still wanted her, wanted them, then she would be a widow no longer. She nodded.

"Then come. Lucifer is over here." He led them to the side of the barn.

"Lucifer? What happened to Spartan?"

"That is a long story"—he paused to entangle them—"one that will perhaps keep until I get you both to an inn with a soft bed."

They drew near to the barn and Fanny balked. "Are they . . . are the ruffians . . . dead?"

With a sharp laugh, Matthew shook his head. "I decided not to soil my hands with their blood. Well, with more of their blood. The two inside will find it hard to eat anything more substantial than a coddled egg for a month."

That got Fanny to giggling, releasing the tension that had wound itself tightly around her since Davies had put them out of the carriage hours ago. Her shoulders sagged and she put out a hand to grab Matthew's arm to steady herself. The warmth of his body seeped into hers at an astounding rate. So much the better. She suspected she would never be warm enough after today unless Matthew held her.

He led them to a huge black horse, tethered to a bush. The animal snorted at their approach. "Easy, Lucifer." Matthew set the lantern down and patted the arched neck. "This grand fellow is as much your hero as I. He should be called Pegasus as far as I'm concerned. Brought me here faster than I'd ever dreamed."

"Where did you get him?" Fanny looked askance at the enormous animal, snorting and prancing. Lucifer seemed rather an apt name at that.

"At the Duke of Gloucester in Mickleham. Spartan was spent by the time I got there. I plan to buy him off the inn when we return, no matter the cost. Here, darling," he said, standing Ella on the ground, "let me put your mother on the horse then I'll hand you up to her."

The child whimpered and threw herself at Fanny, sobbing. "Mama."

"It's all right, lovey. Lord Lathbury won't leave us

for a second." Fanny hated to leave the girl's grip, but she had to mount if they were ever to leave this godforsaken place.

"Have you ever rode pillion?" Matthew asked, running his hand over the rump of the horse.

"Perhaps once or twice. Why? Do you plan for all of us to ride?" That raised her eyebrows.

"The child's weight is negligible. And we will go only at a walk. It's some five or six miles back to the Chequers and we need to get you two out of this cold as quickly as possible. If I walk and lead the horse, it will take several hours. Ella, watch how your mother is going to sit right behind the saddle here."

Matthew put his hands around her waist, and she reveled in his touch once more. Never did she ever want him to let go. The night was growing colder, however, and he quickly hoisted her up behind the saddle. Perched on the rump of the horse, she settled herself as best she could.

"Now your turn, my dear." He scooped Ella up, bringing forth a shriek, and deposited her before the saddle. "Hold his mane, Ella." He closed her hand over a handful of the horse's hair. "I'll sit up behind you and hold you the whole way." Swiftly he retrieved the lantern, blew it out, and tossed it back on the ground before grabbing the reins and mounting behind Ella.

The horse stamped impatiently, but otherwise seemed not to be distressed by his full load. A hero indeed.

With a slight nudge of his heel, Matthew started them off.

Fanny grasped him around the waist to steady herself, and although she quickly became accustomed to the horse's swaying gait, she kept her arms around her love, glorying in his presence. She leaned her head against the small of his back. "Did you receive my letter this morning?"

"Actually, no."

Startled, she sat up. "Then how are you come here?"

"It's a bit of a story."

Fanny's horror grew as he related the tale. "He burned my letter before your eyes?"

"Quite gleeful about it, he was." Matthew's back shook slightly with his own mirth. "I suppose he never thought for a moment I'd find you in time. Does the marquess have some other grudge against you, my dear, or has this all been about the fact that I am Ella's—"

"Shhh. Don't tell her now." She didn't want the knowledge of her parentage to come at such a horrible time for Ella.

"Do not worry, my love. She has been asleep almost since we started."

Satisfied, Fanny leaned her head on his comfortable back again. "Yes, I believe that information must have driven him to devise this scheme to murder us. That and . . ." She sighed. So much she'd brought on herself because of her follies. "I more or less threatened to let the news of our affair and the name of Ella's true father come to light when he banished us from the house."

"God, no wonder he was in such a state. He seems to be under the impression society will give a damn."

"And they truly won't, you think?" That fear had been instilled in her by Theale and Lavinia for years.

"Do you think we are the only couple in the *ton* to

have done such a thing?" Matthew's laugh moved her head up and down. "I can name you ten wives at least who have a child not of her husband's getting."

"I don't believe you."

"Shall I name them forthwith? One or two will positively make you gasp." He chuckled and she gave his back a smack.

"No, thank you. I do not need such confirmation. Your mother assured me of the same thing, though again, I did not believe her at the time." If only she had, so much could have been avoided. "So how did you find us? I had written we were going to my cousin's in Copsale."

"A judicious bribe of one of Theale's grooms and then the good luck to find Davies returned to the Chequers. I almost made a grievous mistake there." Matthew's voice had gone grim.

"What happened?"

"I convinced Davies to tell me where he'd put you out of the carriage and was getting it hitched up to come and get you. Which would have taken much longer and been disastrous considering I just got to you in the nick of time."

A chill chased down her spine and she clutched him tighter. "What changed your mind?"

"The smug smile on his weasely face. Something else had to be afoot. With a little more persuasion, he told me he'd hired three men to murder you and Ella." His back tensed and she rubbed it to reassure him. "At that, I leaped onto Lucifer and we pounded the road all the way there. When I didn't see you at the dancing tree, I continued down the road, calling your name, and finally saw the outline of the barn and their lantern glimmering in the darkness."

"Thank God you did, my love." She tightened her arms around him. "Can you ever forgive me for creating all this havoc?"

"You I forgive everything, utterly and completely. The Marquess of Theale," his voice lowered menacingly, "will not escape so easily."

"Do nothing that will end with your being taken from me, Matthew." The thought of him avenging her at the cost of his own life was intolerable.

"Do not worry, love." He chuckled, a lighter spirit restored. "I vow you will not be rid of me for a very long time to come."

Amen to that.

# Chapter 30

Sometime in the hours before dawn Fanny awoke with a slight jolt when Lucifer stopped. Nestled comfortably against Matthew's back, she must have fallen asleep in the night, lulled to slumber by the gentle motion of the horse's smooth gait. Opening her eyes on a lamp-lit courtyard, she stretched carefully and let go of Matthew's waist. "Where are we?"

"The Chequers. What-ho, groom!" Matthew called loudly. Several minutes later a young stable lad stumbled out of the building opposite, shaking his head and pulling on his coat.

"Can I help you, milord?" The boy yawned fiercely, then peered up at Matthew.

"Help the lady down, lad. I need to pass her the child here." He still held the sleeping Ella against him.

"Right away, sir." He darted toward Lucifer's rear and reached up to her. "Grab my hands, lady. I'll catch you." The lad looked no more than twelve, scarcely tall enough to reach the big horse's withers.

But she was too tired to argue. After everything that had happened yesterday, this shouldn't daunt her at all. Leaning forward and trusting again to God, Fanny slid off the horse and into the arms of the lad, who was actually sturdier than he looked. Her feet hit the smooth cobblestones that paved the yard and she slipped, but the boy righted her and she breathed a sigh of relief. Immediately, she turned to Matthew, arms open.

Gently, he picked Ella up, still dead to the world, and lowered her into Fanny's waiting arms. The exhausted child barely stirred and Fanny cradled her against her breast while Matthew dismounted.

"Give him a full measure of oats and all the water and hay he wishes." Patting Lucifer's withers fondly, Matthew pulled a coin from his pocket. "This is yours, lad, if you treat this fellow right."

"Yes, milord." The lad bobbed his head and took the reins, looking up at the big black horse skeptically. "What's his name?"

"Lucifer, but remember the devil was an angel before he fell."

"Yes, milord." Wrinkling his brow, the boy and horse moved off toward the stable.

Arms heavy with the sleeping Ella, Fanny wanted to sink down where she stood. Exhaustion had claimed her, despite her nap on the horse. The thought must have been written on her face, for Matthew plucked the girl from her arms, pillowing her head on his shoulder.

With a sigh, Ella burrowed her head into his neck but did not wake.

Placing his other arm around Fanny's shoulder, Matthew led them toward the inn. Drawn to his warmth and the comfort of his presence, Fanny leaned against him, happy to have his strength to depend upon. Never had she been so tired in her life.

Dark and quiet, the inn's taproom enveloped them with warmth from the banked fire on the far side.

"I could sink down right here and sleep." Fanny gazed hungrily at the hard tables and benches.

"A moment or two more, sweetheart, and I can offer you much softer accommodations. Innkeeper." Matthew called toward a dark doorway that might be the kitchen.

A moment or two later, a middle-aged woman appeared, yawning as she pulled a robe close against her chest. "Can I help you, my lord?"

"I need rooms for myself, my wife, and child."

A thrill shot through Fanny, bringing her wide awake. He'd called her his wife. Suddenly and overpoweringly she wished that were true. She wanted nothing more than to remain at this man's side for the rest of her life.

The woman nodded. "This way, my lord. I've a parlor and bedroom available, though it overlooks the courtyard. I'm Mrs. Jameson. My husband's from home at the moment, but we can still do for you." The woman unhooked a large key from a small brass hook, one of only two such remaining in a row of empty hooks hung behind a desk. "This way if you please. I'll wake Betsy and send her up with warm washing water for you."

"Send her later in the morning." Matthew shifted Ella, and they started up the stairs behind the innkeeper. "I fear we are too weary at the moment to want more than a bed."

The parlor proved well appointed, though Fanny barely glanced at it. She gazed longingly at the door to the bedroom, weariness seeping into every part of her. If she didn't lie down soon, she would drop where she stood.

Quickly stepping forward, Mrs. Jameson lit a lamp, then led them into the bedroom.

The large comfortable bed drew Fanny's full attention. Was it big enough for the three of them? "Ella will have to sleep between us."

"Nay, my lady." Mrs. Jameson darted to the bed and drew out a trundle from beneath it. "The lass can sleep here. Leaves more room for the two of you."

"Bless you, Mrs. Jameson. What a very well appointed inn you have. We'll want breakfast late." He shot a questioning look at Fanny.

She nodded and took Ella from his arms. She lay the child gently in the bed, then sat on the edge of the mattress to remove her dusty shoes.

"A mishap on the road has stranded my wife and child without conveyance. Do you have any sort of carriage that may be rented to take us to London later today?" Steering the woman back into the parlor, Matthew left her and Ella alone.

This afforded Fanny the privacy to remove their daughter's clothes down to her chemise, and tuck her under the covers. The small face, so sweetly innocent in repose, looked the very picture of Matthew as he might have been when young. If all their children could look thus, she would be content. She prayed the horrific events of the day past had not distressed the child enough to cause her sweet nature harm.

Wearily, Fanny stood and stripped out of her clothes, dropping them in a puddle on the floor. Once in her shift alone, she crawled into the bed, pulled the covers over her, and sank into blissful unconsciousness.

A violent dipping of the bed woke her and she jerked upright out of her dreamless sleep with a cry.

"Shhh, it's only me." Matthew's deep voice came from the near darkness right by her head.

"Thank God." She eased back down under the covers. "I need no more villains in my life."

The words brought back vividly the scene in the barn, the ruffian on top of her, his hands fumbling at her skirts. He'd run his rough hands over her thighs, and her skin crawled as though he still touched her. The memory of his open fall, the glimpse she'd had of his thick, eager manhood turned her stomach. At the thought of what might have happened had Matthew not arrived when he did, she turned away from him, shaking violently as tears trickled down her face.

"What is it, my love?" He put a tentative hand on her shoulder and she sobbed aloud.

"That man . . . he . . . he almost . . ." Tears choked her throat.

"Shhh. It's all right. You are safe." He slipped his arms around her, so strong. So secure.

She cried louder as he held her, crooning words of comfort softly in her ear, until her tears were spent and she panted to catch her breath.

Easing toward her until his chest and stomach pressed along her back, Matthew gathered her to him. "Do you feel better now?"

Nodding, she sighed and relaxed against him. "I

feel like a fool. It is over and done with. He cannot hurt me now. Still, I remember—"

"Many feel fear but have the courage not to show it. As you did tonight. There is no shame in letting your fears and hurt go, however you do it." He kissed her cheek. "It is truly over, my love. Try your best to forget it and think only of our life going forward."

She turned toward him, though the darkness hid his face. "Our life?"

"I love you, Fanny. I will say it however many times it takes for you to accept it." His voice softened and he grasped her hand. "I want us to spend our lives together, to see our children grow up together, to grow old alongside you, and in the end, to lie beside you forever into eternity."

Any tiny doubt she may have had disappeared with those words. "I want those things too, my love." She touched his cheek, his night beard prickly beneath her fingertips. "To live beside you, to lie in your arms every night, to bear your children proudly, and love you with all my heart forever."

His body tensed like a great coiled spring. "Then you will marry me?"

"Yes, my love. Of course I will."

"There has been no 'of course' about it at all. Oh, Fanny." He grasped her head and found her mouth. Insistent, he pressed his lips to hers until she couldn't tell where hers began and his ended. His tongue stole into her mouth, stroking and caressing her until she tingled all over. Their tongues tangled and she wanted to melt into the bed with happiness. A kiss of such passion and possession that the world disappeared, leaving only the two of them joined in the darkness together.

Finally, Matthew raised his head, panting. "I had thought we would wait until the wedding, but I believe that is impossible."

The hardness poking her thigh told her he spoke truth. She laughed deep and throatily, pulling him onto her again. "I see no reason to delay our pleasure."

"Then we must marry soon, sweetheart. Unless you no longer care if our next child is said to be born too early."

Fanny went still beneath him, closed her eyes, and swore silently.

"What?" The edge of concern was back in his voice. He sat up, fumbled with the candle on the nightstand, and the flare of a single flame brought his face into sharp relief. Puckered brow and taut jaw greeted her. "What is wrong?"

Putting a reassuring hand on his arm, she stroked the firm muscles. "Nothing, save I suspect we are too late for that to be a consideration, my dear."

His frown deepened, then his eyebrow raised, a look of surprise on his face that made her chuckle.

"Do you mean you—"

Smiling, she nodded. "Yes, I am almost certain I am carrying your child."

"Fanny! Oh, my love." The joy in his voice made her heart sing. Then he shook his head. "But how is it possible, sweetheart? We have not been together since Charlotte's house party. You had said then you believed yourself safe."

"So I did. I'd been drinking the concoction all along. Yet, ever since Charlotte's wedding, when I discovered both she and Elizabeth were increasing, I have recognized the symptoms—unexpected flashes of heat, fatigue, my breasts have been sore and swollen, and I have developed a strange craving for milk in my tea."

He sat back, staring at her with wide eyes. "Milk in your tea? You have never liked it that way."

"Save when I carried Ella." An odd thing that disappeared the very day her daughter was born.

"And your courses?"

"Absent since September." She took his hand, twining it in hers. "Somehow your seed vanquished my Queen Anne seeds." Hesitant, still she needed to ask, "You are pleased, my lord?"

He stroked her cheek, his eyes shining with love. "With all my heart, my love. I am thrilled that you may even now be carrying my heir, or another beautiful daughter. But how did it happen? Your seeds have not failed before." He raised accusing eyebrows at her. "When you took them."

"I have no proof; however, I suspect it may have something to do with that startlingly sensual pagan rite at the Wrotham Harvest Festival. You remember when the Harvest Lord claimed the Corn Maiden?"

His eyes grew the darkest black and he settled himself on top of her again. "That I do remember very well." He kissed her neck, nuzzling along the side until he came to her shift. Growling, he grasped the fine linen material. "We need to dispense with this now."

"Wait." She closed her hands over his to stay them, then pushed them away. "If you tear this garment I will have none to wear tomorrow." Sitting up, she untied the string at the neckline. "You must wait a little as I disrobe."

"Ahhh, you mean to torment me. Go faster." Matthew threw himself full length on the bed.

"Going faster would merely lessen the element of seduction, my lord. Lie back."

With a groan, Matthew complied, lying in her place with one arm beneath his head.

Fanny rose to her knees, pulling the chemise from around her until it covered her completely from neck to knees.

"Why do you assume the Wrotham festival possessed some quality that assisted in getting you and your two friends with child?" Bright eyes taking her in as she slipped the garment off her shoulders, Matthew extended his hand toward her neckline.

"No, I need no assistance from you, my lord. Yet." She blew him a kiss, then pulled the one remaining comb from her straggling hair, bringing it tumbling around her shoulders and spilling down her front covering her breasts further. His sudden intake of breath and a stirring beneath his shirt to her right made her own body yearn for his, deep within her. "I find it interesting that all three of us had passionate interludes that night after witnessing the rite. A fertility rite, if you recall. Charlotte and Nash were actually in the field." She lowered her shift until it barely covered her nipples and raised his shirt, revealing his cock at keen attention.

"I remember." The husky voice only increased her need.

Grasping his member, she slowly stroked up and down. "I also discovered that Elizabeth and Lord Brack shared a bed that night. I scarcely believed it, but she told me it was true."

"For pity's sake, Fanny, I'm about to burst."

She threw back her head and laughed.

A whimper from the trundle bed cut her short and she froze. After a moment, when no further sound was forthcoming, she returned her attention to her impatient lover.

"As you command, my lord." In a liquid motion she dropped her shift, revealing her overly plump breasts, nipples hardened into tiny points, and mounted him, sliding herself onto his thick cock.

He grunted as she seated herself and sighed with the exquisite pleasure of having him deep inside her once more. "You may also remember our interlude in the trees just beyond the field."

"I remember nothing at the moment," he said, cupping her breasts, kneading them, a look of pure bliss on his face.

"Allow me to jog your memory." She eased herself up and down, slowly at first, then faster as he began to counterthrust into her. Leaning over she seized his lips, plunging her tongue into him as her need reached its ultimate peak. Groaning into his mouth, she shattered around him, complete and whole again.

Moments later he strained into her as his release came, calling her name. Sweeter words she'd never heard.

As they lay panting, entwined together in the rumpled sheets, Matthew grasped her hand, lacing their fingers together. "If you will agree, I'd still like for us to be married from Hunter's Cross, in my parish church, All Saints."

"I would like that very much. Will you get a special license?" They need not rush, but if he suddenly worried about Society's gossip, then they should wed as quickly as possible.

Matthew stared at the cracked gray plaster on the ceiling, then shook his head. "I want us to have a proper wedding, with the banns read. Sometime early in the new year."

"But where will I live until then?" The realization hit that she no longer had a place at Theale's house where she'd lived for close to eight years. "We must journey to Copsale tomorrow and explain all to my cousin. She will likely take us in for the few weeks before we marry."

"Absolutely not." He grasped her around the shoulders as though she might disappear on the spot. "You will journey with me to Hunter's Cross and there remain, ever after."

"Won't your mother object?" Lady Lathbury had been friendly toward her even after she learned of Ella's parentage; however, she could not help but wonder how the lady would react to her future daughter-in-law's moving into her home while she was still mistress of it.

"Once she hears the tale of this day, I seriously doubt it. And she has told me she approves of you becoming my wife. She believes us well matched." He squeezed her to him. "So do I."

"And so do I." Drowsily, she snuggled against him. "I am truly glad to hear of her approval. After these past days I need no more discord in my life."

"Only harmony from now on, sweetheart, I promise."

A new life with a true love. Apparently happy endings did come true, if only you had the good sense to see them and accept them. "Yes, my love. Oh, yes."

# Chapter 31

Backed by a small army of four strapping footmen, a grim-faced Matthew arrived at Theale House and knocked at the door.

After Fanny's ordeal, he had ensconced her at Hunt House, along with Ella and a hastily summoned Jane, to allow her and his daughter to recover their strength before journeying on to Hunter's Cross. There they would stay until the wedding. Today, he'd come to retrieve her and Ella's trunks. He expected trouble, but nothing he and four other fit men couldn't handle.

The door opened a crack, revealing a wary butler who kept glancing over his shoulder.

"I am Lord Lathbury," Matthew intoned, using his deepest voice. "I have come for Lady Stephen's and Miss Ella's belongings." He peered at the quivering man until he at last opened his mouth

"You may not enter, my lord." The little man whispered so low Matthew had to lean forward to catch the words.

"What do you mean I 'may not enter'?" He drew

himself up to his full height, now towering over the cowering butler.

The man craned his head back to look up at Matthew. "Lord Theale has given instructions you are not to enter Theale House, my lord."

"Has he indeed?" Well, they would see about that.

With a nod to his footmen, none of whom were shorter than six-foot-one, Matthew pushed his way into the entry hall, his men following behind in a flying wedge, like so many soldiers going into battle. "Where is your master?"

The stunned butler had fallen back before them, his back now pressed against the wall. "I'm certain I do not know, my lord. His lordship roams the house these days. It's difficult to say where he might be at any given moment."

What the devil did that mean? With a sharp glance at the manservant, Matthew surged forward to the staircase. "Take me to Lady Stephen's chamber or I will find it for myself."

"Oh, no you won't." The cracked, high-pitched voice from above jerked Matthew's attention up to the first landing. Lord Theale stood, his excellently cut coat strangely askew, as though he'd been interrupted while dressing, belying the man's reputation of not stirring until he was impeccably dressed. "You are banned from this house, Lathbury. Defiler of wives." His voice rose in a shriek. "Spawn of the devil."

Glancing over his shoulder at the footmen, eyes wide and murmuring to one another, Matthew firmed his lips. "Steady, men." He'd never led troops into battle, but it seemed there might be a first time. "I want nothing but the property that belongs to my betrothed, Theale. Have her trunks and Ella's brought down and we will retire peacefully."

"You'll never take them. Never take them!" Brandishing an imaginary sword, Theale ran down the steps toward Matthew.

Aghast at this strange behavior, yet confident the man would stop when he reached the first step, Matthew stood firm, though the peer's disheveled appearance and erratic behavior filled him with uneasiness. Surely the man would—

Theale reached the bottom step and ploughed straight into Matthew, knocking him back into the footmen close behind him. He stumbled, but the men kept him standing.

"Noyes, call for reinforcements," Theale shouted, picking himself up off the stairs, and finally adjusting his coat.

The butler scurried away.

"Now you'll get what's coming to you, you blackguard. This is for Stephen." Theale pulled his arm back for a blow.

Matthew was a longtime patron of Jackson's boxing saloon, often training at the hands of Jackson himself. That training now took over. When Theale began his swing, Matthew blocked the blow, then jabbed his fist into the marquess's snarling face.

With a loud groan, the man fell back onto the steps, staring up at Matthew, an utterly shocked expression on his face.

At that moment, Noyes arrived with every footman, groom, and stable boy the marquess employed.

Shaking his hand, Matthew signaled his men to

go. Theale's belligerent behavior was completely uncharacteristic of the man, which was troubling. "I will return, Theale, to retrieve Fanny's things."

"And I'll not give you quarter then either, Lathbury." Theale laughed as he sat up, wiping at the blood trickling from his nose.

Noyes ran forward to assist his master to stand.

"Have her trunks ready and we won't have to repeat this scene." Despite the satisfaction of finally planting the odious man a facer, his manner still seemed unusual. Perhaps it was time Matthew paid a call on Theale's heir, Craighaven.

"Hah. Got you on the run, have I? I'll have a go at you again if you come back."

"I'll be back," Matthew spoke under his breath. "And I guarantee you will not like it when I do."

Two days later, Matthew once again knocked on the door of Theale House, although this time he was accompanied by a single man.

Noyes opened the door, his face registering alarm at seeing Matthew. "Lord Lathbury. Please, my lord. I cannot allow you to pass."

"You won't deny me entry, will you, Noyes?" Craighaven stepped from behind Matthew, his tone even but firm.

"Lord Craighaven." Noyes made a full bow to his master's heir. "Please my lord, come in."

Pushing past the butler, Craighaven crossed the threshold into the entrance hall, Matthew following closely behind. "Where is my father?"

"I believe he is in his study, my lord."

"Alone?"

"Yes, my lord."

"Good." Craighaven glanced at Matthew. "This way, Lathbury."

"But, my lord . . ." Noyes hurried after them as Craighaven started up the stairs. "His lordship has expressly forbidden—"

Craighaven threw up a hand in dismissal. "I will take care of the matter, Noyes. Thank you." They continued up the stairs to the first landing and turned left. "It's just this way." His voice betrayed his annoyance with these dealings, yet the man had agreed to confront his father. He stopped before a familiar door. "Here."

Lord Theale sat behind the desk, in his overlarge chair, writing a letter. He did not look up when they entered, and when they reached the desk, Matthew discovered the letter was merely a series of doodles—looping swirls, squares stacked upon squares, never-ending spirals.

"Father."

At his son's voice, the marquess finally raised his head. "Craighaven. Have you come for the holidays after all?"

"I live here, Father. Remember? With you and Mother. I gave up my bachelor apartments a year ago when I married." His son's patient voice told Matthew this conversation had taken place before. Perhaps many times.

"Yes, quite right. Must have slipped my mind." Theale glanced at Matthew and his face transformed into a snarl. "What is that traitor doing in my house? I'll have Noyes's guts for garters."

"He is here with me, Father. I have spoken with Lord Lathbury, who has informed me of your recent behavior regarding Aunt Frances." Craighaven firmed his mouth and continued. "He has shown me proof that you tried to have her and Cousin Ella murdered."

"Lies, all lies." The marquess reared back in his chair. "He cuckolded your uncle. Do you think he will speak truth to you?"

"I have spoken the truth, Lord Theale." Matthew stared at the man with abject loathing. "I informed your son about our meeting here and what you did to Fanny and Ella."

"Lies."

"I have proof."

Theale sat up so quickly his chair scooted back across the Aubusson carpet. "What proof?"

Reaching into his jacket, Matthew withdrew a sheet of paper. "An affidavit, sworn before the magistrate in Southwater and signed by Davies, attesting to the fact that you instructed him to abandon Fanny and Ella along the road and hire men to set upon them and murder them." Clenching his fist, and itching to ram it into Theale's face again, he breathed deeply and instead held the sheet up for Theale to see. "I think you will need to hire another coachman. In return for this sworn statement, I persuaded the magistrate to commute Davies's sentence of death. He's currently in Newgate awaiting transportation. The locals are still searching for the three ruffians who tried to seize them."

Nonchalantly Theale waved the paper away. "That has nothing to do with me. Davies lied to save his own skin."

"The magistrate thought him truthful enough to issue this." Matthew slipped the document back into his pocket lest Theale get ideas about snatching and burning it too.

"Father, attempted murder is a felony." Craighaven had paled, although he'd turned as white as the affidavit when Matthew had shown it to him. "Should Lathbury or Aunt Frances bring suit against you, you could hang. You should be grateful they have chosen not to do so."

"For the moment." Matthew shot that caveat in quickly.

"Pah." Theale gave his son a disgusted look. "Thought I raised a man not a milksop."

"A man who will see reason is no less of a man." Of course, as far as Matthew could tell, reason and Lord Theale seemed to have parted company some time ago. "You are fortunate, my lord, that the attainder of corruption of blood was abolished last year. Had I brought suit and you'd been convicted under that, your titles and properties would have been forfeited to the Crown after you were hanged. Now you will only lose your life." He stared straight into Theale's eyes. "If I bring suit against you."

"Which Lathbury has promised not to do," Craighaven broke in, "if you cease to persecute Aunt Frances and Cousin Ella." Now his son's gaze bored into Theale's eyes with deathly intent. "I have given him my word you will. Do I now have yours?"

With a deeply frowning countenance, Theale returned Matthew's stare. "You and she dishonored my family."

"As your brother did her." Not willing to give an inch, Matthew raised his head. "He is dead and we will be married shortly. Let this matter end now. For if anything should happen to Fanny or Ella, if you attempt the same dastardly actions against them, I will pursue not only you, but your entire family as well. Craighaven will immediately undergo my challenge, and I think you know my reputation with a pistol."

Giving a short nod, Theale swallowed hard.

"I will make sure, my lord, it will not come to that." Craighaven had paled again. The gentleman surely needed to disguise his feelings better.

Perhaps his father's estimation of milksop had not been far off the mark.

Stepping to the door, Craighaven called for Noyes, who appeared amazingly quickly. "Please have Aunt Frances's and Cousin Ella's trunks brought to the entrance hall. Lord Lathbury will take charge of them."

The butler gave a quick glance to his master.

Theale paused, then nodded.

"Very good, my lord." The relief in the man's voice echoed that in Matthew's mind.

"I will take my leave of you then, Craighaven, Theale." Matthew bowed and shot a final angry glance at Theale. "I pray we do not meet again under such circumstances." Turning on his heel, he strode quickly from the room, a huge weight rolling off his shoulders, although he'd continue to be vigilant for a while as far as Fanny and Ella's safety was concerned. Likely until he read Theale's obituary in the *Times.*

His and Fanny's path to love had been difficult in the extreme and he would do everything in his power to safeguard his new-made family for as long as they both should live.

# Epilogue

The blustery, cold month of January proved a busy one for Fanny and Matthew.

After the final ordeal wresting her belongings from Theale's hands, they had arrived at Hunter's Cross in good time to celebrate a quiet Christmas with Lady Lathbury, Lady Beatrice, and his younger sisters, Lady Eugenie and Lady Marianne, who took to Ella as another sister with open arms.

After the holidays, both she and Ella had settled quickly into a routine of work and play at Hunter's Cross. Ella joined Matthew's sisters in the schoolroom, and had taken to their governess, Miss Gleeson, instantly. The girl's studies had since gone at a clipping pace.

Fanny too had taken on lessons in household management for Hunter's Cross from her future mother-in-law, who wished to leave the manor house in good hands when she removed to the much smaller dowager house, situated a quarter of a mile away. Both Fanny and Matthew had urged Lady Lathbury to remain with them at Hunter's Cross, but the lady had been firm, as was her wont in most things.

"My dear," Lady Lathbury had said one afternoon over tea, "once you marry Rowley you will be mistress of his home. There is not room for two of us. You will need to find your footing by yourself and I will give you that chance from the beginning. Rowley's grandmother did not do me that courtesy and I eventually became resentful of her presence in what should have been my house. I will not make that mistake with you."

"I thank you for that, my lady, but I will hate to feel I have turned you out of your home." Fanny poured more milk into her teacup. Why it should taste so good when before she abhorred it was an ever-present mystery.

"Nonsense. I am going of my own accord and am quite looking forward to the extra time I shall have for visiting and my charity work. I daresay I may even travel once you are returned from your wedding trip." The countess's eyes sparkled. "Take care you enjoy yourself, for once you return there will be work to be done."

"I believe I can guarantee a glorious time on our trip to Paris, Mother." Matthew caught Fanny's eye and winked at her.

"If it is more 'glorious' than your time spent here, Rowley, I shall expect reports in the papers of scandalous doings in the streets of the city." Lady Lathbury stared first at Matthew, then even more sternly at Fanny.

Matthew's mouth twitched and Fanny's cheeks heated at the censure.

They had promised to wait to be intimate again

until after the wedding. Daily close proximity, however, had managed to break their resolve several times. The countess, apparently, was aware of their transgressions here, although she may not have been privy to the information that when they had attended Elizabeth and Lord Brack's wedding last week, they had spent the two nights in London in each other's arms. Matthew had assured her the servants at Hunt House were entirely discreet.

"It's only one more week until the wedding." Matthew sighed, sending Fanny a long-suffering look.

"For which I am eternally grateful, Rowley, as you do not seem to know the meaning of the word 'restraint.'" Lady Lathbury fixed him with a stern eye, though her mouth seemed to tremble as well.

Fanny's wedding day, the last day of January, dawned cold and crisp. A sprinkle of snow had fallen overnight, giving the landscape the look of a fairy cake. A fitting setting for her fairy-tale ending. All her friends had come to see her and Matthew wed, two of them bringing new husbands as well. Jane had asked to include Lord Sinclair in her invitation, with whom, Charlotte had whispered the night before the wedding, she'd declared a truce. She and the other members of the Widows' Club speculated excitedly about whether or not this meant Jane had renounced her vow not to marry again.

A single person of the party seemed decidedly petulant. Lord Kinellan had arrived from Scotland to stand up with Matthew. Looking dashing and elegant in his black tailcoat and gray silk waistcoat, Kinellan seemed out of sorts from the moment he arrived. Fanny wasn't sure where the issue lay, with Matthew's giving up his bachelorhood or some other perhaps more personal reason. She'd asked Matthew to ferret it out of him. "Do try to cheer him up, my dear. I would like my wedding attended by happy people."

Despite all the trials and tribulations it had taken to finally get to her wedding day, Fanny had to admit afterward that the ceremony had gone beautifully. The church had glowed with candlelight, fragrant with hothouse flowers from Hunter's Cross. Fanny's smile had stretched across her face and she had glowed with happiness as she and Matthew said their vows before the largest wedding party the vicar said he had ever seen. With her and Matthew's friends, his mother and sisters and Ella in attendance, the church was filled much fuller than usual. Whatever Matthew had said to Kinellan, it seemed to have worked, for he smiled and wished her happy after the ceremony along with the rest of the throng.

The only one of the original widows noticeably without a partner was Georgina. Resplendent in fashionable new gowns, and accompanied by a lady's maid and her King Charles spaniel Lulu, Georgie appeared the picture of contentment.

"The marquess has relented and furnished her with all the things she has needed these past years," Elizabeth confided to Fanny during the wedding breakfast.

"Indeed. What caused his change of heart?"

"I cannot think but that it is my marriage to Jemmy and the promise of an heir that has softened the old blackguard." Elizabeth's words seemed harsh, although she said them with a fondness in her tone.

Always cheerful, their younger friend now looked radiant, her face filled with smiles. "I will travel nowhere now without Lulu." Georgie was regaling Charlotte and Nash with a tale about the silky little dog with the round soulful eyes. "She is my protector, even though King Charles spaniels are not normally kept for such reasons. However, her great-grandmother was my protector when I was young and Lulu has inherited those same instincts."

"You are looking marvelously well, Georgina. Elizabeth tells me your father has repented his harshness toward you. I am so glad to hear it." Fanny hugged her friend. Today she wanted everyone to have joy in their lives.

"Thank you, Fanny. He has, at least in some respects. I do have Clara now as my maid, which is a blessing. And he's given me Lulu, for which I'm very grateful." A shadow chased across Georgie's face. "I only wish he would stop his marriage negotiations with Lord Travers. Unfortunately, on that he will not budge, even though I've pleaded with him." She frowned. "Perhaps I should set Lulu on him. He might better see reason if threatened by tiny sharp teeth. If he would simply allow me to go to London for the Season this year, I feel certain I could find a nice, likeable man with a title that would satisfy even Father."

"Can Jemmy not talk reason into him?"

"He has tried," Elizabeth spoke up. "But Lord Blackham is adamant about it. I'm not certain why Lord Travers. A rather disagreeable man, for my tastes." She turned to her sister-in-law. "I am sorry to say it, Georgie, but it is true."

"You need not tell me, Elizabeth." Georgie gave

her a Friday face. "I've been privy to his nature, unfortunately, for some time now. Father has had him come meet with me about the marriage twice. He never seems to say much, but he says it with authority. I have managed to find excuses to put off the wedding, but I don't know how long I can continue to do so."

"Don't give up yet, Georgie." Hugging her, Fanny whispered in her ear. "We will put our heads together and find a way to rescue you from this marriage."

"I pray you can, Fanny, for I would certainly wish for a happy wedding like yours and Matthew's, or Jemmy's and Elizabeth's. Or mine was with Isaac." Tears shone in her eyes. Her late husband had been the love of Georgie's life. "Anyone would likely be better than Lord Travers."

"We will call a meeting of the Widows' Club the instant Fanny returns from Paris and try to find a way for you to have a happy-ever-after too." Charlotte embraced their friend and all the women clustered around Georgie. If there was a way, together they would find it.

The candle Matthew had set on the bedside table had burned low. The rhythm of their breathing had slowed at last to almost normal as they lay entwined, tangled in sheets that might need to be repaired. Fanny would swear she heard one of them rip as they had tussled in the midst of their lovemaking. "I don't think we have done this much damage to the bedclothes since our first tryst in your rooms in Albemarle Street."

A chuckle came from Matthew's side of the bed. "I

remember having to come up with a reason why the bed listed to one side after your first visit. The servants simply shook their heads and said nothing. A bit of gold goes a long way to secure silence."

"And now we have no need to sneak, or bribe, or—"

"Or hide under beds it is devoutly to be wished." Matthew shivered and slid down under the covers.

"Exactly," Fanny giggled and snuggled next to him. "We have had enough of those days. Days of revenge." Sobering, she shook her head. "Who would have thought that one act of vengeance would almost end in my death and the death of our daughter? No matter how much I thirsted to make Stephen pay for all he had done, I could never have imagined how badly my scheme would misfire."

"Still, it brought us our daughter, and soon perhaps a son to join her." Matthew pulled her over for a kiss. He had kissed her many times tonight, each seeming more passionate than the last. "Most importantly, love, it brought us back together, as we were meant to be from the beginning."

As sated as she had been minutes ago, his kiss set her aflame once more. To judge by his cock, miraculously stirring to life again, her husband appeared likewise insatiable. Yes, they were indeed well matched in all ways that counted. Although, if they did not show more restraint, Fanny began to doubt she would be able to walk come the morning. "I suppose, then, I shall give up my thoughts of revenge on Stephen. There is no way to strike at him, or Theale for that matter. Save for something that will transcend death."

"I believe I have a scheme, my love, whereby you can perform an act of vengeance on Stephen and his brother you have scarce dreamed of." Drawing her toward him, Matthew melded his lips to hers.

When she could next breathe, he loomed above her, his body pressing her down into the mattress, the weight of him as delicious as any other part.

"The best revenge you can devise, my love," he continued, settling once more between her thighs, "will be to live long beside me as my wife, and love me well for all the days of our lives. Your most perfect revenge will be that neither of them will find the happiness, joy, and contentment with which we have been truly blessed."

"Then bless me again, my love." Wrapping her legs around him, she urged him forward.

"As always, it is my great pleasure to do your bidding, my love." He leaned down to capture her lips again. "Every time."